Special Collectors' Edition
39/100
ANGRY ROBOT

Darkness Falling

"Crowther's twisted rapture is a fast-paced, character-driven, funny, gruesome apocalypse."
Stephen Baxter

"I was reminded of the best of Stephen King. It's the smartest and most compelling end-of-the-world alien-zombie story I have ever read."
Adam Roberts

"This book is told with a sure hand and careful attention to detail; it's frightening where it should be, sensitive where it should be, and enthralling throughout."
Mike Resnick

"Peter Crowther is crafting the first great post-apocalyptic saga of the new century, one that may dwarf even such a benchmark work as *The Stand*."
Lucius Shepard

"Anything that has Pete Crowther's fingerprints on it is evidence of quality. Snap it up."
Joe R Lansdale

"As intensely menacing and gruesome as any George Romero film. A virtuoso 'tour de force' by Pete Crowther."
Ramsey Campbell

"His writing is master storytelling at its finest – gripping, chilling and beautifully told."
Sarah Pinborough

"Peter Crowther's a remarkable writer."
Locus

"*Darkness Falling* is fast-paced, un-put-down-able, and immersed in popular culture… truly terrific."
Jack Dann

ALSO BY PETER CROWTHER

Escardy Gap (with James Lovegrove)
Fugue on a G-String
Gandalph Cohen and the Land at the End of the Working Day
The Hand That Feeds
After Happily Ever

Collections

The Longest Single Note and Other Strange Compositions
Lonesome Roads
Cold Comforts
Songs of Leaving
The Spaces Between the Lines
The Land at the End of the Working Day

PETER CROWTHER

Darkness Falling

FOREVER TWILIGHT
BOOK I

ANGRY
ROBOT

ANGRY ROBOT

A member of the Osprey Group
Midland House, West Way
Botley, Oxford
OX2 0HP
UK

www.angryrobotbooks.com
The death of light

First published in this 100 copy limited edition hardcover
by Angry Robot 2011

Portions of this novel have been previously published as the novellas *Darkness Darkness* (CD Books 2002) and *Windows to the Soul* (Subterranean Press 2009)

A catalogue record for this book is available from the British Library.

ISBN: 978-0-85766-173-9
Ebook ISBN: 978-0-85766-170-8

Set in Meridien and Agency by Argh! Nottingham.

Printed in the UK by the MPG Books Group, Bodmin & King's Lynn.

For my beautiful granddaughters Orla Plum, Edie Serene and Elsie Blue – may the four of us sit down one evening not too far away, to enjoy the intoxicating frisson of unease that comes with the telling of a spooky story at bedtime.

The night has a thousand eyes,
And the day but one.

FW Bourdillon, *Among the Flowers*

We like to think we live in daylight,
but half the world is always dark;
and fantasy, like poetry,
speaks the language of the night.

Ursula K Le Guin

Darkness, darkness
Be my pillow
Take my head and let me sleep...
In the coolness of your shadow,
In the silence of your deep.

The Youngbloods, "Darkness Darkness"

PROLOGUE

When they were barely minutes out of Denver, and not many more to go before a bright light was to change their lives forever, Martha Mortenson said to her husband, Ronnie, "You want to borrow my glasses?" saying it in that oh-so-smart voice she used when she was wanting to make a point.

Martha was always wanting to make a point these days. It wasn't anything personal – though that was kind of a dumb thing to say about the way you spoke to your husband, and Martha would have been the first to agree with that: after all, conversation between a couple *should* be personal – but it was just the way things were now, in the fourteenth year of their marriage. The fourteenth year of their bloodless war.

The marriage wasn't going to last a whole lot longer, though neither of them knew it at that time.

Ronnie felt his cheeks redden as he turned around to face his wife. "Sorry, miles away," he said lamely. He continued swallowing in an attempt to clear the blocked noise in his ears. It was like he was overhearing conversations from another room, carried along a corridor to where he was sitting. Where he was sitting was in Row S, right hand side of the plane, Seat 5: Martha was in 6, next to the window, and Seat 4, next to the aisle, was empty. Ronnie thought that maybe he should have occupied the aisle seat and left the middle one empty. But it was too late now.

Martha adjusted the glasses perched on the end of her nose, gave one final glance at the girl in the aisle struggling with her bag in the locker above where she was sitting and snorted without humor as she returned her attention to her newspaper. "Yeah, right. I'd say it was more like just a few feet."

"What?"

"You said 'miles'," Martha said, nodding at the backside of the girl in the aisle. "More like a few feet."

He looked across at her.

The lead article in Martha's newspaper featured a photo of a young woman with an open smile, one of those pictures taken in photo booths for passport purposes. The headline read:

MUMMY-MAN'S FOURTH VICTIM FOUND IN WOODLAND

Then, in smaller-sized type beneath it:

Denver Police no closer to finding killer's identity

Mummy-man! Ronnie made a noise with his mouth. These serial killer names were getting more and more outlandish. This latest one was so-called because his preferred method of dispatch, apparently, was to bind his victims from head to toe in gauze bandage until all incoming oxygen was blocked off. Then, presumably – nobody actually knew for sure because all they did was discover the bodies, and the bodies weren't saying anything – presumably he sat and watched them die. Or why else would he go to all those lengths? At least there was no evidence of sexual assault, so not all bad news. *Hey, Mrs Jones, we found your daughter, bound up in gauze, dead as last night's pizza wrapping... but at least she wasn't assaulted. So let's crack open a bottle of Moët and raise a toast.*

Ronnie felt his seat shudder. He had already suffered a few pulls and judders from the guy immediately behind him, the guy using Ronnie's seat back as a means for adjusting his vast bulk, a process which seemed to involve the guy jamming his head into the gap between Ronnie's and Martha's seats and then breathing stale garlic all over them. Another reason, maybe, for changing seats. Hadn't these people heard about the weight crisis?

"You OK back there?" Ronnie said, glaring between the seats.

The big man in the seat immediately behind Ronnie shrugged, saying, "What?", hands held out, palms up. This was a man who had never heard of dieting, didn't know diddly about deep vein thrombosis and hadn't yet learned of the invention of toothpaste. He was jammed so tightly into his seat that they were going to need a crane to get him free. Ronnie suddenly dreaded when this guy was going to need to go for a pee.

Shaking his head, Ronnie decided not to respond but instead turned his attention to Martha. "What the hell's *that* supposed to mean?" he said.

Ronnie was feeling a little antsy. He wasn't a good flier at the best of times, and ten after five in the goddam morning on a flight that was already more than seven hours behind schedule – with Denver airport probably still visible behind them as they climbed to a cruising altitude – and now Martha was playing her famous bitch-of-the-fucking-year role. Factor in that they wouldn't be back at home in Atlanta until mid-morning, long after the cock-crow – "sparrow-fart," as his father used to say – arrival they had envisaged, and he just wasn't in the mood for pissy remarks.

"Dad was right," was all Martha would say.

Ronnie returned the snort with interest. "Hold the goddam front page," he said with a sneer. "Your father was *never* right. Your father has made a life's work out of never being right." He rustled the pages of his *Rolling Stone* for emphasis and was immediately annoyed to see the cover had broken from the center staples. "One whacked-out hair-brained fuck-up scheme after another and what's he got to show for it?"

"A happy marriage."

"Oh, yeah, right. Second time around, though. Anyone should be able to get it right once they've had a little practice." He paused for a moment and picked up the ball he'd unknowingly tossed to himself. "Hell, I reckon even I would be happy second time out."

"Just say the word, Ronnie," Martha said without looking up, sounding for all the world like a female Ralph Kramden. "Just say the damn word and you can give it a go." She nodded again at the girl in the aisle. "Think she's maybe a little old for you, though. She must be pushing twenty-three if she's a day."

It had been quite a while since Ronnie had been on the sunny side of twenty-three. Or even thirty-three. Now, the specter of forty – the Big Four Oh – straddled the horizon like a storm cloud, and the once-thick (if not actually bushy) head of hair had thinned out, exposing areas of pale scalp around the crown and a receding hairline that Ronnie's mom said made him look like Robert Taylor. Ronnie hadn't known who Robert Taylor was until Allie Mortenson dug out an old copy of *Movieworld* and pointed out a photo of the actor to her son. "It's called a 'widow's peak'," Allie had said, before going on to explain that a widow's peak actually referred to the same V-shaped hair-point on the forehead of a woman. "Means they'll outlive their husband." Ronnie had just nodded and filed it away with other trivia such as the origin of the term "take a rain check", while thinking – somewhat guiltily – how nice it would be to outlive Martha.

He looked up from an article on Don DeLillo and stared at the side of his wife's head. Ronnie had started to read DeLillo's *Underworld*, and loved the long prologue about the baseball and Sinatra sitting in the bleachers and everything, but after that he couldn't figure out what the hell was going on and he'd just up and left it one day, turning instead to re-reading Avery Corman's *The Old Neighborhood*, which he did every few years, wrapping himself in the novel like it was the old pair of corduroy pants he'd had at Cornell and which Martha had seen fit to throw out with the trash one spring-clean-up.

In the trash, along with their entire relationship.

Maybe that had been the beginning of the end right there.

There had been a time when things had been great for Ronnie and Martha, blowing along like the warm breeze that typifies summer and a worry-free relationship. But then things had started to sour a little, just like, Ronnie supposed, they soured in the relationship between Steven and Beverly Robbins in Corman's novel. It didn't happen fast, like one day you wake up and everything has changed; it happened slow and secretively, building up like silt along the banks of a river. And pretty soon, you can't take a step without sinking up to your waist.

That was the way it was for Ronnie and Martha, childhood sweethearts but adult combatants. Ronnie wished he could have understood DeLillo's book about the baseball because he figured there was a lot of stuff in there that could be pertinent. He liked the novel's slightly mystical and even mythical tone but that was something special where baseball was concerned. And Ronnie knew all about that. After all, he had read Bernard Malamud's *The Natural*, Roger Kahn's *The Boys of Summer*, Philip Roth's *The Great American Novel*, and all of Bill Kinsella's baseball yarns, particularly *Shoeless Joe*, Ronnie's favorite – he'd loved the movie starring Costner and had actually wept in the theater, which Martha just hadn't been able to understand.

"You know," Ronnie had said to Martha as they'd made their way back to Ronnie's rusting Mustang (he'd loved that car), "I sometimes think you have no soul." And Martha had laughed and grabbed a hold of his crotch, squeezing gently, saying in a voice that was softer and more sultry than it seemed it had been ever since, "Yeah, but I have a place for this fella. But first you got to get your fingers wet."

Ronnie winced, partly at the memory of the grossness of what she had said and partly – maybe the bigger part, if truth be told – at the fact that it had turned him on so. Turned him on sufficiently that he had nearly piled the Mustang into a ditch outside of Morganstown Woods.

Maybe that was the first nail hammered into the coffin right there. There was no real romance involved in their relationship – just sex. Sure, there had been good times, but it had gotten so Ronnie could actually count them, each of them specifically, and when he would run out, it was always the same times that he'd identified.

There had to be a first nail and that was surely it, now that Ronnie stopped to think about it... here at ten thousand feet and still climbing, leaving Denver airport some five hours late, heading home to Atlanta after spending a grueling weekend with Martha's father, Frank, and her stepmom, Lucinda. It had been almost sixty hours of pure torture for Ronnie. Hours of sage nods from Frank, hands in pants pocket, head lifted, chin thrust out as he chewed a non-existent piece of cud and considered every damn thing that was mentioned as though it was a momentous decision. And similar hours of the ever-attentive Lucinda, smelling of lavender, peppermints and cigarette smoke, all swirling, flouncy cotton dresses like the ones Mary Tyler Moore wore in the re-runs of the old *Dick Van Dyke Show*.

Yes, maybe they should get divorced, pack it all in, Ronnie thought, watching Martha watch his face, her eyes flitting from side to side like insects, looking a little nervous now, nervous because she couldn't quite figure out what the hell Ronnie was thinking about. He liked that, took a certain amount of pleasure out of seeing her mentally wrong-footed.

The in-flight PA system beeped and the seatbelt sign flashed off. Ronnie suddenly realized that the girl in the aisle had been standing up messing with the locker while it had still been illuminated. He wondered if that girl might have been more attentive to him… might have shown some warmth. But maybe all was not lost – Martha had just given him an exit line. But the thing was, did she mean it?

"Are you *serious*?" Ronnie asked her, keeping his voice soft and thinking of the guy in *The Old Neighborhood* who left the ad agency he'd built from scratch and went back to the streets where he'd grown up in Brooklyn, working as a soda jerk and playing handball with the kids around the block, learning just what was important in life and leaving behind all the shit that his world had gotten clogged up with. Like all the shit that Martha dished out day in and day out, like her fucking life depended on it. But when she turned to him, Ronnie momentarily felt like a heel, like he'd wounded her deep down inside, a deep cut that nobody would ever be able to see but which would take years to heal over.

She shook her head gently, squinting at him, turning her mouth up in that oh-so-practiced sneer. Behind her head he could see the clouds still roiling outside the window. "What is it with you, Ronnie?" she said, venom in the whisper.

He turned away, either unable or reluctant to say anything more, knowing that a turning point had appeared, a fork in the road that could decide his direction – and Martha's direction – for the rest of their lives. He stared at the seat-back just a few inches away from him, hoping to see some kind of sign appear – some little nugget of homespun guidance.

When had all the arguing started?

He glanced down at his *Rolling Stone* and wondered whether all relationships soured after a time. What was it they said about monogamy? A triumph of civilization over instinct? Something like that. In his mind, he pictured Martha on her back, in the old days, staring up at him – "I do so love you, Ron," she used to say to him, repeating it over and over as he worked away inside of her, each word followed by a small gassy exhalation as he withdrew and thrust, withdrew and thrust.

He looked up and rested his head back on the seat. Maybe she had done. Then. And maybe he had loved her, too. Then. What had happened since that time – twenty-some years – was called life.

The girl in the aisle was still struggling with the locker. As she stretched up, she exposed a gap of flesh between the bottom of her sweater and the top of her jeans, and just above the jeans was a telltale strap of the top of a thong. He stared first at the thong and then at the cheeks of the girl's bottom, watching it wobble deliciously as she strained at the bag.

Martha leaned across Ronnie's knee, creasing the *Rolling Stone* still further, and shouted to the girl – "Miss?" – and flipped her on the ass with her rolled-up newspaper.

The girl turned around frowning, then saw Ronnie watching her and broke into a tight smile. The girl had a slight overbite and when she smiled it caused little dimples at the sides of her mouth.

"Miss? I'm here? Hell-oo?"

Her smile fading, the girl shifted her attention to Martha just as the stewardesses inched forward with their trolley.

"Martha, just leave it," Ronnie said.

The girl looked puzzled. "Yes?"

"Martha, what are you *doin–*"

"I wonder if you could do my husband a favor while you're doing that?" Without waiting for a response, Martha continued, "Could you remove your pants completely so that he can get a really good look at your ass? I'm sure he'd be grateful. He's doing his best to study it, but, well, you know how it is. His eyesight's not what it once was." She straightened out her newspaper and, looking over the headlines again, added, "Mind you, there's a lot about him that isn't what it once was."

The girl clearly didn't know how it was or maybe she just didn't like being made the center of attention.

A tall man wearing chin stubble, an Atlanta Braves t-shirt and a frown so intense that Ronnie thought you could maybe stand a mug of coffee on his brow got to his feet over by the opposite window and started shuffling his way towards the aisle. Ronnie now saw that the man had some kind of tattoo on his right bicep – there were two clawed feet and a spiked tale descending from the t-shirt sleeve.

"Bobby," the girl said. It was a cautionary statement.

"Can I help you, ma'am?" Bobby asked. His voice was altogether more refined that his appearance suggested it would be and Ronnie couldn't help but smile. The man's eyebrows met on the bridge of his nose and Ronnie wondered if this was ever a bone of contention between him and Thong Girl. He imagined her looking up into his face when they were in the midst of their undoubted intimate raptures and her attention being drawn to the black hedge running above his eyes.

"Ma'am?" the man repeated when Martha didn't respond. "You hear me talking here?"

"Forget it," was all Ronnie could think of to say though he was all too well aware that it was hardly throwing water onto a fire. So he added, "My wife," waving his thumb over his shoulder, "doesn't fly too well."

Martha muttered "asshole" from behind him and Ronnie saw the Neanderthal's eyes darken.

"She means me," Ronnie said, trying to lighten things with a chuckle.

Sensing something wasn't going exactly according to plan, one of the stewardesses edged her way past the trolley. Her face a mask of perfectly made-up bonhomie, she said, "Is there some kind of a problem here?"

"This guy called me an asshole," said the man. Jerking his thumb at Ronnie.

"It was my wife," Ronnie said, shrugging. *Oh, right, your wife. Well, that's just right fine and dandy, sir. You have a nice flight now, you hear!*

The stewardess's face clouded. "Sir?" Then she looked down at Martha. "Ma'am? Is there a problem here?"

Ronnie rested a hand on the stewardess's arm and immediately wished he hadn't. She looked down at his hand without withdrawing her arm and waited for Ronnie to remove it.

"I'm just trying to get my bag in here is all," the girl explained from the aisle. Her rather nasal whine dampened the fire that looked set to burn and Ronnie bent down to retrieve his magazine.

"This woman, she was bad-mouthing my sister," the neanderthal explained, waving a carelessly pointing finger in Martha's direction. Ronnie felt rather than saw Martha sink further back into her seat.

Bobby the caveman started to say something more, shifting his attention between the girl and the stewardess, and then Ronnie and Martha, before starting all over again.

"It's OK, Bobby," the girl said. She hoisted her pants and waved him into the aisle. "Maybe you could get it in there..."

"That's OK, sir," the stewardess said. "Miss, you really need to take your seat."

The girl nodded at the overhead signs. "I thought we were OK to leave our seats," she said. "The belts sign has gone out."

"Can you keep the noise down there?" a gruff voice sounded from behind Ronnie's seat. The man's southern accent made "there" into the two-syllable extravaganza, "thy-arr", and the question was immediately followed by a wave of pure garlic fumes. Squinting at the ferocity of the odor, Ronnie turned to face the stewardess fully expecting to see her hair blowing back and her uniform to be in tatters. But she wasn't looking.

"Yes, miss, but we're still only just airborne." The stewardess's smile was gentle but firm. She had seen it all before, and most of it more than once.

Ronnie's seat was pulled backwards and the bulk from Row T lumbered into peripheral vision.

"People are tryin' to slipe high-arr," the voice announced.

Ronnie turned to look at Martha and just hoped that the man would sit down.

"Take your seat, sir," said the stewardess.

"But the sign is out, ma'am," Bobby offered.

"Yes," the stewardess replied. She was turning away from the bulk in Row T but her arm and outstretched finger were still pointing at the guy behind Ronnie. "If you could just keep the aisle clear until we've handed out the refreshments, we'd be really grateful. Let me handle the locker. You can check it later. That OK?"

The girl sighed, nodded, slipped past Bobby and sat down.

The sumo wrestler in Row T rejoined his seat with a loud noise that Ronnie guessed was part springs throwing in the towel and part fart. Well, at least it might sweeten the goddam garlic. He smiled at the thought and glanced up at the stewardess. She wasn't smiling. Her nametag said "Vicky" but Ronnie didn't think she looked like a Victoria. There were a lot of kids these days who were christened by their nicknames.

After one final glare at the stewardess and then at Ronnie and Martha, Bobby resumed his seat across the aisle, presumably to continue his consideration of the secret of fire and nursing the scuff-marks he got on his knuckles from his hands trailing across the ground when he walked around. Ronnie looked up to see if there was any action from Vicky the stewardess's ass when she turned around to maneuver the girl's bag into the locker but it was a regulation tight blue skirt – nice, but no major points-winner – with a mauve blouse tucked into the waistband so tight it would have taken a quarterback to pull it free.

"Jesus, Ronnie," Martha said.

"What?" Ronnie said, slamming his magazine onto the tray jutting out from the seat in front. "I'm thinking here."

"Sir? Ma'am?" Another stewardess's face appeared over the seat.

"Heh," Martha laughed, "looks like we could have a second feature for that front page. Ronnie Mortenson *thinks*. That's like one of those–"

The stewardess gave a practiced smile. "Cold drinks?"

"I'll have a club soda," Martha said icily.

"Sir? Something for you?"

"That's like..." Martha was continuing. Once she got onto one of these rolls, Ronnie believed the only thing could get her back to earth was a swift clip with a piece of uncut timber.

"Jack on the rocks," Ronnie snapped. *And then I'd like a parachute so I can bail out of this plane, this relationship, and this goddam life.* He scanned this new stewardess's chest for a nametag and, without actually thinking about what he was doing, he lifted himself from his seat to get a better look.

The stewardess looked up just in time to see Ronnie scanning her breasts. "Nuts?" she asked.

Was that a smile tugging at the corners of her mouth? Ronnie thought that it was. He nodded and smiled, sinking back a little but not completely into his seat. *Yeah, nuts,* he thought. "Sure," he said. "Let's do the whole thing." He spotted the badge and made out three letters: J–A–S...

"Pardon me?"

Ronnie shook his head and let out a tiny smile. He shuffled further back into his seat.

"That's like..." said Martha again.

Ronnie turned to her and sighed. "Martha, will you just leave it? Will you just let it rest? OK?"

The stewardess placed two small packs of salted peanuts on Ronnie's tray, followed them with a coaster and, finally, a glass with ice cubes and a miniature bottle of Jack Daniels.

Ronnie unscrewed the Jack and poured it over the ice. "You see what you almost did there?"

"What did I almost do, dearest?"

"You almost started world war goddam three is what you did."

In the aisle, her backside bouncing against the arm of the empty seat next to Ronnie, Vicky the stewardess had finally managed to secure Thong Girl's bag in the locker and was now busy trying to make the locker cover close.

J – A – S. What was that? Jasmine? Ronnie couldn't think of anything else. *Jasmine*: nice name, he thought. Just as he was about to accept the proffered club soda – and was in the process of considering whether to tip it onto Martha's head – a girl screamed from somewhere down nearer the split between standard and business. He looked across and, almost immediately, the entire aircraft lit up with the brightest light Ronnie had ever seen.

It was a soundless flash that filled his brain and just for a second he thought maybe they'd been blown up. But there was no explosion, only a collective gasp from Martha, alongside him, but even that seemed to be cut off mid-way through. And then there was a dim clatter of things falling to the floor.

The light was so bright that Ronnie pulled his hand back and clapped the palms of both of his hands to his eyes. As he rubbed, there were more clunks of things falling over. He felt something bounce on his right shin – the nuts – and instinctively reached to steady his drink.

"Jesus Christ," he said, removing his hands from his face, "what the hell was–"

But the stewardess whose name began with the letters J–A–S wasn't there. The trolley edge was in exactly the same spot as it had been just a couple of seconds earlier, but now the woman who had been handing out the drinks and the little packs of peanuts (and whose breasts Ronnie had been committing to memory by simple virtue of trying to find out her identity) was nowhere to be seen. And the plastic glass of club soda had apparently dropped onto the headrest of the seat in front of Ronnie – there was no sign of the glass but Ronnie's tray was pooled with liquid. He waited for the guy in front – was it a guy? He couldn't remember – to stand up and ask him what the hell he was doing. It looked fairly likely that someone was going to rearrange Ronnie's face: the least likely was Thong Girl, then her tree-swinging brother, then Vicky the stewardess, plus maybe her friend Jas-something-or-other, possibly the deep south lardass behind him with his death-breath weapon of mass destruction or, perhaps most likely now that he had somehow been involved in spilling her fucking club soda, his own wife.

Ronnie looked across the aisle with the intention of sharing an exasperated grimace with Bobby the Atlanta Braves fan and thereby removing just one of the problems stacking up against him, but even the caveman had disappeared. He leaned forward – no sign of his sister, Thong Girl, either.

And now it felt as though there was a problem with the engines or something. The plane seemed to be dipping forward.

Ronnie bent forward to see if he could see the top of the woman's head in the aisle seat of the row in front of Bobby and Thong Girl but the seat was empty. There *had* been someone there, hadn't there? Maybe not.

He turned to Martha. "Must have been some kind of–"

And then he stopped.

Martha wasn't there.

(1)

It was always the same.

Rick was sitting in the car, reaching into the glove compartment in the dash to pull out a pack of *Juicy Fruit,* feeling his fingers touch the paper, a long, torn-off strip of yellow – even though, in the dream he could not experience the feeling of touching things and the dim light inside the glove compartment of the old DeSoto didn't permit the luxury of color definition – taking his eyes off the road, just for a second, taking his eyes away from the snow-streaked slopes of the Bighorn Mountains straddling the horizon, with I-90 snaking its way right for them, Lovell somewhere up ahead, over west, and Ranchester sitting way behind him, hearing the little voice in the back of his head, the one he used to talk to himself, hearing himself have it tell him–

Hey, the road! Better keep your eyes on the road, dog-breath!

–he shouldn't let his attention drift, feeling a little tired (which was why he'd thought of the *Juicy Fruit*), thinking maybe he should roll down the window, let in a little air, seeing it all again, knowing that it was a dream and that he only ever thought all those thoughts the once, just the one time, and that this time was like he was playing a part, making the same moves all over again, even though he knew these were the wrong moves to make, then, calm somehow, calm inside of himself even though it was all going to happen again, seeing the guy being chased out of a wide parking area on the side of the road by a girl in cut-off blue denim shorts, the two of them laughing, then seeing *them* see *him,* watching their faces slide down on themselves like candle wax flash-fried, their smiling mouths first drooping at the corners and then their eyes widening, catching out of his eye corner the two bicycles propped against a pile of logs, Thermos beside them, and some kind of plastic carton, and all the time Rick bracing himself, his arms locked out holding the steering wheel, the yellow *Juicy Fruit* pack dropped to the floor beneath his feet, forgotten but–

So, just how much value d'you place on a stick of gum, huh, Rick?

–remembered in the dream, then slamming his feet on the pedals, nearly standing up on them, his backside off the DeSoto's seat, feeling the wheels lock, talking to himself–

Shitshitshitshitsh–

–and being distantly aware of the dust clouds billowing at the sides of the car, seeing the faces of the guy and the girl–

She had freckles, didn't she Rick? You remember that, don'tcha... you remember seeing her face in that much detail just before–

–before the car drove through them, the two of them first doubling over towards him, folding over the hood, the guy reaching out at the last minute to push the girl (it was his fiancée, Rick found out later... much later), and the girl disappearing somewhere – one minute there, the next minute gone – and the guy coming up over the hood, smacking down onto it and then up against the windshield and then rolling and tumbling up over the roof, hearing his body bouncing along its length while Rick felt the telltale judder of the DeSoto's tires going over something in the road, then looking in the rearview, even as the car was finally slowing down, and seeing the guy's body falling onto the road like a rag doll–

A very red rag doll, huh, Rick?

–with another shape lying behind it a few yards back, and then the car coming to a halt and the engine cutting out and there being no sound at all, just Rick staring at that rearview willing the two unmoving rag dolls to get to their feet, dust themselves down and give him the bird–

Hey, asshole, whyn't you come back and finish the job... think there's a couple of bones here seem to be still in one piece...

–but Rick knew the rag dolls would not move and he knew that the worst part of the dream was now waiting for him, crouched down like a feral cat behind a creaking cellar door, daring him to peer around and sneak a glance into the darkness: now was the part where he got out, hearing the soft clicks of the DeSoto's engine cooling down and the creak of the suspension as he swung his legs out onto the dusty road and pulled himself up to his full six-two, smelling the scorched smell of brake linings mixed with the cool fresh air blowing down from the mountains, glancing across to the pull-in and seeing the bicycles and the Thermos–

Hey, come on, quit fooling around now... coffee's getting cold...

–feeling the sudden need to pee but, instead, forcing his legs – those two wobbly tentacles that didn't seem to have a single bone between them – to carry him back along I-90 towards the two shapes lying in the still swirling dust, neither of them moving, knowing deep down that they wouldn't move just as they hadn't moved when it had first happened and they didn't move any of the other times, the reprise-times – like now – when they had to go through the whole thing again in Rick's dreams, knowing all this but, as each step brought them closer, straining to see a sign of movement, a sign of–

Someone shouted out and a light burned into his brain. Then it was gone.

Rick opened his eyes, suddenly aware in that instant that he had been dreaming again – the same old dream – and that he had shouted out. He looked around the porch and listened: it was silent. He listened again. No, it wasn't just silent it was... empty – no insect noises, no distant hum of an occasional late-night traveler negotiating the twists and turns of the highway way below.

There was a dull *crump* noise from somewhere outside, somewhere way off, out on the road. Then the silence returned.

As though in response, a burst of applause exploded from behind and Rick suddenly remembered he'd left the TV on.

"What the hell time is it?" he asked the night. No answer. It had to be before 4 am which was when his show started – there was no way Geoff would let him sleep through that.

He bent down and lifted the bourbon bottle and the glass from the wooden deck, set them on the table alongside the lounge chair he'd been stretched out in. As he considered one last swift shot before he went inside to bed he gave a mental vote of thanks to all-day and all-night TV. There was always something on and even though he had not been watching it, the sound was reassuring when he sat out on the deck staring over to the forest-clad hills in the distance, listening, as he did most nights, to the sound of the canned laughter on one of the sitcoms while he waited for the sun to drop down out of sight.

As he made to go inside he heard a muffled explosion.

When he turned back, he could see a fire on the road across the fields. It was a vehicle of some kind, a truck maybe.

Rick went inside.

(2)

In the few days leading up to Martha Mortenson's disappearance (and the disappearance of a whole lot of other folks, too, as it was to turn out), Virgil Banders had watched one particular house very carefully before deciding to make his move.

He had hired three cars, a different one each day: a Subaru, a Mercedes, and finally a Honda flatbed pickup, parking around the corner from the adjoining street, down by where she lived and, finally, with the flatbed, up by the Expressway that joined into the I-25, using a big hover-mower to cut the grass alongside the road. He had hired the mower from Toolland over on 4th Street – it wasn't cheap but then one had to invest. *Got to speculate to accumulate,* Arnie Banders had told his son, Arnie never amounting to much at all until the day he drifted off on a soup kitchen cot, coughing blood and long since moved away from the family seat.

Arnie had been Virgil's first, Virgil only sixteen years old at that time, and the world was a happier place somehow, Clinton in his second term and riding all the hoo-ha about the White House BJ with Monica like a seasoned pro – which, of course, was exactly what he was. It was with this scenario as a background – a good few years before the whole world (it *seemed* like it was the whole world, anyways) got so mightily pissed at the good ol' US of A that they actually started killing themselves to make that point, flying airplanes into buildings for Chrissakes – that Virgil checked to see nobody was around and then climbed up and sat astride his old man, one knee on each elbow and his ass on his daddy's crotch, and then pressed the pillow down on the old man's face, the pillow covered with Virgil's old Levi Timberline coat, the corduroy one with the fake fur-type collar.

"You left me," was all he had whispered into Arnie's ear, and then, even softer this time, "with her." And he had pressed the pillow some more, even feeling his father's nose through all the filling, that's how hard he was pressing.

The old man hadn't had any strength left at all, just shuddered a little as the blood-and-mucous phlegm came up into his mouth, old Arnie sputtering his last and maybe wondering why his boy was doing this, him sick and all. What had he *done*? If the boy would just move that goddam pillow then maybe he'd just up and ask him right out, maybe sort out this mistake young Virgil was making here.

But no, it didn't work quite that way. And it wasn't a mistake. "Think of it as a nightcap," was all Virgil said by way of explanation, and as far as Arnie Banders was concerned, it wasn't much of an explanation at all.

When it was done (and it didn't take too long at all), Virgil slipped back onto the floor and wiped the gunge off of the inside of his jacket before pulling it on. Then he went off to find someone, tell them that his father had shuffled off the old mortal coil, Virgil all teary-eyed.

Walking along the corridor after all the hoo-ha had quieted down and his dad had been covered over by the sheet, Virgil saw that his hands were shaking. But he felt good. If anyone had asked him why he'd done it, why... Virgil didn't think he'd be able to come up with an answer. Save for maybe that... that it felt good. And feeling good was what it was all about. Wasn't it?

In fact, it felt so good that he did it again.

Several times. So many times, in fact, they'd given him a name, the folks in the newspapers. "Mummy-Man" they called him, and "the Smotherer". Virgil liked both of those, made him feel special, like a superhero or something. And they – well, the papers and the cops, but mostly the cops, Virgil guessed – they were turning it into some kind of contest. Saying how it was a cry for help – that he wanted to be caught (the newspapers quite rightly deciding that the killer was a male) and so on.

But Virgil didn't want to be caught.

He liked doing what he was doing, particularly since his mom had been diagnosed with terminal lung cancer, her taking to her bed and too concerned with other things even to think about Virgil playing with her honeypot, the main one of the other things being her breathing oxygen out of the cylinder, that hoarse breathing, like a ruptured bellows, rasping all the time, her sitting in front of her game shows with a mask on her face, old arthritic hands clasped on her stomach, clasped but shaking.

"I'm going out, mother," Virgil would say. "To work," he would add. She didn't know what he meant and was too breathless all the time even to bother asking, but there was an air of menace in his voice and she knew it didn't bode well for someone somewhere.

Then one night he had come home and Alice Banders's hands were not shaking any more.

They had buried her last week, Virgil's Aunt Deidre and his Uncle Demain – *I mean, what the hell name is that? De-fucking-*main*? I ask you,* Virgil told the guys at work, at the print shop down on Second – the pair of them putting in a lot of tears but managing, through sniffs and coughs, to ask what was happening to the house that Virgil's daddy, good ol' Arnie Banders, had seen fit to leave to her when he'd passed away last year, and him so young and all, dying of a heart attack like that, my, oh my, it was such a tragedy and all, the good Lord working in mysterious ways and no denying, and Virgil telling them, his voice just a little shaky, that his mom had left it all to him and he was maybe gonna live there for a while before selling up and maybe doing a little bit of traveling, seeing some places he'd only read about, places like Venice, with the roads of water, and Paris, with all its pavement coffee bars and pretty women.

Virgil surely did enjoy the company of a pretty woman, no doubt about that at all.

That latest of them, this Wednesday evening in late February, was one of the prettiest. He had seen the girl at school, back when he used to go which was before he dropped out to concentrate on other things – like looking after his damn fool mom – and he'd taken what his grandfather used to call a shine to her. Of course, to his grandfather, that shine was probably best explained by an overall breathlessness and hot feeling around the crotch area as young Virgil imagined the girl – her name was Susannah Neihardt, but everyone called her Suze – parading around in tiny panties and maybe an already unfastened brassiere that hung loose on her small breasts. But that wasn't strictly true. Oh, the breathlessness was there and the hot feeling around the old pecker station, but the imagining was a shade different.

What young Virgil thought of at night, safe in the sanctity of his bed, a much more pleasant place since he was no long required by his mother to provide her dreaded nightcap, was Suze Neihardt bandaged from head to foot, the bandages tight around her little titties and her furry area down below (Virgil's mom had called it her honeypot), the girl rasping for breath, her eyes popping out under all that whiteness as she tried to arch herself to draw in just one more tiny insect's breath of air, feeling all her stomach and intestines wrap themselves up, trying to come up her chest and her throat and her mouth to venture out into the world to get their own life-giving oxygen fix but not knowing that all there *was* was cloth, bandage cloth, pulled tight around the mouth and nose and eyes, so tight that her nose was squashed flat and her lips pulled back against and above her teeth, resting on her upper gums, in fact, contorting her face into a rictus grin.

And with those thoughts in mind, Virgil could always get a response from the old pecker.

And so it was that Virgil had taken to following her most days, making sure he stayed well back and out of sight if she turned around. He had thus discovered where she lived and, thanks to a real stroke of good fortune that must surely point to the fact that providence was smiling down on him, he had been able to watch her in some detail from the old record store across the street – *The Vinyl Countdown* – watching her house as he rummaged through the bins in front of the store windows (old Al Kooper, Big Brother and Seatrain albums for a couple of bucks apiece, all stuff he'd read about in his mom's old magazines, tall stacks of *Rolling Stone*, *Crawdaddy*, *Fusion* and *Creem*, plus old British mags like *ZigZag* and the more recent *Mojo* and *Uncut*), seeing the girl come in and go out, seeing her open and lock the door on only two days – Tuesdays and

Wednesdays. The other days some woman (her mother, he guessed) greeted her, either at the door – which was always unlocked on Mondays, Thursdays and Fridays – or in the main room at the front of the house, the woman getting up out of her chair and hugging Suze like they'd just found each other again after being separated for years.

So he'd decided on a Wednesday, the middle of the week, the worst days over with and the anticipation of the weekend still to come. He'd noticed when, while visiting with his Uncle Demain, he took in his mom's old Ford rust bucket to have the muffler replaced, that the repair shop, *Tin Lizzie's* over on Fontaine (on account of the proprietor, Elizabeth Macready, widow of Manny – "Just don't ask how come we can have a Macready named Emmanuel," is what Virgil's mom was told by old "Doc" Svenson soon after the marriage, when Virgil was still just a tyke with his mother's more peculiar affections still to be shown), had a pile of clean coveralls sitting on a dusty spin-chair in the reception area, the kind of chair you always found in those old aluminum diner cars, the coveralls colored a bright orange with blue seams on the pants and sleeves and around the pockets, and sporting a very nifty logo on the back – a big heap of mufflers and car tires stuffed into what looked like a big old square zinc bath with the words *Tin Lizzie's* stenciled on its side. Virgil helped himself to one of them, put it in his rucksack. Then the next day, this very day, a Wednesday, eight o'clock in the evening, he went calling on Suze, a big brown bag filled with crepe bandages, rang the bell just as bold as you please, hands neatly covered with a pair of plastic gloves he'd also picked up at Tin Lizzie's, his heart racing like a trip hammer, checking over his shoulder down the street to make sure nobody was watching him, even checking across the street in *The Vinyl Countdown* and half expecting to see his own self standing there, looking across at him, holding an old Mike Bloomfield or Love album, shaking his head–

don't do it, boy, don't do this thing no more.... just turn around and walk aw–

–but the store was closed at this time of day and, anyway, she'd opened the door by then and said, "Yes?" in that sing-song voice of hers, and Virgil, who had already checked down the street and up the street and across the street, Virgil, whose heart was racing and whose blood was pumping away, Virgil who had a stiff one in his pants big enough for a rooster to perch on, why... Virgil, he just pushed the girl right back into the house and marched in just as ripe and ready as you like, the girl stumbling backwards, her eyes suddenly wide, eyebrows raised, taking in Virgil's face and his outfit and the plastic gloves, and Virgil closing the door behind him to make sure they weren't disturbed.

And they hadn't been.

Virgil had had the girl strip all her clothes off right there in the lounge, Virgil first pulling the curtains closed and not bothering about the fact that it was daylight and–

wouldn't folks get a tad suspicious about curtains being drawn and all?

–the girl sobbing all the time even though Virgil kept telling her he wasn't going to hurt her at all, no, not *at all*, ladeez and gentlemen... just going to have a real good look at whatever she had to offer, wanted to see it all, and then Virgil seeing the dim realization in Suze's eyes, those wonderful little green eyes, seeing her see that this wasn't going to have no happy resolution when the end-credits rolled up the screen – nossir, this was going to end bad, mighty bad, because the guy in front of her hadn't taken any trouble at all to cover up his face and he must know that she would be able to identify him to the police–

and why was he wearing plastic gloves, we all might wonder...

–and it was right then, with Suze already stripped down to her smalls and unhooking her brassiere, that she made a run for it and that's when Virgil had had to swipe her a good one upside that pretty head, swiping her with the thing that was closest to his right hand, a porcelain jug with a deep ruffled handle imprinted with fluffy clouds, and Suze had gone down hard and fast, like someone dropping a sack of potatoes, just flopping down on the polished wooden floor and lying still.

Virgil had removed her panties – closing his eyes in case he glimpsed her honeypot – and her brassiere, avoiding looking at her titties, and then bound her up real tight, bandages around her wrists and forearms and then across her belly and the small of her back, making her almost lie to attention before he started wrapping her up. By the time she came to, Virgil had covered her feet, ankles, shins, knees, thighs, hips, waist, belly and arms, chest, shoulders, and neck. And he had covered her mouth with duct tape so that her eyes darted side to side, flicking, like a deer's or a horse's eyes, nervous, anxious, fearful. Virgil liked that: fearful. Green and fearful.

When he had started to wrap the gauze bandage around under her chin, slowly but surely removing those final bits of flesh, the girl had begged, begged silently, amidst hoarse grunts, communicating only by movements of her head and her legs, moving those legs the way Virgil imagined a mermaid might move her tail, just one glorious long piece of flesh and scale.

And the best thing about it all was–

How's momma's little boy, then? Does Virgie wanna play with momma's secret place? Virgie the Pooh... the little boy who likes to lick the...

–there was no honeypot to be seen. No titties, neither... though Virgil had seen Susannah's breasts – just a flash, mind you – and they was no way like his momma's, big pendulous and veiny orbs, each with a flattened-out nipple area sprouting a couple curly dark hairs.

Just a minute or two later, Virgil sat back on an orange and green chair in the kitchen area, his feet propped up on the bar, as Susannah squirmed and wriggled. Virgil tried to imagine what it felt like, the breathing, hoarse and raspy, straining for tiny pockets of air that might prolong life just another minute or so, just another few seconds, and another, and maybe just the one more. And that was when the old woman had come back in, just a little while before midnight. And he never did find out where she had been, the old woman, nor what her relationship had been to the soon-to-be-late Susannah Neihardt.

Suze, well, she didn't know what the hell was happening, her down there on the floor and all, trussed up like a hog come Christmas, sucking in nanoparticles of oxygen – did oxygen even have nanoparticles? Well, Virgil didn't rightly know, but he did know he had to do something about the old woman so – saying "Hey, hey, take it easy, lady," holding his hands out, palms up, still wearing the plastic gloves from *Tin Lizzie's* and sporting that big cheesy smile of his, mouth turning up at the corners as he glanced down at the writhing bundle–

Only, hey, it ain't writhing no more and, is it my imagination or does it suddenly smell a little ripe in here?

–getting up from his chair, carefully avoiding touching her (but fully prepared to bring the old fart right down in her tracks if she looked set to spring for the door or holler out for help) and closing the door, nice and softly, no rush, no hysterics.

And then he hit her.

There was nothing available for Virgil to grab a hold of so he simply used his hand, his big right hand, clenching the fingers into a fist and bringing it around in a sweeping movement so that it was the middle sections of his fingers that connected with the side of the woman's face. She went over with barely a soft moan, her glasses flying off and skittering across the floor, with one lens skidding on and disappearing under the tasseled frill of a worn armchair, and the plastic bag – groceries, Virgil saw, though what the hell she was doing shopping for goddam groceries at this time was anyone's guess – scattering produce, loose vegetables and cans mostly, all over the floor.

When she was down, she didn't make any noise there either, just kicked her feet out in a little flurry of movement, and swung her arms around like she was a little human windmill, her tiny fists clenched with the thumbs on the outside and not tucked under the fingers. None of the movements connected with Virgil so he left her to thrash around while he went for the brown ducting tape. Then he set to securing the woman's arms and legs, placing a thick piece of tape around her mouth to stop her making any noise (just in case it ever occurred to her to do so, which, as far as Virgil was concerned, no longer seemed particularly likely).

When the woman was secured, Virgil pulled her back into the kitchen and laid her up against Suze. Then, with a deep sigh, he pulled out one of the kitchen chairs, a tubular steel framed job with garish yellow seat and back that were made out of either highly polished and veneered wood or some kind of heavy duty plastic, the shapes of them like amoebae, some kind of flashback to the kitsch designs of the 1950s and 60s, stuff he'd seen in his Uncle Demain's collection of *Saturday Evening Post* magazines back when he was a kid, cutting them up and sticking all the car advertisements into lined notebooks.

The woman was lying very still, watching him. He had taped her wrists behind her back and ran a length or two of the brown tape around her elbows. It couldn't have been comfortable – the woman lying kind of half on one side, the points of her elbows clearly making her unable to lie flat – but she wasn't complaining.

She was watching him.

He saw a little cut on the side of her nose, running up to her left eyebrow. It had bled a little but wasn't bleeding now.

The woman's eyes were darting from side to side. After a minute or two, she slowly moved her head to look at the bandaged bundle lying alongside her. Virgil thought he heard a muffled word – *"Hoozahnnah?"* it sounded like – and the woman nudged the bundle a couple times. But there was no response. That's when the woman turned her head back to look at Virgil, the eyes cold and accepting, knowing that there was no way this man was now going to be able to let her live (and that was assuming there had ever been a time when that had been a serious viable option). She blinked a couple of times and looked around. Maybe this woman was not Suze's mother after all. Virgil frowned and watched her. The woman was altogether too calm and calculating, looking around like she was Harrison Ford or Tom Cruise, scanning the place for a means of escape or of overpowering Virgil.

Virgil didn't like that. He didn't like that at all.

He got to his feet and walked across to the doorway and flicked the light switch, flooding the room. "And Virgil said, 'Let there be light,'" he said. "'And lo,'" he added, waving his arms majestically, "'there was light.'" He nodded, looking around the kitchen and the living area. "'And it was good.'"

When he looked down at the old woman again, Virgil thought he could see the makings of a tear, or perhaps just a tiny streak of moisture down the side of the woman's face, like a slug trail. That was better. Some emotion.

Virgil hunkered down beside her and smiled. "This isn't going to have a good ending, you know," he said, his voice matter-of-fact and sounding for all the world like he was going to try to help her, like–

So I tell you what I'm gonna do for you here today… I'm gonna forget you came in here and I'm gonna forget you ever seen me…. hell, I'm even gonna forget you know this woman over here–

–a sharp market salesman peddling his wares from door to door.

"You know that, don't you?"

The woman looked from one of Virgil's eyes and across to the other. She didn't respond.

"You hear me? You hearing what I'm saying to you here?"

Nothing.

"Nod your head if you can hear me."

No nodding of head. And then, barely distinguishable from an everyday movement of the head, there it was. It could, of course, have been a tic, an involuntary twitch, a spasm of muscle and cartilage. But it wasn't.

"You hear me?"

This time she nodded almost enthusiastically.

"OK, here's what we're gonna do, me and you." He got to his feet. "I'm gonna go sit down a while and think things over. And then we're gonna…" He looked over at Suze and then back at her, waving his hands and shrugging his shoulders. "…and then, why, we're gonna finish up is what we're gonna do."

The woman didn't move, just watched him.

"How's that sound to you? That sound OK?"

Nothing.

Virgil walked into the lounge and flopped down onto the sofa. He reached for the TV remote and flicked the button. But he was asleep before a channel came on.

Virgil dreamed strange dreams on regular days but on irregular ones, those days when he went out and did some of his special work, his dreams were downright bizarre. Even by those already impressive standards, this one was a classic.

Virgil's mother was there, which wasn't unusual in itself but she was sitting with a woman who Virgil did not immediately recognize, though she did seem familiar. It was only when the two women commenced to removing their clothes that Virgil saw that the second woman was the one he had recently bound on the floor of Suze Neihardt's house, Suze still lying there on the floor, all wrapped up but now with her head exposed. And now, not exposed, because Virgil's mom had thrown her brassiere over the poor girl's face, and Virgil must have said something to her because his mom looked hurt, halfway into rolling down her hose – Virgil saw that his mom's voluminous pants had a pot of honey drawn on the front, like one of those pots that Winnie the Pooh always had a paw into. And now the second woman, she turned to Virgil, scowling at him as she patted Virgil's mom's head, stroking it as it rested on the woman's shoulder.

And then the woman held up a finger as though for Virgil to watch what happened now.

Virgil's mom lifted her head from the woman's shoulder and the pair exchanged what appeared to be a knowing glance before craning their necks and looking up. In the dream, Virgil duplicated the action and suddenly found that he was staring into a night sky.

And then – *pow!* – everything dissolved into a blinding flash.

(3)

At later times, when reflecting, and when things got even stranger and the knot in his stomach made him wonder if his time was almost up, Ronnie Mortenson would think back to that moment as the cusp of his two lives. The *then* and the *now,* a knife-edge precipice between everything that had gone before and which had prepared him, and the time to put such preparedness into action. And even when things seemed to be at their most bleak – most notably in the troubles still to come in New York and the fraught time in Central Park in a strange and deserted Big Apple overshadowed by an alien edifice that rivaled even the much-missed World Trade Center – Ronnie thought that, perhaps, just *perhaps,* mind you, the *now* far outweighed the *then*. For it was at that moment, when he turned to the empty seat that had, until moments – moments? What were moments? Nanoseconds, more like – ago, been occupied by his wife, that Ronnie Mortenson finally came of age.

"Martha?" Even as he said it, Ronnie knew that it was a ridiculous thing to do. And even as he bent forward to look beneath her seat, he knew that that was an equally ridiculous thing to do. The next thing would be to lean over and stare out of the window, see if she was sitting on the goddam wing like that gremlin thing on the old *Twilight Zone* episode.

A clattering sound from the aisle made him turn around.

A young voice shouted for daddy and then mummy.

Things were falling from trays all around him. Something was happening to the plane.

The owner of the voice – it was a girl's voice, Ronnie realized – was crying now. He unclipped his belt, allowing the *Rolling Stone* to fall to the floor, and got to his feet.

The Boeing 757-200 series could carry between 178 and 239 people, depending on the individual plane's specification, and not counting cabin crew, in a series of three-seat rows on either side of a central aisle. Up towards the front of the plane, the legroom for the rows improved slightly and, right at the front, in first class, the rows became two-seaters on either side of the aisle. By Ronnie's estimate, the late-running – very late-running – 10pm flight from Denver had been maybe eighty or ninety per cent full when they left the ground. Ronnie checked his watch: it was after five in the morning.

And now the plane was empty.

The entire section of seats – with, as far as he could make out, just two exceptions – were completely empty. The two exceptions were Ronnie himself and the owner of the voice that had cried out. In front of many of the seats, small viewing monitors were showing programs: Ronnie could make out a cartoon – it looked like *South Park* – and, on another screen, what appeared to be some kind of news or current affairs show, with a man holding a microphone walking to and fro across a stage. There was no sound from the screens – that was piped up through the earphones plugged into the seat consoles. Ronnie could see them all as he looked, could hear them all whispering to themselves, some on the floor, some on the actual seats themselves, some lying on the seat-arms.

Ronnie hardly dared breathe. It all seemed so incredibly wrong that he thought he had to be having some kind of dream. He glanced back at his seat half-expecting to see himself still sitting there, maybe asleep or (even more likely, he thought) sitting staring sightlessly at some indefinable middle distance, a globule of drool hanging from his lower lip, a spreading pee stain around his crotch and a steadily increasing smell of manure drifting up from his *Fruit of the Looms*. But the seat, now that he was out of it, was empty.

He shouted out what he thought was going to be "Hello?" but it came out more like some kind of bestial howl.

A young girl got to her feet somewhere near the front of the left-hand section, maybe around Row D or E, and screamed at the top of her voice. Ronnie recognized the scream from somewhere – the scream from before, from just– How long ago? A minute? Two minutes? It was her.

The plane was turning downwards at an increasingly steep angle and Ronnie stumbled forward, partly into the aisle and hitting his right shoulder on the back of the seat in front of him.

"It's OK," Ronnie shouted, trying to regain his balance. He held his hands up, palms turned towards her, to demonstrate just how wonderfully alright it was all going to be.

OK? Yeah, right. Everyone on the plane except for Ronnie and some third- or fourth-grader had disappeared and he was trying to convince the kid that everything was hunky dory. He tried to move fully out into the aisle but he couldn't do it. He was pinned against the seat-back in front of him – the now worryingly empty seat in front of him, the one with the splash of Club Soda pooling on the little blanket that lay crumpled up on the seat – and he twisted away from that to land sprawling in the aisle on his hands and knees, before slumping forward onto his face and starting to slide down the carpet. He collided with the trolley, pushing it partly into the next but one set of seats where it thankfully jammed.

Jesus Christ! What was happening? It could only mean that the plane was in a nosedive. Ronnie turned onto his back and lifted a leg, fully expecting it to continue upwards with little or no involvement from himself, but it just lifted and stopped. Happy that there seemed sufficient gravitational pull on his leg to return it to the carpet – thus implying that their descent was not wholly vertical – he pulled himself upright by the trolley, turned around and took in the emptiness.

Now the engines were roaring.

He held onto the headrest corner and started down towards the flight deck. The plane still had a definite tilt, and the engines now sounded as though they were about to burst free from the plane and go off by themselves, but at least things did seem to be calming. He had no idea why he thought that. Perhaps this was what people who were about to die felt right at the end: a sense of almost religious calm. He thought about the usual safety presentations at the start of any flight, when the cabin crew advised the placing of one's head between one's knees. This was, in the opinion of one of the comedians Ronnie had seen on the TV, in order to kiss your ass goodbye. Ronnie didn't think that was going to be necessary this trip. Which meant one more good thing. Should that be one *more*, or just one?

There was somebody else still here. Somebody in the flight deck.

Ronnie looked across at the windows but couldn't make out anything but dark sky and occasional cloud. What *should* it look like out there? He turned around and kept walking.

The girl was in the left section of the plane, way up from where Ronnie and Martha had been sitting. Now she was in the aisle, up ahead of him, falling over, holding her head and screaming at the top of her voice.

"My *mommy*," she shouted. "My mommy's *gone*. Where did she *go*?"

The girl was blonde haired, wearing a blue paisley patterned dress over wrinkled yellow stockings made out of a corduroy-type material. She wasn't wearing any shoes.

"Hey, hold on," Ronnie said. "I'm on my way." *Huh, big deal*! he imagined the girl thinking. But this was all just a dream of some kind, wasn't it? How could a planeload of people just up and disappear in the space of seconds when they were a couple miles up in the air? It was a dream. That was all it was.

"Mommy!" the girl sobbed hoarsely. "Mommy!"

Each row of empty seats that Ronnie passed was littered with magazines, headphones still plugged into the armrests, trays down with packs of candies and chocolates, bottles of mineral water – some with their tops off, on their side, contents spilling out over belongings – paperback books lying on the floor or on suddenly flattened plane blankets that Ronnie was sure had covered legs and stomachs just a minute or two earlier. And there was the proof: not one single book or magazine was tented cover-up. They had fallen either open-pages-up or closing to lie crumpled and creased.

In other words, none of the people reading them had been prepared for what had happened.

And just what had that been? Ronnie thought.

The girl was pulling herself up the opposite aisle, heading for the rear of the plane. Ronnie braced his hands against two opposing headrests and tried to keep from falling forward.

Falling forward? That still didn't sound too good. How long could they continue to dive before they hit the ground? Without asking for it, an image suddenly shot into Ronnie's head: the image was of their plane hammering forward into the ground on a more or less vertical trajectory. Ronnie wondered what that would feel like. What was it going to be like, if you viewed it in slow-mo, to feel your body suddenly crushed between an unforgiving ground and a fairly determined thousand-ton airplane following it at several hundred miles per hour?

That was something the medical authorities always said, and it was something that Ronnie had never been able to sign into. They said, "It would have been fast. He/She/They wouldn't have felt a thing."

Well, that was all fine and dandy, but when you had to move from the one state of living and breathing into the second state – i.e. not living and breathing – there was surely going to be a brief moment or two in which you would experience that cessation of life or, at least, its imminence. Like the scene in the *Armageddon* movie when Bruce Willis is sitting on the state-sized asteroid holding the push-button that's going to blow the colossal hunk of real estate (and himself as well) into just so much dust. Pushing that button would take a whole lot of doing, Ronnie had argued with Martha when they left the movie theatre. It's just a movie, Martha had insisted. But Ronnie couldn't get it out of his head. You must be able to feel it when you decimate all the miles of arteries and your lungs and your kidneys, your heart, your eyeballs, your teeth, hands and feet, fingers and toes. Your balls. Your pecker. The way he saw it, death was gonna hurt. And it was gonna hurt big time. The end of all things. Plus a deep dish helping of profound pain.

He tried to put it out of his mind, although his back-of-the-brain comedian wasn't having it. Question: What's the last thing that goes through a man's mind in a nosedive plane crash? Answer: his ass.

No, it didn't sound good at all. More than that, if everyone was gone – everyone apart from him and the girl – if all the passengers had disappeared, then why couldn't the same thing have happened to the pilot?

"Who's flying the plane?" Ronnie asked nobody in particular, trying to keep his voice steady but shouting it out, above the sound of the engines roaring and things still falling behind him. He thought he knew the answer to that one.

All at once, the plane engines seemed to ease up a little.

At the same time, the PA system beeped and a man's voice came on.

"Ladies and gentlemen? As I think you might just have noticed, we had some problems there for a few minutes, so my apologies for any concerns we may have caused," the voice said. It was slightly hesitant but making some effort to be assured and confident. Ronnie had an idea what was causing that hesitancy.

"We're leveling off," the voice continued, "but we're turning around and heading back to Denver International. There are no problems with the plane. I repeat, there are no problems whatsoever with the plane."

The voice paused.

Yeah, what's it like up there where you are, Mr. Pilot? Ronnie thought. He looked across at the girl, who was staring up at one of the PA loudspeakers from which the voice was coming. She had calmed a little, and Ronnie knew how she felt. He was looking at one of the speakers, too. There was something reassuring about the voice, a touch of refreshing normalcy in a bizarre situation. He felt like the people who went to see Jesus must have felt, a kind of serenity, a lifting of the spirits. They were no longer alone – he and the girl. And just for one second, one fleeting wonderful second, Ronnie thought that maybe the pilot would be able to explain what had happened to them. After all, he had already said there was nothing wrong with the aircraft and that they were simply returning to Denver.

Ronnie imagined the airport, a working everyday airport. OK, it was two in the morning, so it would hardly be bustling but there would be people there. *Wouldn't* there? Perhaps it was just some sort of...

But there nothing he could think of that explained what it had been – except for a passing flying saucer that had beamed some kind of ray on them and picked up everyone on the plane. Everyone except for Ronnie, a kid and at least one pilot. And praise the lord for that last one. Amen, brothers and sisters. And you betcha, we'll *all* of us gather at the river for that one!

The girl looked across at him and rubbed her arm across her face to wipe her eyes and nose.

"One final thing," the voice said. "Would one of the cabin stewardesses come up to the front of the plane please? Thank you. I'll– We'll be keeping you posted on any other developments but we expect to be landing in Denver in around thirty minutes. Thank you once again."

I'll – change that to: *We'll* – yeah, right. Just one pilot. The other or others had just up and vanished, right back into the magician's hat with all the other rabbits.

The girl waited for a few seconds, looking around at the debris of interrupted life, and then, her face crumpling under a threatened fresh onslaught of tears, she said, verbally underlining key words, "My *mommy*. Where *is* she? She was *talking* with me and *then*–" She shook her head. What she was about to say made no sense. She was – what? – eight, nine years old? Even in the world of fairies and Santa Claus, of bogeymen and talking animals, a world she obviously still inhabited, there was nothing could prepare this kid for her mom disappearing from right under her nose when she's sitting right next to her on an airplane.

When he was just a few feet away from her, having sidestepped bags, pillows, blankets, bottles of water and various other icons of normality, crunching along on a myriad spilled peanuts, Ronnie crouched down and held out his hands sides upwards and palms facing each other, like a cross between going-to-clap and come-over-here-to-daddy. Ronnie knew he wasn't the girl's father but he wanted to do something that might make her feel a little easier.

"Hey?" he said.

The girl waited a few seconds, looking at Ronnie between splayed fingers fixed to her face. "Hey."

"You OK?"

"My *mommy*..."

"I know, I know. Take it easy now. What's your name?" he asked.

The girl was starting to shake and Ronnie saw a pool of water between her feet. "Angel," she said, her voice soft. "Angel Wurst." Then, "My mommy... where's my–"

"That's a lovely name," Ronnie said as he reached out a hand to move a curl of hair from her eyes.

The girl nodded. "Thank you," she said. "My name is really Angela but my daddy said he breathe-iated it to Angel."

"Well, it's lovely."

The girl nodded again.

"And just how old are you, Angel Wurst?"

"I'm nearly seven," she said, sniffling. "Where's my–"

Still six years old. Ronnie shook his head at her. So much for his estimate of eight or nine.

"You know," he said, "I'll bet your mommy's with my wife, Martha." He shook his head and made a tutting sound, looking around conspiratorially. "They're hiding from us. And everyone else is too, come to think of it," he added, whispering now. "They've all snuck off and left us. Like magic."

"Magic?"

Ronnie nodded.

"My mommy *wouldn't* leave me," Angel Wurst said.

Ronnie felt himself still nodding. That was surely true. He pulled a blanket from the seat alongside him, dislodging an Annie Proulx novel and sending it clattering to the floor. He held out the blanket.

"Here," he said. "Come put this on. You look cold."

The girl shifted from one foot to the other, holding both hands to her face. "My *mommy*!" she said. "I want my *mommy*. I don't *want* a blanket."

The PA system beeped and the man's voice returned. This time, it didn't sound quite so casual.

"Hello out there. Can anyone hear me?" It was as though Ronnie and the girl were eavesdropping on the pilot's (*was* he the pilot? Ronnie hoped so) conversation with the control tower, only Ronnie knew that he wasn't speaking to the control tower. This guy was speaking to the one-time crowded cabin behind him, a cabin from which he was getting no sign of life. Just like, Ronnie imagined, the cockpit of the plane, in which he was suddenly and inexplicably alone.

"We need to go see the captain," Ronnie said.

The girl looked around up towards the front of the plane. "The captain?"

Ronnie nodded. "He sounds scared, doesn't he?"

This time it was the girl's turn to nod.

"Well, we need to go see him tell him we're OK. See if he needs any help."

"What about my mommy? What if she comes back while we're–"

Ronnie smiled as reassuringly as he was able. He couldn't bring himself to tell her what he thought, couldn't tell her that he didn't think Angel Wurst's mommy was coming back, just as he couldn't bring himself to tell *himself* that Martha wasn't coming back – Martha, whose guts he had hated just a few minutes ago but whom he would now dearly love to see and take in his arms. *Was* it only a few minutes ago? Ronnie checked his watch. It was turning two in the morning. They should be back in Denver within just a few minutes. But what would they find there? That was the $64,000 question.

Oh, and there was a good one just before it: could the owner of the juddery PA voice land them back on the ground in one piece? Time to find out, he thought.

"Come on," he said to Angel Wurst, and the two of them started down the aisle towards the front of the plane.

Ronnie could feel her straining at him, pulling back from the door at the end of the aisle. As they approached the stewardesses' compartment just before business class, Ronnie saw trays of pre-packaged meals and plastic drink cartons strewn over the floor. He stopped just before they reached the area and hunkered down beside the girl. She was still shaking but she stared up into Ronnie's eyes. Ronnie recognized that look. It was a craving for assurance. She wanted him to say that everything was going to be OK because, even with the limited take on things that six slim years allowed for, she was pretty damn sure things were just about as bad as they could be.

"Angel?" Ronnie said.

The girl didn't speak, just nodded, though Ronnie saw her eyes sliding to the side and her head threatening to turn just a little so that she could see what was in the stewardesses' station. Because she sure as hell knew something was there – that was another thing Ronnie could see in the girl's eyes.

"Angel," Ronnie said again, "we're going to have to give a lot of help to the pilot."

"I dunno how to steer a plane," she said. "My daddy let me steer his car one time, sitting on his knee, but a plane is a lot bigger than my daddy's old-mo-beel."

Ronnie just stopped himself from correcting her.

"No, sweetie. You won't have to steer the plane." He jabbed his thumb into his own chest and added, "Heck, I won't have to steer it either."

He got back to his full height and gently eased Angel past the station while he continued to talk.

"No, the pilot will do all the steering, but I reckon we'll have to help him."

The girl looked up the aisle towards the door into the flight cabin and then looked back at Ronnie. "They're gone, aren't they?"

"Who's that, honey?"

"The men in the–" She looked up at the cabin door again and then said, "The men in the cockpit."

Ronnie looked into those two green eyes before nodding slowly. "I think they might be," he said.

"They're hiding too, right?"

"They're hiding, too."

Angel Wurst said, "*Where* are they hiding? I didn't see that part."

"I don't know where they're hiding, honey."

"My daddy calls me honey," she said. Her bottom lip started to quiver.

"Hey, what am I thinking of! We need to get you to a restroom. Get you cleaned up."

"Cleaned up?"

"I thought I saw you'd spilled your drink," Ronnie said, sliding into kindergarten diplomacy. "Didn't you get some on your pants? And down your legs?"

The girl frowned and then her eyes lit up. "No," she said, "I think I might have done a pee-pee."

Despite the situation, Ronnie had to smile. No diplomacy needed here, folks. Just tell it right as it is and skip the bullshit: *Hey, gramps, I think I pissed myself so will ya get it cleaned up already?*

He sat Angel Wurst in a big comfortable chair in the business class and went back to her seat to retrieve her *Little Mermaid* bag. Minutes later, with Ronnie looking the other way – "You sure you're not looking? My mommy tol' me never to take my clothes off in front of a stranger." – Angel changed into clean pants. Soon after that, they were rapping on the cabin door.

"Hey, come open the door," Ronnie shouted.

There was a *whoop!* from inside and a clattering of locks being turned and then the door opened.

A small, jowly man with disheveled hair – and not too much of that – pulled the door wide and peered myopically at Ronnie and the girl. Ronnie half expected him to say, *Yeah? What is it? I'm watching TV here and I already gave at the office.* Instead, the man started to sob and, raising his hands to his face, he knocked his glasses onto the floor. Angel promptly stepped forward and placed her foot on them. Even in her bare feet, she managed to shatter one of the lenses.

Jesus Christ! Ronnie thought. "Hey, take it easy," he said, taking hold of the man's shoulders and backing him into the cabin. There was something about the guy that was familiar. But he sure as hell didn't know any airplane pilots.

The cockpit was small. Just two seats were jammed between, in front of, and beneath a huge range of dials, switches, levers and knobs. Lights flashed and flickered, needles went around and around. And from the two pairs of headphones sitting one on what Ronnie decided to refer to as the dashboard and the other on the left-hand chair, a thin crackle of static sat on the air like the sound of the highway from across the fields where he had grown up in Cuyahoga Falls.

"They just went," the man said, shaking his head, the mixture of amazement and sheer disbelief still on his face. "Disappeared," he said, accepting the glasses from the little girl and slipping them right back onto his nose. He pulled at his necktie – which was already undone – and undid the top couple of buttons on his shirt.

"They're all hiding," Angel offered. "But we don't know where because I didn't see that part."

Hiding?" The man frowned first at Angel and then at Ronnie, squinting up at him through his broken glasses, the eye behind the smashed lens blinking constantly.

Ronnie watched him all the way, trying to dispel the image of Piggy in *Lord Of The Flies*, and flared his eyes as he helped the man into one of the seats. "Yeah, they've done a good job of it, too. There's only us two back there. Everyone else has dis– *hidden* themselves."

Ronnie was about to say something else but instead turned to the girl. "Hey, what did you say?" he asked.

"They're all hi–"

Ronnie shook his head and hunkered down alongside the girl. "Was it you who screamed? Just before the big light?"

Angel Wurst nodded her head, blonde ringlets jiggling over her ears.

"I'm going to get back to the controls." The man in the cockpit shuffled back into the left-hand of two leather seats and took hold of the steering column.

Ronnie looked around the cockpit, saw all the dials, the blinking lights, the switches and levers. "You OK with all this?"

"I'm OK," the man said, his voice soft, and he looked down at the girl who was staring through the front window into the swirling clouds. He leaned forward so that his face was almost touching Ronnie's. "So long as I don't have to land." He nodded and flashed his eyes a couple times. "You know what I'm saying here?"

"Well, we sure as hell can't stay up here forever."

The man nodded, turned his head and jiggled his eyebrows a couple of times. The jiggles said it all. They were in deep doo doo.

"Can we do something to help? Hey, this is Angel, by the way."

The girl nodded sheepishly and looked down at her *Little Mermaid* bag.

"I'm Karl," the man said, and he adjusted his glasses, still squinting a little at the broken lens.

"Ronnie," said Ronnie. He slapped Karl on the shoulder a couple of times and then reached over and tousled Angel's hair.

"Hey," he said, "we never finished, did we?"

Angel frowned.

"You said something before?" He let his voice drift off and when the girl still looked puzzled, Ronnie added, "You said something about not seeing that part?"

She nodded.

"What did you mean?"

She shrugged.

Did you *see* something? Is that why you screamed?"

She looked down at her bag.

Ronnie glanced sideways at Karl, who had turned in his chair, and then looked back at the girl. "Angel, if you saw something that might help–"

Then, right out of the blue, she said, "I saw it in my head."

(4)

The light had come around two hours into the Songs for Sleepers section that ran from one am until five. The show was a mixture of mood music, Melanie Grisham's sultry voiceovers and intros, and occasional phoned-in calls from folks either unable or unwilling to sleep, for whatever reason.

Some of them might be nursing bad relationships, some might be holding down nightshift jobs at the packing plant over at Carlisle, across the hills, or the trucking depot down at Dawson or even propping up the counter at Martha McNeil's Diner down the road in Jesman's Bend – affectionately known locally as the one-horse town to end them all ("...and even that one is lame," was how Rick usually ended those discussions). And one or two of them had some kind of psychological disorder, but Melanie didn't mind that. She reckoned they posed less of a problem to the world phoning her in the middle of the night – telling her they wanted to get into her pants and asking her about her pussy (Melanie's 15-second tape delay always kept such remarks off the air but she always managed to tell them she didn't own a cat) – than if they were out there roaming the streets, drinking their cocktails of oblivion and strength out of brown paper bags and talking to the moon... unless someone happened along they could talk to instead, someone who would be better off home and wrapped up in bed.

The light flashed and then disappeared. Just like that.

At a little after 3.15, the whole world had turned white, just for an instant, and then everything had gone back to normal.

Melanie was cueing up a CD of Perry Como's greatest hits – her mother's favorite – flicking forward to track 11, 'Magic Moments', when, suddenly everything in front of her had turned white. It wasn't just a glare from outside – like the headlights of an approaching car washing across the windows, except there weren't any windows connecting to the outside world in the studio – it was everything in the room, including the air itself: all definition had disappeared, a momentary white blindness, and then back the way it had been just seconds before.

"Jesus Christ!" Melanie hissed, yanking her hand back from the track button on the CD rig like the rig was a hot stove and she'd just touched it. "What the hell was that?"

Geoff rushed out of the sound booth and stood in the center of the room, looking around at the equipment, a copy of *Men's Journal* hanging from his hand. "You OK?" he asked when he was satisfied that nothing had blown.

Melanie nodded. The Sinatra song was coming to an end. She waved Geoff quiet and pulled the mic boom across to her. "Yeah, nobody told those stories like Old Blue Eyes," she said into the gauze, her voice smoky and just the right side of hoarse. She pressed the play button on the CD player. "We're gonna leap right on now with one of my mother's favorites. I'll be back to talk to you after this – a few 'Magic Moments' from Mr. Perry Como." As the first orchestral strains cut in, Melanie said, "And anyone out there needs someone to talk to in these lonely hours, just give me a call – you know the number." She pushed the boom away and wound up the volume.

She leaned back on her chair and held her hands straight out in front of her. They were shaking. She looked across at her husband and took a deep breath. "What was it?"

Geoff shrugged. "Nothing in here, that's for sure."

He ran a hand through his thatch of sandy hair and breathed deeply.

"So where was it, if it wasn't in here?" Melanie pointed across to the wood-paneled sidings that went all around the room. "Can't even see outside."

Rick appeared in the sound booth and started waving. Geoff waved him to come inside.

"There's a car, truck maybe, out on the forest road," Rick said as he came into the studio. "On fire."

"That must've been it," Geoff said. "Don't see how we could see it in here, though."

Rick looked from Geoff's face to Melanie's. "That must've been what?"

Melanie shook a Marlboro from a pack on the console and lit it. "Some kind of light," she said, blowing out smoke in the thin stream, watching it curl up below the light. She placed the cigarette on the lip of a Coca-Cola ashtray and flicked through a CD rack.

Rick frowned and thought back to sitting out there on the deck at the back of the station, remembered the dream and waking up from it. "No, the light came first."

Geoff walked across and shook himself a cigarette out of Melanie's pack. "Before the truck?"

"I don't know for sure it's a truck. Could be a car. But it's burning."

Melanie seemed to have found what she was looking for. She flipped open a CD case and slipped the CD into the second player, cueing a particular track. "You boys want to talk about it in the booth? I've got a show to do?"

They walked out and secured the studio door.

"I think we need to go out, take a look," Rick said, watching his brother flop onto the sofa. "Could be somebody's hurt."

"Uh uh. I'll call Eddie at the station. Let *them* go." He blew out smoke and adjusted himself, fought back a yawn. "You say it was on the forest road?"

Rick nodded.

"Mm hmm, could be they're even nearer than we are." He reached over to the desk and lifted the phone, keying in the number with his other hand.

"Many calls?"

Geoff shook his head, listening to the *brrrt brrrt* in the earpiece. "Never are this time, after two, two-thirty. Folks are all curled up doing what they should be doing–"

"Or what they *shouldn't* be doing!" Rick added with a big smile.

"And it's a big amen to *that* one," Geoff said returning the grin.

"Leastwise, they ain't wanting to talk to folks over at the radio station, and that's a fact."

Rick leaned against Geoff's desk and scanned the walls, taking in the posters and the Vargas calendar months – there were twenty-seven of them, some of them more than thirty years old. He smiled and shook his head. "Mel never say anything about those?"

"The Vargas girls?"

"Uh huh."

"Why would she say anything?"

Rick gave a little shrug. "Like maybe she thinks they're a little tacky."

"Tacky!" Geoff snorted. "They're art. Ain't nobody ever drew a woman like Vargas." He slammed the phone down on the cradle and picked it up again, re-keyed the numbers.

"Busy?"

Geoff shook his head and slouched back against the cushions, the phone at his ear again. "No answer."

"Who's on tonight?"

"Eddie – Eddie for sure – Shirley maybe? Don... Troy?"

"Didn't Barbara deliver yet?"

Geoff shrugged.

"I think she did. A girl, as I recall. Janey told me, over at the deli? It's my guess Troy will be home nights for a couple weeks."

"Well, maybe." Geoff stubbed his butt out in a saucer on the sofa's arm. "Still should be somebody picking up calls, though."

"Geoff, I think we should maybe go out there ourselves. Right now."

Geoff put the phone back on the cradle. He frowned up at his younger brother. He tried to see himself in Rick's face but couldn't. Rick was taller – at six-two, a good three inches – with dark almost black hair and a swarthy complexion. Geoff, meanwhile, was light-skinned – always a problem in the height of summer – and maybe a little on the stocky side.

"What about Mel?" he asked. "Leaving her here all alone?"

Rick waved his arms expansively. "I'll wake Johnny."

Geoff snorted. "He'll be so thrilled."

"Has to be done."

"You enjoy making him pissed. You know that, don't you?"

"Like I say, has to be done."

"But you *do* enjoy it."

Rick nodded and smiled. "OK, OK, I enjoy it."

As Rick left the sound booth, chuckling, Geoff's own laughter died away and he glanced in at his wife. And then at the telephone.

"You wanna die, right?" Johnny spoke without opening his eyes, his head almost completely buried face down in his pillow. "Whoever you are, you got bored with life and decided you wanted to try dying."

Rick removed his hand from John Meshtik's bare shoulder and sat gently on the side of the bed. "Johnny, you have to get up."

"Who says?" Still no movement.

"I say, Geoff says."

Johnny smacked his lips again and turned around. He shielded his eyes with his hands and looked up at Rick, squinting at the light from the hallway over his shoulder. "And why is that?"

"There's been an accident, out on the forest road, and we're–"

"What kind of accident?"

Rick shrugged and pushed the door closed, returning the room to gloom.

Johnny turned around and opened his eyes so they were slits. "Ah, thanks – that's better. What kind of accident?"

"Don't know till we get over there. Truck maybe, on fire."

"You call the Sheriff's office?"

Rick nodded. "Geoff did. No answer."

"No answer?" Johnny sat up in bed and lifted his watch from the side table. "It's after 3.30 in the damned morning. What could they be doing down there at this time?"

"Lines could be down," Rick said and then realized that that couldn't be true. He had heard the phone ringing when Geoff had dialed.

"And why would the lines be down?"

"Jesus Christ, Johnny, just get out of the fucking bed. We're going down to see if someone needs help."

"OK, OK." Johnny pulled the sheets back and swung his legs out, yawning. "But why would the lines be down? There a storm?"

"Uh uh." Rick got up and opened the door again. "There was some kind of... some kind of light. Just before the truck crashed. It if is a truck... and if it did crash."

"If it didn't crash, why is it on fire?" Rick glared and Johnny sniggered, holding his hands up. "I'm getting out of bed, see? This is me–" he got to his feet and adjusted the waistband of his shorts"– getting out of bed, OK?"

"OK."

He pulled a pair of jogging pants from the bureau behind the door and stepped into them. Then he slipped an already buttoned creased shirt over his head and gave a mock bow. "Johnny is ready."

"I'm pleased."

They walked out into the hallway and made for the stairs down to the studio floor and the outside doors.

"You said there was a light?"

"Yeah, like a flash – lightning. Everything went white for a few seconds, then came back to normal."

"Sounds like we're gonna get a bitch of a storm." Johnny took hold of the handle into the studio and stopped. "You guys take it easy out there."

Rick nodded. "Look after Mel."

Johnny's eyes opened wide. "Hey, that's right. It's just me and the Lady Melvin... maybe she needs me to look after her, keep her warm against the nasty storm."

"Yeah, in your dreams."

When Rick stepped outside, his brother was already pulling the Dodge around the front of the building. Rick looked across the sweep of the valley to the forest road and saw the smoke. It didn't look as bad as it had done before, but maybe that was because the first rays of the sun were showing behind the hills, turning everything lighter, making everything seem less hostile, less mysterious.

Geoff leaned over and flicked up the door catch. "Get in," he said.

They drove in silence.

The sky behind the hills was lightening up all the time and by the time they had reached the vehicle – a flatbed pickup they knew was owned by Jerry Borgesson – shadows were already showing themselves.

"Jerry's truck," Geoff said as they pulled in behind it. Rick didn't say anything.

The truck was plowed into the bushes at the right hand side of the road. If it had drifted to the left, it would have gone over the side and straight down the steep wooded incline to the valley bottom. Rick looked across at Honeydew Mountain and saw the radio station straddling the flat middle section below the horned crown, tried to imagine Melanie speaking in husky tones into the mic, holding her early morning audience in raptures.

Geoff had moved around to the driver's door and his voice interrupted Rick's reverie. "He's not here," Geoff shouted. "Nobody's inside."

The fire had not done much damage although smoke was still fuming out from the buckled sides of the hood. Geoff reached in and switched off the ignition and the thin, watery headlights disappeared. Rick walked around the other side of the truck and looked inside the cab. It was empty, as Geoff had said. He opened the door and climbed inside.

"Can't get this side open," Geoff said through clenched teeth as he pulled at the handle. "Must've been damaged in the crash."

"There's nothing in here," Rick said. He was looking specifically for blood or damaged dashboard or windshield to indicate Jerry Borgesson's bulk or head slamming into it. But the interior looked as good as new – or, at least, as good as fifteen years old would allow. There was a creased Polaroid of Jerry's wife, Shirley, slotted behind the rear mirror fixing plate, a half-eaten pack of mints lying on the plastic shelf housing the speedo, and a confusion of crumpled paper bags, breadcrumbs and apple and pear cores around the pedals. All pretty much the way Jerry's truck should be. Except for the fact that there was no Jerry.

Geoff moved back from the door, hands on hips, and turned around. He shouted Jerry's name and waited.

"You think he's hurt? Crawled off somewhere, maybe, to get away from the fire?"

"Something like that," came the reply. Geoff shouted again.

Silence reigned.

"Hey, Rick? You notice anything?"

Rick moved across to the driver's seat and rolled down the window. Leaning on the sill, he said, "Like what?"

Geoff turned around and glanced at him and then glanced quickly away, as though what he was thinking was too preposterous even to verbalize it. "There's no sound," he said.

Rick leaned further out of the window and listened. Geoff was right. The entire valley was as still and as silent as a grave. No bird sounds. He sat back and shuffled around in the seat so that he was facing forward. He took hold of the steering wheel gingerly, allowing his hands to acclimatize themselves around the worn leather and the smoothed finger sections, fighting back the images of the young man and woman whose faces had stared at him as he ran them down. It was almost six months ago now but it still felt like yesterday.

He had sold the DeSoto to a dealer over in Carlisle, and though Geoff had reasoned with Rick that it wasn't Rick's fault and that it was just an accident – could happen to anybody – Rick wasn't having any of it. Now, all this time later, the feelings were not getting any better – if anything, they were getting worse, with the dream coming to him every night now instead of every few nights the way it had done immediately after the accident.

Rick looked across at the passenger door. "Geoff?"

"Yeah? You found something?" Geoff was kicking through the undergrowth at the side of the road above the incline.

"I just realized something."

"Yeah? What?"

"I opened the door." He turned to look at Geoff. "I opened the door to get inside here."

"And?"

"Well, if Jerry was hurt – or even just dazed – why would he close the door after him?" Rick pretended to stagger out of the cab and then turned to close the door. "Why would he do that?"

Geoff shrugged. "Truck-proud? Hey, I don't know."

"Doesn't make any sense. Doesn't make any sense him not turning off the ignition, either... particularly with the engine on fire." Rick removed his hands from the steering wheel and rubbed them down his trousers. They were clammy.

"He's probably lying somewhere out in the bushes," Geoff suggested, though the suggestion didn't sound all that convincing. "Or maybe–" he turned around with a big smile on his face "–maybe he walked into town! Yeah, that's it. That's what he's done. He's walked into town." He clapped his hands together. "He's walked into town because there's nothing else for him to *do* at four o'clock in the morning. Come on, let's drive on."

Getting out of the cab of Jerry's flatbed pickup was a huge relief for Rick though he didn't know whether that relief was simply a throwback to memories of the accident or something else. Something else entirely.

(5)

Virgil had heard – or maybe seen – something in *his* head, too. But what was it? He came awake and listened. *Had* he heard something? Was that what had awoken him? Or had he been dreaming?

The television was showing one of those teen comedies that were simply not funny, and Virgil pressed the mute button, cocking his head on one side. Was it somebody at the door? He got up from the sofa and turned to the kitchen.

The bandaged and gauze-wrapped body of Suze Neihardt lay exactly where he had left it. But the brown-taped old woman was nowhere to be seen.

Damn! That was what he must have heard – the old bird sneaking out of the house, like to call the cops. Not stopping to wonder why she hadn't called them from in the house itself, Virgil ran to the kitchen, taking care to check around corners, keeping his head down. How had she got loose? But there was no time to answer – or even ask – such questions. She was loose, certainly. Of that there was no doubt.

Now in the kitchen, Virgil checked over towards the back door – it was closed. Surely she would not have had the presence of mind to steal away into the night, closing the kitchen door gently behind her? That just seemed too ridiculous.

But Virgil was beginning to feel that an even more ridiculous solution to the problem was uncoiling itself in his mind.

He turned to the floor, frowning.

There was no tape, scrumpled up in sticky wedges – as, of course, it would have been immediately on her escape.

He looked across at the body of the girl.

And would she have left the girl, that old woman? Virgil did not think so. He wasn't sure of the relationship between the two but he was sure that there was a bond between them.

"No," he told the disinterested kitchen, "something isn't right here."

But hold on there a minute, hoss. The girl is dead, long gone, kaput. Why risk your freedom to start messing around with a taped-up corpse, particularly when the guy who taped her up is sitting right there, in your living room, snoozing on your sofa.

No," he told the silence. And he said it again – "No!" – emphatically, this time. Something smelled in Denmark.

Virgil went to the kitchen drawers, pulling them open one by one: bread knives, steak knives, carving knives, skewers, forks, carving forks.

He slammed the last drawer closed and stopped right where he was standing, and he listened.

But he couldn't hear anything.

He was about to move again but then he froze. And concentrated. He had been right before: he couldn't hear anything. But it was more than that: he actually could not hear even the slightest noise, even from way off in the distance.

He had a sudden mental image of police cars parked up and blocking the street in both directions, stopping traffic and passers-by. But how could they know he was here? And how could they–

The old broad, that's how they could know. The cunt had gotten out and blown the whistle. And any minute now – any *second* now – there would be a knock on the door or a ring on the bell, and a deep voice that took no bullshit from any jumped-up little assholes like Virgil Banders would say, *Police,* spreading that word into two, *"poe"* and *"lease"*, and then "Open the goddam door, kid!" maybe shouting through a loudhailer. Then maybe there would be tear gas, like on the old prison movies starring Jimmy Cagney and George Raft. Did they still use tear gas? Virgil guessed they did.

He lifted his right hand to his mouth and chewed on his thumbnail.

But hold on now, how come the old fart had closed the door after her? No, that didn't make any sense at all. If she'd gotten the door open then she'd have hared off down the path to the sidewalk, hollering for all she was worth, and he would have heard her. That and maybe there'd be a bunch of people standing out there on the step.

He checked his watch. Coming up to 5.30.

No, there wouldn't be any bunches of people at 5.30 in the morning.

He looked again at the back door and this time saw that the key was turned in the lock. He walked to the front door, saw the deadbolt pushed across. OK, OK, this was looking better.

So the woman had somehow gotten herself untied, and–

Virgil shook his head. No, that just wasn't right. And he said so, looking down at the still and bandaged body of Suze.

"There's no way she could have undone that stuff," he announced. "And if there was, she would have left the scrunched-up tape. But even if she was so clean and tidy that she put the tape into a pocket or something, there was no way she would disappear." Virgil shook his head. What she would have done in that situation would have been either get the hell out or introduce her intruder to a kitchen knife or a skillet.

He glanced across at the stairs.

Maybe she was up there. He moved closer to the foot of the stairs and bent his head so that he could see right up into the darkness at the head of the stairs. He couldn't hear anything.

He moved back from the staircase, checking behind him for the old fart suddenly–

Boo! Try this carving knife in your kidneys, sucker!

–appearing from around back of the sofa or the curtains.

There was nothing else for it. He had to check upstairs. But first, he also had to check outside.

Virgil moved across to the curtains and pulled the left one back about an inch, so that he could put his face against the wall and look down the street. It was deserted. No traffic.

No *traffic*? OK, so it wasn't six o'clock yet but there should be signs. They were close to the meat packing plant over on Roylston and refrigerated trucks were moving in and out of there all day every day.

He looked some more.

And this time, he looked closely. Just for a moment, he thought he saw a shape out there, a shape like a woman just standing there over in the shadows on the sidewalk opposite but then the figure either backed off or it was just the window-pane, a trick of the glass and the darkness outside against the light behind him. And now, over behind the Jansson warehouse complex near the overpass, he thought he saw some more movement. But when he focused in on it, like Clark Kent, he saw it was only a piece of paper, maybe a potato chips bag, blowing in the wind.

"There's nobody out there," Virgil told the house, and somewhere, in the deepest part of his bowels, his stomach groaned a faint agreement.

Virgil looked at the door, then at the body and then back at the staircase. First things had to be first.

He found the knife in the third drawer along from the washbasin – third time's a charm – a long-handled job whose handle looked to have split: someone had wound some kind of green twine around it. Virgil hefted it from hand to hand, checking the balance, and then he moved quickly but calmly (*businesslike,* his mom would have said) out of the kitchen, flipped the light switches at the foot of the stairs and ran up two at a time, sliding his back up the wall and holding the knife right out in front of him. When he reached the upper landing he kicked open each door, starting at the end of the corridor, working through the bedrooms all the way to the restroom, and then a kind of storage cupboard piled high with freshly ironed clothes and linen, and finally a bathroom at the other end. With each room, he marched right in there, kicking at things, knocking things off of the tops of dressing tables and bedside cabinets, checking inside wardrobes and behind doors, even behind curtains which were still bunched up at either side.

In the second bedroom, he stopped for a minute and looked out of the window.

It looked as though the whole of the neighborhood had ground to a complete halt. There was a part of him then, then while he was standing at the window, which just wanted to see a pair of car headlights snaking along the road, or maybe some old guy, a derelict or a wino or a bum, a druggy... any damn thing at all. But there was nothing.

He stood there challenging the old fart-woman, wherever she was, to come at him from behind, screaming an old fart-woman's scream as she whacked him across the shoulders with a broom handle or a Dictionary, or maybe jabbed a knitting needle into his side . . . whatever. He just suddenly felt afraid of being alone.

The next room, he went into without all the noise and the bluster. He knew she wasn't in there. Not under the bed, not in the fucking closets, and not outside clinging to a tiny ledge up above the street. No, the windows were closed, the shit-to-fuck doors were closed, *every* fucking thing was closed. And seeing how every fucking thing was, indeedy, locked up tighter than a nun's snatch, and the fact that she just wasn't anywhere to be found, just what exactly–

Hey, no, don't put the thought into words, man, don't beard this monster in its lair cos it's just as like to whip your pants down and chomp on your pecker, ripping it right out and leaving a bloody stump down where the curly hairs grow...

–did that mean?

Virgil backed up until the backs of his knees touched the bed and stopped, still staring out of the window. He lifted his hand to his mouth and started chewing on his thumb.

He went back downstairs, clumping loudly.

"Hello?" he shouted.

There was no answer.

So, she had gone out. She'd somehow managed to get herself untied–

And how the hell did she manage to do that, *oh wise one?*

–and instead of introducing her captor's head to the flat side of a heavy pan or putting a hole in his chest from a snuck-away Saturday special she kept maybe in the hallway drawer or a secret cookie jar on a kitchen shelf, she had quietly left the house–

Miraculously locking the door again.... from the inside – *don't forget that one, Sherlock....*

–and gone to look for help.

Virgil chewed his lip, eyes darting to and fro as he took in all the possibilities.

So, if he accepted that – because, after all, what else *was* there, true believers? – then he needed to get the hell out of there.

Virgil didn't know where the next thought came from – maybe it was from the great Central Casting of all secret thoughts – but he lifted his hands and looked at them. The plastic gloves had gone.

"Shit!"

He ran into the kitchen, checked the counter-tops and ran back into the hall. Nothing there. He glanced up the stairs, half-expecting to see the old fart standing there with a gun in one hand and the gloves in her other, hanging like a limp prophylactic: *unassailable evidence of a gross misdeed, your honor.* But the stairs were clear. He turned back to look at the window, concentrating to hear the first faraway *wee-wah* sound of an approaching cop car. But then, maybe they'd sneak up on him, not give their presence away with a siren.

Virgil shook his head. "Think!" he snapped at himself, emphasizing the urgency of the instruction with a slap to the forehead with the heel of his right hand.

Did the woman – the old fart – did she know him? No sir, she did not.

Did he have any priors? No sir, he did not.

So no fingerprints recorded anywhere? Uh uh.

No DNA samples to be gotten from hair follicles or skin scrapings or dried-up blobs of jizm? Nope, nada.

He glanced down at the body on the kitchen floor.

And the alleged dead person? No such animal, mein Kapitan.

Virgil rushed to the front door, flicked off the room light and turned the key. As he edged open the door he expected a light to wash over him – the same light from his dream, perhaps – and a bullhorn voice to croon across at him from the street: *OK Banders, make it easy on yourself and come out with your hands held high.*

Virgil wished he had a gun. He wasn't about to let them put him in prison, nosirree. He wasn't going to let his sweet and untainted ass become jerk-off meat for some 300-pound tattooed love-boy with more gaps than teeth. He would have gone out in a blaze of glory, gunned down by the cops as he raced out into the yard brandishing his piece – *I'm at the top of the world, ma!*

He looked back into the room and felt a sudden calm come over him.

"Fuck it," he said, and he pulled the door open wide.

The street was empty. The old Honda flatbed was still at the curb, no police car was parked behind it or across the front of it, and there were no sudden blasts of light freeze-framing him against the house front. Nope, he was all clear.

Minutes later, he was staggering down the path to the sidewalk, the bandaged Suze Neihardt over his shoulder like a roll of carpet. He pulled down the flatbed gate and dropped the roll on. Then he fastened the gate and pocketed the keys, checking around some more. Boy, it was quiet. He checked his watch. It was coming up to 5.45. There should be more traffic than this.

No, strike that last one sports fans. There was no fucking traffic at all.

Virgil walked a little way up the sidewalk, turning around every few feet and walking backwards and then turning again and moving forwards. When he reached the intersection he stopped and looked back. The door to Suze Neihardt's house still wide open. He suddenly didn't seem to feel that was important anymore. Something just was not right here. He stopped and looked around. Nothing.

He walked across the street and back up the other side until he reached the vinyl store, checking both ways, maybe even hoping, from somewhere deep down where hopes start out that he would see a cop car turn a corner a couple blocks up the street and swing out towards him, the siren starting up like a wildcat's howl.

But there was still nothing.

Nothing and nobody.

"Hey," he said, his voice soft and almost drowned out by the early morning breeze, "this is not right."

Virgil stepped out into the street. When he reached the midway mark, he looked around again. Then he lifted his hands up to his face, cupped them around his mouth and shouted out, "Hello?"

The wind soughed through the skeletal branches of a couple of small cedar trees and a newspaper dispenser along the sidewalk.

Virgil bent over backwards and shouted again, louder this time – much louder. "Anybody there?"

He felt his heart miss a couple of beats, skidding around in his chest someplace, as he jogged back across to his pickup.

"Hello?"

Nothing.

He picked up a piece of broken cement and hefted it in his hand as he checked the windows of the houses further along the street. Then he pitched it. The rock hit a piece of wall between the first and second floor windows of the next-but-one house to Suze Neihardt. He figured the dull clunk it made followed by the resounding clatter as it landed on something metallic should have caused those drawn curtains to pull apart a little and some guy to lean out–

What the hell's goin' on down there, for fuck's sake? People's tryin' to sleep up here ! It's goddam six ay emm in the fuckin' morning!

–and give Virgil the benefit of his feelings on the noise, but when nobody appeared, he looked around for another piece of rock, this time one slightly bigger.

The rock sailed through one of those second floor windows, billowing the curtains out and spraying glass shards all over the sill and the bedroom floor. The noise reverberated but, when it faded, it left a silence that was somehow much louder.

And nobody appeared.

Maybe the people in that house weren't home. Maybe they'd gone to stay with their son and daughter-in-law in Des Moines or Cedar Rapids, leaving the house empty and silent behind them. He hefted another piece of rock, this time through the lower window of the house behind him. More shattered glass, more billowing curtains. More goddam silence.

"Hey, now just wait up a minute here!" Virgil shouted. He strode purposefully across to the first house he'd hit and hammered on the door.

When nobody appeared, he hammered some more, and kicked.

And then he took a step back and did a series of flat-foot kicks until the door sprang open in a flurry of wood bits, the security chain twanging and sending something skittering along a wooden floor inside. Virgil stepped inside the house, flicking on a light switch.

"Knock, knock!" he shouted.

No answer.

He moved across to the staircase and shouted up. "Sir? Ma'am? There's an emergency here..."

He waited. Nothing.

"I'm coming up."

He went up the stairs, clumping all the way.

"Coming up the stairs, now... no cause for alarm... we got an emergency here..."

On the upper landing there were two doors facing him, with another over to his left. The one to his left and the right-hand one of the two facing him were closed.

Virgil moved straight ahead, pushed open the door and flicked on the light.

At first, he thought there was someone in the bed but then he realized it was just the sheets, pulled up and rumpled as though encasing someone – perhaps *two* someones? he wondered – who was no longer there. Yes, now that he looked closer, he could see that the pillows were pulled down a little way from the headboard and scrunched at their lower ends, as though a shoulder had until recently been jammed into each of them, and each was indented in the middle where a head had lain. A paperback novel was tented on the side table of the left side – Robert B. Parker's *School Days* – and a pair of house shoes (slippers but made of leather with thicker soles and heels) was neatly placed just below the bed edge. A blue toweling dressing gown was lying in a heap next to the slippers. Pieces of broken glass littered the floor and lay on top of the dressing gown and the slippers.

He moved around to the other side and saw another pair of slippers, this one backless and topped by plumes of yellow fluff. Virgil looked at the side table and saw a pack of Pepto Bismol chews, a dainty watch, a pair of rimless glasses and a *Good Housekeeping* magazine.

Virgil leaned over and placed a hand beneath the top sheets. It felt vaguely warm in there.

"What the hell is going on here?" Virgil whispered.

He backed out of the room as slowly as he could, scared – deep, deep down where the irrational has a face and an expression and, all too often, a set of very sharp teeth – that if he turned his back then someone or maybe something would crawl its way out from beneath those still-warm sheets and pounce noiselessly on him.

Back on the landing and still facing into the room he had just left, Virgil turned left and saw the other closed door.

His heart pounding now, he moved along the landing and pushed the door – it started inwards with the faintest squeak and then continued to open even when Virgil removed his hand.

He didn't turn on the light here. He could see enough.

It was clearly a child's room, a boy's. Posters of Wolverine out of the X-Men movies, Jerry Seinfeld and Angelina Jolie in her Lara Croft outfit all looked down at him as though questioning why he was here. A shelf against the side wall housed a run of Stephen King paperbacks while on the shelves below it sat piles of comic books.

Virgil turned to the bed. It was the same as the other one: indented pillow, rumpled bedclothes, the works. It was as though the occupant of this bed – and the ones from the one in the other room – had somehow been spirited away.

Virgil moved back into the light of the landing and, just for a few seconds, he considered looking around the place to see what he could steal. There must be money here, maybe some credit cards – though the increased security measures made that a no-no these days. But then the idea popped out of his head just as fast as it had popped in: where had these people gone?

Virgil went back along the landing, giving a wide berth to the open doorway of the main bedroom, and jogged down the stairs two at a time.

He checked all the rooms downstairs, not sure what he was looking for but increasingly convinced that whatever the problem was in this house might well extend outside.

And he was now almost certain that the old fart had not set herself free and walked off. She'd gone to wherever it was that the couple upstairs and the kid in the small room had gone.

On a hunch, Virgil walked across to the telephone and lifted the receiver. He punched in 411 and waited for an operator. The phone rang a couple times and then went into a solid tone. He cleared it and re-punched. Same thing. There had to be a sensible answer to this.

Right on, man... like maybe all the operators just stepped out for a smoke – same thing with the folks upstairs, sneaking out from their beds without disturbing any sheets, just stepping out at five o'clock in the morning for a smo–

One more time. He punched the numbers: 4-1-1.

Same thing again.

Virgil went back outside. The sky was lightening over to the east. The city should now be coming awake but there wasn't a sound anywhere.

He walked into the street and looked back towards the west and downtown Denver. A thick pall of smoke was filling the sky over there. He hadn't noticed it earlier because it was still dark, but he could see it now. It was a lot of smoke.

So what was it? Terrorists? But terrorists couldn't remove people from their beds without disturbing the sheets. And anyway, why was *he* still here? So many questions.

And no goddam answers.

A few minutes later, he was heading west with Suze Neihardt's body bouncing around on the flatbed. As he moved out of the suburbs and onto the deserted interstate, where the buildings flattened out and offered further visibility, Virgil could see that the ceiling of smoke was coming from several drifting plumes, like mini-tornados, each of them twisting and turning into the early morning.

Cars and trucks were littering the blacktop, some of them just pulled up against the metal sidewalls and some turned over or actually half through the walls. A little way along, he saw a pale green Pontiac convertible turned sideways right in the middle of the road. Virgil stopped and got out, walked across to the car and pulled open the door. No handbrake had been applied but the car was a manual shift so he guessed that it had simply stalled when–

When the bad thing happened, right? When the bad thing happened and everyone on the planet got themselves wiped out... erased – everyone except him, of course...

–and had just run to a stop. Virgil slipped into the driver's seat, shuffled the lever to park and turned the ignition. It started first time. He checked the gas gauge – three quarters full.

Virgil looked across at the Honda, the rust, the dented side-panels, the cracked headlamps, and then looked down at the plush green upholstery of the Pontiac. It was no contest. Shifted into first and turned the car around slowly until he was facing the city again. Then he pulled Suze Neihardt's body off of the flatbed and moved her across to the Pontiac, where she had a nice warm trunk all to herself.

A few minutes later, he was on his way again.

And best of all, he had Flaming Lips on the CD player.

Life was good. It was strange, but it was very good indeed. And all the signs were it was going to get better.

Virgil Banders, the Last Man on Earth.

He liked that. It had a nice ring to it.

Wayne Coyne must have thought so, too: *With all your power / with all your power / with all your power...* he and the guys sang.

"Yeah yeah yeah yeah yeah," Virgil chorused, the words drifting out of the open window of the Pontiac and floating up, way up, into the early morning air to mingle with the smoke that hung over the city like a graveyard mist. A gentle rain had started up and it seemed to Virgil Banders like a spray sent to clean the world.

(6)

Over in Lakewood, just a few miles from where Virgil Banders was driving his stolen car through the silent streets, Sally Davis also felt cleaned by the rain.

Sally had been out on the street since the bright light had filled her world, standing there wide-eyed, her hair hanging a little lank and limp around her face. She was dressed only in a skirt and cardigan sweater, her arms folded about her midriff like one of the women from the fuse factory over near the Project. Watching, feeling thc rain patter on her head, her head tilted to one side, seeing it spread darkness across the sidewalk. It felt real good. In fact, it seemed to freshen the voices inside in there, seemed to liven them up with renewed energy and vigor.

Maybe the light had been lightning. Maybe there was a storm coming. She craned her head back and looked up into the early morning sky which, despite the rain – little more than a cooling wet mist, if she were absolutely honest – was cloudless.

Yes, well, Sally nodded to herself, there *could* be a storm coming – but it wasn't no regular meteorological event, and you could take that one right to the bank. Yessir. You didn't need to be one of those guys on the weather channel, waving their arms about pointing to cold fronts and hot areas. Hell, it was plain to see. Sally breathed deep and smacked her lips. She could taste energy in the air and in the misty rain, could taste electrical charge.

The voices agreed.

Sally had heard the voices even before her husband Gerry had left the house that fateful morning seventeen years ago last August – the fifteenth if anyone was wanting total precision – when good ol' Ger drove out to Fenham's Woods, parked up his Chevy and scattered his brains all over the back seat. No note, no explanations, no goodbyes.

Just a cooled-off shotgun and a crotch full of fertilizer, Sally had heard the policeman who took her downtown tell one of his colleagues, a desk sergeant, Sally assumed, the sergeant watching Sally over the patrolman's right shoulder, leaning on his desk kind of awkward, like he needed to go pee or something, giving Sally an uneasy smile. But Sally had known the sergeant didn't want to pee. He wanted to shut the other guy up, what with her standing there right behind him, her purse in her hand, all disheveled. Wanted to tell the cop to quiet it down but not quite knowing how. Wanted to tell him to shut the fuck up, maybe, cos the guy's old lady's standing right there, large as life, wondering what the hell was going on.

And then the patrolman had finally cottoned on, turning around real slow, his voice, while not stopping, lowering a little, like someone had the volume doodad on the TV remote and was just running it down, the way Sally Davis did during a commercial break in her favorite TV show, *Six Feet Under* maybe (my, but Sally surely did enjoy that show) or *Desperate Housewives.*

Yessir, that was Sally, OK, sure as shooting. One mighty desperate housewife – particularly back then (it was raining *that* night, too, Sally suddenly realized, standing out in the street and an otherwise empty world, just her and the rain, and the silence), with good ol' Ger's mortal remains still cooling off down in the precinct house basement, covered over with a sheet and a rubber-banded note fastened to his big toe:

Davis, Gerald Mortimer

And maybe with his date of birth on there, too:

3/27/58

And maybe the way he'd died:

Suicide

Or even:

Sucking on a double-barrel shotgun.

Standing out in the rain in a deserted side street in an uncharacteristically quiet Lakewood, Sally recalled watching the patrolman all those years ago, recalled his face starting to redden like one of Cora Pohlsson's McIntosh apples brought to ripeness in fast speed the way the people at Disney used to do on their *Wonderful World* TV programs.

As he had started to stammer out an apology, Sally told him no matter, patting his arm with an impassively calm touch. Then she had turned around again to sign for her husband's rings – the gold-plated band with the sun face that his parents had bought him for his twenty-first and a worn-thin wedding band that looked as tired, tarnished and lack-luster as had its wearer – car keys, and a handful of money comprising a ten and three fives plus a couple of quarters, a dime, a nickel and a mess of pennies. She would keep this little collection with her at all times from that moment on, at first not realizing that she still had it and then, later, attaching some kind of ghoulish, talismanic importance to it. She rattled them now, feeling their warmth in the deep pocket of her corduroy skirt. Listened to the sounds they made as they rolled and bounced into one another, like puppies or kittens at play.

She looked around and breathed in deep. Somewhere over in town, something was burning. Sally could see the smoke over the houses, could smell it in the air. Maybe that was what she had smelled before, not a storm coming. Maybe there had been an accident of some kind.

But no, not an accident. She knew that, deep down. The world had been mysteriously vacuumed of life and sound. She knew even without going to doorways and knocking or ringing bells, pressing buzzers, knew that there would not be an answer. She didn't know what it was nor why it had happened. She just knew it had happened, the way you sometimes knew things without any reason. Instinct. That's what it was.

She guessed it had been instinct years ago that had told her Gerry didn't love her any more. (Sally preferred to say 'Didn't care for her any more'.) But she was prepared to go with it and not make waves. After all, she could have been wrong.

But then the voices told her, and they didn't use Sally's preferred phraseology. They told her it was because Ger couldn't take it anymore and that he didn't love her, that he had *never* loved her. That last part, Sally found real hard to take. She couldn't believe that. No way. And so, on the evening of the first anniversary of her husband's suicide, she had driven out to Fenham's Woods, parked up the car – she was still driving the old Chevy, though her sister Maizie had said for her to sell the car, but Sally couldn't do that – and she positioned herself outside the car, waiting for Gerry to show up and do it all again. Like a repeat performance, or an encore, maybe.

And sure enough, he had showed up, at a little after 11 o'clock, when the sun was almost at its highest and the farm buildings and the patches of trees on the sloping hillside across from the car parking area seemed like a half-finished painting, shimmering in the heat haze.

Gerry Davis was shimmering, too, sitting in the driver's seat, large as life and close enough to reach out and touch. Only she knew that he wasn't alive and couldn't be touched. Not anymore. Sally could see clear through him to the window winder on the driver's door.

As he lifted up the ghost of his old shotgun, Sally got up from where she was sitting and knocked on the window, asking her husband if it was true that he didn't love her and hadn't ever done so. He turned to her, not looking at all surprised that she was there, nodding, sad-faced as he mouthed the word 'yes'. It was true: he had never loved her. Then, with the slightest of shrugs, he slipped the shotgun barrel into his mouth – the mouth that, one time, long time ago, had kissed Sally's mouth or her cheek or sometimes the nape of her neck, or maybe whispered sweet nothings to her the way all lovers did – and pulled the trigger.

Because he was turned to face her, across the passenger seat in the front, a whole load of blood and tissue and bits and pieces scattered across the front seats and onto the back window. Those bits and pieces were mostly brain, she would suppose hours later when, sitting in front of her beloved television set watching Gus Grissom in *CSI*, her mind replayed the entire incident in single-frame Technicolor. Good old Gus Grissom. Sally loved that show, too, but only that one, not the spin-offs: *Miami*, with that guy from the old *NYPD Blue* show, who always wore shades and stood around with his hands on his hips; and the *New York* variant, even though she liked Gary Sinise well enough.

It answered the question posed by one of the voices that visited her from time to time: why wasn't Gerry facing forward when he pulled the trigger? What was he looking at across the passenger seat?

She figured it was *her own* ghost, come from the future to ask him if he loved her. Sally had always wondered if ghosts couldn't be from something that *would* happen instead of always something that *had* happened. That clinched it for her.

Her husband's body was no longer in the car when Sally Davis drove back home but the interior smelled of hot metal, gunpowder and shit. When she got back to the house her checked cotton two-piece – a matching skirt and blouse item she'd bought for $29.99 from the Kmart catalogue one time for a special meal with Gerry's boss, Richard – was soaked through to her pants. But when she went inside and peeled everything off there was no stain to be seen and the skirt was as dry as sun-bleached grass.

Sun-bleached grass. That about summed up their marriage, too: dry, arid and parched – devoid of life, bereft of hope and singular in its monotonous promise of sameness.

They had had money. Gerry was an account executive at Willard and Drew, a successful advertising broker firm just down from the Art Museum on 14th Avenue Parkway, and they didn't really want for anything. Except, as far as Sally was concerned, just one thing: children. Sally Davis wanted a child in the worst way. She wanted one so badly that it hurt.

It hurt most on summer nights when she and Gerry used to take to their separate beds and Sally would try to read her book, half-listening all the time to the sound of her husband snoring and the gentle creaks and sighs of the house settling down and sleeping without her. Leaving her behind... behind and still awake.

It was then that she would imagine what it would be like to have another small body lying in a cot by her bed, smelling of fruit purées, talcum powder and the almost indefinable pinkness of new flesh. Then she would get up and go over to Gerry's bed, roll him over on his side so that his snoring wouldn't interfere with her imagining of the baby's soft breath rolling in and out of its tiny mouth.

Sally had bought maternity clothes which she wore when Gerry was out of the house, stuffing them with cushions and an assortment of underwear and hose and walking around splatter-footed, holding onto her back as though the weight she carried were pulling joint and muscle. She did that for seven months and then, one magical day, she stood in the kitchen – Gerry was out at the office – and she pissed herself. *"My waters!"* she cried jubilantly, and she rushed to the bathroom and tore off her clothes, threw them into the bath and pulled the doll she had bought from Gamble's toy store out of its hiding place behind the central heating boiler in the airing cupboard. She rubbed the doll between her legs until it was completely wet and then the two of them got into the bath together.

Sally had dried the baby off on the boiler during the afternoon and then, at night, when Gerry was asleep, she powdered it, dressed it in a pretty one-piece from TJ Maxx and took it into her bed. Pretty soon it was nuzzled up against the warmth and sustenance of her breasts which, she was delighted to discover, had started to lactate to such a degree that she had to wear small tissues in the cups of her brassiere.

Before long, Sally was rolling Gerry over so that he wouldn't wake the doll that slept so soundly in a Gamble's bag beneath her bed.

She shook her head at the memories and, re-folding her arms, she pulled her cardigan sweater tighter around her.

As the years went by, the child grew older. Sally knew that it was a girl but what *kind* of girl? She could never fully decide.

Did she like broccoli and carrots?

Did she like to watch the rain running down the window in the autumn and early spring?

What was her favorite color?

Sally did not know the answers to any of these questions. So many of them, and so many possibilities, so many alternatives.

Sally knew that if she were to talk to her child as it grew older then it would have to talk back to her. Communication was, after all, a two-way thing. Thus, it had to have a voice of its own. But the voice that she would have to provide would need to be a composite of all the myriad possibilities of its life. The answer was simple: she would give it many voices.

"Like me," a scrawny voice whispered in the silence.

"Yes," Sally said, nodding her head, "just like you."

"And me!" said another voice, testily.

"And you," Sally agreed, smiling.

One by one, the voices came, looking for assurances, looking for warmth. And each one of them received those assurances before disappearing once again.

Sally remembered the voices starting.

Some of them came only in the spring, when the trees started to grow new leaves and Gerry performed his annual repair work on the Chevy. Maybe, she often thought in the later, lonelier years, maybe even then, as he hummed and whistled away beneath the car's hood or lay spread-eagled beneath it, his face scuffed with oil and grease marks, maybe then he was already making at least mental preparations for blowing off the top of his head in that very same car.

Some of the voices came only in the summer, filling Sally's head with the electricity of heat-haze and the scent of freshly-squeezed lemons whose resulting questionable vintage was sold by the roadside from huge aluminum bathtubs by tow-headed kids for a dime a plastic cup. It was one of these voices, these blue-sky birdsong confidences, that told Sally her husband had never loved her.

"Have you forgiven me?" a low voice inquired.

Sally considered this, her eyes taking in the empty streets around her. "You told me what I needed to know," Sally said at last.

"Yes," croaked the voice – and was that the hint of a smile creaking around those words? – "but have you forgiven me?"

A few seconds went by before Sally was able to say, "It's very hard," her voice barely above an exhalation of air.

She looked at her watch. Almost six o'clock.

Other voices came to her mainly in the autumn, when the leaves started to wither and drop and the air smelled of exhaust fumes and garden fires, whispering to her, full of sadness and thoughts and questions.

And still more came to her in the heart of winter, those cold and introspective months when the bone-cold winds blew through Colorado and the world was silent and still, and the snow filled the sidewalks and piled up against the trees in the fields. These were the dark voices, cold tones, lost and alone and unloved, filled with the poison of aggression and bitterness.

But while each of the voices had special characteristics and an individual personality, all of them had one thing in common: they all called Sally Davis *mommy.*

And though she loved them all, in a sometimes frightening confusion of different reasons, her special affection was for the voices of the winter. For it was these that most matched the coldness and emptiness of her heart. It was the winter voices that told Sally about the woman across the street, and about her daughter.

And Sally liked to go outside and watch through the windows, secretly, late at night. But tonight, the storm had come, bringing with it the mother and father (and maybe a handful of aunts and uncles and even grandparents) of all lightning flashes, Sally standing out in the drizzling rain and the darkness, her hand endlessly kneading the tattered notes and the couple of quarters, a dime, a nickel and a mess of pennies nestled in her pocket, and a voice had said to Sally, *Nobody is in there, mommy.*

And then, with the voice still whispering to her in her inner ear as the rain ran down through the wool of her cardigan sweater and a lick of wet, greasy hair dropped over her eyes, Sally looked around at the world and recognized in an instant that–

"Something has happened here." Sally Davis said these words to an unhearing and unsympathetic world, speaking them in hushed tones and, somewhere in the sky behind her, across fields and woods and black-topped roads going here and leaving there, a rumble of thunder sounded a somber agreement. "Everyone has gone," she said. "And left me."

Where could they have gone to? It didn't make any sense, no sense at all. It had been the flash of light, she reasoned, nodding again, wiping her rain-soaked hair back from her forehead. That much was surely beyond dispute. She would never have noticed the flash if she had slept normal hours like other people, but there was always so much to do for the children…

"We must leave," Sally said, her voice now defiant.

"Where shall we go?" one of the voices asked.

Sally looked around the street, stepped from the sidewalk onto the pavement and tried to think. Where could they go? Where might there be others? After all, if she had survived whatever it had been, then it stood to reason that there might be others.

"The mall," said a voice. "Let's go to *the mall.*"

"*Yes,*" came a supportive voice, "the mall."

"Oh, *can* we?" whined another.

"Mommy, *can–*"

Sally waved her arms around, while the very tiniest part of her, a part now virtually buried without even the tiniest trace after all these years, wondered what she must look like. What she must sound like, so many voices, so many facial expressions to accompany them…

But those thoughts popped out of her head at exactly the same time as they popped in, leaving nary a single trace of their having been there at all.

"Very well," she said, interrupting any further badgering from her brood. "The mall it is."

And all of the entities that comprised Sally Davis turned their collective back on this strange and quiet new world and headed for something they knew more about. The mall.

(7)

Meanwhile, about an hour, hour and a half before Virgil and the bandaged Suze Neihardt took to the road in a commandeered Pontiac convertible and Sally Davis and her cerebral progeny slid behind the wheel of Sally's old Chevy, with the still lingering smell of husband Gerry's atomized brain cells and dried blood defying even the strongest air fresheners bought from the filling station over in Wheat Ridge, the late running and rapidly descending 10pm Denver to Atlanta flight had problems of its own, with the revelation that one of the remaining three people spared whatever had – well – had 'done something' with all the other passengers, this girl, she had just admitted that she saw things in her head.

Only the sound of the aircraft could be heard for some time, Karl having turned back to face front and Ronnie looking at the girl, watching her face, waiting for her to say something else. In the end, he just repeated her own statement – and threw in a question mark.

"You see things in your *head*?"

"Great," Karl snapped, more to himself than anyone else. "Now it's starting to rain."

Angel pulled open the zipper on her bag and then closed it again, time after time, nodding quickly all the while. And as she was doing this, and without looking up, she said, "I often see things in my head."

And there it was. A simple statement of fact. *I sure do like ice cream. I like to stay up late and read my comic books. Oh, and yeah… I see stuff in my head.*

Ronnie watched her over and over for another half-minute or so before saying, "What did you see, honey?"

And she told him. She told him how she had been talking with her mommy and then she had experienced some kind of surge in her head – like someone had poured boiling water inside through her ears, she said, which was the way it always happened – and in that split second, she saw everyone on the plane, no matter what they were doing, awake or asleep, reading or eating or talking or watching something on their little personal video screens, everyone just blinked out. She shook her head and reached out for her mom, screaming (which is what Ronnie had heard), but before Angel had been able to tell her mother – to warn her – her mom had started to ask her what the matter was but it had come out as only *What's the mat–*. And then she and pretty near everyone else on the delayed 10 pm out of Denver–

And maybe everywhere else, let's not forget that one…

–just up and sidestepped into another world.

"Does this – these little dreams – do they happen often?"

The girl nodded, keeping her eyes down looking at the zipper on her *Little Mermaid* bag, which she was still opening and closing, opening and closing.

Did this mean anything? Ronnie was beginning to think not and then–

"We're going to be OK," Angel said. Then she frowned and turned to look at Karl's back. She didn't say anything more before she returned her attention to her bag.

"OK, Karl," Ronnie said. "You heard the lady. We need to get us back into the airport."

Karl grimaced. "Yeah, well, that may be a little more difficult even than you'd imagine."

When Ronnie jerked his head questioningly, Karl continued.

"Come see."

He gestured Ronnie into the other plush leather seat and motioned for him to get in. Outside, all they could see was cloud. Karl settled himself back and fastened his seat harness. "I think we should do this," he said. Ronnie followed Karl's example.

In front of them was a huge windshield, split right down the center by a metal divider. Another window was fixed onto each side, much closer to them than the front windshield thereby enabling both Ronnie and Karl to look out almost immediately down.

The sky looked clear beneath them. A thick bank of cloud sat just off to the right and quite a way below them – Ronnie couldn't gauge how far – and rain was misting the windshield. Below that, more cloud was bunched up like cotton candy. Suddenly, the cloud opened up and Ronnie saw right through to the ground. It was just a mess of lights and distant roadways, a few buildings.

"Can you turn on wipers or something?"

Karl frowned and ran his fingers across lines of switches, levers and buttons. "Must be here someplace." He stopped at a set of three switches, leaned forward for a closer look, and said, "Hey, our luck's in."

"You really think so?" Ronnie said.

Karl flipped one of the switches and a pair of wipers started to move side to side across the windshield.

"You know," Ronnie said, "I kind of expected something a little more, I dunno, more technical, I guess."

Karl shrugged. "Whatever does the job does the job, right?"

Ronnie leaned over to the side window and looked down. "Where's that?"

"Outskirts of Denver," Karl said. "We're going to be on the ground in just a few minutes."

"I think I'd prefer the phrase 'landed'." Ronnie turned to the other man and smirked. "Too many connotations in 'on the ground'."

"Roger that," Karl said, and he adjusted his glasses.

"How long before we... you know?"

"Before we 'touch down'?"

Ronnie nodded.

"We should be down there before six."

"When's sun-up?"

Karl looked across to the east and shrugged. "Hour, hour and a half maybe. We'll be seeing signs before then–" He looked across at Ronnie with a warning glance but he didn't have to say anything. Ronnie understood. The pilot meant that they'd be seeing signs of the sun rising only if the landing went OK. Ronnie nodded, just one brisk nod, to let Karl know that he understood. Karl continued, saying, "–not too much, just a lightening of the sky."

They sat like that for a minute or so and then Ronnie asked, "You know why we were delayed?"

"All I know is they were talking about disturbances."

"Yeah? What kind of disturbances?" He shook his head. "Will you *listen* to me?"

"What?"

"I'm sitting here in an airplane that was filled with people a half-hour ago but which is now empty except for me, a seriously reluctant pilot and a six-year old kid straight out of *The Sixth Sense* and I'm discussing what time sun-up is going to happen and asking you why we were delayed taking off."

Karl shrugged. "Nothing much else to do."

Ronnie wished they had the past few minutes to go through again. And he would have preferred Karl to have a fully functional pair of glasses for the job that lay ahead.

"You want to go sit back in the main seats, honey?" Karl called over his shoulder to Angel Wurst, who was still standing in the doorway.

Angel turned around without answering and looked back into the main seating area. It looked lonely and somehow threatening. She didn't know what had happened to her mom and dad. If only she could see where they were inside her head, but when she tried to concentrate on them, thinking hard about their faces, all she got was static, like the white noise that came on the TV screen when someone disconnected the cable lead. She only knew that first they were there and then they were gone. And she didn't like the wide expanse of seat backs facing her – or watching her back once she had sat down (if she were to sit down, of course). She thought about what might be raising itself out of those seats when she wasn't looking.

"Uh uh," she said, and turned back. "I wanna stay with you." She plopped herself down on the seat behind Ronnie.

"That OK? If she stays up here, I mean?"

Karl shrugged. "Why not." He turned to Angel and nodded at

the seat harness straps behind her shoulders. "Can you pull that onto yourself, honey?" he asked.

Angel did as she was told and Karl nodded to her, gave her a wink.

"So, disturbances? You said about disturbances?"

"Oh, back in Denver? Caused the delay?"

Ronnie nodded. "What were they, these disturbances?"

"Some kind of electrical interference in the sky is what I heard. They'd died down by the time we took off."

Ronnie knew now who Karl reminded him of. It was the actor who played the guy in the *American Splendor* movie – and the wine-freak in *Sideways*. Ronnie loved those two movies. Paul something or other. Italian-sounding name.

He could hear Angel tugging at the harness and not seeming to get anywhere so Ronnie got up from his seat and fastened her in. When he returned to the leather seat, clouds were swirling past the nose of the plane.

"The rain gonna cause us any problems?"

"Well, let's just say it would be easier if we didn't have it. But no, I don't see any problems coming from the rain." He glanced aside and gave a little ironic smile. Ronnie knew exactly what that smile said. He flashed back on the scene from Butch Cassidy and the Sundance Kid, when Newman and Redford are about to leap from a cliff into the water far below, and Redford says he can't swim. "Can't swim!?" comes Newman's response. "Hell, the fall'll probably kill ya!"

Ronnie shook the image and its implications out of his head. "Anything you need me to do?" he asked.

"See the wheel-thing right in front of you?" Without waiting for an answer, Karl added, "I want you to push on that. Gently at first but then harder. OK?"

"OK." Ronnie reached out and took hold of the steering contraption. It was like a half steering wheel, curved around at the top with each side dropping to a point. He held onto it and felt the vibrations. It felt good.

"You got that?" With the engine noise having increased, Karl was now having to shout.

Ronnie nodded. The plane was starting to tip downwards.

Angel Wurst grabbed her seat arms. She was sitting sideways-on behind Ronnie and so, by turning her head to the right, she could see out of the windshield or by looking straight ahead, she could see out of the window alongside and running behind Karl the pilot.

"We're on our way," Karl shouted. "Hey, I really am pleased to see you guys, I can tell you." He pushed forward on various levers and pulled back on a couple of others. Then he nodded to the earphones curled around a handle on a section of housing. "There's nobody out there, you know," he added, his voice lower now. "Nobody out there at all."

"You sure?"

"Uh huh. Tried every frequency. And I'm not even hearing static, you know? It's just silence. There's nobody there."

"They can't *all* have gone," Ronnie said, hoping that he didn't sound as desperate or as scared as he felt. "I mean, *we're* here, right?"

Karl didn't say anything, just looked sideways at Ronnie and then glanced back at the girl. "The three of us, huh? Some cavalry," he said. "I never thought I'd wind up as a savior of the human race." He twisted a dial and watched rectangles of green overlay each other. "But we got to get down out of the sky first."

Ronnie said, "She says we're going to be OK." He slapped Karl's arm and kept looking straight ahead.

Outside, the cloud swirled about them like fog and then suddenly cleared. Stretching ahead of them was empty air and darkness, dotted here and there with wispy cloud-trails. Below that, Ronnie could see the distant sprawl of Denver, and the endless gray strips of the I-25 and the I70 feeding into it, like tied ribbons come together on a parcel. Immediately beneath them was Denver International Airport, some twenty-five miles to the north-east of the city. They must have turned around and were coming in over Laramie and Cheyenne.

It was quite a scene. But the most fascinating part of it was the fires. They were everywhere – out on the Interstates, along the airport runways and amidst the spires and buildings of distant Denver – plumes of smoke twisting and twirling lazily into the early morning sky.

Ronnie heard Angel Wurst draw in her breath.

"It was like a meteor storm," Karl shouted finally. "When it happened – whatever 'it' was – we lost altitude,. dropped like a stone. I was in back–" He pointed to a table immediately behind them and to one side of the small cabin. "–checking weather charts. Then–" He snapped his fingers. "–poof! Everyone was gone.

"Out there, planes were just... just falling out of the sky. I watched them, man. Five, six, maybe more. I never want to see anything like that again."

Ronnie said, "There probably wasn't anyone on them."

Karl shrugged. "Maybe not anyone who could fly, you mean."

Ronnie didn't say anything to that one. He knew what the other man was thinking, what he was picturing in his head: plane passenger cabins pretty much deserted apart from one or maybe two people, maybe a half-dozen of them, standing up – or trying to stand up – as the plane they were on just nosedived right out of the sky. At that instant, Ronnie fancied he could hear their screams, drifting on the wind around them, brought into the plane by the strangeness of the situation because no sound ever truly dies but just keeps on going around and around, getting fainter and fainter.

"OK, but they could also have been completely deserted," Ronnie said, wishing it with all his heart.

"Maybe. But it was the sheer helplessness of humanity that got to me. That make any sense at all to you?" He glanced sideways at Ronnie, who was watching him closely.

"Giamatti!"

"Excuse me?"

"That's his name, the guy you look like. Paul Giamatti." Ronnie shook his head. "Nobody's ever told you that?"

"Uh uh." Karl faced forward again. "Should I be pleased? I mean, not that they haven't told me but that I look like this guy."

Ronnie shrugged. "Well, you know what you look like."

After a few seconds' thought, Karl said, "Yeah."

They sat in silence for a minute or so and then Karl said, "Here we are, making all these scientific breakthroughs and then along comes something that just stops us in our tracks. I mean, you know, what the hell happened to everyone?"

"They're hiding is all," Angel Wurst shouted from behind Ronnie, though she didn't sound convinced.

"Anyway, it took me a while to level her out, but I managed it. I just sat here, trying to figure out how everything worked together while I watched billions of dollars of aircraft drop out of the sky." He shrugged.

Ronnie felt a sinking feeling in his stomach. Who *was* this guy? He just sat there trying to figure out how everything worked? *Jeez, Louise,* Ronnie thought. *Looks like I may yet get to wear my sphincter as a baseball cap.*

"So–" He tried to choose his words carefully, playing it super-casual, not wanting to get the wrong answer. In a few minutes, it wouldn't matter anyway. "So you're not a pilot?"

Karl gave a snort and a chuckle. "Hell, no," he shouted. "Wish I was."

He pushed forward a little harder on the wheel and the plane seemed to let out a rattle, dropping and steadying and then dropping and steadying again, like it was making a little protest, but then it seemed to even out again.

"I'm heading for JFK, so hopping to Atlanta and then on to New York on the red-eye. They need a maps-man for an early-morning hike over to Beijing – that's what I do, by the way."

"Cartography?"

Karl glanced at him with a big grin. "Hey, that's right. How'd you know that?"

Ronnie shrugged. It was just another example of the things you pick up as you go through life: like the word "adrenaline" from one of his friend Tommy's father's comic books – *Strange Adventures* #110, as he recalled, with 'The Hand From Nowhere' being the lead story; the word "desultory" from a Simon and Garfunkel song (he had also picked up a love of Emily Dickinson from Simon and Garfunkel's "The Dangling Conversation"); and a kind of love-hate relationship with Melville and Whitman, courtesy of the author Ray Bradbury. When they had first started going out together, Martha Baez ("Hey, no relation," she always liked to tell people) had told Ronnie he had poetry in his soul. When she had told him that, they had been almost naked on the small bed in the spare room of his parents' home in Cuyahoga Falls, Martha's face a mask of love and admiration. How times changed.

"–so I said I'd do it," Karl finished saying.

Ronnie nodded, hoping that he wasn't going to be expected to comment on anything that Karl had said.

He waited a few seconds and then said, "You say there were lots of crashes. How come there were so many planes out there? I mean, at this time – two in the goddam morning, for Chrissakes."

"When we left Denver, there was a backlog of traffic to move out because of the disturbances, plus several circling to come in. I'd say maybe a dozen, fifteen, something like that." He shook his head and made a clucking sound. "Just fell to earth like stones."

Then the penny dropped with Angel. "Does that mean that everbody on those planes..." She let her voice trail off. It was something she couldn't get her head around. If everyone – everybody – on those planes was hiding, even the pilots and stewardesses, then it was a pretty dumb trick. They'd just committed themselves to a fiery death. Unless, of course, they were hiding *off* the plane. And even a six year old was going to find that particular cut of meat just a little tough to chew on. But that was a place Ronnie didn't want to visit with Angel Wurst anytime soon.

Ronnie looked at the fires and, as he looked, he could make out the wreckage more clearly, huge clumps of twisted metal burning in thick palls of smoke and flame. It wasn't so much the wreckage but the fact that there were no services to be seen – no fire engines, no helmeted men hosing water and foam onto the smashed aircraft. He looked at the distant buildings and imagined the silence within them – the empty lounges and coffee shops, the stilled luggage conveyer belts, the control tower with its myriad screens of glowing green lines. "What happened to everybody?" he said again, his voice barely above a whisper.

"I'm going to try put her down on the I-25," Karl said, so matter-of-factly that he could simply have been deciding which color sweater to wear today.

"Why not the airport?"

"The wreckage. We wouldn't necessarily see all the pieces, and there could be a lot of pieces." He was really shouting now, over the sound of the engines.

"What about all the traffic on the highway?"

"At 5.30 in the morning?" Karl shook his head. "But I'm going to need some help."

Karl explained what he needed Ronnie to do and within minutes they were ready, the three of them buckled into their seats and watching the world come up to meet them.

And what a world it was.

Aside from Karl mentioning occasionally that Ronnie should push on this lever or pull on that one, the trio sat in complete silence, wisps of cloud disappearing around and about them as they lowered their altitude. The Interstate now immediately below them looked like a stock-car racetrack. Two huge long-haul rigs were jack-knifed into a rack of roadside stores, the Taco Bell franchise effectively demolished apart from its sign, which was still sputtering around the cab of one of the rigs. A third rig was upended in what appeared to be a recently ploughed field in front of a sprawling trailer park. A thick ribbon of fire – Ronnie assumed it had to be gas from a ruptured tank – led up to the cab. It appeared to be burned out.

Without exchanging a word, both Karl and Ronnie noted the absence of any police or rescue services or medical assistance. Ronnie shifted his focus on the windshield and saw the reflection of the concerned face of Angel Wurst looking over his shoulder. What did she think to all of this? It didn't make any sense at all to Ronnie, who had been down here on the planet for four decades: so what did someone make of it all when they hadn't even put in *one*?

"See that?" Karl said, apparently needlessly until he added, "No doors open."

And it was true. The cabs of all three rigs were closed up tight, same as the doors on all the cars they passed over.

"Everbody's hiding," Angel Wurst said from the seat behind Ronnie. Ronnie just didn't have the heart to say anything. In fact, he kind of wished he'd not started this hiding myth. It was going to make it all the harder for the girl to face the facts when the time came.

Yeah? And what facts are those, Mr Ripley? the tiny inquisitive voice whispered in Ronnie's head.

Holding steady on the steering column and maintaining an even green line on the bright dial to his right, Ronnie took the opportunity to glance around at Angel. She was looking out of the window, twisting around in her seat and using the back of Ronnie's as an armrest. She must have sensed him looking because she looked up into the reflective section of the window just as Ronnie had turned his attention to watching her reflection. She forced a kind of half-smile – that was the best way to describe it, as far as Ronnie was concerned – and just for a few seconds, he wondered if she was sitting there worrying about how she was going to break it to this asshole in front of her that everybody wasn't hiding. Everybody had gone permanent *bye byes*, maybe never to be seen again. Maybe the girl was thinking about Ronnie's wife, Martha.

Ronnie winked at the girl's reflection and turned back front again, momentarily feeling guilty – he hadn't thought about Martha since... since the whole thing had happened. Where was–

"You OK?" Karl's voice disturbed his reverie.

"What? Oh, sure, OK as I can be, I guess."

Karl nodded. The plane was now about two or maybe three hundred feet above the highway, the left side – did they call it left in the flying manuals, or was it port or starboard? – slewing over towards a group of taller buildings coming up.

"Push it, push it," Karl snapped.

Ronnie pushed.

The plane leveled again and the nose rose, the wingtip narrowly missing a jumble of cars and a crippled eighteen-wheeler that had pushed into the stonework of a group of buildings that looked like bank offices or a realty office. A ruptured fire hydrant was spewing water in a cascade and the street was flooded at an intersection that led to another trailer park.

"Lot of trailer parks," Ronnie observed.

"Sign of the times," Karl said after a few seconds' consideration. Then, "We're gonna have to take it up again and swing back. Do the run all over again."

"Yeah?" *Shit,* Ronnie thought. He was amazed that they had got to this point still alive. He didn't think they could do it again. "Problems?"

"Just that, we're not careful, we're gonna run out of road. And it's getting a little clogged up down there." He adjusted the glasses on his nose and pointed. "You see? So much for me saying there'd be no traffic cos it's two in the morning."

The road looked like a skating rink with cars, vans and trucks the skaters, every one of them sprawled out unconscious, some by themselves, others piled one on top of another, and some driven into store windows.

Ronnie turned around again and said, in a quiet voice, "Still think we're going to make it?" Asking the girl annoyed him the way it had annoyed him once when he had gone to a fortune-teller (Madame Carnocki, he recalled now, sitting in the co-pilot's seat of a plummeting Boeing 727 on the day that the world's population had been magicked away without so much as a tap of a wand or an Abracadabra!) at nearby Kent County Fair back when he was a teenager, asking the woman if maybe Valerie Skijsmik would be able to see beyond the braces on his teeth. The woman dressed it up in some kind of mumbo jumbo bullshit about his needing to exude confidence and it would be so – *and that'll be fifty cents, thank you very much* – but young Ronnie could no more exude *that* than he could poop a turd through the eye of a needle. And now here he was again, making the same damn mistake, looking around for a shoulder to lean on. He looked at the approaching road, felt the shuddering vibrations of the aircraft, feeling like it was about to fall right apart and scatter the contents of the plane and their three fool bodies onto the littered blacktop, and he made a mental note, a promise, a note to self, that he would, in future, face whatever life threw at him with a kind of acceptance that did not require any platitudes or hollow encouragements, any assurances or conciliatory winks and nudges. What would be, would be and what wouldn't, wouldn't. It was as simple as that. *Que sera, sera,* as the old song had it.

But just this time, he waited for her response.

Angel Wurst smiled at him, a strange kind of smile, slightly crooked and not wholly truthful Ronnie thought. Then she glanced sideways at Karl, looked back at Ronnie and then concentrated her full attention on the windshield.

Ronnie turned back to Karl and settled in his seat again. "You think anyone else is still around down there?" He didn't feel any further need to dress up the conversation for Angel, and Angel didn't say anything, just kept looking out of the window.

Karl pushed more levers, checked more dials. The fact that he hadn't answered provided the answer that Ronnie himself feared. The world was empty. Deserted.

"I take it you do know what you're doing?"

Karl gave a half-smile and a sideways glance. "Some. Not a whole lot, mind you, but some."

"We gonna make it down there without breaking our damn necks?" He deliberately avoided looking at the girl.

"We're sure as hell gonna try," Karl said.

"Pretend you're just reading a map."

Karl nodded without turning. "That's what I been doing all the time."

The plane leaned over to the right, turning a full circle to head back to where the I-25 still had a good twenty or so miles before hitting the outskirts of Mile High City. Now they were able to look to the right and see the true state of the world post the Big White Light. Fires seemed to be blazing everywhere but, as far as they could see – not foolproof, admittedly, from this height, speed and angle – there was no movement.

"Looks like the aftermath of riots," Ronnie shouted.

"See over there?" Karl asked as they veered back around again, watching the highway come back into prominence. Ronnie followed the other man's pointing finger. Way over in the distance shone a beautiful gold light, bathing the sky above it like a halo. "The mall, one of the biggest I ever saw. Open twenty-four-seven."

"Yeah?"

Karl turned to look at him. "Reckon it'll be quiet in there right now. Unnaturally quiet, mind. Maybe the PA's still playing the old muzak loop but aside from that, it'll be quiet.

"I tried calling all kinds of frequencies and–" He nodded to a cell-phone sitting on what Ronnie supposed was the plane's dashboard. "–all kinds of numbers, back before you came and knocked on the door." He shook his head. "All quiet. Nobody home."

Ronnie waited for more but then they started their approach again, the I-25 looming long and straight in front of and below them, stretching out into the distance, the blacktop littered with crashed vehicles and smoking fires.

"Nobody home," Karl said again, this time just to himself. Then, "You both belted in?"

"I'm belted," said Angel Wurst.

"Does it really matter?" Ronnie asked, but he kept his voice low enough that neither of them would hear.

"Are you belted up?" Angel's voice was kind of high-pitched and a little indistinct but Ronnie caught it and checked the girl's reflection in the windshield. She was looking across at Karl's back but he hadn't heard her. Ronnie focused on the road – it seemed so close that he felt they must surely be running along it already, but he knew they weren't. Not yet. But soon, he thought, very soon.

"Here goes," Karl shouted, the words coming between clenched teeth.

The plane shook and groaned as though they were flying through a gale. Ronnie looked at different dials, saw needles spinning or edging into solid green areas but couldn't make out their significance, if there was any. In the end, he stopped looking at them and instead just stared out of the window. The road was coming up fast but somehow its proximity beneath them seemed to remain constant.

Then Karl shot a hand out and pulled back on a thick handled switch and something started to whine beneath them.

"That the wheels?" Ronnie asked, without taking his attention from the windows. Alongside him, the wing scraped across the front of an eight- or nine-story building, scattering glass and concrete debris over the road. He glanced to the right just in time to see the word "LOANS" painted onto the brick before the wing-tip scored through it in a puff of dust. The plane juddered and the wings wobbled.

Directly in front of them, a white stretch limo lay on its side.

Ronnie shouted out in excitement – one of the rear doors was open. He scanned the road as quickly as he could but they were moving too fast for him to spot anyone. And anyway, wouldn't whoever was out there come and wave at them?

It's a goddam plane, fuckwit! the little voice said. *You don't flag down a goddam airplane.*

Ronnie nodded to himself and tried to imagine what might be going through that someone's head, whoever he or she was. Maybe a celebrity, being driven around in one of those ridiculous cars. Had they gone right up into the city? He glanced up at the horizon and saw the buildings towering a few miles away like a fabled El Dorado mirage.

Karl was up out of his seat now, the belt still around him but bracing himself like a jockey, pushing on the steering column.

A bank of telegraph poles appeared from nowhere on the left and the wing scythed through them like a knife through butter, though there was a flurry of sparks. Then one of the poles shot towards them and caromed off the airplane's nose, dragging another three or four poles, all attached by the overhead wires, to spread across them.

"Shit!"

"No, that may help," Karl said, grunting at the strain of keeping the plane steady. "Slow us down."

"Like a parachute, right?"

Karl nodded. When he turned to Ronnie he was smiling, a little crooked sarcastic grin and a suspicious frown on his face. "You sure you're not a pilot?"

"Funny."

Karl adjusted his glasses again and faced front, chuckling.

"I'm scared," Angel Wurst's small voice said from behind Ronnie. So small, in fact, that it was amazing that Ronnie even heard it above the scream of the engines and the buffeting of the cabin, with things bouncing about on the floor around their feet.

You're *scared!* Ronnie thought. *And you're the one been telling us we'd be OK. Smell that? That's how scared I am.* He reached a hand back and patted the girl's leg.

"We're going to be OK," he yelled. "Nearly down now." He turned to Karl. "Aren't we?"

Karl didn't answer.

Ronnie felt his attention being drawn to the girl's reflection, knew she was watching him in the windshield, waiting for him to ask *her,* but he wouldn't. Wouldn't give her the satisfaction. What did she know anyways! He closed his eyes and tried to think of a prayer.

Gentle Jesus, meek and mild
Look upon your little child

The plane lurched and then jinked to the side, grinding noises coming from somewhere beneath where they were sitting. The trunk and rear fender of a car appeared just below their line of vision and then disappeared off to the side.

Pity me my simplicity
Suffer me to come to thee

Ronnie stared out of the window to catch a glimpse of it, to see what make it was, though he did wonder just for a few seconds why that could possibly be important: he guessed it was to make some sense of the completely senseless situation they were in.

A streetlamp buckled forward as the left wing hit it, the grinding noise making Ronnie wince and run his tongue over his rear teeth. The impact wasn't enough to slow them down with any significance but it did manage to slew the plane's nose towards the left. A retail park appeared set back on the left, its parking lot mostly empty save for a handful of vehicles. One of them, a small flatbed truck – *a Dodge, maybe,* Ronnie thought, in that oh-so-casual way one picks up meaningless minutiae at a time of great stress and concern – had its lights on. Though there was no chance he would be able to hear anything, Ronnie leaned forward – he suspected the engine would be running: someone had come out of a restaurant or a coffee house, turned on the lights and the engine and *pow*! end of story. He glanced around the storefronts and saw a 24 hour McDonald's with its lights on. As he watched, the right wing tip caught a U Haul van and spun it around, the van's wheels buckling and the tires popping like blown-up paper bags burst in a handclap, before sending it crashing into a drugstore.

"You any idea what these things cost?"

"The plane?"

"Yeah."

"They can deduct it from my next paycheck."

"I never knew pilots got paid so well."

"I'm a cartographer, remember?"

Karl was trying to pull the nose back straight again but was having difficulty. A Texaco gas sign with a "Turn here for gasoline" logo of a little hunched-up driver with lit-up eyes hit the right side window and scattered glass all over them before scouring along the side of the plane, but at least it turned the nose slightly to the right again.

"That's a little better," Karl shouted, still struggling, "but we're going to hit the buildings."

It sounded as though he was talking only to himself and Ronnie braced himself again on the dashboard. "OK," he said. It seemed so ineffective. *Oh really? That's nice. Thanks for letting us know.* "Angel?"

"Yes?"

"I want you to brace yourself, OK?"

"OK."

The plane suddenly leapt upwards and then crashed down again, then slumped to one side.

"We lost a wheel housing," Karl said.

"How bad is that?" Ronnie barely stopped before adding, *on a scale of one to ten, with ten being the worst.* The truth was, at this stage, he didn't really want to know.

There was no answer. Then, "OK, here we go. Either of you like books?"

The gaudily-lit windows of a Barnes and Noble store were coming towards them.

Somewhere, a car horn was honking, honking, honking.

A dull *whump!* sounded but Ronnie couldn't tell whether it was outside or from behind them. Then it didn't matter: shards of glass cascaded through the front windows while concrete and masonry – and books, lots of books – showered down around the plane's nose.

Another crash – definitely from behind them this time – and a strained scraping sound were followed by a security alarm someplace outside, the wail dopplering towards them and then past them.

Angel shouted.

"You OK?" Ronnie yelled over his shoulder.

Angel didn't answer immediately. She was too busy leaning forward and looking straight down the aisle of the passenger cabins. Many of the overhead lockers had sprung open, catapulting bags and coats and – Angel noticed – an acoustic guitar and a saxophone case, the black case sprung open and the instrument now lying just a few yards from the door to the cockpit.

"Angel?" Ronnie was straining to turn while keeping his hands on the dashboard.

Angel shouted, "I'm OK," and then, "all the stuff's falling out of the lockers." But nobody responded so she settled back into her seat.

The plane sloughed to the other side now. *The other wheel housing,* Ronnie thought. He considered asking Karl–

Hey, how many wheels did we have when we started out?

–but the map-reader seemed a little too preoccupied.

Ronnie turned from the chaos outside and watched Karl instead. He was pulling on what looked for all the world like a giant trunk- or gas-cap-release lever, the tendons on his neck standing proud like guiders. Karl placed his free hand on top of the other, the right onc, and doublcd thc powcr of his pull. Ronnic saw his thumb going white.

"Hey. We're slowing down," Angel Wurst shouted.

It was true. Ronnie looked down aisles of bookshelves, the flooring buckled and littered with books – paperback books, hardcovers, fiction, non-fiction – it all seemed so normal. But Ronnie didn't think there'd be anyone in to buy anything for a while. Maybe never again. Who knew. So yes, they were slowing down, but the momentum of the plane was still such that they could not force themselves forwards in their seats. A piece of wooden planking suddenly sprang out from beneath a coil of matting, the matting swirling like coffee steam and the planking sliding forward, propelled by some constriction behind it, such constriction presumably the result of the impacting plane nose on the front of the store. Yin and yang. Cause and effect. All of the above.

"Shit!" was all Karl seemed able to come up with, and as he reached down to hit the release catch on the seat-belt contraption, the plank came through the left side of the already shattered windscreen, breaking up what few sections of glass remained and carrying on forward until it hit Karl on the right shoulder and spun him and his chair around the way a storm will send a garbage can lid pirouetting along the sidewalk. Then the plank kept on going though Ronnie assumed it was the plane that was carrying on while the plank remained stationary. He certainly hoped that the resounding *crack!* was the chair being torn from its mountings and nothing at all to do with the map-reader's shoulder.

Karl went face down, still attached to his chair seat buckle system.

Ronnie turned around to watch him and saw the pilot (yessir, he was a pilot now!) get somehow twisted around so that he was on his side staring down the plane, out of the pilots' cabin – the door was hanging askew as though it had been blown open: how had *that* happened? – through into the First Class area and then Business Class and finally, way down the plane, Standard or Economy or whatever word they used to dress up "inferior". As Ronnie turned around again he was suddenly aware of the ridiculousness of the different grades.

And then he realized that nobody was holding the wheel.

Ronnie reached out and grabbed a hold of the steering column and pushed it forward. It seemed like the right thing to do and Ronnie dearly hoped with all his might that the plane would not suddenly lift itself up and head off into the sky again, trailing behind it a three-story Borders storefront and a few thousand books. *Just one more time around the park, driver and then take us home.*

But no, they were coming to a stop, the plank now having pushed itself right over Karl and lodged into the corner housing at the rear of the flight cabin. He couldn't move anything except for his left arm and hand. The plank had turned over the entire seat housing and pinned him to the floor. Even his head he couldn't move – it was jammed against the radio and listening equipment. And his glasses were gone again.

Karl ran a mental hand over his body searching for breaks or – even worse! – leaks. Breaks could be fixed, he'd always thought, might even fix themselves, given time. But leaks of the dreaded red stuff usually signaled problemo alert. He seemed to be OK, although his shoulder felt like it had been pulverized with one of those little wooden hammers you use to tenderize steak. Karl thought his shoulder was pretty much 100% tenderized.

The sound of a belt buckle release was followed by heavy breathing and a scuffling noise. Then Karl heard Ronnie say, in a soft voice which he knew was not directed at him, "Are you OK?" Then he heard the girl – he'd forgotten her name now: Emily something? – he heard her say sure, she was OK.

"That was quite a ride," she finished off.

He heard Ronnie agree. And then another snap of a belt buckle and more scrabbling, until Ronnie's face suddenly appeared in front of him.

"How you doing in there?"

"I'm a little cramped. And I think my shoulder may be shot."

"Shot?"

"You know, messed up. Took the full force of that wood right on it. Doesn't hurt too much right now but I'm guessing it will soon."

Ronnie nodded and looked around somewhere off behind Karl's back.

"How's it look? I can hardly move a finger in here."

The girl appeared – Angel, not Emily (where the hell had Emily come from?), Angel Wurst – and gave him a smile. "Great driving," she said.

Karl forced a smile – something was sticking into his back, maybe something that had broken free from the seat, which he was still pinned into beneath what appeared to be a series of wooden planks, a lot of electrical wiring, some powdery masonry and some ripped carpeting. There was even a book – Karl could see the page edges though he didn't know what it was. But he was too uncomfortable to think about reading. And anyway, his glasses were gone again.

"Can you see my glasses anywhere? They're gone again."

"I'm going to check you out back here," Ronnie said. "Give me a minute." He moved off to Ronnie's left of vision and Ronnie felt a slight easing of pressure on his left leg. Then, with a grunt from Ronnie, the pressure returned, quickly followed by Ronnie.

Angel shuffled herself forward so that she was able to reach her right arm beneath Karl's neck. She moved her arm around and then, with a yelp, pulled it out again. She was holding Karl's glasses.

"Good girl! You think you can fit them onto my nose?"

"You're jammed in real tight back there," Ronnie said from somewhere over near the instruments. "I don't see any way I'm going to get you out, particularly as the entire floor of the third story of Barnes and Noble Bookshop seems to be resting on your seat."

Karl felt an immediate wave of panic and it was all he could do to keep from weeping and begging. They were going to leave him here. They couldn't do that. *Could* they? "So, what... what are you gonna do?" he asked.

"I think all we can do is look for some help, maybe bring some tools to try cutting through some of this wood." He slapped one of the planks for emphasis. "No way we can move it ourselves."

"You think there's anyone out there?"

Karl could feel cold air coming into the cabin and he strained to hear a voice calling out to offer help, but there was only the gentle soughing of the wind and ticking noises as the aircraft settled around him. He'd done OK. Karl closed his eyes and felt a single tear force its way out.

"Anyone's guess," Ronnie said, so long after the event that Karl had forgotten the question he'd asked. "No sign of anyone so far."

"How do we get out?" Angel asked.

"You can hit the emergency switch on either of the exit doors. It'll blow the door and run an inflatable chute – you can slide down onto the tarmac."

"And how'd we get back? With tools and all?"

Karl could not have explained the feeling of excitement he felt at that moment so instead he shook his head, hoping the emotion would pass and enable him to speak. "With difficulty," he said, unable to keep the smile from his voice. "I'm just glad that coming back is on your agenda."

Ronnie reached a hand into the debris and patted Karl's face. "Hey, you think we were just going to leave you?"

Karl looked up at him and shook his head, frowning. "Nah," he said.

Ronnie smiled back and nodded. "OK," he said. "We'll see you later." He patted his face again. "You did good."

"You too."

Minutes later, Karl watched the backs of Ronnie and the girl walk down the aisle to the center door. He heard the door pop and clatter outside someplace and then the *whoosh* of the chute. After that, and the distant sound of muted voices and running footsteps, there was only the wind and the faint sound of pages flickering.

(8)

The two or three miles down into Jesman's Bend were as silent as the valley had been just minutes earlier.

The initial euphoria of Geoff's solution that Jerry had walked into town was eroded almost as soon as they were back in Geoff's Dodge. The reason, quite simply, was the radio. They picked up KMRT OK, heard Melanie introduce Andy Williams singing 'Can't Take My Eyes Off You', smiled at each other–

Yep, everything is just fine...

–and then Rick went and spoiled it all by turning the tuning dial.

He couldn't have put into words why he turned the goddamned dial but he did it. And–

Nope, everything isn't just fine... Everything isn't just fine at all...

–all they could pick up was static.

"Maybe it's some kind of massive electrical charge," Rick ventured. "Blown out..." he waved his arms like a huge flower opening its petals "I dunno... blown out all the transmitters or something."

He looked across at Geoff and saw his brother raise his eyebrows.

"And," Rick continued, "we can only pick up Mel because we're so close to our own transmitter."

Then, turning out of the curve alongside Frank and Eleanor Dawson's house into Main Street, they saw the blue and white wrapped around the fire hydrant.

"I don't think so," Geoff said, his voice suddenly sounding tired. "I don't think it's that simple."

Geoff slowed right down as they went by the car. It was Don Patterson's, easily recognized by the furry tail on the radio antenna. Most times either of them saw that furry tail, they had to smile. But this time, it just didn't seem funny. This time it seemed awfully sad. Almost pitiful.

"No point in getting out," Rick said.

"Uh uh. Car's empty."

"Maybe..." Rick started to say something, suggest some way that such things could happen in their town that would make everything seem right, but he gave up after just the one word and closed his mouth tight. There was no maybe about it. Something was awfully wrong.

Further along Main Street, Martha McNeil's Diner was ablaze with interior lights. Geoff pulled the Dodge into the sidewalk, parked it between an old Chevy two-tone that was more rust than paint and a little continental job with a floor-shift and a rear-mounted engine, and they got out.

The street was more than silent: it was like a canvas before the paint got put onto it. Empty, devoid of life instead of just sleeping.

"You know," Geoff said, placing his hand on the hood of the Chevy like he was seeing if the engine was still warm, "why do I feel that we're not going to find anyone here in town?"

Rick's face was pressed up against the diner window, looking past his own reflection into the strip-neon-lit interior, staring at the littered counter, the plates of half-eaten food, mugs of coffee, pieces of cutlery lying some on the plate, some on the counter and one or two on the floor behind the foot rail. He shifted to one side so he could get a look into the back, where Martha herself did the cooking, best plates of pancakes and flapjacks in the State. The kitchen was deserted.

"Where'd they go?" Rick said stepping away from the window and out onto the street. He didn't expect an answer and wasn't disappointed when he didn't get one.

"You think maybe it was some kind of radiation?" Geoff turned around and looked at his brother. "I'm just grasping at things here, you understand."

"Hey, grasp away."

"Well, like maybe the military came in and evacuated everybody."

"Including Don from his smashed up car? Jerry from his pickup? And how come they didn't come for *us*? How come nobody even called us up and *told* us?"

He turned around, hands on hips, and shook his head. "And how'd they do it so fast? And–" He pointed down the street away from the stores, where the houses sprouted picket fences and grass so close-cut you'd have thought it had been trimmed using scissors. "Nobody leaving their door open. We knock on those doors, there's gonna be no reply. So, if they all just high-tailed it out of here with the military, in such a dad-burned rush, how come everyone remembered to close their door?"

"We don't know for sure that–"

Rick stepped onto the sidewalk, his shadow disappearing into the broadening shadow of the diner's roof. "So let's find out."

"Rick..."

"Yeah?"

Geoff looked at his kid brother's face, studied the eyes and, in them, saw the same fears and uncertainty that sprawled in his own heart. Rick was bigger than him but Geoff always felt the need to care of his kid brother. "It'll be OK," he said, and winked.

They stepped inside the diner, listening for sounds and hearing nothing.

All that was needed to complete the effect was an occasional tumbleweed blowing across Main Street and maybe the wind whistling around the saloon swing doors. But there were no saloon swing doors in Jesman's Bend.

In fact, there was nothing there at all... at least nothing alive.

Martha McNeil's diner had been as silent as the grave. Plates of food half-eaten, mugs half full of coffee – now cool to the touch – a jacket slung over one of the booth stools (Jim Ferumern's, his wallet still in his pocket: forty-six dollars in bills plus a picture of his wife, Jacqui, and the two boys – Geoff didn't remember their names, if he'd ever known them – and a bunch of coins that slipped out of a side pocket and clattered to Martha's linoleum floor), and a magazine lying open on the counter beside a half cup of coffee and a Danish with a bite out of it: *Book,* open at a spread about a bookstore in New York, *The Mysterious Bookshop*. Turning the magazine over to look at the cover, Rick dropped crumbs onto the counter from the open spread – the kind of crumbs that made him mad when he was reading: crumbs on the magazine – he always knocked them off or took more care eating.

Further down the street, houses were empty and silent. Knocks on doors and names called out by Geoff and Rick brought no response. Not even from Luke Napier's terrier, gone from the lavishly-built dog kennel by the front of the house with its restraining chain lying curled up in a tangle alongside a bowl bearing the word "Duffy" in scrawled paint.

Most of the doors were still locked against the night, even though by now, with all their looking and checking, it was almost six o'clock. Those that were not locked opened onto silent homes, some of them with TV sets playing – some showing old movies and sitcom re-runs but some (the ones tuned into stations showing live material, Geoff guessed) showing static, and radios mostly playing the same, though on one or two they heard Melanie's smoky voice announcing a new song. They felt like thieves, stealing into the sanctity of friends' houses, breathing their air, smelling the smells of their homes. When they spoke they spoke in whispers, eyes pulled wide open in an effort to strengthen their hearing that they might discern even the tiniest movement, the laziest turn-over in bed. But the beds, when they found them, were like everywhere and everything else: empty, the sheets on many of them bunched up as though wrapped around slumbering figures that had suddenly blinked out of existence, pillows indented beneath nonexistent heads.

The lights in the gas station glared dimly against the strengthening sunlight but Gram Kramer was nowhere to be found, though his prized leather jacket hung stiffly by the side of his stool in the windowed booth overlooking the pumps, a copy of the *Enquirer* open on the counter and a burned away cigarette butt lying on the counter, a long perfectly formed funnel of undisturbed ash lying in the ashtray beside it. At least here there was some sense of normality – the radio was tuned into their station and Melanie's voice suddenly drifted in on the closing strains of Ray Charles's "I Got a

Woman", speaking to all those people who had loved ones "way over town". Her voice now had a sense of urgency, a sense of needing somebody to respond to what she was saying. Rick wondered what Mel and Johnny had been talking about up there on the mountain; wondered whether they'd started making telephone calls and finding nobody home. Nobody home anywhere.

"You need to give her a call," Rick said without turning.

"Uh huh," Geoff said. "I'll do it from Eddie's."

There were two blue-and-whites parked outside the sheriff's office, which meant that there should be somebody inside. Even without the cars, there was no way Shirley Pakard would leave the office unattended. And how come nobody had wondered why they couldn't get a response from Don Patterson, his car wrapped around the fire hydrant on the outskirts of town? The answer was there was nobody to make that call, nobody to wonder why the response didn't come in.

Rick strode up to the door and pushed it wide.

"Troy, Shirley?"

Only a little over one hour ago, Rick and Geoff had edged into places shouting out names and other things to go with the names – things like, "Hey, what's happening?" and "Come on, time to rise and shine," – but they had given that up after a while. Now they just burst into homes and through doors and even the shouted names were half-hearted at best, the volume of the call lessening each time.

Rick pulled a notebook from his jacket pocket and slumped into Shirley's chair. He pulled the phone across the desk and started to dial.

"Who you calling?"

Rick leaned back and looked up at his brother. "Mom."

Geoff looked at his watch, about to say something – something like *don't call her yet, too early* or *let's not worry her about this... there has to be a logical explanation* – but he knew those would just be excuses. The fact was he feared the same thing that his brother feared, though neither of them was prepared to put it into words. He leaned against the desk and waited.

When Angela Grisham's voice came on the phone, Rick's face lit up like a fourth of July fireworks display... but when that voice kept on talking without waiting to hear what Rick had to say – telling him she couldn't get to the phone right now but instructing him (even though the long-ago recorded voice didn't know who she was talking to) to leave a message – his face collapsed. He returned the phone to the cradle. "It's almost six o'clock for mom – she should be there. Whatever it is, it stretches out to the West Coast."

Geoff said, "Try Mel's brother, Bob... New York." He recited the 212 number from heart and watched Rick prod the keypad.

"What time is it there?" Rick said as he listened to the ringing tones.

Geoff checked his watch. "Around nine. He should be there." Bob and Linda McAuley worked from home, running a small press publishing operation in the Village. They were always there, at least one of them. But not today.

Rick shook his head. "No answer."

Whatever it was, it stretched right across the country.

They didn't like to think how much further it went.

"You gonna call Mel?"

Geoff shook his head. "Let's just get back to the station," he said.

(9)

They were in the 16th Street Mall and it had to be getting late – Ronnie could see the sky darkening through the glass roof. He checked the watch on his wrist once again, forgetting for the God-knew-how-many-times that the thing had been at 5.46 or so ever since the crash. He looked around.

"You OK there, Samantha?" Angel Wurst asked her doll. The doll conveniently waved its arms, with just a little assistance from Angel. They had found Samantha in a store called *Going Back* on one of the upper levels. Ronnie thought that was maybe a strange name for what was a toy store but closer investigation of the price tags suggested that this was no common kids' store but something altogether different.

"What's nostalgia?" Angel Wurst had asked when Ronnie had tried to explain what the store was about, but then her attention had switched to the muzak – "What's that song? My mom loves that song." It was the second time he knew about – he suspected that maybe he'd heard it once before those – that he'd recognized a saccharine sweet instrumental rendition of Simon and Garfunkel's "The Boxer". To Ronnie, it was like a sign – he loved Simon and Garfunkel.

It had taken them almost four hours to reach the city limits, three hours of which they'd done on foot and another hour in a succession of vehicles beginning with a 4x4 of indeterminate manufacture, a private hire cab and, finally, a crimson Chevy with gloriously large tailfins. Ronnie had felt like he was in *Happy Days* – or at least happier days than he was in right now. They had found the Chevy parked up with its door open and engine still running outside of what appeared to be a 24-hour newsstand, just beyond a multiple vehicle pile-up at which they'd had to ditch the cab – the stand was decked out in all the usual magazines and newspapers, lit up and just sitting there as though the owner had stepped around back for a pee.

The last hour or so they had picked their way slowly along streets littered with car wrecks, some of them serious – cars through store windows – and some just looking like they'd run out of gas and drifted up against other car fenders or mailboxes. On an overpass coming into the city, Ronnie had seen a break in the railings and broad-black skid marks leading up to it. The skid marks suggested that someone had fought for control – someone maybe blinded by a bright light but not removed by it – but that someone had lost it and veered over towards the rail. He didn't stop the Chevy to check for signs of life below the rail: he could see right from where he was that it was a long way down.

They had reached the 16th Street Mall a little after one o'clock and Ronnie had just slumped back in the seat and closed his eyes. Angel was already sound asleep in the back seat, her legs curled up and her hands clasped beneath her cheek, all wrapped up in a tartan blanket. He had gone out like a light, reliving the experience in the plane, the light, Martha's disappearance – hell, *everyone*'s disappearance – and then meeting up with Karl, the map-reader turned pilot.

When he had woken up it was after four o'clock in the afternoon and it already seemed to be getting a little overcast. The sky over to the east was slashed with ribbons of dark cloud that appeared to be snaking their way westwards. Ronnie had checked over behind him, to the west, and it looked fine over there so he put it down to maybe an approaching storm – it was too early for sunset. And anyway, the sun always set in the west.

He had woken Angel who didn't say anything at all, just rubbed her eyes some and then checked the seat alongside her. When Ronnie asked how she was, Angel simply said, "I'm not good in a morning." He imagined her picking the phrase up from one of her parents and immediately wondered if she would ever see them again. Or if he would ever see Martha again, Queen Bitch Mistress of the Mouth, but now strangely missed. He suddenly felt a frisson of affection for her. But no sooner had it made its presence felt, the frisson was gone.

They had walked across an eerily semi-deserted parking lot that seemed to be around the size of Ronnie's old campus at Kent State, where the National Guard had shot the students back in May 1970 – that was almost 15 years before he'd started but the wounds were still open, the blood still wet. They went up to a wide array of glass doors under the legend "East Entrance". As they approached the entrance, the doors opened with the vaguest swish noise, drew them into the muzak-filled chromium warmth and closed again right behind them. Ronnie had thought of the Romero zombie film, where the survivors were holed up in a mall, and he'd given a little shudder.

That was hours ago now.

By Ronnie's reckoning, they had been in the Mall for three hours, maybe even a little longer. The next thing he had to do was get a hold of a new watch. He felt naked without the time on his wrist, naked and vulnerable.

There was no doubt the Mall had been reasonably busy whenever what had happened had happened but the place was completely deserted – just the muzak echoing along the corridors, and an occasional fountain gurgling in a never-ending spray. Here and there, soft drink containers and fast food packets – hamburger cartons and KFC cardboard buckets – were spilled on the concourse, their contents fallen out into alien shapes and unpleasant-looking mounds of fat and grease.

They had walked up and down, gone up the escalators, travelled up in the elevator, had coffee and soda plus almond croissants in a *Passin' Thru* (where Ronnie had to make the coffee), found the toy store where Angel had picked up Samantha (because she had whispered to her, Angel had said, her brow furrowed with abject sincerity) but the one thing that wasn't here was a hardware store or an outlet that specialized in tools. As far as Ronnie was concerned, they needed a heavy-duty battery-operated chainsaw and maybe an oxy-acetylene torch.

Leaving the table, Ronnie had actually considered taking their plate, mug and glass across to the counter – even thought about leaving a five dollar bill near the till area – but the thought didn't last long. As time went by, he was pretty sure he wouldn't ever think of doing it.

Another hour or maybe even a half-hour later, Ronnie and Angel Wurst lifted pre-packed sandwiches – a triple-decker pastrami on rye and an egg and cress in a seeded baguette – out of the cold cabinet in Stephenson's Pharmacy, completing the banquet with a couple bags of potato chips and a mineral water and a Coca-Cola. "My mom never lets me drink Coca-Cola," Angel confided to Ronnie, keeping her voice low and conspiratorial as she swung her legs over the edge of her plush leather stool at the Pharmacy counter, her egg and cress double-decker in the one hand and the Coca-Cola bottle – clearly a rare treasure for the girl – in the other. She chewed a little, took a big swallow, legs still swinging, took a drink of the coke, and then said, "You think we'll ever see her again?" It sounded like she was saying, *Hey, you think it's gonna rain tomorrow?*

"Your mom?"

Angel nodded, took another bite out of the sandwich and delicately added a large potato chip into her mouth.

"I don't know, honey," he said, narrowly banishing the pedant in him that cried out to inform the girl that, never having seen her mother, he clearly could not see her *again*.

"I wonder where she is. And my dad."

There was nothing Ronnie could think of to say to that so he let the silence say it for him. The silence and the muzak.

And then there was something else.

It was Ronnie who heard it first, far off, and he wondered if it was maybe in his head. He looked around at Angel, eyebrows raised questioningly, and she nodded.

"Telephone," she said.

"Telephone," Ronnie said, the word assuming mantra-like significance. "Someone's ringing the phone."

They stood up together from the pharmacy counter stools and tried to get their bearings.

"It's coming from out there," Angel said, nodding towards the empty corridors of the shopping mall.

"Come on."

Ronnie took a hold of the girl's hand as they ran out of Stephenson's Pharmacy and into the spacious walkway of the mall. They stopped, listened some more, silently praying for the phone to keep ringing, and Angel Wurst lifted her arm and pointed in the direction of the escalators. "There," she said.

Ronnie started running and then realized that he couldn't go full speed while holding the girl's hand. "Here," he said, turning to her and crouching down. "Let me carry–" She was shaking her head.

"What's the matter? I can carry–"

"It's stopped," she said.

Ronnie turned in the direction they had been running and all he could hear was the distant thrumming of the air conditioning or the escalators, or maybe both. A cheesy instrumental version of "Sweet Caroline" started up.

"This music sucks big time," Angel announced, pulling a face.

Ronnie was nodding as he stood up.

"You think maybe it was Karl, the pilot man?"

"He doesn't know we're here."

"I thought you told him we were coming–"

"He doesn't know the number."

He took a hold of Angel's hand and again they walked in the direction of the escalators. "I think it was coming from around here," Ronnie said as they reached a central area which saw walkways continuing in three directions. He scanned the area around the escalators but couldn't see any telephones.

"Maybe it was from one of the stores," Angel offered.

Ronnie checked the stores – sporting goods, chocolate, all-year Christmas goods, a music store, a cheap-and-cheerful cut-price women's wear store, a lingerie store, a Starbucks coffee wagon, a Barnes and Noble and a big toy store. "I don't think we'd have heard it if it had been in the stores." He looked around some more and noticed a pair of blue doors on the way to the restrooms with a stenciled

PRIVATE
STAFF ONLY

across them. One of the doors was propped open with one of the metallic standing platforms that they used in the bookstores when they needed to reach the high shelves.

"Let's check in here," Ronnie said.

Inside the small corridor behind the doors was a world away from the glitz and glamour of the main mall. The corridor was the same blue as the outer doors, but the paintwork was scuffed and chipped. Down here they could hear a deeper hum.

"Generators," Ronnie said, feeling Angel grip his hand tighter.

"I don't like it down here," she said.

"It's OK, we have to–"

ring riiing

ring riiing

Ronnie pulled her down the corridor until they reached a door marked "Floor Supervisor" which he then pushed open to find a small office area that led onto a single open glassed room in the corner. The outside office featured three desks, a copier, a water cooler, a large trestle table littered with papers and two fax machines. It was the telephone on one of these desks

ring riiing

ring riiing

that was ringing.

Ronnie let go of Angel's hand and moved over towards the desks, hand outstretched.

It wasn't the first one, which he passed quickly by, and it wasn't the second.

"It's that one," Angel said, pointing at the desk immediately in front of the glass office. Ronnie did a side-step and lurched across the front of the desk, his fingers making first contact with the handset just as the

ring riiing

was abbreviated to

ring rii-

followed by a dull click. He lifted it anyway and snapped into the mouthpiece – "Hello?" – but all he could hear was a dial tone. "Hello?" he said again, even though the tone was still there. People do that, he realized now. All that stuff on movies and in books, when you think that people just didn't do that kind of thing, it was all true. People really were that stupid.

"They hung up?"

Ronnie nodded and replaced the handset.

"Maybe they'll call again. They done it twice now."

"Could be they've done it other times," Ronnie said. He looked at the desk. There was a small calendar on it, tented open with a little marker strip with a crimson square poised over Thursday 12 April.

He moved around the desk and sat in the chair. He lifted the phone and keyed in *69. A pre-recorded voice told him that the caller withheld their number. "Thanks," Ronnie said needlessly. He had to fight off the urge to ask the voice to wait, stay a while, *talk to me...*

"Why'd they bother whiffolding their number?" Angel inquired, her forehead furrowed.

"They didn't actually withhold it now," Ronnie explained. "It's already set up that way, their phone." He watched the girl's eyes trying to make sense of what he was saying.

"Why?"

Good question, he thought. He shrugged and said, "Some folks just don't like people to be able to call them back by hitting star-sixty-nine."

Angel sat on the edge of the next desk from the one where Ronnie was and started swinging her legs. "So what now?"

Another shrug. If he kept this up he was going to be deformed. "We wait? We go? I just don't know."

He lifted some papers, flicked through them, left them be. Then he sniffed the air.

"What is it? You smell something?"

Without answering, Ronnie bent forward and rested his nose against the desk, right where his arms had been, and he sniffed some more.

"Perfume," he said.

"Is that good?"

"Uh uh. Not in itself, it isn't good. But it's started me thinking."

He started pulling open side drawers, found a pair of Scholl sandals with the wooden bases, a small box of Earl Gray teabags, a mug with World's Best Mom stenciled on the side of it, a crumpled pair of women's underwear, an old newspaper – just two sheets of it, carefully folded – a paperback novel (*B For Burglar* by Sue

Grafton), spine badly creased, some grocery store bags, all neatly folded and in a small pile, and a couple of tangerines. He picked up the paperback and opened the cover – a name was written on the synopsis page in blue ink:

J. Talbert

"No luck?" Angel asked as Ronnie closed the final drawer.

"Somebody called J. Talbert. Unless somebody else loaned it to her, that is."

Ronnie returned the book to the drawer and moved around the other desks.

The one immediately inside the door had a triptych photo montage featuring a smiling woman in the center panel flanked on either side by a boy, the one on the left maybe around twelve years old and the one on the right a little older, with that pubescent awkwardness in his stance.

Ronnie moved to the last of the three desks. A nameplate on the middle of the desk announced that this was the property of J. Peter Baldone. "Bet he keeps the nameplate just in case he forgets," Ronnie said, unable to keep the smile out of his voice.

Angel said, "Are we going back to the airplane?"

"Sure we are," Ronnie said. "But we need to get some stuff to help Karl. And we should find out who was calling."

"I'm hungry."

"Again? We only just ate."

Angel shook her head emphatically. "No," she said, slurring the word to let Ronnie know he was out of order. "Not 'again'... '*still*'. I didn't have enough to eat the last time."

Ronnie moved into the glass office and checked the filing cabinet. "OK, we'll finish up here and go get another sandwich." The cabinet drawer opened effortlessly.

Ronnie flicked through the card markers on the filled slots – Vacation, Rota, Bank details, Insurance, Head Office and so on. He pulled out the Vacation and Rota folders and flicked them open.

There were five names on the vacation listing: DeShaun Maniker, JP Baldone, Jennifer Talbert, Matthew Bodowski and

Philip Kahn. He replaced the file and continued flicking through the rest of the drawer. He was disappointed to find that there were no personnel records, so no addresses or telephone numbers. He slid the drawer closed again.

"So, Jennifer Talbert," Ronnie said, "world's best mom, who is calling you here today?"

"You think it was maybe a fren?"

"It *could* be a friend," Ronnie said. But he didn't think so. If everywhere had been affected the same way, then he thought that the last thing on people's minds would be to call friends at work. No, this call had to be from family. Maybe a husband, calling to see if his wife was OK; a mother or father, calling their daughter; or kids, looking for mom.

Ronnie looked at his watch. And then cursed. He still hadn't got himself a new one. But no matter, it was hours since the light. If it was someone local then they would have driven down here long ago. Plus, if the husband were at work himself, then he probably wouldn't have a number block on his work or business telephone. So, realistically, that left out a husband. Or "significant other" as the politically correct lobby would have it.

So, parents? That was the second one in Ronnie's list of options. But he didn't buy Jennifer Talbert's parents as being the kind of people who put a number block on their home telephone. No, that was something a younger person would do. He looked at Angel. She was oblivious to what was going on in Ronnie's head, busy straightening Samantha's dress.

He moved back to Jennifer Talbert's desk and sniffed some more. It was a younger perfume. It wasn't middle-aged but it wasn't a twenty-something. Ronnie closed his eyes and tried to picture her.

"You OK?"

He snapped his eyes open and gave Angel a smile. "I'm fine. A little tired, maybe, but I'm fine."

"So not a fren?"

"Nope. Not a friend. It was home calling. Not her husband but her son or her daughter."

Angel giggled and slapped Samantha against her leg. "Hey, how'd you know *that*?"

Ronnie shrugged. "I think maybe I'm picking up the power from you," he said, holding both index fingers against his temples and crossing his eyes at the girl. Angel giggled some more.

Glancing around the main office, Ronnie saw a stack of directories on one of the filing cabinets. He went across and pulled off the residential volume, turned to the *T* section and started running down the names, flicking pages until he reached the *Ta*'s. "Boy," he said, more to himself than to Angel Wurst, "there are some strange names in here." Then he stopped. "Ah, here we go, Talbart, Talbatt, tuh tuh tuh, *Talbert*!" He ran his finger down the listing, tutting, and then stopped. "Hey," he said, turning to Angel, "if the person calling her was at home, then Jennifer Talbert's number won't be listed."

Angel shrugged helpfully, eyes wide. Whatever the problem was, she was pretty sure it wasn't her fault.

Ronnie went back to the cabinet, closed the open drawer and pulled open the drawer above it. He flicked through the file sections until he came across Personnel, which he pulled out. There were eight folders in there, including some names he hadn't come across. But the main thing was that Talbert, Jennifer was there. He lifted the folder clear and opened it.

Jennifer Talbert was 36 years old, married to Theodore Allan Talbert, and they had two sons, Theodore Brian Junior and Wayne Allan. There was a number to call for emergencies but it was her husband's, Jennings and Milhause Risk Assessment. There was no number for her home.

"You reckon this is an emergency?" Ronnie said as he lifted the receiver of the nearest phone and started to key in numbers. The line was dead. He replaced the receiver, lifted it again, and prefaced the number with 9. He got a tone. Then he dialed.

"Who you calling?"

"Ted Talbert."

Angel made a face. "Who's he?"

"His wife works at this desk. I'm calling him to see if he's been trying to call her."

Angel made Samantha do a little walk and then sat the doll down on her knee.

The number cleared and Ronnie heard a ringing. Somewhere over town, in a suite of offices whose windows were painted "Milhause Risk Assessment", a telephone was ringing. He pictured the desks and the nice paintings on the walls, the water dispenser over in the corner, the coffee machine, maybe – all of these things. But it was deserted. Nobody had come into work today.

"Damn!" was all Ronnie could think of to say that he felt he could get away with in front of a six year old.

"Can we go get another sandwich?"

"OK, honey." Ronnie pulled a sheet of paper from a scrap tray on J. Peter Baldone's desk and scribbled down Jennifer Talbert's address. Then he replaced the folder and slipped the paper into his pocket. Minutes later they were back at Stephenson's pharmacy choosing more sandwiches.

"What kind of stuff?"

"Huh?" Ronnie was partway through a thick chocolate doughnut and he had caramel icing around his mouth.

"What kind of stuff you wanting for Karl?"

"Oh, OK. Stuff to help him get free."

Angel tore another piece out of the day's second sandwich and dropped the rest of it onto her plate, going instead for the potato chips.

"You think you really should have had more potato chips?" Ronnie had just narrowly avoided asking her what her mother would say when she found out her six year old daughter had been stuffing herself with carbohydrates. He figured the chances were not good that Angel would ever see her parents again. Or that he would ever see Martha.

Angel ignored the question and instead asked, "You think he's OK under all that wood?"

"I think so, sure. I *hope* so."

"You gonna take him some food?"

Ronnie snapped his fingers and patted Angel on the shoulders. "Hey, you're quite a catch, aren't you? That's good thinking there, Angel." He finished his water, stifled a belch and pushed his empty plate forward. "Let's go choose him something from the cabinet. You done?"

She nodded and slid from the stool.

"I need to go to the bathroom."

Ronnie looked around until he saw the RESTROOMS sign. "Over there, honey. I'll get Karl a sandwich."

"And potato chips," she called over her shoulder as she ran through the pharmacy.

"And potato chips," Ronnie agreed.

When Angel started off along the corridor to the restrooms, Ronnie opened the cold cabinet again and checked the sandwiches. There seemed little point in leaving any of them: they didn't know how plentiful food was going to be so he may just as well take the lot. He slipped behind the counter to look for something to carry them in.

(10)

Rick and Geoff didn't go back to the station, not right away. Geoff had second thoughts and headed the Dodge out of Jesman's Bend the 18 miles to Dawson. But it was a wasted effort.

They heard the horn plaintively wailing long before they had passed the tracks on the town outskirts, its drone hanging on the wind like a half-remembered tune or the tired buzzing of a wasp trapped against the window pane in a deserted room.

The cause was an old Lincoln, all chrome and fins, its front end sitting in the double-fronted window of a deli on Milton, where the street curved slightly to the intersection with Boedeckers. They didn't stop to look but, as they passed the Lincoln, driving slowly, praying silently for any movement, Rick wondered whose car it was and why he or she was out so early in the morning. It was almost ten by that time but they both assumed the smash-up happened in the early hours, same time as the light.

A little further along, another car and a delivery truck had met head on at the intersection. The car was a wreck and the delivery truck had jackknifed onto its side so that it was spread right across the road. A few yards beyond, they saw a bicycle lying by the side of the road, a burlap sack of spewed-out newspapers littering the sidewalk. If they wanted to go any further they would have to park up and proceed on foot. Without saying anything, Geoff slowed down and made a turn back the way they had come, back past the smashed Lincoln with its horn still wailing like an abandoned child – and, just like such a child who had been crying for attention for a long time, the horn's voice was growing hoarse.

Going back, they passed more empty streets and empty houses, with the only sign of movement being the flag over the courthouse, flapping in the wind.

They hit Jesman's Bend for the second time at a little before midday, pulling up outside the station at 12.20. The sun was high and the shadows long. Neither of them was looking forward to the darkness, though they couldn't explain why.

This time they didn't stop.

Melanie was sitting on the rail outside the station's front entrance, coffee cup in one hand and cigarette in the other, its smoke drifting peacefully up into the air as though everything was absolutely normal.

"We're on strike," she announced as Geoff stepped out of the Dodge.

He nodded.

Rick walked up to her and tousled her thatch of blonde hair, closing his eyes and breathing in the smoke. "My, but that smells good."

Melanie squinted into the sun and gave a sorry-looking smile to her husband. "There's nobody there, is there?"

Geoff shook his head. "How did you know that?"

Melanie shrugged, took a pull on the cigarette. "No calls, no movement out on the road, no answer from people *we* called – some of Johnny's friends, my brother–"

"Yeah, I called Bob, too." Geoff stretched his arms behind his head and arched his back. "He could be out."

"Hey, don't bullshit a bullshitter, OK?"

Rick made for the open doors. "I'm getting a coffee. Anyone else."

Melanie shook her head but Geoff said he'd have one.

When Rick had disappeared, Melanie asked Geoff what he thought had happened to everyone.

"I have absolutely no idea. No idea at all. None of it makes any sense." He plopped onto the rail beside her and leaned forward on his knees. "We drove down to Dawson, same thing: everywhere silent and deserted. Abandoned cars smashed through store windows, truck upturned in the street... Jeez, Mel, I'm worried."

She threw the butt to the ground and put her hand on his hands. "Don't be. We're OK, that's the main thing."

"But what if they've all gone for good? What if we're... what if we're the last people on the planet?"

"We won't be."

"Why not? And anywise, we don't even know why *we* weren't taken or–" he waved a hand in the air "–disintegrated, or whatever it was happened."

The sound of footsteps made them both turn.

"Maybe we just live right," Johnny said. He was leaning against the door drinking Coca-Cola from a can, wrap-around dark glasses reflecting the sun. He looked like a young Marlon Brando: scuffed motorcycle boots, tight jeans and tight sweatshirt with the short sleeves rolled up onto his shoulders, a bulge of a cigarette pack in the left one, like a rectangular epaulette. He exuded attitude.

"Doesn't make any sense," Geoff said again.

Melanie got to her feet and threw coffee grounds onto the soil at the side of the path. "Have you noticed how there are no birds?" She walked a little way to the Dodge, its engine clicking in the heat. "And no insects?"

"There ain't no nothing," Johnny announced. "Took everything, whatever it was."

"But why not us?"

"That, Geoffrey, is the $64,000 question."

Melanie threw her head back and sniffed. "You think maybe it's poisonous... the air, I mean?"

Johnny shook his head. "Whatever happened happened fast – if it was something in the air then we'd have noticed it long before now." He stepped out and shucked himself onto the rail. "It was the light. I didn't see it – as you know – but that's what it was."

"Maybe it was a comet or something."

Melanie looked across at her husband. "Like that movie, *Day of the Triffids*? That was some kind of comet, wasn't it?" She glanced over at the grassland rolling down the side of the valley to make sure she couldn't see any monster plants staggering up to keep them company.

"But whatever it was," Johnny said, his voice soft but insistent, "it still doesn't explain why it didn't do us. And it doesn't explain what's happened to all the bodies."

Melanie shook her head and went inside.

"We were inside," Geoff suggested. "But, no, that doesn't work either. Lots of folks – in fact, pretty much everyone – were inside, most of them in bed. Like you," he added.

Johnny looked back to make sure Melanie hadn't reappeared. "But maybe not New York," he said. "New York is two hours in front of us – that would have made it five, five-thirty there, when the light came."

Geoff let out a deep sigh. "Then it's happened all over the world."

Johnny took a slug of soda and nodded. "Could be."

"Except for us."

"Except for us." Johnny took another slug of soda and crushed the can.

"So it wasn't simply being inside that helped us," Geoff said, studying his tented fingers. "And it wasn't anything to do with here–" he waved a hand at the surrounding hillside "–because all the birds are gone."

"And the insects," Johnny added with a chuckle.

"Yeah, every cloud has its silver lining."

They both laughed.

Geoff got to his feet and looked at the station building. "So maybe it's got something to do with our building that doesn't apply to any others."

"Either that or we've been spared."

Geoff looked across at Johnny to see if he was smiling.

"You serious?"

Johnny shrugged and pulled his pack of cigarettes from his sleeve. "Why not? Makes as much sense as anything else."

"Well I don't feel like Bruce Willis right now. Or Schwarzenegger. Truth told, I feel more like Woody Allen." He turned back to face the station. "Nope, it's the station. Has to be."

"OK: why? Why the station?"

Geoff clapped his hands together in frustration. "God, I just don't know – the roof? Something in the concrete, maybe?"

"Like what?"

"Johnny-"

"I'm not being difficult – at least not deliberately – I'm just trying to eliminate the things that don't make any sense."

"*None* of it makes any sense."

"Agreed. But special concrete makes less sense than most things."

"Yeah, OK. So not the concrete."

"What about us? I mean, us ourselves?"

Geoff shook his head. "If it were just me and Rick then maybe that would work, our being brothers. But you and Mel, too… it doesn't work."

"Hey, what about something to do with the station itself?"

"I don't follow you."

Johnny blew smoke up into the air as he jumped from the rail. "The station… broadcasting!"

Geoff's eyes narrowed as he considered it.

"Sound wa– no, not sound waves – radio waves," Johnny continued. "Maybe there's something about radio waves that protected us. I mean, we pump a lot out from here, right?"

Geoff waggled his head from side to side, not really having an answer. This is the time, he thought, we suddenly need for one of us to have majored in some-damned-thing-or-other, to suddenly spout up with an answer for everything, just like they used to do in the comic books and those cheesy old black-and-white movies they kept showing on the SciFi channel, the ones starring Richard Carlson or Marshall Thompson.

He looked across at Johnny, the thirty-something dyslexic Lothario with the Springsteen wardrobe and the in-your-face deejay patter. Then he thought of his kid brother, twenty-eight-going-on-fifty, still unable to drive a car almost half a year after an accident that just wasn't his fault, and Melanie, beautiful Melanie, a siren in military-style baggy dungarees whose body sang him to sleep most nights when it was she – the high school dropout with the background of parental abuse – who most needed the attention.

And himself, The Proprietor of KMRT – K Mart, as the guys in town delighted in calling it – the failed advertising executive who couldn't stand the rat race, staring the big four-oh down the throat and not liking the smell that came out of there – a smell like flowers that had passed their prime, old perfume gone still and bad. Atomic Knights they were not. If the future of the planet – of mankind itself, maybe – were their responsibility then maybe it was time to send the audience home. The game was as good as finished even before it had gotten started.

"Hello... Planet Earth to Geoff... come in, Geoff..."

He shook his head and gave a weak smile. "Sorry. Drifting."

"Uh huh. Drifting where, oh great one?"

He reached over and lifted Johnny's pack of Marlboro from the concrete standing by his feet. "Just drifting." He shook a cigarette out and Johnny tossed across a matchbook, most of whose matches were twisted out and bent over, their heads blackened like dead soldiers. He pulled a match free, struck it, held it to the cigarette and inhaled. It tasted good... tasted normal.

He looked up at the sky through the blue-gray of the swirling smoke and said, "There's one thing we haven't said anything about."

"Yeah?"

"What happens tonight? What happens if they – or it, whatever it was – what happens if it comes back to finish the job?"

Johnny looked around again. Geoff thought it must be because of Melanie: Johnny didn't want to say anything that might cause her concern. Geoff liked that. It raised Johnny in his esteem and he made a mental note to have a word with Rick to get off his case, not ride him so much. They all needed each other's support if they were going to get through this, whatever "this" was.

"... already given that some thought," Johnny was saying. "Right at the start, when Mel and me figured out for ourselves that the world had suddenly gone AWOL and we were left holding the hill against the enemy, I wondered if... if this thing has been an intentional thing by–" he waved his hands in the air, "–by whatever, then maybe they know we're here. Maybe they know they screwed up with the people up on the hill in that wacky-looking building with all the antennae sticking out of the top." He frowned and lowered his voice. "And maybe they're going to come back for us... tonight."

"So you're suggesting?"

"We get the hell out. Now!" He slapped the rail with his hand and the ring on his finger made a dull chime.

"That's fine if–" He tapped his index finger. "One, they know they screwed up and, two, they know where they can get us. But it's a bad idea if they just send the light again, same way they did this morning, and we're suddenly out there, somewhere, away from whatever it was that protected us."

Johnny was nodding. "Hadn't thought it through that way. Maybe they won't come back: maybe it was just a random thing, something that happens once in every zillion years or so, something natural." He said the word "natural" as though it was something unpleasant.

"Maybe."

"But you don't think so."

"No, I don't think so. I never heard of anything natural that could remove folks from out of their beds and out of their cars, just like that." He snapped his fingers. "Except maybe in *The X Files*."

"So they're coming back."

Geoff nodded, took a final pull on the butt and flicked it onto the path.

"So, which one is it to be? Move off or stay put here?"

Geoff leaned back and breathed out a final cloud of smoke. "You're putting *me* in charge?" he asked, tapping himself in the chest incredulously.

"Seems to me like you're the best we've got."

"Well, that convinces me what a sorry state we're in."

"And it's amen to that, oh Great One."

They both forced a smile at that and turned to watch the sun, lost in their own thoughts as, silently and slowly, it made its way across to the far horizon. They couldn't see it doing it, of course. But they knew that it was.

It was almost 8pm, the sun so low in the western sky that only the burnt orange memory of it remained over the wooded hills surrounding distant Carlisle, when Geoff and Rick were finally satisfied they had secured the station for the night.

In the hours since Geoff's conversation with Johnny, the four of them had been busy. Geoff had assumed the mantle of Chief of Operations, a role that had seemed to meet with everyone's approval. He had sent Johnny and Rick back into Jesman's Bend to get provisions while he and Melanie went around the station shoring up shutters and doorways and windows. Then they cleared the garage space of all the junk they had collected over the months, making room for the Dodge.

They watched in silence, each of them lost in their own thoughts, as the overhead door closed on its electronic pulley, stuttering the way it always did around the halfway mark, when Geoff had to slap the remote with his hand before pressing the wide button again. It caught with the one slap – it usually took more when they were raising the door, which is why they had abandoned the garage as a store for the Dodge in the first place – but when it *did* start again, there seemed an element of finality to it and Geoff looked down at the remote with the steady confidence that he would never use it again, as though he would never open that door again. He looked across at Melanie and forced a smile when he saw her watching him, frowning. He waved the remote. "I love these things, you know."

"So I see. What is it they say about little things pleasing little minds?"

He leaned over, kissed the side of her face and gave her a knowing wink. "There's a couple bigger things I get a lot of fun out of, too." He brushed his hand lightly against Melanie's breasts and gave a lascivious grin.

Melanie shook her head in mock disgust and pushed him away. "God, you are such a sleazebag, you know that?"

Geoff smiled as the descending door removed the last glimmer of the Dodge and the door clanked to a stop. "There, that should do it," he said.

He turned to Melanie to hand her the remote for a second but she was pulling weeds from the side of the concrete apron. Geoff hadn't the heart to disturb her, lost as she was in the simple act of tending and tidying. He bent down and laid the remote on the ground and went across to check the door. It was secure. It rattled in its runners, but it was secure. Geoff reckoned that anyone with the capability of doing what they'd done would probably be able to beat down a few doors but he had kept that to himself. The chances were, anyway, that everyone else recognized that same fact but they, too, had kept it quiet. The activity had kept them all busy.

"All done?" Melanie asked.

Geoff turned and nodded, smiling at the tufts of weed in his wife's clenched hand. "How about you?"

Melanie frowned and then saw Geoff looking at her hand. She let out a high-pitched giggle and tossed the weeds across at him, Geoff ducking and dodging back around her to the door. Melanie chased him and, when the station door was satisfactorily locked and bolted, she fell into his arms.

In that embrace they were lost and they were safe, a million miles away from the strangeness of the deserted town and the abandoned trucks and cars, a thousand light years away from marauding lights in the night sky.

"I love you, honey," Geoff said, his voice little more than a whisper.

Melanie nodded, blinking her eyes once. A wave of profound sadness washed over her and, just for a second, she felt that they would never leave this place, and that this was the final embrace she would share with her husband.

"Hey," Geoff said, tapping Melanie's nose with his finger. "Lose those bad thoughts."

"How'd you know–"

"It's my job," he said.

Melanie rose onto the tips of her toes and found Geoff's mouth with her own, flicking her tongue across into his tongue, closing her eyes in the throes of the immense and indescribable pleasure of their touching, and of his smell.

Johnny and Rick had got back a little before five, quiet and even solemn. Geoff hadn't asked them about town – there was no reason to do so: he'd seen it for himself. Instead, while Melanie set to work making fresh coffee and plates of sandwiches, Geoff had watched the two men unloading bags of canned goods and bread into the station's large galley kitchen, filling cupboards and stacking things until the assembled produce coupled with the seemingly impervious security had made them all feel a little easier. Even gung ho.

As the afternoon had trembled over into early evening – and the shadows lengthened and lengthened until, the light fading fast, they faded into watery gray stains and then disappeared completely – Geoff had Rick and Johnny take it in half-hour turns to sit on the roof with Geoff's old binoculars, keeping a watch for any sign of movement on the road leading down into town.

With the lessening light had come the lowering temperature and, a little after 7.30, Geoff watched Rick finish securing the shutters on most of the windows. It was the final job that needed to be done. Geoff had said that it was probably best that they kept lighting to a minimum, and even then only as absolutely necessary. Rick stepped back, lost for a moment in the results of his work, and then suddenly remembered that when they went in they would be in the dark. He turned and gave a half-hearted smile.

"Done?"

Rick nodded and looked around. It had all the appearances of a final look, a last glance before they slipped the black bag over his head and then the noose. "I used to love this time of the evening at this time of year," Rick said. There was a softness to the words and to Rick's voice that Geoff hadn't heard before. Or, at least, he didn't recall hearing them. Rick sighed. "But now, with all the noises gone, and us–" He waved a hand at the gathering gloom and nodded to the station. "–scurrying around in there in total darkness like moles, it's like..." He searched for the words. "It's like I'm standing in a painting, or in one of those hologram setups on the Star Trek shows. Like the dinosaurs in the *Jurassic Park* movies – everything seems to be there but when you get up close to it, it's not the same." He looked around at his brother and pulled a face. "Am I making any sense here or just blowing wind?"

"Yes, you're making a lot of sense."

The countryside seemed to be sitting out there, waiting – but waiting for what? That was the question. There was no sound, no light and no energy anywhere in the world. Geoff imagined flying up into space, right from where he was standing, and soaring over the towns and the cities, over the plains and the forests, over the multi-lane highways and the towering skyscrapers, all of them empty, silent and deserted.

"You coming in?" Johnny's voice broke the stillness.

"Yeah, we're all done out here. See anything?"

"Uh uh. Quiet as the grave."

Geoff would have preferred a different analogy but he took the point.

"Isn't this about the place in the story where you're supposed to say 'It's quiet... *too* quiet!'?"

"Yeah," Rick said, ever the movie buff, "like the old Foreign Legion movies or the Indian uprisings, where a handful of guys are stuck in the fort with a bunch of their dead comrades propped up on the battlements, hoping to fend off one final attack before the cavalry arrive."

"Think they'll get here, Geoff?" Johnny shouted down from the roof. "The cavalry, I mean."

Geoff didn't think so. He didn't think there was anyone to help them repel this enemy, whatever it was and wherever it had come from. But he wasn't about to tell them that. The secret of good leadership is to preserve optimism, even in the face of insurmountable odds. But "It'll turn out," was as much as he could manage, and even that stuck in his throat like a fishbone.

"Yeah," Johnny said, and he moved back on the roof and sat down against the door. Out of sight of Geoff and Rick.

"You really think that? That it'll be OK?"

With a final look around outside, his hands thrust deep into the pockets of his denims, Geoff silently bid the world goodnight. Then he said, "Yes, I really think that."

He turned around and stepped into the station.

Rick followed him and Geoff locked the door, dropping the two security deadbolts into place. The sound was like a cell door and the darkness that engulfed them was like a waiting grave.

All that was then left to do was check the windows and then join the others.

"I was wondering," Rick said as they made their way up to the studio, having satisfied themselves that the building was as secure as they were likely to be able to make it. He was carrying a small pencil flashlight that cast a shuddering circle of white on the floor in front of them.

Geoff said, "What about?"

"How long will the food last? I mean, you know, if everyone *has* gone and we're the last people–" He stopped himself saying "alive" and just left it at that.

Geoff held open the door to the main corridor. "We *won't* be the last people. Something will–"

"But if we are, how long will the food last?"

Geoff led the way to the studio, trailing a hand along the wall for guidance. "Indefinitely. The canned stuff, years certainly."

At the door to the sound booth, Rick stopped and pulled on his brother's arm. "And if there are no animals? Nothing to kill and eat?"

Geoff punched him lightly in the shoulder. "Then we'll become vegetarian. Learn to grow things. Vegetables." He opened the door and Melanie looked up from the console. Johnny was in the studio shielded by the soundproof glass, bent over a box of CDs with a candle glimmering beside him and the pinpoint glow of the system lights above his head.

"All secure, Number One?" she asked, shielding her eyes from the flashlight's beam.

Geoff saluted. "Aye, aye, Captain."

Johnny stood up and waved a CD case, suddenly surprised to see Geoff and Rick in the sound booth with Melanie. He leaned over the desk and dislodged a stack of CD cases, then flicked the mic on the desk. "Shit, can't see a damned thing in here," he announced. "Anyway, I found it." He glanced an apology to Geoff. "I was getting lonely out there – and it's so quiet. I thought we could liven things up with a little music." He sniggered.

Melanie smiled. "Found what?"

Johnny waved for her to wait and fumbled the CD into the console deck, turning the control dial. He pressed a button and then stood back, the broad grin on his face illuminated by the candle's glow.

The strains of the Carpenters' *Calling Occupants of Interplanetary Craft* filled the booth. Melanie laughed up at Geoff and Rick. She laughed even louder, clapping her hands, when Geoff pointed for her to look in the studio: Johnny was standing, legs and arms outstretched – the candle in his right hand – swaying side to side to the music.

Rick thrust his hands into his pants pockets. "So what do we do now?"

"Now," Geoff said, "we wait."

It was just past nine o'clock.

(11)

Karl thought he had heard something a couple of times, like people moving around in the plane, sneaking up from standard class into business or first but he figured it was just the bodywork settling. All in all, he guessed he'd been pretty lucky – though, no sooner had Ronnie and Angel left him, he would have given a fortune for a restroom. In the end, he just had to let his muscles relax and pee his pants. He was thankful that, at least at that point, he didn't need to take a dump. But, as he knew all too well, that time would come and he would have to face it like a man.

The shoulder went into spasms of pain interspersed with bouts of pins and needles, and he didn't have enough room to move himself around in order to alleviate it. After a while – which was what, exactly? an hour? two hours? *five* hours? – he developed a crick in his neck from trying to keep facing down the aisle into the main cabin, and he just let his head slump forward against the floor. He dozed a little, woke every now and again because he heard people talking around him, people like Gerald, the captain of the flight out of Denver, and Lizbeth, the senior stewardess, Jayson, the co-pilot, and then, after lifting his head, drifted off once more.

It must have been around midday – because he could feel the sun burning into the back of his leg and could see the light of it spreading across the cabin floor – when he definitely heard voices from outside, one of them shouting to someone else. He tried to call out – *Hey, I'm in here! Anybody... Come help...* That kind of stuff; but after a few clatters and clanks – they were *throwing* stuff at the plane? kids, it must be, Karl thought – the voices grew softer and, after a few more minutes, Karl straining to hear any noises at all from outside, the voices faded away so completely that Karl wondered whether he had ever really heard them at all. For didn't one of those voices sound like him, Karl Sjovin, and one of the others his big brother Stanley? But Stanley had been dead now these past 22 years, so...

He allowed his head to slump forward again against the floor of the cabin, thinking suddenly that it seemed more luxurious than it had been before.

And then, despite his hunger, his bowels gave a little nudge, the nudge coming in the shape of a winsome fart – *You win some and you lose some,* his grandmother had always told him: *The secret of life is recognizing which is which* – the fart drifting out of his ass like a cross between a wandering bee hopping from one pollen-filled flower-head to another and a cartoon trombonist who had inadvertently swallowed the mouthpiece to his instrument. He held on for a while, clenching his buttocks for all he was worth, but then he just had to let go. The only good thing was that he figured the smell would be gone by the time Ronnie and the girl got back.

Come to think of it, how long had they been gone out there?

Karl wished he could see his watch. The light had moved up the floor some – it was now sitting in the doorway to the main cabin – and Karl thought he must have been sleeping more than he'd originally figured, because surely it was too early for the sun to have moved so far on.

But then he went to sleep again.

He woke up when someone called for him. It was his mother. He turned around and was delighted to discover that he was in his bed, his very own bed back in Cedar Rapids, his mom standing at the door with that mock look of annoyance she always put on, right foot tapping, hands on hip. "Come on there, soldier," she was saying to him, "time to get a move on or you'll be late."

Then, even before he could respond, "Hey, big guy!" came from the hall, the words all alone as they started out but then, almost immediately, accompanied by his father's wave and a big smile as he walked past Karl's bedroom door.

"I'm not too good, mom," he explained.

His mother leaned against the door jamb and nodded, her smile leveling out. "I know, sugar," she said. And his father came back and leaned immediately behind her, him looking the same way, too – kind of sad somehow, and loving. His dad put an arm around his mom and Karl saw the fingers of his dad's hand squeeze.

He sat bolt upright and–

–cricked his neck. He wasn't in bed at all. Outside, someone sniggered. Those damn kids again. He rested his head and felt a sudden unimaginably strong sense of profound loss. He had just lost both of his parents again – it was as though those brief seconds in the dream, watching them standing once again at his bedroom door, they had been fully alive, and he had been seven or eight years old, with all the sunlight of youth pouring through his windows and his curtains.

Karl turned his head to look at the windscreen and felt suddenly very weak. The patch of sky visible above the still lighted sections of Borders bookshop was dark, a few intermittent stars blinking on and off all those millions of miles away, sending their light to him so long ago and yet it arriving only now. He slumped once more and felt humbled.

"Mom," he barely managed to say, "I don't feel so–"

(12)

Inside the restroom at the mall, Angel didn't notice the body immediately: it was the smell that got to her first.

Boy, someone had dropped a real load in here, as her dad would say, teasing her mom when he followed Sally Wurst into the bathroom back at home. But this time, someone really *had* done a number. The smell was infinitely worse than anything created by anyone in the Wurst household, or anyone even just paying them a visit. It was a real pungent aroma, though Angel, swinging her doll by her side, didn't know pungent from parsnips. She held her nose and spoke to Samantha.

"Gee, Sabadtha, dat reardy shticks!" Angel said, her fingers gripped tightly on her nose. She was pleased to see that Samantha seemed oblivious to the whole thing but, just to be safe, she pressed the doll's face against her chest and, grimacing, checked the cubicles to see which one the offending smell was coming from.

That was when she saw the body.

The woman was lying on the tiled floor over by the washbasins around the corner from the cubicles. Angel saw the woman's foot first, just the one foot, the leg attached to it sprawled out and crooked at the knee.

Angel gasped and then moved sideways to the wall, which she leaned against before edging slowly forwards, watching as more of the unfortunate woman came into view.

By Angel Wurst's reckoning, the woman was maybe around one hundred years old and had skin that looked like her grandma's dark brown leather sofa, all wrinkled and, in some places, worn into a different color altogether.

"Hello?" Angel said, her voice soft and nervous. She half expected the woman to wake up suddenly, shaking her head – *Hey, how about that, sweetie, I done fallen sound asleep and fell right on my ass in the restroom!*

But as she moved a little further forward so that she was almost to the washbasins, she saw that it was unlikely that the woman was going to move anywhere at all. There was a thick, deep red pool – so deep red, in fact, it was almost black – spread around her head like some kind of fancy hat, or a peacock's tail feathers, all fanned out like a halo. And there was a puddle of what Angel hoped might be pee between the woman's legs, though from the smell, the color and the consistency, she thought it was likely that the woman had pooped her pants.

Moving away from the wall, Angel stepped closer to the woman's body, one tiny step at a time, heel to toe, heel to toe. As she got nearer, she saw the woman's face. It was all twisted up, either in pain or surprise. No, that wasn't surprise: it was absolute fear. She had seen something, something that had struck terror into her. Angel turned around and looked at the line of washbasins. That's when she saw the bags.

One was a small valise with the outline of a cat embroidered or crocheted on the side. That one was standing on the shelf above one of the washbasins. When she glanced into the basin, Angel saw that it was filled with water and there was a thin film of soap in there, too.

The other bag was a briefcase kind of affair, like the one Angel's daddy took with him when he went into the office each morning. It was standing on the floor, leaning against the wall beneath another basin. This basin was empty but there was a mascara pencil lying on the floor, its end broken off. Like it had been dropped – dropped when the person who had been holding it had suddenly – *pop*! – up and disappeared right out of the restroom along with the other woman, the one using the washbasin.

Angel closed her eyes and saw it happen. There was a flash, a real blinder, the place filling with whiteness that seemed to last for ages. In the middle of the whiteness, two women over by the washbasins – not just the one with the pencil, there was a second one – seemed to flare up and then just disappear, as though they had never been there. The other woman – the woman on the floor, Angel saw now – clutched at her chest and screamed out. It wasn't a high-pitched scream, more like an anguished groan. Just that and then the woman hit the floor, shaking from head to foot for a few seconds as the whiteness subsided, and then she was still.

Angel opened her eyes and looked around at the cubicles: all the doors were partly open except for one. She bent down and looked along the floor beneath the door but couldn't see anything except for the toilet pedestal. She guessed that the door would be locked if she tried it.

She looked back at the old woman on the floor and saw that she was still clutching her sweater with her left hand. Wasn't that the side that your heart was on? Angel thought that it was. That meant that she'd had a heart attack. (The very idea of a person being attacked by their own heart was something Angel would have to try tackling a little farther down the pike, because, right now anyway, it just seemed plain foolish.)

The woman's eyes were wide open, real wide, wide like the eyeballs might just fall right out onto her cheeks, and she was frowning, too. Angel leaned over and looked down into the eyes and she saw, right then and there, the difference between alive people and dead people. This woman had nothing *inside* her. She was like one of those dummies in the store windows – the ones where the shape was right and everything but there was no life in their faces. There was no life in this woman's face either.

But no, it was more than that: it was more than simply no *life* – there was no *person* either. Fleetingly, Angel wondered what the woman's name was – or should that be *had been*? No, she reckoned not: the woman shouldn't lose her name just because she was dead.

Then she wondered about the woman's family, about what she was doing here in this big mall with the cheesy music playing all day every day. Angel moved her head slowly to the right, keeping watching those eyes, and then moved it over to the left, still watching the eyes, waiting for them to give the game away and follow her.

Nah, Big Girl, she's dead, Samantha the doll whispered in the back of Angel's head. *But what if the someone who* made *her dead, the same person who made the Big Light, what if that someone is still here someplace; what if that someone is still here, hiding in that locked cubicle over there...*

Angel looked up from the body and stared at the cubicles. "Hello? Is anyone here?"

She half imagined a pair of feet appearing on the other side of the cubicle door – maybe bare feet, covered with hair and maybe with long nails and all dirty – the feet slowly lowering themselves down onto the floor in there, and the sound of the cubicle bolt being pushed back across, and then the door opening, and whoever – *what*ever – was in there suddenly standing between Angel and the outer door.

Angel started to back up towards the door she came in by until she finally came right up against it.

Then the door pushed open and she screamed.

"Jesus Christ!" Ronnie shouted and he backed straight out of the restroom again, dropping the brown bag containing the sandwiches, potato chips and mineral water he'd picked up for Karl. He was retrieving them from the floor when Angel appeared out of the restroom.

"I'm sorry about that," Ronnie said. "You'd been a long–"

"There's a woman."

Ronnie was crouched down dusting off the bottle and he jerked his head up. "In there?" He nodded at the restroom door.

Angel nodded back enthusiastically. "She's dead."

"She's dead?"

Another nod. "Pooped herself, I think," Angel added, explaining the cause of death succinctly.

Ronnie handed over the brown bag – "You stay here, and don't go anyplace until I get back," – and disappeared into the restroom.

The music system was now playing another song that Angel recognized, this time with singers. They were singing about leaving on a jet plane, and the fact that they didn't know when they'd be coming home again. They sounded sad.

Outside it was getting darker.

Angel hugged Samantha tight and told her everything was going to be OK. She hoped the doll would believe her.

• • • •

"You still need to go?"

That was the first thing Ronnie said to Angel when he emerged from the women's restroom a few minutes later. And truth to tell, Angel had forgotten about the whole reason for going in there in the first place. But now that she had been reminded...

Angel nodded her head enthusiastically. "I didn't go in there," she said, nodding to the women's restroom.

"Then go use the men's," he said, pointing to the door just a few yards along the corridor.

Angel laughed incredulously, old beyond her years. "You want me to go pee pee in the *men's* room?"

"Angel, it'll be fine," Ronnie reasoned to the girl. "There *are* no men around," he added.

Angel looked across at the door with its little stick-man icon. "No bodies?" she asked.

Ronnie shook his head. "Uh uh. I went in there myself and it's completely clear."

"You're sure no bodies... like in the stalls?"

Ronnie wasn't sure whether he needed to address his response to the girl or the doll she was holding, seeing as how the girl's question had been delivered in a somewhat squawky voice and had been accompanied by much head and arm movement from the doll. So he did both, shifting his eye level from one to the other the way he might do in any conversation with two people. "There are no bodies in there at all. It's completely body-free."

Angel ran along and disappeared – albeit cautiously – into the men's restroom.

She came out a few minutes later looking much more relaxed.

"That was my first dead body," she announced when the two of them started walking off back to the Mall's main walkway. "I wasn't scared," she added. "Not really." "Me, either," said the squawky voice, before Ronnie could say anything in response. Just as well, he thought, because any additional comment from him could fall well short of being optimistic.

Back in the mall it was becoming dusky now. They had to get back to the plane but Ronnie had no idea where to get the equipment he needed. Then he saw a metal door with JANITORS stenciled on it standing partly open along a tiny alleyway.

They went through the door, Angel Wurst hanging tightly onto Ronnie's shirt flap as though her life depended on it – and who could say that it didn't – to find a spacious storage area with benches and lockers. It was clear that no expense had been spared for the mall's employees – the muzak played even in here, though Ronnie was not sure whether that was a good thing or a bad thing. Particularly when "The Boxer" came around again. Maybe it was some kind of indoctrination or brainwashing. He imagined shift changes in here, with the employees changing their clothes, thinking about breaking free of the drudgery but always–

I am leaving, I am leaving… but the fighter still remains…

–turning in the following day.

Ronnie found various tools, a whole collection of saws, hammers and chisels hanging on the wall from special plugs fixed on by what appeared to be masonry nails. He considered taking a couple of them but decided he probably wouldn't achieve much with them – sawing through wooden flooring in such an awkward position. He tried not to think about what condition Karl was going to be in when – *if* – they managed to set him free. That shoulder of his had taken a lot of punishment.

"There are some more cabinets around here." Angel's voice was immediately followed by a brief run of clanging and banging as she tried various doors, obviously without much success.

"I'll come around," Ronnie shouted.

There were four cabinets, all big jobs, standing around eight feet off the ground and double-locked top and bottom. Ronnie went back to the wall tools and selected a thick-handled hammer and a couple of heavy-looking chisels. A few minutes later, he had forced the locks on all four of the big cabinets.

"They look a mess now," Angel observed.

"Had to be done," Ronnie said. He rummaged around inside the first one – there were two big rolls of insulation, a few more tools, a battery-powered drill (Ronnie couldn't see any attachments of drill-heads but he guessed they might be in one of the other cabinets), a battery-powered sander, a full-length floor polisher and a box of sanding pads. There was also a pile of wiring reels with a plug on one end and a socket on the other – he lifted a couple out and stood them on one of the benches.

"Why you getting the ones with the big doo-dads–" Angel pointed to the battery attachments for each of the tools. "–instead of those?" Now she pointed to the pure electrical versions, each considerably more compact.

"The doo-dads are batteries, and batteries means we can use the tool without any electricity."

Angel looked at him with wide eyes and a wavy smile. *Nah, you're putting me on… how could you work the tool without–*

Ronnie shrugged. "There are no wall sockets on the airplane, are there?"

Angel didn't respond. Ronnie figured she had no idea what he was talking about. Six years old was a long ways back from where *he* was standing, he had to remind himself.

Instead, Angel said, "You think anyone's going to be mad?"

Ronnie backed out of the first cabinet and moved along to the second.

"I hope not."

The second cabinet had rolls of posters, boxes of cloths and polishes and a whole rack of overalls.

"Shit," he said. Then, realizing, he added, "Sorry, Angel."

"That's OK. My daddy says that words can't really hurt you. But sticks and stones can."

"That's right." Ronnie closed the door on the second cabinet and moved on to the third. "Your daddy's a smart man." He opened the door and there, alongside tall clippers and coils of rope, sitting all by itself on a shelf at the back, was a chainsaw. Just one. And best of all, it too was battery operated. He stepped back and triumphantly held the saw aloft. "*Voila*!"

"Vwahla?"

"Sorry, getting carried away there." He shook the saw with both hands. "This is what we were looking for."

"Does it work?"

"Let's find out." He flicked the main control switch and then pressed the start button. There was nothing. He flicked the switch back to where it was and pressed the button again. Still nothing.

"Shit," said Angel.

Ronnie nodded and barely managed to keep from smiling as he removed the battery from its clips. He went back to the cabinet and lifted various boxes, checking contents and muttering to himself. There had to be a spare battery. *Had* to be.

Ronnie found two extra batteries in the fourth cabinet. He clipped one of them into the saw and pressed the button. Nothing. He let out a deep sigh, flicked the control switch and pressed the button again. The saw burst into noisy life.

"OK," he said, "I think we're in business."

Ronnie dropped the spare battery in with the provisions and held the bag out to Angel.

"You think you guys can manage these?"

Angel nodded. "Sure. Are they heavy?" She held out her hands.

"Not too bad."

Ronnie loaded the bag into the girl's arms, watching her groan a little, and then took the bag back. "Hey, better idea. Let's go get ourselves some neat new shoulder bags, then all the weight will be taken without it breaking us both in two."

Angel liked that idea. "And you can get another watch."

"Hey, right."

When they left the janitors' area and went back to the mall walkway, Nancy Sinatra was telling anyone who would listen that her boots were made for walking.

When they left the mall around twenty minutes later, it was actually starting to get quite dark. But when Ronnie checked his new watch – just $1,300 and change, including tax – but he'd gotten a great discount – it was barely seven o'clock. He stopped and shuffled the two new bags on his back, one on each shoulder. Angel stopped right alongside and echoed the shuffle with her own bag – Ronnie had put her in charge of the provisions, which he said was the most important job.

"Strange," Ronnie said, looking over to the west.

Angel followed his line of vision. Way over in the distance, the sky was light, shot through with veins of deep orange and red, but the darkness that seemed to be threading its way over their heads, coming from behind them, was different from the usual nighttime dark. They both turned and looked to the east.

"It's night over there already, isn't it?"

Ronnie nodded. "Yes it is. The sun rises in the east and sets in the west. So the first light of morning starts over there." He looked down at the little girl and saw that she was watching the horizon. "Over there is New York, Angel. You ever been to New York?"

She shook her head. "My daddy has," she said. "My mommy, too. They went there for their honeymoon." She turned around to face him, her eyes half-closed in a scholarly fashion. "Acksherly," she added, "I *have* been to New York."

"You *have*?"

She nodded. "But I was in my mommy's tummy."

Ronnie watched Angel look down for a moment at her doll and then she looked back at the horizon.

"Something's going on over there," she said, matter-of-factly.

"Going on? Going on how, Angel?"

She shrugged. "I don't know… not yet. But something's going on." She turned around to face Ronnie and said to him, very gently, "In Central Park."

"Central Park?"

Angel nodded slowly. "But they're not there."

"Who's not there in Central Park?"

"My mommy and my daddy. And your wife. They're not there." She turned away again. "It's a special dark over there, isn't it?"

Ronnie looked up. Overhead, the sky was darkening the way it should darken at this time – after 8pm, he saw by his new watch – in April. But further away to the east, the dark was absolute, impenetrable. The more he looked, the more he could see it. There were stars showing through above them but the further eastwards he looked, the denser it became. Until at last, right over on the horizon, it was pure black. An absence of all color.

"Yes," Ronnie agreed. "Special dark. But it shouldn't be."

"Is it a problem?"

Ronnie shrugged. "I don't know."

Angel pulled on Ronnie's sleeve and stopped.

"What is it?"

Angel was looking around the parking lot and then back at the mall building. "I dunno. Something," she said.

"You hear something? The phone again?" There was no way they'd be able to get back into the mall and up to the office to answer it before the caller rang off again, but Ronnie was prepared to give it a shot.

Angel closed her eyes tight and concentrated.

"There's another body," Angel whispered.

"Another body?"

Angel nodded. "She can't breathe."

Ronnie looked around the lot. There were maybe thirty, forty cars parked up in bays, one car wrapped around one of the tall lighting poles and another one, a big 4x4 gas guzzler, lying over on its side amidst the flowers on one of the decorative border areas. It could have been modern art.

"In the car?"

Angel opened her eyes and looked across at the 4x4. "She's in a tight space," she said. "She's dead."

"I thought you said she couldn't breathe?"

Angel nodded, her eyes lidded and sad.

Ronnie shook his head and smiled crookedly. "So, dead folks don't *need* to breathe, honey."

"I know. Not being able to breathe was how she died."

His first inclination – and maybe every inclination up to around number eight or nine – would normally have been to think the kid was either overimaginative or missing a few slates from the old roof area. But that was when Martha was still around and planes landed in airports, not taxiing along highways piloted by map-readers who demolished bookstores when they landed. "Wait here," he said.

Ronnie walked across to the 4x4 and leaned over to look in one of the side windows. It was empty. He turned and shouted to Angel.

Then he walked across to the little Chrysler that was wrapped around the light standard – same thing: empty.

"Nobody's here," he shouted as he walked back.

Across to the east, the sky looked like a purple and black bruise.

"I think it could be a storm," he said as he reached the girl. He didn't feel convincing and he saw from Angel's face that it was coming over to her as well. "We'd better get moving."

"What about the body? I saw a body."

Ronnie shrugged. "Nothing we can do. And if she's – you said it *was* a she, yes?"

Angel nodded. "Yes."

"Well, if she's already... you know..."

"Dead?"

"Right. Dead. If she's dead, well... she's dead." He patted her on the shoulder and squeezed reassuringly. "Come on, we got stuff to do."

As they were getting back into the Chevy, Ronnie heard the unmistakable sound of a car door-lock being released. He turned around and scanned the cars until he saw a man rising to his full height a couple of sections over to the left, standing up from what looked like a Volkswagen or some other little beetly European job. Ronnie squinted and felt Angel's hand take hold of his own.

"It's OK, honey," Ronnie said. For some reason, he could feel his stomach knotting. It was as though there was suddenly an intruder in Paradise. Here he was – or here *they* were – all alone and in charge, and now some newcomer was going to be involved. And after this guy, how many others? And the sky was a blacker black than it had any right to be. Everything felt wrong somehow.

"Hey," Ronnie shouted over, moving away from the Chevy. Angel held his hand tighter.

"Hey," the man responded, slamming the Volkswagen door closed, the guy wearing patterned overalls of some kind with colored beading on the sleeves and pockets. "Just about given up on finding anyone else," he said as he came closer, threading his way through the cars.

The man was in his early twenties, moving with the easy gait of self-assurance, swiping his long hair back from his forehead.

"Hey, how you doing?" Ronnie asked, holding out a hand. "Ronnie Mortenson. Boy, are you a sight for sore eyes."

"You too, sir," said Virgil. "Virgil Banders." Virgil took a hold of Ronnie's hand with both of his and clasped it, still shaking long after the greeting was over and done.

Ronnie nodded. "And this here," he said, turning to usher Angel into the conversation, "is Angel."

Virgil nodded and smiled. "Angel," he said, holding out a hand.

Angel's face remained still and completely bereft of any expression. She reached out towards Ronnie, took a hold of his pants leg and moved in closer to him, hiding her head behind Samantha the doll and a handful of material.

Ronnie patted Angel's head and put his hand on her neck. "You been in the mall? Nobody there."

The boy nodded. "Took a walk around a little earlier. Place is deserted." He glanced back at the girl, saw her watching him. "She nervous around strangers, your daughter?"

"Oh, she isn't my daughter. We met on the plane."

"Plane?" Virgil looked around, frowning.

Angel tugged on Ronnie's jacket.

"Late running out of Denver." He shrugged.

"Where you headed?"

"Atlanta."

Angel tugged a little harder.

"So how'd you, you know, how'd you wind up back here? Plane didn't take off, right?"

"No, the plane took off OK. But then, just a few minutes after takeoff, everybody just–" He snapped his fingers.

"*Hey*!" Angel snapped.

"What is it, honey?"

She pulled Ronnie so that he lowered his face level with hers and cupped her hand around her mouth. "The man," she whispered, "he knows about the body."

"What?"

"What's she saying?"

Ronnie shook his head and gave an apologetic smile. "She's a little shy."

"Right."

Ronnie turned back to Angel. "He seems OK to me, honey," Ronnie whispered into the girl's ear.

"He knows," she said again. Then she folded her arms around her doll.

Ronnie straightened up and smiled at Virgil Banders, the two men just standing there watching each other. Then, pulling Angel close to his side again, Ronnie said, "Hey, you see anything? I mean, you see folks, well, vanish?"

"They're hiding," Angel muttered glumly.

Virgil shook his head. "Uh uh, I was asleep. Woke up and–" He snapped his fingers. "–all gone. Poof! Like a damn magic trick." He gave another smile, glanced down at the girl, and said, "Drove over here to see if I might find anyone." He clapped his hands. "And, hey presto, I found you guys."

Ronnie nodded, still smiling.

"Lot of wrecks out on the highway," Virgil Banders said, waving his right arm over in a southerly direction. "Took ages to find my way through on some of the roads."

"So... nobody at home, right?"

The boy shook his head. And then shrugged. "I don't know. Haven't been back home yet. I was at my girlfriend's place. Fallen asleep." He winked at Ronnie. "You know what I'm saying here?"

"I remember it pretty well. Been a while, but I do remember."

They both chuckled at that, the boy more than Ronnie, with Angel looking from one to the other with a quizzical expression on her face.

"So what happened, you think?"

"Pardon me?"

"What happened? To everyone, I mean?"

Virgil shrugged. What was wrong with this asshole? It was like he was trying to trip him up all the time. And the girl. He didn't like the girl, not a bit. And it was sure as hell certain she didn't like him either. Why had he told the guy he'd *driven* up here? He glanced at the girl and saw she was watching him. She knew. That was why he'd not mentioned his car. Somehow, the girl knew that he'd tucked good ol' Suze Neihardt up in the Pontiac's trunk. He didn't know how she knew, but she knew. And you could take that one to the bank. He suddenly felt inexplicably relieved that, when this very undynamic duo showed up, Virgil was checking out a Volkswagen – V for V, seemed appropriate – that just happened to be the only other car on the lot with its keys in the ignition. The car had been parked at cross angles to the ones in the bays and had run up onto the curb. He had pushed it down and straightened it and was busy going through a glovebox of CDs – hip hop shit and some classical stuff – when he had seen Ronnie and the girl. Virgil looked at the girl now, smiling. He wondered how easy it would be to wrap her up, this brat, wrap her real tight so she couldn't breathe, watch her little body squirm, see the gauze around her mouth pulling in, and then out, in, and then out...

"Hey, I was gonna ask *you* that one, sir. I was asleep, don't forget."

"There was a light." Ronnie rubbed his chin, smiling. "It sounds stupid, you know? Like some kind of road to Damascus thing?"

Virgil frowned. Where the hell was Damascus? Must be out of state.

None of them said anything then for a few seconds until Virgil asked how they'd got the plane down.

"There's one more of us. He's a map-reader, was in the cockpit at the time. It was him brought us down."

"Where's the plane?"

Ronnie thumbed over his shoulder. "Back out of town, down I25 about ten miles or so."

"The other guy? He make it, too?"

Ronnie nodded. "Got a bit beat up, piece of Borders store flooring came straight through the windshield and has him pinned down." He shook the bags at Virgil. "We got some things we hope to get him free."

"You need any help?"

"You bet!"

Virgil turned to Angel and gave her his warmest smile. "That OK with you, Angel?"

She didn't say anything, just kept looking at him.

"Like you say, shy," Virgil said.

Ronnie nodded and looked over to the sky in the distance behind the boy. "You ever see storm clouds like that?"

Virgil turned and whistled. "Boy, looks like we're in for something."

There seemed to be a small wheel of blackness, thick and pure, way over in the distance down on the horizon, and the duskiness was spreading out from it.

"Still a ways off," Ronnie said. He rattled the Chevy's keys. "But best we get started before night comes. Be good to get Karl out of–"

"Karl? He the map guy?"

Ronnie nodded. "Best to get him free and all of us holed up someplace warm before it hits."

Virgil took a hold of some of the packages. "Lead the way," he said.

"What about your car?" Angel asked.

"My car?"

"Oh, I forgot you have a car," Ronnie said, slapping his forehead.

Virgil shrugged. "Doesn't matter. I'll travel with you." He gave a little half-smile and waved an arm around. "Can soon pick up another one any time I have a mind to. But I kind of like the little foreign jobs."

"I'm betting there'll be plenty more to choose–"

As they started to walk, Angel yanked on Ronnie's sleeve.

Ronnie stopped and looked down at the girl, fighting off – just for a few seconds there – an urge to snap. Instead, he said, "What is it, honey?" in an exasperated tone.

Angel tugged at his shoulder and pulled him down towards her.

"Sorry about this," Ronnie said to Virgil. "She's been through a lot."

"Hey," Virgil said, shaking his head, "no sweat. Not going anyplace." He watched the girl frowning at him as she shuffled around out of his sight and leaned in close to the big guy's ear. Virgil decided that he would like to put Angel Wurst through a lot more. An *awful* lot more. He figured he knew what was coming and smiled to himself.

Ronnie stood straight again and turned to Virgil. "Can we see your car?"

"My car? She wants to see my car?" He looked over at Angel. "Why'd you want to see my car, girly?"

"I–"

"Like I say," Ronnie said, "she's been through a lot. Can we just take a look at your car? No big deal. Just a look."

Virgil shrugged. "Sure," he said. "Keys are in it." He smiled a big smile and slipped his hands into his pants pockets. "Figured it would be safe."

Ronnie nodded. "I'll leave all the stuff here."

Virgil watched the two of them moving through the parking lot towards the Pontiac, unable to shake this feeling of anxiety. He waved when Ronnie turned around, saw the girl turn around at the same time, the two of them almost at the Pontiac. He could imagine the conversation:

He's got a what in the trunk?

A woman... and she's all trussed up. Dead.

Dead?

Yes. He killed her, that man... that Virgil Ban–

They had stopped. It was the girl – wouldn't you fucking know it, the little cunt – she'd stopped right in her tracks alongside the Pontiac, and she was turned towards it now and looking at it, holding her goddam doll under her arm.

"Everything OK?" Virgil shouted.

He saw the guy lean close to the girl and say something. The girl didn't move.

"Mine's the vee-double-you." Virgil cupped his hands around his mouth to make sure they could hear him. He stepped forward. Shit, maybe he was going to have to deal with this right here and now. He looked down on the pavement for something he might use if it came to it, something he might be able to beat this little shit's goddam nosy fucking head with, but there was nothing.

Virgil had now moved one row of cars closer to them, appearing confused, a little quizzical, trying not to draw any attention to himself. Then, all at once, the girl looked around at Virgil, stopped him dead in his tracks, just as the man – Ronnie, his name was; Virgil would have to remember that – reached out and grabbed a hold of her free arm and pulled her away.

Virgil stopped right where he was and watched them.

They were at the Volkswagen now. Virgil tried to ignore them and looked over to the right, four or five cars. He saw the Pontiac. In his mind, he imagined good ol' Suze coming back to life again right there in the trunk, hammering on the inside with her forehead until Ronnie and that little shit-wipe went over to find out what was going down. Then it would be, *Well, hey there... what do we have here. Let's remove this wrapping Angelkins – what's that you say? Why,* that *man? That man over* there*?* He *did this to you? Whatever for? Virgil? You come over here right now and exp–*

He was looking up into the sky, over to the east, and it was unmistakably darker than it was overhead. No stars. He did a double take. It was kind of like two different pieces of sky, captured on photographs and spliced together badly.

"Forgot about the trunk!"

Virgil shook the thought away and looked over at Ronnie. He was walking around to the front of the car.

"Forgot that the trunk is in the front," Ronnie shouted, and he gave a little self-deprecating shrug as he tugged on the handle and lifted the trunk lid. Standing right next to Ronnie, Angel was watching Virgil, her eyes burning into him.

Virgil wanted to shout over, tell the girl to get the fuck away and stop staring at him like that, but instead he just smiled at her, gave a little wave before sweeping his hair back and returning his attention to the sky.

Angel kept right on staring, just as Ronnie said, "Nope, nothing in here – just a few canvas sheets, a tool kit, a–" He paused and rummaged, rustling paper. "–and a bag of old paperback books." He closed the trunk. "No bodies. Not even one," he said.

"She's here," Angel said, annoyed to hear the whine in her own voice as she looked around desperately. "I know she is. She's in the other car. The blue one."

Ronnie put an arm around the girl's shoulder and started to move back to join Virgil. "Well, if she is here someplace then there's two things." He held up two fingers and, as he folded one of them over, he said, "First off, she's dead. You said so yourself, right?" Without waiting for the girl's confirmation, he continued. "So, honey–" He said the word "honey" as an afterthought, amidst all the talk of death and destruction. "–there's nothing we can do for her. And secondly–" He folded over the second finger. "–it's got nothing to do with Virgil. Though I grant you," Ronnie added softly as they came closer to the boy, "he's a strange one."

Virgil watched them approach and couldn't stop the smile. "Everything OK? Did I pass your test?"

"Yeah, you passed the test," Ronnie said.

Angel Wurst didn't say anything at all.

(13)

In the hours that followed, once they had satisfied themselves that the station was reasonably secure, the quartet ate a light supper of cold meats and salad, bagels filled with pâté and humus, coleslaw and pickles, and then, while Johnny had played his hard rock session leading to midnight, Melanie, Geoff and Rick sat out on the roof staring across the quiet and empty world. When the night finally spilled over into morning and it was Melanie's turn at the turntable – they still called it the turntable even though most of the music was now played from a three-disc CD setup – Rick and Geoff agreed to have a last smoke before turning in.

There was something inexplicably threatening about the silent blackness of the trees across the valley that made the pair uncomfortable and, without saying anything about their thoughts to each other, they sat in silence yearning for the sanctity of the station. Feeble though they were in the grand terms of the cosmos and whatever things might be marauding their way through it, the walls of the station seemed to promise some kind of barrier to all that might be out there. Maybe, Geoff thought as he took a last lingering look at the outside world, that was how the people had felt back in the 1950s when they carried out those ridiculous safety precautions against atomic bomb attacks – hiding under flimsy wooden tables with their hands over their ears – or like squirrels and rabbits that curled themselves up against the wheels of an oncoming car.

They went inside without speaking.

It was almost two o'clock when the light came again.

Johnny and Geoff were asleep – Johnny in his room and Geoff on a cushioned camping mat stretched out on the floor in the sound booth – and Rick was sitting across from Geoff reading *Mad* magazine in the glow of the flashlight, with his feet propped on the CD shelves. Melanie was playing tunes and songs and huskily breathing her patter into the mic, hoping against all reason that someone would call her on the telephone – if for no other reason than to complain. It was an interesting playlist after all, the usual late night, early morning aural fodder of Bennett, Sinatra, Holliday and Mitchell having given way to The Chemical Brothers, Philip Glass, Will Smith and Captain Beefheart. As the strains of Frank and the Mothers' "Bobby Brown" faded, the world went white.

Rick jumped to his feet dropping his magazine.

"Wh– What's up?" Geoff rolled to one side and thumped his head on the table leg. "Shit!" he said, rubbing the side of his head as he squinted up at his brother. "That hurt. You say something?" he asked groggily.

"The light. It came again." Rick was at the glass looking into the candlelit studio. Melanie was looking around her, checking to see if anything had changed.

"Go get Johnny," Geoff said. As Rick left the booth, Geoff leaned over and switched on the connecting mic. "You OK, Mel?"

Melanie nodded. And then, as though reconsidering her first answer, she gave a shrug. Who the hell knew? It was a fair point.

"Now what?"

Geoff allowed the question to sink in while craning his head to one side to see if he could pick up any sounds from outside. *Now what?*

He looked around the booth, searching for an answer. Then his gaze settled on the telephone sitting on the table.

When he looked up again, Melanie was pulling the broadcasting mic towards her. Geoff hammered on the window and shook his head. "Not yet," he said. "Let's just wait a while, find out if anything's happened."

"Why don't I make an announcement? See if anyone's there."

Geoff shook his head again and lit a candle – Rick had taken the flashlight with him to get Johnny. "No, not yet."

"Can I at least put a record on?"

Geoff thought on that one a minute. What was the harm in that? *Well,* a small voice said lazily, in a small back room inside Geoff's head, *the harm in that is letting folks know we're still here – isn't that why you're wandering around in the darkness?* "No," he said, trying to sound casual, like there was some damned good reason – maybe there was a damned good reason but Geoff couldn't actually visualize it. "Let's not do anything yet."

Melanie sat back down and lit a cigarette. "I'm smoking too much," she said, her voice thick with disappointment in herself. "But the light is just so good."

When Rick came into the booth with Johnny in tow, the flashlight beam playing around their feet, Geoff had the telephone handset in one hand and was keying in numbers with the other.

"Anything?" Johnny asked around a yawn.

Rick switched off the flashlight and said, "Who you calling?"

"Sheriff's office."

Geoff finished keying and waited. The phone rang.

"We gonna go outside?" Johnny said. "See if anything's happening."

Geoff glanced into the studio and watched his wife – or, more accurately, Mel's cigarette tip – swinging side to side in the swivel chair, in small erratic movements.

Rick said, "Shit, nobody's there."

"Come on, let's do it," Johnny said. "Let's go outside."

Geoff was about to hang up but Melanie stopped him. "Give them a couple of minutes."

Geoff hit the squawk button and dropped the receiver onto the cradle. The sound of the telephone *brrrrt-brrrrt*ing all the way down in Jesman's Bend sounded sad and lonely. Around the *brrrrt*s, Rick said, "Anything's better than just sitting here." He turned around with his back to both Johnny and Geoff and then turned back. He ran his hands through his hair and took a deep sigh. "I mean, that's what we were waiting for, isn't it? We were waiting for the light... and we got it. So let's go out and–"

Geoff raised his hand.

Rick frowned petulantly.

Johnny said, "What?"

Geoff turned to look down at the phone. It was silent.

"It's stopped ringing," Johnny said.

"Hey, you win tonight's star pri–"

"Quiet, Rick." Geoff watched the phone, leaned closer to the squawkbox.

"Whyn't you pick it up, for Chrissakes?"

Geoff looked at his brother. Then at the telephone. No, it *wasn't* silent – there was a sound coming from it, but what was it?

"You know," Johnny said, his voice soft and careful, "you know what that sounds like?"

Geoff looked at him.

"It sounds like someone listening."

Geoff returned his attention to the telephone. That was what he had heard. Johnny was absolutely right – maybe it was something inherent in human beings, that you actually could hear when someone was listening to you on the phone. He'd done it plenty of times, called someone up and asked them something and then he had actually been able to hear them thinking – or, indeed, listening. It wasn't a sound of breathing or of movement, but simply of existing.

Hey mom, someone's existing *on the phone.*

Yeah, well make sure they clean it up when they're through.

Mel's voice broke the silence. "What's happening out there?"

Geoff hit the audio button killing the dead sound and then hit it again. The dial tone sounded friendly and reassuring. He re-dialed quickly.

"Geoff?" Mel said. Her voice sounded scared.

"It's OK," he said.

No it isn't, the voice in Geoff's head whispered. *It isn't OK at all and you know it.*

No sooner had the final number connected than the busy tone echoed around the booth. It sounded for all the world like an early warning siren.

Geoff hit the audio button and the tone stopped. He stepped back from the table.

Johnny plucked a cigarette from the Marlboro pack with his mouth. "Maybe it was someone picked it up and–" he lit up and continued around a cloud of smoke, "–and they didn't like to say anything."

Rick moved over to the chair and plopped into it. "Know what I think?" he said, "What about if maybe–" He used to his hands to suggest a surface and objects above that surface. "–maybe the vibrations of the telephone's ringing unsettled something and–"

"Aw, come on, man!"

"Shut the fuck up, Johnny and let me finish, OK?" Rick turned back to his brother. "So, the vibrations of the phone unsettle something, like something on a shelf above the desk... a manual or something. Anyway, and this something drops down onto the desk and–" He clapped his hands together. "Blam! Knocks the receiver off the hook."

Johnny blew smoke and shook his head.

"Hey, all I'm saying is it could happen, right?" He ignored Johnny and looked at Geoff. "*Right?*"

Melanie came through the linking door to the studio. "Mind if I join in?"

Nobody answered.

"Geoff, all I'm saying is it *could* happen, right?"

"OK, it could happen." He hit the audio button and redialed.

"Who you calling, honey?"

Geoff held a finger to his lips.

The final number clicked home and for a second nothing happened. Then the familiar noise of a ringing tone sounded. Geoff hit the audio key and clasped his hands around his stomach.

"Oh God," Rick said, his voice sounding small in the cramped booth.

"Will someone tell me what's going on?"

Johnny put his arm around Melanie's shoulder. "What's going on, dear Melvin, is another book has just bounced off of Don Patterson's desk and flipped his phone receiver back onto the cradle." He shook his head. "I mean, shit like that could make Ripley's *Believe It Or Not.*"

"We have to go out," Geoff said. "We have to go outside and take a look around."

Johnny dropped his butt to the floor and ground it with his boot heel. "Now why did I just *know* you were going to say that."

(14)

"It's getting too dark," Ronnie said.

Angel Wurst and Samantha the doll looked at him through the driving mirror. Without looking at the girl's expression, Ronnie knew she was questioning his reason for the statement.

"There should be more stars," he added by way of explanation. I mean, he thought, what the hell kind of a statement was that? *It's getting too dark.* For fuck's sake. It was like in the movies when someone always said, *It's too quiet.* It didn't mean diddly. What they were really saying was that their gut instinct was warning them of impending danger. He hunched forward over the wheel and gazed up into the sky. Why the hell was he worried? It wasn't darkness that had gotten them into this sorry state of affairs, it was light… a very big light.

"Just ignore me," he said to the rearview as he straightened up again.

Why was he doing this? What was the point in having a conversation with a six-going-on-seven year old about the gnawing feeling in his gut that all was not as it should be? And even if she could contribute something, wouldn't Ronnie's apprehension – *was* it apprehension he was feeling? – scare her all the more? After all, the kid had just lost her parents. "Lost" being the operative word: "misplaced" would be one almost as good.

"What time *is* it?"

Ronnie glanced down at the clock on the dashboard. "Coming up to a quarter after eight." He glanced out of his side window into the gloom, gazing up at what appeared to be elongated streamers of black fluttering across the sky from the right as they trucked back down the littered blacktop towards the plane. Then he looked across at the boy, Virgil: the sky on the horizon on his side of the car was still filled with a little bit of color. Angel followed his stare.

"Where's that?" she asked.

"Where's what, honey?"

She pointed over at the last remnants of the setting sun, a wide maroon bruise shot through with pink-tinged clouds.

"You go all the way over there and you'd be in California. After that, you'd be in the Pacific Ocean."

"No," the girl said. Her tone suggested she had dropped the additional word "dummy" right at the last second. "I mean is it north or south or east or west."

"That's the west," he said. "That's the side the sun sets on." He swerved the Chevy suddenly to avoid a Toyota Camry that was up on its side.

Angel nodded. "Doesn't the sun ever set on the other side? The east?"

Virgil laughed.

"The way things are right now, girly," he said, "seems to me *anything* is possible." He laughed some more but stopped when he looked across and saw Ronnie's stony expression. He looked away out of the window.

They had talked about what had happened, each of them running through possible scenarios, while Angel Wurst listened. Ronnie had considered trying to change the subject on several occasions, but what was the point? They had all lost people – Angel, her parents; Ronnie, Martha; and the boy, Virgil Banders, his mother. There was something about Virgil that Ronnie did not entirely cotton onto – he felt that Angel was a little unsure, too: and what was that stuff about the dead body that the girl had gone on about? The body – a woman's body – that was unable to breathe?

But the really big question was what had happened.

Virgil had suggested a few comic book ideas and one or two possibilities that Ronnie thought he recognized from TV shows, notably *The Twilight Zone* and that one where they took control of your television set. But nothing they could think of between them came even close to making any sense at all, though Ronnie suspected that, in terms of the explanation being measured on a Richter scale of pure "sense", they were not in Kansas anymore.

"Nope." Ronnie couldn't keep the smile out of his voice. He looked at Angel in the mirror. "The sun always rises in the east – the first people to see it being New Yorkers – and it sets over in the west, watched all the way down by Californians. Boring, isn't it?"

The girl nodded enthusiastically.

When Ronnie turned to face the road, he could see the wounded plane taking up most of the Mall parking lot. Another half-mile or so and he could see the partially destroyed Borders building, the huge glass frontage slipped down around the plane's nose like a too-big tiara.

"Here we are," he said, "home sweet home."

They parked the car up around the plane's tail and got out, hoisting bags and tools onto the walkway that ran along where, on a busy day, the hoods and trunks of the cars would be. Today, this evening, the row was empty. They swung open the doors and stepped out into the gloaming, each of them in his or her own way feeling as though they were stepping down onto the alien dust of another planet.

With Samantha the doll tucked firmly under her arm, Angel walked across to the end of the chute and looked up. "How we gonna get up there?" she asked.

Ronnie paused, with the chainsaw strap around his shoulder, and looked up the chute. She had a good point. It was a good twenty or thirty feet up to the hatchway – if the plane hadn't lost its wheels then it would have been more.

He looked around at the spreading pile of stuff by the car and tried to figure out what would be best: for him to go up first, thereby leaving Angel on the empty parking lot, or for the girl to go up – assuming she could, of course: hell, assuming *he* could, of-fucking-course! – and into the plane, with whatever it was that she might find in there.

Ronnie didn't doubt for a minute that everything would be OK up there just as it would be OK down here in the parking lot, but there was something about either scenario that just didn't sit well with him.

He walked up to the end of the chute and shouted up. "Hey, you OK up there?"

For a few seconds, Ronnie thought the worst. And then Karl's voice came, clearing his throat, saying, "Yeah, still here." And then, "You took your time."

"Time goes nowhere when you're having fun," he shouted back, and then he turned to Angel and made a comical face. Angel put a hand up to her mouth to shield a snigger. Ronnie was pleased to see that the girl's earlier concerns seemed to have gone away.

"OK, just hang tight – we're coming up . . . but it might take us a little while to figure it out. But hey, I almost forgot . . . we brought some help."

"The fire brigade?"

"Not quite. But it's a start. Say hi to Virgil."

Virgil shouted "Hey," at the same time as Karl's weak attempt at a welcome, and everyone laughed some more. They could have been out on a picnic instead of being the last people in the world – or, at least, in their little part of it.

"We'll get you out of there, no problemo," Virgil shouted. "Your man Ronnie here looks to have brought every damn tool in the shopping mall."

"No worries," Karl shouted. "Take your time. I'm not going anyplace... save the bathroom, and the sooner I make that call, the better."

Ronnie turned to Angel and crouched down in front of her. "You think you can get up that chute?"

She looked up at it, frowned and then nodded. It was an emphatic nod.

"You think maybe you can carry some rope?"

"Where's the rope?" she said, delivering the question in a weary no-nonsense kind of way that suggested she did this kind of thing every day of her life.

Ronnie pointed to a coil on the ground beside the Chevy. "You can put it around your shoulder – maybe even over your head?"

"And what do I do with it when I get up there?"

"Jeez, Louise, we gotta tell you *everything*, girly?" Virgil asked.

"I'm not 'girly'," Angel snapped back at him. "I'm Angel."

Virgil held up his shoulders, palms outstretched. "Hey, go easy on me, OK?" When he looked around at Ronnie to share the joke, there was something in the way Virgil smiled that didn't sit well with Ronnie. It was a crooked kind of smirk, a laughing-up-your-sleeve thing that made Ronnie uneasy.

"*What?*" Virgil shrugged the question over at Ronnie, tipping his head back and thrusting out his chin. "Just having a bit of fun, is all," Virgil said, shaking his head and turning to the girl, hunkering down so that he was on her level.

Ronnie explained in minute detail and then shouted to tell Karl that the girl was coming up.

It took barely three minutes before Angel came sliding down the chute, chuckling uncontrollably, having reached only around the third-of-the-way mark. Ronnie held onto his frustration and laughed with her. Virgil smiled and watched, turning to Ronnie as the girl reached the ground.

"Looks like fun," Virgil said.

"It's slippy," Angel said.

"You think you can try again?" Ronnie asked.

Angel Wurst nodded with a profound certainty.

"You having a good time down there?"

"We're getting there," Ronnie shouted back. He turned to Angel. "OK, second time."

"My mommy always says the second time's the charm," the girl said.

"No, that's third time," Ronnie said.

"My mommy always says it's the second time," she said, with a steely determination.

And, this time anyway, it was.

Angel managed to hook the rope around the bulkhead struts of the plane's nose, one of them buckled inwards and resting on Karl's seat. Also resting on the seat, they discovered when the trio gathered around the trapped map-reader after ascending the rope in a haphazard clamber, was a pair of six-inch-square wooden planks – flooring planks, Virgil said (rather obviously, Ronnie thought: he'd pretty much made up his mind not to like the boy though he couldn't think whatever for – and, if he were completely honest about it, he felt a little guilty because of it).

"We can saw through the planking," Virgil Banders said, wafting a hand in front of his face not entirely subtly (the stocky map-reader having clearly soiled himself), "but we still won't get the seat free."

Nobody said anything at that for what seemed like several minutes, Karl's upturned but side-on face checking the faces of his cohorts in an attempt to read what they might offer as an alternative solution. *Guess we'll just have to leave him where he is, then,* Karl fancied he heard the boy say, but it was just the little girl, Angel, talking to her doll.

Karl wasn't comfortable with Virgil though he couldn't explain why.

The boy seemed pleasant enough, if a little circumspect and possibly even secretive, but then he was of that age. And, with a decidedly disenchanted son of his own, Karl knew all too well about young men of a certain age. So he made allowances. Most important of all, of course, was that he get free from this trap, and the boy – Virgil Banders – seemed to know what was required and, best of all, how to achieve it. *Virgil Banders,* Karl thought as the others set about the task before them, *such a remarkable name: a name destined for greatness, even, or perhaps for what passed for it in these troubled times.*

And so it was that within a half-hour of exertion on the part of all concerned, increased discomfort (which, had he been asked beforehand, Karl would have sworn was not possible: he had been in absolute agony for several hours now and his usually flip and savvy banter had disappeared) and a stream of profanities that, at the beginning, everyone had sought to excuse and apologize for, respecting the delicate years of young Angel Wurst and her doll companion, Virgil managed to chainsaw through Karl's leather and heavy-duty plastic seat and right down the full length of his torso, drawing blood – and a considerably voluble yelp – only once. When Virgil and Ronnie pulled the map-reader free, Virgil optimistically (and perhaps recklessly) attempting to provide additional support by jamming a shoulder under the bulkhead strut, it was all Karl could do to keep from weeping right out loud. The past few minutes, maybe ten or fifteen, he had become convinced that he was going to die there, pinned down in his pilot's seat after his first ever landing, slowly starving to death. With the racking sobs, however, and his newly freed body, came a flood of flatulence (and a slight follow-through, which Karl decided to keep to himself).

"Phew-eee!" proclaimed Angel Wurst, her nose upturned.

"Let's get him to the bathroom," Virgil said.

Karl let out a deep groan when Ronnie took hold of him beneath his armpits, shaking his head anxiously and moaning "nononono, please no," at the top of his voice.

"We have to move him," Virgil said.

Ronnie noticed the boy smirking as he glanced down at Karl's trousers, as though looking for evidence of the map-reader's unfortunate bowel explosions, and he immediately wanted to slap him. Instead, he said, "We can't move him yet – you heard him. It could be that he just needs a few minutes to allow his muscles to readjust to their freedom. Or–" Ronnie added, shrugging, and trying to make what he was about to say sound less downbeat than it warranted, "–it could be that there's been some internal damage."

Damage? What the hell are they talking about here, Virgil thought. Damage was surely a word used for the breakdown of things, not for the destruction of flesh and bone. The very thought of that gave Virgil a pleasing hot flutter around his crotch.

And now Ronnie was addressing the girl – Virgil liked the look of *her*, but she clearly didn't seem to have gone a bundle on him – telling her to go back into the main area of the plane and sit down.

"Hey, we staying *here*?" Virgil said, unable to keep the whine from his voice.

"We can't move him," Ronnie said.

Virgil seemed to consider that and weigh up the implications. Whatever his findings were, he decided to keep them to himself – wisely, Ronnie thought. Virgil shrugged and said, "Ho-kay," doing it in a kind of sing-song *I don't give a shit* voice, and, thrusting his hands into his pants pockets, he edged past Ronnie into the plane's main cabin.

Ronnie didn't say anything – what *could* he say, for Chrissakes? – as Virgil went past him, but he saw the unmistakable bulge of an erection in the boy's trousers. He wondered just what it was that had so excited him. He shouted in for Angel to come sit up front next to the flight cabin where he could keep an eye on her. If Virgil thought anything about that then he certainly didn't show it – at least, Ronnie thought as he watched the boy make his way down the aisle, not from the back.

When Virgil and the girl had gotten themselves ensconced, Ronnie leaned over Karl and patted his shoulder. "OK, flyboy," he said, "it's party time."

"Huh?"

"I'm gonna wipe you down, put you into some clean pants."

Karl started to protest but Ronnie *shhh*'ed him.

"You want to bring the girl back in here? And Gilligan?"

Even feeling as wretched as he did, Karl could not hold back a snort at that one. He knew he'd recognized the boy from somewhere but he just hadn't been able to place him.

"It'll make you feel a whole lot better, believe me."

"I believe you," Karl said, stretching his head to look along the aisle. When he was satisfied that they were not likely to be interrupted, he added, "But I'll tell you, it's gonna be messy in there."

Ronnie patted the other man's shoulder. "You can be the son I never had."

(15)

The night was cool and the sky was clear. It was 2.37, and it was refreshingly lighter and less claustrophobic than the darkened station.

Geoff went out onto the roof first, turning off the flashlight beam while they were in the corridor and even then squeezing through the outer door so as to avoid any suggestion of movement should anyone be watching the side of the station. He wasn't taking any chances. When Rick asked why, Geoff simply shrugged. Melanie followed with Rick.

Keeping his back to the outside wall, Rick edged his way to where the small wall started and then crouched down. On all fours, he scurried crab-like along the wall's side until he was in the center, overlooking the valley and the beginning of the forest road. There, immediately beneath the station, the road crept to the right as though it was going straight down the side of Honeydew Mountain and then hit a fork: the right hand tine of the fork carried on towards I-90 while the left snaked around to travel the full length of the exposed saddle and ran down into the woods that led on into Jesman's Bend.

Once he was in place, Rick shifted into a sitting position and lifted his head so that he could see over the wall.

It was Melanie who broke the silence. "See anything?"

Without turning around, Rick shook his head. "Don't know what I'm looking for," he said. "But there's nothing unusual."

The outer door squeaked open behind them and Johnny emerged

onto the roof. He held out a pair of binoculars to Geoff. "Try these," he said. "They've got infrared."

Geoff took them and duck-waddled across to his brother.

"Why'd you buy those?" Melanie asked in a trembling voice. She was feeling a chill in her bones that had nothing to do with the temperature and everything to do with the clandestine nature of being on the roof, speaking in whispers with the lights out.

"Dunno," Johnny said. "Seemed like a good idea at the time, I guess."

Melanie nodded, apparently satisfied with the answer, and watched Rick lift the glasses to his eyes.

Johnny suddenly craned his head back. "Hey, you hear that?"

Geoff hissed for him to keep quiet.

"What?" Melanie whispered.

"Listen."

They listened.

"I don't hear anything except the crickets," Melanie said at last, unable to keep the trace of exasperation out of her voice.

"Kee rect," Johnny said. "The crickets. They're back."

"Oh ye–"

"What's that?" Geoff whispered loudly, pointing across the valley where, just for a second or two, a light had shone out of the blackness.

Rick moved the glasses over to the left of where he had been looking. "Where?" he said. "What was it?"

Geoff shifted to the other side of his brother and rested his chin on the wall. "I don't know... but it was something. A light of some kind."

"Like a flashlight?"

"Let me have the glasses." Rick handed them over and hunkered down. "It was around about..." Keeping his elbows on the wall so as to steady himself, and keeping his head, neck and hands in perfect unison, Geoff slowly moved his sweep of vision along the forest road to where the trees grew dense. "...round about where we saw Jerry Borgesson's truck."

"So what kind of light was it?"

"Does it matter?" Geoff said.

"What I mean is," Rick said, lowering his voice so that Melanie and Johnny couldn't hear him, "could it have been the cab's interior light?"

Geoff didn't answer right away. Then he said, "Yes, it could have been that." He lowered the glasses. "How'd you fancy a hike?"

"What, down the forest road to the truck?"

"It's the only thing I can think of." Geoff looked around and saw that Melanie and Johnny had moved across to the far side of the roof, overlooking the valley edge, away from the road. He turned back to his brother and said, "I just want us to be sure about what's happening before we let everyone know we're still here." He shrugged. "I know maybe I'm being paranoid, but that thing with the phone. I mean, how come nobody said anything? You know as well as I do that someone had picked the receiver up... but they didn't speak." He watched his wife leaning over the roof, saw Johnny hold onto her waist and lean over alongside her. "Then they put the receiver back. There was somebody there... I know there was. But they didn't speak. Or–" He stopped and looked down at the binoculars cradled in his lap. "Or maybe they couldn't speak."

"How do you mean? Like they were being held captive or something?"

"Or something."

Rick let out a low whistle that was more air than note.

"And now, maybe Jerry *is* back at his truck. Right now. Maybe he's down there, crawling about on the floor of his cab trying to figure out what's wrong with it. And then again, maybe it's not Jerry."

"Hey, maybe there's nobody there at all."

Geoff nodded, tapping the binocular side with the ring on his middle finger. "Yeah, that too. But the way I figure it is we don't want to start driving around drawing attention to ourselves until we know what's going on, or until we've at least got a reasonable idea and we've verified that things are almost back to the way they were before the first light hit."

"OK. We walk down to Jerry's truck and see what's happening."

Geoff slapped Rick's knee and made to get up.

"But Geoff," Rick said. "What if... what if, you know, things aren't the way they were... or the way they should be? What then?"

The faint and far-off sound of an engine turning over prevented Geoff from having to respond. Melanie and Johnny ran across, each of them whooping with joy at the sudden return to familiarity, but Geoff snapped for them to keep quiet and get down out of sight.

"Hey, what's the matter, man?" Johnny whined. He pulled himself against the wall next to Geoff while Melanie, frowning, put her arm around her husband's shoulder. "Jerry's trying to get his truck started." He shrugged. "So what's the big deal?"

"Yeah, we can go down into town and find out what happened to everybody," Rick added.

Geoff was still looking through the binoculars when the engine fired into life. When he spoke it was a mutter. "You know, I'd've bet a dollar to a dime he'd never get that thing started."

"So what's so bad about that?" Johnny asked, peering over the wall as he watched the distant road leading down into Jesman's Bend. The sound of the truck driving off was now unmistakable.

"And there's something else."

"What?"

Geoff handed the glasses over to Johnny. "Here, take a look."

Johnny raised the glasses and scanned the road until he caught sight of the old truck moving down the road, disappearing for a few seconds each time a clump of trees came between it and the station. Johnny grunted.

"What is it?" Melanie said.

"Hey." Rick's voice was little more than a throaty whisper. "He doesn't have his lights on."

"Well, first off he gets the truck started," Geoff said quietly to Melanie, "which is pretty good going considering the thing was on fire when we last saw it. And then he drives without his lights on."

Johnny tutted. "So? Maybe they were damaged in the crash." He handed the glasses back to Geoff.

Geoff nodded. "Yeah, maybe so. I guess it's surprising that there's any life left at all in the engine. But if there is life there, then I'd've thought there'd be enough for the lights. But there's another thing."

Johnny sighed. "What?"

"How fast do you reckon he's going?" He cut across Johnny's and Rick's groans. "I mean, approximately."

Rick's face grimaced. "Thirty, thirty five?"

Geoff nodded. "At least. And we all know what that road's like, yeah? It bends and turns and winds like piece of dropped string."

"What are you saying, honey?"

"What I'm saying is that Jerry's driving that truck like a stock car racer." He looked through the glasses again and then put them down, turning around and slumping with his back against the wall. "He's out of sight now, heading into the last stretch before town."

They all slumped back alongside Geoff, like condemned men facing a firing squad. Melanie was the first one to break the silence.

"Maybe it doesn't mean anything, Geoff. Could be a lot of reasons."

The truth, however, was that she couldn't think of one. Geoff was right: the road down through the trees into Jesman's Bend was treacherous and, even if his lights were *not* working and he was still determined to get into town, Jerry Borgesson would have driven a lot slower. Over the years, many experienced locals had fallen foul of misjudging the tight bends on the Forest Road – and that was often in daylight or with their lights on. Jerry driving the truck away at a fast speed in total darkness didn't make a lot of sense at all. And they all knew it, deep down, where it really mattered.

"So what do we do now?"

Geoff turned to his brother. "Well, we decide – democratically. My view is that two of us walk down into town, while it's dark. That way, maybe we can find out some more." He shrugged and tried a big smile. "Hey, it could be that there's nothing, right? Could be that Jerry was just busting to get into town and his lights weren't working and he thought, fuck it, I'm going anyways, and I'm going as fast as I can. We don't know what these folks have been through, or even where they've been through it, so we maybe have to make a few allowances for strange behavior."

"But we should still be cautious – is that what you're saying?"

Geoff nodded and slapped Rick's leg. "We should still be cautious."

"So, who's it gonna be?" Johnny asked, verbalizing everyone's thoughts. "Who's the lucky twosome?"

(16)

Just before the light came back, Angel Wurst screamed.

Ronnie had cleaned up the map-reader, removing his soiled pants and shorts and washing him down. Karl had been right – it *was* a mess in there – but they'd laughed about it and had somehow managed to get the job done without Virgil or the girl coming in to see what was going on. By the time they were through, Karl seemed to have recovered some of his flexibility and he attacked with considerable gusto the sandwich that Ronnie had brought for him. But the likelihood of getting Karl down the inflated chute was slight to non-existent. He was in too much pain, with simple movements a huge chore, and that pretty much ruled out Karl jumping from the plane hatch onto a balloon and sliding his way down onto the book-strewn floor below.

So, the decision was made to make the best of a bad job and stay in the aircraft for the night, tackling the thorny problem of getting Karl onto the ground once daylight had returned.

Karl went back to the cockpit and sat in the seat only recently occupied by Ronnie – it was arguably the most comfortable seat on the plane, if a little tight around the backside, in that it seemed to enclose Karl's entire torso. He couldn't decide which part of him ached the most, though the shoulder that had taken the brunt of the wooden planking when it came through the windshield was odds-on favorite.

Ronnie and Angel – and Samantha the doll, of course – took seats close to each other in the business class section; Virgil Banders lifted the armrests on a bank of three seats in the main compartment and stretched out.

Sleep had drifted over them a little after midnight.

Angel Wurst had been the first one to succumb to the aftermath of a grueling day, and then Karl, who had forgone the pilot's seat for something more "material" and had soon propped himself up in one of the luxury class seats with his legs stretched out a little awkwardly on one of the produce trolleys that Ronnie had softened for him with blankets and pillows.

The resulting snoring prompted Ronnie to move back in the plane to sit with Virgil Banders and maybe give the boy a second chance to redeem himself in Ronnie's eyes, but all attempts at conversation amounted to little – if anything at all – with Virgil apparently more interested in playing the tape loops in the plane's entertainment system.

Ronnie hadn't even realized that he'd fallen asleep.

He had gone back to check on Angel Wurst first, seeing that she was curled up and cuddling the doll he'd "stolen" for her from the *Going Back* store in the mall. Then he had checked Karl – so sound and silently asleep now that, just for a few seconds there, Ronnie had thought that the map-reader had died from some internal injuries that they could only guess at. But he'd hunkered down alongside the other man and, his face barely inches from Karl's, had watched and listened until he was satisfied that the man was breathing.

And that was about it.

Then the scream.

Ronnie opened his eyes and saw that he had moved back to the row of seats just three rows behind Angel, who was now standing out in the aisle, her hands to the sides of her face, screaming for all she was worth.

"Angel, it's OK, it's OK," Ronnie said, getting to his feet and then slipping to one side and clattering into the abandoned trolley – he must have had his legs awkwardly in the seats because his right foot was all pins and needles.

"Jesus Christ!" Virgil Banders shouted from somewhere behind Ronnie. "What the hell..."

The girl continued to scream.

Now that he was fully in the aisle, Ronnie could see Karl the map-reader propped up on his left arm, looking dazedly down at the back of the girl and rubbing his head.

Ronnie moved towards her, holding out his arms, telling her that everything was going to be OK, dragging his sleeping foot behind him and grimacing each time he put it to the floor.

Karl shouted something that Ronnie couldn't hear and, almost at the exact same time, Virgil shouted that they needed to get some sleep.

And then the world went white.

Ronnie moaned and fell to the floor, his arms lifted to his face. The whiteness was so pure that he feared that it had maybe removed his sight. His eyes now closed, he got to his feet and stumbled forward again towards the still-screaming girl. He dare not open his eyes yet to see if the light had gone again but here in his head it was as bright as ever, the kind of light that you see in animated movies when the cartoon cat sticks its paw into the electric socket and lights up all of its insides like an X ray. Eventually, he connected with the girl, wrapping his arms around her and hugging her close to his chest, patting her back and saying "there now," and "it's OK," time after time.

And then it was gone again.

Ronnie could tell that the light had gone without even opening his eyes. He could think again. When the light had been there he had not been able to do anything at all, with every single movement completely automatic.

"Was that it?"

Virgil's voice came from just behind Ronnie's head.

"Was that the light?"

It was just about the dumbest question that Ronnie had ever heard but, at the same time, it was completely understandable.

"That was the light," Ronnie said. Angel Wurst had quieted down and was hugging Ronnie as tightly as she could. He thought he knew why: the light had taken her parents and now she was scared it was going to take these other people as well. But then he remembered the girl had started screaming even before the light came. He pulled her away from him and held her at arms' length.

"Angel?"

She sniveled and opened her eyes very slowly.

"Angel, why were you screaming?"

"The... the light," she said.

Virgil Banders appeared at Ronnie's right shoulder. He knew now that the light they had just experienced was the same one that he had seen in his dream, back at Suze Neihardt's house.

"What was it?" Virgil asked, addressing the question to the girl.

"*I* don't know," she sobbed. "Why should *I* know?"

"Angel, why did you start screaming *before* the light came?"

The girl looked up at Ronnie and rubbed the sleeve of her sweater across her face. She took a deep sigh and then glanced first at Virgil and then back at Ronnie. "I already told you."

"What did she tell you?" Virgil asked.

Karl half-crawled out of his seat and landed in the aisle in a heap. Pulling himself to his feet, his arm pressed tightly against his stomach as though he had been gut shot, he said, "What's going on? Lot of noise."

"It was the light again," Ronnie said, his voice flat. What the hell was going to happen now? He almost dreaded stepping out of the plane to find out.

"I sometimes see things before they happen," the girl told Virgil Banders. Ronnie thought it spoke volumes about just how distressed she was that she was prepared to exchange dialogue – if not exactly pleasantries – with the young man who had so recently joined their party.

"You mean like... a clairvoyant?"

The girl glowered at him. "My name is Angel Wurst, not Claire Voyant!"

"How come I missed it?" Karl asked. "I was awake."

"You must have dropped off," Ronnie said.

"No, a clairvoyant is someone who sees things that–" Virgil was about to say *things that aren't there,* and then he remembered how the girl had acted earlier about the car. He smiled and looked down at her. She was a pretty kid, no question. It was almost a shame that he was going to have to do what he was going to have to do. But, shit, he was going to have to do it, and that was all there was to it.

"Who sees things that other folks can't see," he finished. And he reached out to tousle the girl's hair. Angel flinched and Virgil looked around at the others. They didn't appear to have noticed.

"How you feeling?"

"Shit," Karl said and then he groaned and looked over at Angel. "Sorry Angel."

"That's OK," she said, hugging her doll tightly and edging backwards away from Virgil Banders.

"Her dad says it all the time," Ronnie offered, deliberately choosing the present tense to give Angel a feeling of things being OK and of maybe having a chance at carrying on the same way sometime. But Ronnie didn't feel things were OK at all. And he didn't think for one second they would ever go back to the way they used to be. He couldn't explain why he felt like that, but he felt that things were actually a whole lot worse than they had been before.

"What time is it, anyway?" the map-man asked as he accepted Angel's hand of support.

"Well, by my very smart new watch, it's just after two."

Karl staggered back towards the cockpit with Angel still holding his hand. "Hey," he shouted, "I thought I just saw a light."

Ronnie and Virgil followed them and soon they were all standing in the glass-strewn cockpit craning their heads forward to look out of the ruined windshield and up, through the debris of Borders bookstore and out into the night beyond.

There wasn't anything to be seen, though Ronnie was pleased that the sky looked altogether normal. There were stars everywhere.

"Maybe it was a shooting star," Angel ventured.

"Mmm." Karl did not sound convinced.

"Nothing there now," said Virgil.

There wasn't. The sky was empty – apart from the stars – with no signs or even suggestions of movement.

"I say we try get some sleep – some decent sleep – and maybe we'll feel more up to investigating in the morning," Ronnie said. He reached out and turned around Karl and Angel and ushered them back down the plane. Virgil stayed in the cockpit.

"Jeez, you landed this thing?" Virgil called after them.

Karl, groaning, was in too much discomfort to respond.

"Well, we're here," Ronnie said.

Virgil ran his hand over the banks of dials and switches and levers. "You deserve a medal, man," he said at last.

Karl slumped back into one of the business class seats and breathed a sigh of relief. "Christ, I feel like I've been beaten within an inch of my life."

"Probably more like a centimeter."

"Just as well we didn't go metric."

Angel sat in one of the other seats and looked out of the window. "That's a *lot* of books," she said. "You think we're going to be in trouble when everyone gets back?"

Ronnie got to his feet and laid a tiny airplane blanket around the map-reader. "With any luck, we'll be long gone by then."

"Hey, guys," Virgil called. "I think Map-man may be right. I could have sworn I just saw a light out there."

"What kind of a light?" Ronnie asked as he moved back to the cockpit.

"I dunno. Kind of like... like a searchlight?"

"Maybe they're back already," Angel suggested.

"Nothing there now," Ronnie said.

They stood for another few minutes and then Ronnie said, "Like I say, let's get some shuteye and see what the morning brings."

A few minutes later they were asleep.

(17)

Sally Davis had been asleep, too. And hadn't seen the light, so to speak.

Sally had spent the day getting to the mall, arriving in the late morning in a garishly metallic orange Citroën something-or-other that sat up like a dog, hunkering down on its rear wheels and lifting from the front, when she turned on the ignition. She could have had her pick of cars but it was that one that appealed to her the most. Of course, she could have used Gerry's beloved old Chevy, that, when the air was just right, still smelled of shit, cordite and decaying flesh, but she felt like a change. This brave new world that seemed to have been thrust upon her (without her having asked, she wanted it known to anyone interested) clearly called for changes. She told the children as much, abandoning the car near the visitor information center on California Street and walking over to the Denver Pavilions. It was closed.

She had to eat, however, so she smashed a window of nearby *Bagel Shmagel* with a tire iron she purloined from a Subaru 4x4 that had ploughed into the window of a sportswear store – setting off the alarm – and helped herself to some bagels, cream cheese, smoked salmon and a pack of potato chips. Once she had made her sandwiches, she took one of the tubular steel chairs sitting around the Formica tables and smashed the flashing light box on the wall. The alarm didn't stop but it sounded a little woozy. As she was taking her seat outside on the street, it finally petered out and silence returned. Nobody appeared to have heard the alarm – as good a piece of evidence that she was definitely alone as she could possibly wish for.

She sat out on one of the benches and watched the silent world as she ate, always half-expecting a car to come into view from Welton or Greenarm or Tremont, or maybe someone to appear suddenly out of one of the stores or maybe a hotel apartment and give her a wave. But there were no cars and no people. Not even a bird or an insect, as far as she could make out.

After a few minutes, she went back into the *Bagel Shmagel* and helped herself to a piece of blueberry pie from the freezer display unit. The unit had gone off since she'd attacked the alarm system and the pie was just the right temperature. Back out on the street, she poured a half-dozen thimble-sized cartons of half-and-half onto the pie – she'd found the cartons next to the coffee machine but she couldn't figure out how to get it working. A shame, she thought then, that whatever had happened hadn't happened in the middle of the day, when everything everywhere would be open and accessible and functioning.

She finished the pie, dumped the plate, fork and mess of little brown half-and-half cartons into a trash container on the corner of California and 16th and set off to find who knew what.

The voices seemed to have been asleep since she left the house but now they skittered around in her head like moths. *What's happening?* seemed to be the favorite question, along with *Where are we?* And *Where are we going?* Plus, of course, *Where is everyone?* After a curt "Downtown," Sally couldn't bring herself to answer them anymore. Then the voices stilled and she felt them watching and waiting, could feel their attentions focused through her eyes as she wandered along Glenarm Place looking for someplace to go. Over in the east, the horizon was darkening. She stopped and frowned at it, shielding her eyes as she studied it some more.

No, it was more than just darkening with the onset of dusk. It looked like black ink spilled into some kind of viscous liquid, the ink swirling around and spreading itself, the thin tendrils thickening into ribbons and the ribbons merging to form swathes of dark material like an old-fashioned cape blowing slow-mo in the wind.

But Sally turned around and headed down 17th Street to the Brown Palace.

Teddy Roosevelt was the first US President to avail himself of the Brown Palace's opulence, landing at the hotel back in 1905. Then came Taft, Wilson, Truman and Ike. When President Harding stayed there in 1923, a report announced that, for a few hours at least, the White House would be located on the eighth floor of the Brown Palace Hotel. "That's where *we* shall sleep tonight," Sally David told the building's ornate façade as she climbed the steps to the lobby.

The noise of the vacuum cleaner was disconcerting to say the least. It was like an angry bee, trapped in gossamer webbing from which it had been trying to extricate itself for almost an entire day. Sally could not help but wonder at the plight of the unfortunate woman – she guessed it would be a woman – plucked from her duties just fourteen or fifteen hours earlier, the machine left in mid-sweep, poised between spotlessly clean carpet and a small stretch of pile blighted with the most miniscule of dust specks. She walked to the wall socket and removed the plug, plunging the lobby into what at first seemed to be a stultifying silence, until Sally heard the faint strains of piped music. "Delibes's *Lakme*," she said, hugging herself. The voices twittered the way they were so often wont to do. "I *recognize* it," she added.

She strode up to the wide mahogany desk and tapped the bell with the palm of her left hand. "I shall stay on the eighth, I believe," she announced grandly, throwing her head back and wafting an invisible scarf from her chin and neck. "Certainly, madam," she responded in as close to a baritone as she could muster. The voices were amused. Tickled. What joy. What fun they were all having here, and no denying.

The first room she went into – 811, luckily she had thought ahead and had taken six keys from the master board in the glass case behind the reception desk – had an unmistakable air of occupancy, coupled with unmade beds. Sally preferred to think of them as unmade, rather than as the ruffled scene of a double abduction, the sheets suddenly deflated onto mattress that was previously covered by leg and backside, arms and belly, the pillows indented, pressed in by invisible and now forgotten heads and faces. Fighting off an urge to tiptoe, Sally backed out of the room.

The second was the same.

The third was empty.

The third is always the charm, one of the voices whispered to Sally.

And she had to admit that it was.

Room 815 was truly palatial, though not ostentatiously so.

"I feel at home," she told the voices. And they agreed.

She went to the window and looked down onto the empty city as the sky above it started to darken. She hugged herself again and leaned her forehead against the glass. "I feel safe here," she whispered. It was the first time she had felt that way since watching her husband eat his final meal of buckshot.

(18)

Maybe it wasn't entirely democratic but, to Geoff, the way they had decided on who was going to go out into the night made a lot of sense.

Geoff was first up because, well, because he was effectively in charge. It wasn't put quite so bluntly during their brief discussion but it was understood that Geoff seemed to have the best handle on what was going on, so it seemed logical that he was out there making decisions as events presented themselves.

Melanie stayed behind because she was the expert when it came to transmitting, and if Geoff and whoever didn't return from their expedition, then transmitting needed to be a real weapon in their limited arsenal. Geoff had no idea why he should not return but there were so many unanswered things that he was playing it safe.

Playing it safe also meant that Melanie – who figured large in all of Geoff's considerations – was reasonably mobile. And the problem there was that Melanie didn't drive. She had taken a few lessons with her father, back when she was sixteen, but she had never pursued driving as such, being content, as were most New Yorkers, to take the subway, buses or, on special occasions, cabs when she needed to go somewhere. This meant that Geoff had to leave a driver behind, which excluded his brother from the list of possibles. Ever since the accident, more than six months ago now, Rick had been unable even to consider driving. When he simply got behind a steering wheel, Rick would break out in cold sweats, shaking hands, dried-up mouth, the full business. So leaving his brother to look after his wife wasn't an option for Geoff.

And so it was decided.

Geoff and Rick stepped out from one darkness and into another at 3.11.

With a soft smile and a final stroke on her husband's arm, Melanie stepped back into the station and allowed Johnny to secure the door. Rick watched, wondering whether to say anything but, glancing around at the road which disappeared into the night, he didn't feel very reassuring.

Away from the pull-in apron in front of the station doors, the road drifted gently downhill. They kept to the grass sides to avoid even the slightest noise of their shoes on the blacktop, coat collars pulled up against the night. It felt strange to be out there at this time, but the sound of an occasional rustle and cricket *chirrups* from the undergrowth made for company of sorts. It also made for several jumps as each of them thought that the sounds meant that someone was sneaking up on them. But that didn't make sense, any more than their being out here in the first place made sense, and pretty soon they had moved into muted conversation.

As they turned left to head on down to town, Geoff stopped and looked back at the station, nestled into the side of Honeydew Mountain. He would have given anything to be up there right now, just passing time, doing this and that, chatting to his brother and maybe Johnny, listening to Mel's show. He gave a single wave to the station and turned to face the road, suddenly aware that Rick was watching him.

"You OK?"

"I'm fine."

Rick pushed his hands still further into his jacket pockets, at the same time hugging it tight around his legs. "How far to town?"

"From here? Three miles maybe. Four at the outside." Geoff kicked a stone and sent it spinning into the long grass. "Should be there in an hour, hour and a quarter if we take it slow and easy."

"Well..." Rick stepped out and began to walk, bending his head back, taking in the stars and the endless blackness of space. "Let's just hope we get a lift back."

Geoff said, "And it's a big amen to that."

"At least this way it's downhill."

Geoff grunted acknowledgment. No matter how hard he tried and no matter how optimistic he allowed himself to become, he could not imagine that they would be getting a lift back to the station. In fact, he already felt that he would never see his wife again. Right now, walking down the road, that realization was easier than it had been back at the station. Back at the station, with Melanie framed in the doorway, there were options open to him: for one thing, he could change his mind and stay put. But now, with the wind on his face and in his hair, and his coat around him, he felt primed for primed for action; a grunt, deep in-country and miles from home, prepared for whatever the enemy threw at him.

As they reached the spot where they had seen Jerry Borgesson's truck, Geoff realized that he had seen the same thoughts captured in Melanie's eyes. She too didn't expect him to be back. He took his hands out of his pockets and, with his right hand, felt for the wedding band that had been there since their wedding day. It felt good. Whatever happened, nobody could take that away from him, or take away the years they had enjoyed together.

They stopped and looked around.

"See anything?" Geoff called to his brother.

Rick glanced back and when he saw that Geoff was watching him, he shook his head and continued to plod around the thick grass beside the road. After a couple of minutes they met again on the road and continued on towards Jesman's Bend.

They walked in silence for more than a half hour, Rick occasionally clearing his throat and glancing across at his brother, while Geoff merely forged ahead. He had worked his way into a routine, placing one foot after the other and mentally striking off the yards to town. And all the time he concentrated on sending a message to Melanie that told her how much he loved her and how she should not be bitter whatever happened to him tonight. Just now and then, he got a wave of guilt about dragging his brother along to share in whatever was waiting for them. But he hadn't had a choice. Maybe Rick would get around to driving again – and Geoff certainly hoped that was the case – but he could not leave it to chance, not when Mel's life was dependent on it. Then even that thought brought its own wave of guilt, as he realized he was effectively saying he didn't mind Johnny getting killed but he did mind if it was his brother. But surely everyone thought that way. What was it they said about blood being thicker than water?

Rick was aware of Geoff looking at him. He didn't respond. He was in what he called The Graveyard, a place in his mind when he imagined a pair of dead people were walking along behind him, shuffling their tire-marked torsos and stretching out their wattled, sore-covered and bloodstained arms to reach for him. He knew the two of them well, though he had forgotten their names since the hearing. Sometimes he imagined they were right alongside him, standing back amidst the cover of the trees, ready to waddle out in that off-balance way the dead have of walking, and sometimes he imagined they were waiting up ahead, ready to step out into his path–

Hey, asshole, whyn't you come and finish the job... think there's a couple of bones here seem to be still in one piece...

–like a couple of old Wild West gunslingers. But mostly he thought they were behind him, moving one mud-caked foot after the other, gaining on him. He turned around and walked backwards a couple of steps while he scanned the road behind them. It was deserted.

"Hear something?" Geoff whispered.

Rick turned around and shook his head. "Just checking."

"Listen."

They stopped and listened.

Up ahead, occasionally hidden by the wind through the trees, was the unmistakable sound of industrious activity. A lot of activity.

Hammers hammered and engines *vroom-vroomed*, their sound muted and hoarse, straining. The wind picked up the sound like a playful dog, ran with it first one way and then the other, taking it out of earshot and then dropping it again, louder now.

"Sounds promising," Rick ventured. He glanced to his right at a big bush that seemed to be moving strangely, the way maybe a bush moves when a couple of dead people are holding it close to them. But it was just the wind, of course.

Geoff didn't say anything.

They walked a couple more steps and stopped again, both of them together. "Doesn't seem right to you either, does it?" Geoff said.

Rick had to admit that it didn't. It didn't sound right at all. The main thing that was wrong with it was that, even though the sound of activity was reasonably loud now, with the first houses just around the next clump of trees, there wasn't a single voice to be heard. No muted shouts or far-off conversation. No laughter, no music.

It's life, Geoff, but not as we know it.

Geoff hissed and pointed to the trees. Rick understood straight away. If they ducked off the road and into the trees before the bend, they could come up on the ridge that overlooked the town without anyone below being able to see them. That way they could check things out before actually having to advertise their presence.

Rick led the way through the bushes and checked behind every few steps to make sure that the lumbering sound of twigs and branches being either snapped or displaced was in fact his brother and not anyone else. The hoot of an owl from somewhere over to their right suddenly made Rick feel silly. What the hell were they doing clambering about in the woods when it was obvious that everything was entirely normal?

He pushed past a large branch, holding it to one side but failing to notice that the ground fell away into a deep ditch whose earthen sides were a maze of exposed roots. The sense of falling away was horrible. Rick felt as though he had stepped off the edge of the earth, and was doomed to plunge forever through space. He held onto the large branch with one hand and, even as his feet went away from him and he plunged forward, he threw up his free hand and grabbed the end of the branch, momentarily swinging forward and then being swept back into a huge bush. The branches cut and pierced his skin, one narrowly missing his eye and instead getting entangled in his hair. Rick let go of the branch and fell into the bush, settling after a few seconds and trying hard not to breathe loudly, though he suspected anyone within twenty yards would have heard all the commotion.

The hand on his arm made his jump but it was only Geoff, smiling despite his obvious concern at all the noise. "You OK?"

Rick allowed his brother to pull him to his feet and then rubbed himself down. He nodded. The branches had scratched his face and managed to tear open his jacket and shirt, and raise thick welts on his chest and stomach – he tucked his shirt back into his pants, wincing at the pain. "I'll live. Think anyone heard me?"

Geoff shrugged. "We'll wait a few minutes just to be on the safe side."

They waited and listened.

The noises of industrious work continued seemingly unabated and there were no telltale branch snaps or rustles to suggest that anyone had heard Rick's plight. Geoff patted Rick on the shoulder.

"Come on, I'll lead the way this time."

Geoff moved off. He slid slowly down into the ditch and waved for Rick to follow. As he moved away, Rick felt the unmistakable feeling that someone was watching him. At the top of the ditch, he turned around–

Hey, asshole, whyn't you...

–but there was nobody there.

He slid down and followed Geoff across the floor of the ditch and then up the other side. They made their way slowly and with hardly any noise at all until they emerged once more at the side of the road. Ahead of them, they could see Main Street stretching over to the right and out of town towards Dawson.

There were no lights on, and hardly any moon, but what natural light there was enabled them to see that the folks down in Jesman's Bend were having problems sleeping. So they'd gathered in the town square where they had brought various vehicles onto the grass and were busy working on them.

"I don't get it," Rick whispered. "What the hell are they doing?"

"Never mind that," said Geoff, "why are they doing it without any lights?"

They watched and kept quiet. Then Rick said, "Geoff, they're all wearing dark glasses."

"And gloves," Geoff added.

Don Patterson stood up after being bent over into the engine of Luke Napier's Eldorado, which already seemed a little strange because Luke himself was across the street hitching some kind of wire siding to Martha McNeil's flatbed pickup. "What–"

Geoff shook his head and put a finger up to his mouth.

After another couple of minutes, Don Patterson, who had been standing with another couple of men – Rick couldn't tell who they were but one of them limped like Jim Ferumern – walked back to the Eldorado and slid behind the wheel.

"You see that?" Rick whispered.

"What?"

"Yeah, it was Jim."

"No, you see the way he walked?"

Geoff nodded. One-time quarterback Jim Ferumern was walking like he'd shit himself, slow and easy straight-legged steps, his arms held awkwardly, each about a foot away from the side of his body.

Ferumern pulled the door closed and turned the ignition a couple of times until the engine caught. Then the others stepped back a few feet – each of them displaying the same cumbersome gait – and Luke Napier's Eldorado slowly lifted into the air, wobbled a couple of times and then dropped back to the ground. As Don got out of the car again, another vehicle – neither Rick nor Geoff could identify the make or figure out who the driver was – rose into the night sky from somewhere down Derwent Street and angled over Main and moved slowly out to the east. Nobody on the town square so much as gave the vehicle a second look.

Neither Geoff nor Rick spoke. They just watched.

Down towards the end of Main, an open top pulled up into the sky out of the filling station. This one angled around and moved northwards.

Back down in the town square, Don Patterson was doing something beneath the Eldorado's hood. He stood up for a second and took off one of his gloves – then he bent over again.

Geoff slithered backwards and rested his head on the grass. "I think it's time we went back," he said.

Rick turned to face him, his eyes suddenly wide in either disbelief or outright fear. "Geoff–"

Geoff reached out a hand and steadied his brother. "Take it–"

"*Geoff!*" Rick hissed, nodding to something behind Geoff.

Geoff turned slowly and saw the imposing shape of Jerry Borgesson standing just a few yards to the side. Jerry was not looking at them. He was wearing dark glasses and he was standing straight-legged with his hands – his gloved hands – by his side staring down into the town square. All the activity from down below seemed to have stopped.

Geoff said, "Hey, Jerry…"

Jerry Borgesson turned slightly and half-looked in their direction, like a wily old fifth grade teacher glancing at a couple of errant pupils he'd caught giving him the bird behind his back. They couldn't see Jerry's eyes through the dark glasses – real nifty-looking jobs, like the ones the flyboys wore when they were flying billion dollar stealth airplanes – but the expression on his face spoke eloquently. *Hoo, boy,* the expression seemed to say, *are you guys in for it* now!

Lifting his left leg outwards, causing him to sway a little, Jerry started to turn towards them. And then he lifted his arms and started pulling off his gloves.

(19)

Melanie watched Geoff and Rick walk down the path away from the station with a sinking feeling in the pit of her stomach. She stepped back, half turning away while Johnny stepped forward and locked the door, pushing the dead bolt into place with a sound of grim finality.

"He'll be OK, Mel," Johnny said without turning around.

"I know," she said, though she wasn't exactly sure. "It's just that everything seems so, I dunno – so *strange*. I just don't feel comfortable with anything."

Turning around to face Melanie, with the sprawling radio station looming up and around her, empty, and without any shows being transmitted, Johnny knew exactly what she meant. Even the most familiar and dependable of things seemed to have assumed an air of mystery.

Melanie looked up at him and gave a trembling smile. He knew she was close to tears, fighting them back not just for her own sake but for his too.

"C'mon," he said, "let's go up on the roof. That way you can keep an eye on him, make sure he doesn't come to any harm." Even as he was saying it, Johnny wondered if he was doing the right thing. What if they were sitting up there watching Geoff being torn apart by some raging pissed-off flying-saucer-lagged lizard monster from Alpha Centauri? *Yeah, but apart from that, Mrs. Grisham, how did you enjoy the show?*

But second thoughts were far too late. Melanie's eyes lit up like a kid's at Christmas, and Johnny hadn't got the heart to sound a note of caution. It would teach him to think first before he spoke.

"That's a *great* idea." She ran ahead of Johnny and hit the stairs to the roof two at a time. "Quick, before they're out of sight."

"If you're gonna do it, Lizard Man, don't do it where we can see you," Johnny mumbled. Then he followed.

They crept out onto the roof, bent double, and made their way to the wall overlooking the concrete apron. The moon was about half-full and the clouds kept eating into what available light there was. Even so, they had a clear view of two figures making their way down the lane. As the figures reached the fork that turned left to head into town, one of them stopped and turned around. Johnny and Melanie couldn't make out who it was but Melanie knew deep in her heart that it was Geoff. "Take care, honey," she whispered to the night. Then, right on cue – as though he had acknowledged the communication – the figure waved his arm and turned around. And they continued down towards Jesman's Bend.

A few minutes later, they had disappeared behind the trees.

"What do you think they'll find?"

Johnny shrugged. "Well, either everyone is back or they're not." He patted his jacket pockets for his cigarettes.

Melanie slumped down against the wall and crossed her legs. "I hate it."

Johnny found the pack and shook a Marlboro free. "What? Him going off without you?"

She nodded. "Well, that. But it's the *waiting* that gets me." She drew her knees up and wrapped her arms around them. "It's the same when he's just going out to the store, even going out of the *room*. I don't like to be apart from him. You know what I mean?"

Johnny shrugged and lit the cigarette behind cupped hands. "I guess. I ain't never been that close to anybody. Not even my folks." He pulled on the Marlboro and blew out smoke. "I *was*," he added, "but then my pop died. Took a long time about it, too."

"What was it?"

"Cancer." He held up the cigarette. "Lungs. Only took him a couple of weeks to go once it had been diagnosed. But they were sad weeks. Seemed like forever."

"How old were you?"

"I dunno. Thirteen, maybe fourteen."

"You don't know exactly? Like what year he died?"

Johnny sat next to her and handed her the cigarette when she held out her hand. "Nope. He died. And that was that. Didn't seem important to know the year, or the day or the time."

"You must know the time!"

"It was late one night. I was watching TV and my mom called for me. I knew it was bad because her voice was strange."

"Strange how?"

He took the cigarette back and tapped the burning end against the wall, shaping it into a tiny glowing cone. "It was cracked and formal-sounding. She never spoke to me like that, before or after." He put his head back so that it rested partly on top of the wall and sighed.

"I went on up to their bedroom and pop was lying in bed, same as he'd been doing for the past couple days... but he was different."

Melanie didn't say anything. She waited.

"It was my pop but he was different. Like everything that actually *was* him – you know, all the stuff that made him who he was – like everything that made him who he really was had just up and left, leaving behind the body he wore." He took a drag on the cigarette and blew a couple of smoke rings.

"Anyway, seeing my mom so sad – I mean she was *devastated* when pop died – seeing her that way convinced me that relationships were bad–"

"What was that?"

"What?"

Melanie turned around, pulling her head down so that her eyes were level with the top of the wall. "I heard something."

Johnny stubbed out his cigarette and he too shuffled around so that he was looking over the wall. "Can't see anything."

Everything looked exactly the way it had been before. The clouds had left the moon uncovered and visibility was good. Johnny scanned the patches of road between the trees but couldn't see any movement. "They'll be well out of sight now," he said.

"No, it wasn't from the road," Melanie whispered. "It was nearer.

Much nearer." She twisted onto her knees. "I'm going to go take a look."

"No." Johnny shot out his arm and took hold of Melanie's knee.

"What?"

"I don't think you should do that."

Melanie considered it for a few seconds. Then she said, "What does it matter if we're seen? If someone – some*thing* – is down there then we ought to know about it, don't you think?"

"Maybe it came from inside, downstairs someplace."

"Like what?"

Johnny shrugged. "I don't know what," he hissed. "Something falling over maybe?"

"Like what?"

"Will you stop with the 'like what'! I don't know *like what*... just *something*. There's a lot of stuff down there. Maybe it was a CD case slipping off a stack... something like that. Something completely innocent."

"And maybe it wasn't."

Maybe it's the Lizard Man come to pay you a call, Johnny's secret head-friend whispered to him, *and he's brought various bits and pieces belonging to Geoff and Rick... dripping red pieces...*

He shuffled the thought as far back as he could, out of sight.

"Shit, I'll look," he said, and he clambered up and leaned over the wall.

The concrete apron was deserted.

He scanned the grass and then looked across towards the bushes and trees that lined the driveway. Nobody there. No Lizard Men.

"All clear," he said.

Melanie scrabbled away from the wall. "I'll check inside."

Johnny thought about stopping her but decided against it. The station was secure – they'd spent long enough making sure that nobody but nobody could get inside unless someone let them in. He turned around, fighting back another thought: namely that he didn't want to go back into the station himself. And he hated himself for thinking such a thing – and then hated himself some more for letting Melanie go alone when, deep in the secret places inside his head, he feared that whatever she had heard it might not be a CD case falling off a stack.

He closed his eyes and stretched his neck back, feeling the tension ease a little. He heard a muffled grunt from the passageway and then a hissed "Shit!" Almost immediately Melanie called out that she was OK. Then more mumbling. Johnny smiled to himself and waggled his head from side to side. The tension eased a little more.

He opened his eyes and stared across at the town road, scanning for any signs of movement. The treetops looked still as paintings, shades of black against the deeper black that formed the woods at the far side of the road.

Johnny turned to the right and, slowly dropping his head, followed the road back, past the fork and all the way up to the concrete apron in front of the station. When the top of the wall in front of him appeared, Johnny moved his head slowly to the left, scanning the concrete.

Troy Vilawsky didn't register anything when Johnny's eyes met the deputy's dark glasses. He just stood there, arms hanging by his side but each of them standing a little away from his body, like he was an old-time gunfighter, his head tilted back and seemingly watching Johnny.

Johnny felt exposed. He nodded, a sinking feeling–

Why the hell's he wearing dark glasses when it's pitch black?

–starting off in the pit of his stomach and slowly–

And what the hell's wrong with his arms?

–working its way upwards like bile and–

Better still, when did he start wearing gloves, for Chrissakes?

–threatening to explode into his mouth.

"Hey, Troy? How's it hanging?"

Troy didn't respond.

The deputy had moved into Jesman's Bend a little over four years ago, transferred across from the coast, from some town nestled in the greater Los Angeles smog belt, for a break from the drug and gang warfare. "Some folks are made for that kind of shit, and some folks aren't," Troy had told the folks in Martha McNeil's diner couple of mornings after he'd moved in, his shirt pressed like a marine drill sergeant's. "Me, I'm made for things being a little quieter."

It wasn't that Troy was slow in coming forward when he was needed, nossir. It was Troy pulled the man and woman from the blazing Subaru up on the mountain road that time, even went back a couple of times to get their little girl but she was long gone and the fire held him back. It was a blessing really: the girl had flown forward between the front seats and smashed into the windshield. Wasn't anything anyone could have done for her, not even Troy.

And it was Troy who tackled Jack Salliday when he'd had just a little too much tequila, and finally managed to get the serrated knife out of Jack's hand before Jack slit his wife's throat with it, Conchita Salliday having passed around just a few too many favors to the guys at the truck stop over on Boedecker Street down in Dawson. Conchita had taken a skillet to the back of Troy's head while her ever-loving husband had proceeded to slice open the deputy's right side, the fleshy part just around from his belly. And Troy hadn't pressed charges that time either, making sure instead that Jack Salliday straightened himself out some and stayed away from the booze and home more with his wife. "Might solve a lot of problems," Troy had told Jack.

And now here he was, standing out in the night air wearing wraparound dark glasses like he was a Hollywood heartthrob or something. He didn't look relaxed and he didn't look tense. He looked wrong. He just stood there glaring up – at least that's what Johnny figured he was doing behind those dark glasses: glaring.

Johnny shuffled his way to a crouched position, his knees against the wall, and he nodded towards town. "Everything OK, in town I mean?"

Still nothing, but now at least Troy turned around stiffly, like Jim in *Taxi*–

Town? Whut's "town" mean, man?

–and looked in the direction Johnny had indicated.

As if on cue, Gram Kramer stepped out from behind a bush, ignoring the bush's branches scraping across his face. Gram's arms were hanging the same way as Troy's, awkward and lifeless. And he was wearing the same dark glasses, too.

Johnny glanced down at Gram's hands. Yep, the gloves were there. All present and correct.

Johnny nodded. "Hey, Gram. How're *you* doing?"

Gram walked stiffly over to Troy and stopped. Troy turned around and joined Gram in looking up at the roof, at Johnny.

Johnny forced a slight laugh. Nope, things were most decidedly *not* OK in town. "Hey, come on guys, talk to me, will ya? At least tell me why you need to wear shades at four o'clock in the goddam morning." There was a noise from deep inside the station, deep down right underneath where Johnny was crouching.

Troy and Gram turned their attention to something right in front of them.

Johnny frowned: what *was* right in front of them?

He heard only the faint strains of Melanie's muffled voice but it was loud enough for him to figure out what she was shouting – shouting through the door, the door with the covered peephole that allowed folks inside the station to look out and see who was standing outside.

Hoo boy, she was shouting, or something like that.

And something like, *Am I glad to see you guys.*

Then Johnny heard Melanie shout out his own name, and he imagined the inevitable fumbling of her small and petite hands on the lock and bolt system that would undoubtedly follow – maybe was underway right now, even as Johnny struggled to his feet and made for the hatchway leading into the station.

Just hold on there, Melanie was probably saying as she fumbled, *and we'll have you inside in just a few seconds...*

As he plunged through the doorway into the blackness of the station's interior, Johnny didn't think that having Troy and Gram inside right now was a particularly good idea at all. Halfway along the corridor, when he heard a roll of loud thuds against the door, he had a sneaking suspicion that Troy and Gram didn't agree with him.

"Mel!" he shouted at the top of his voice, suddenly realizing how good it felt to make a loud noise. "Don't open the door!"

(20)

Sally Davis was about to have trouble with her own door.

Sally did not recall going to bed but she must have done because here she was slipping out of it. Outside it was pitch black.

What had awakened her? It was certainly a noise of some kind, though Sally didn't know what. She sat on the edge of the bed and strained to hear, absently smoothing the bedspread with her hand. There was no repetition of the noise, if that was what it had been.

She slipped silently from the bed and padded across to the door, bent down and looked through the spyhole.

"The lights have gone out," she told the room.

My oh my, but how interesting.

She stood up, hand on the door handle. "Why would the lights go out?" she wondered aloud.

Generators? one of the voices suggested.

She took her hand away, frowned, and leaned forward again to the spyhole. She could hear a slurring sound.

If there really was someone else, someone out there in the hallway, if she really was no longer all alone, then why did her heart feel as though it were skipping beats all the time? And why did her hand place itself firmly at her side, scrupulously avoiding that door handle?

Sally leaned closer to the door, her head resting on the polished oak, and she squinted through the spyhole.

The fisheye lens effect showed the corridor starting up on the left, dropping down towards her door, and then lifting up again to the right, heading for the elevators, like a smile – Sardonicus, perhaps, or the constantly laughing sociopath out of the Batman comic book.

No, it wasn't generators that had taken the light from the corridor, turning it into a shadowy place bereft of familiarity and imbuing it with only the suggestion of edges and planes. Then, as the slurring noise grew, a dull light shone down the corridor, and in that light, for the briefest of moments before Sally withdrew her eye from the spyhole, she saw a small boy walking slowly and awkwardly along the corridor from the direction of the elevators. And the small boy was wearing gloves and sunglasses.

Sally's hand went up immediately to her mouth, but not fast enough to prevent a small gasp breaking free. Some deep-rooted part of her told Sally that it was important for that little boy not to know she was there. *Why?* she whispered mentally to the voices of the child/children who lived inside her. *Because,* they whispered back in a cacophonous concordance of misery tinged with acceptance: *He is like us. He does not truly exist.*

Sally leaned forward to the spyhole once more.

Two things, she noticed.

First, the boy had stopped right outside her door, the dull light bathing his left side as he stared – Sally *presumed* he was staring: it was difficult to know, what with the sunglasses – up at her door, his head on one side.

"He's listening," she whispered. And sure enough, the boy's head twitched, like a cartoon version of a radar might twitch if/when it saw/sensed incoming craft.

That was when she noticed the second thing.

The dull light that now bathed the boy, intermittently sweeping across the other side of the corridor, up and down the wall, was coming from a luggage trolley coming down the corridor from the direction of the elevators. Standing on the trolley was a black man wearing a checkered cowboy shirt: he, too, was wearing sunglasses and gloves. He was maneuvering the trolley by working the knobs and levers on a small box attached to the front; the light, meanwhile, was coming from what appeared to be two car headlights whose wires were intertwined around the rail that ran across the top and from which guests usually hung their tuxedos and party dresses.

Best of all, however, was the fact that the trolley was not actually on the floor, but rather floating a foot or two above it.

Sally took a step back, raised a hand to her mouth and turned to look at the room.

Mommy?

A solitary slap sounded against the room door, shaking it in its frame.

Suddenly, the opulence of the swish eighth floor suite disappeared. Instead, it now seemed little more than a very comfortable prison cell.

Her heart was beating fast.

A dull thud sounded from the door, around the bottom, and she guessed that the airborne trolley had come to rest right outside. Now there was another slap. And then another, this one higher up. The black man.

Sally stepped forward, her hand stretched out towards the door chain. She took a hold of it very carefully, trying not to make a sound–

After all, there's no reason they should know we're in here mom–

–and then jumping at the sound of another trio of slams, two low down and the other higher. "They know we're here," Sally whispered.

A further single crash, delivered with new intensity, made her drop the chain and it clattered against the door.

Everything went silent.

She leaned forward and checked the spyhole – and then wished that she hadn't. The black man was right in front of her, the boy by his side. They were looking at the little glass on the door. The black man's face was smashed in, blood running down from his forehead and nose.

He's battering the door with his head, Sally thought, thinking the thought casually – *I think it may rain today* or *I must remember to get the meatloaf out of the freezer* – without even the vaguest hint of surprise.

(21)

"Back up, Geoff," Rick hissed. "For God's sake, back up right now."

"Jerry...?"

"It's not Jerry." Rick glanced down at the crowd in the town square. "It's not *any* of them."

The people were starting to amble – there was no other word for the movement they were making: they were ambling, a slow and formless motion forward – towards the grassy slope that led up to them. He turned around and saw that Jerry Borgesson was also ambling, thrusting one leg out in front of him, swinging it around like it was stiff or something, like he couldn't bend it at the knee any more, and then, when the first foot had connected solidly with the ground, swinging the other in the same half-arc, his arms swinging by his sides. Then Jerry brought the arms up and held them out, the fingers flexing all the while like they were reaching for something.

"It *is* Jerry, for God's sake," Geoff said, his voice soft so that only Geoff himself could hear, in a tone that might just as easily have said, "No, it's not a lump... it must just be a bruise or something," while he was inspecting his balls in the shower.

"Geoff, back up. Now!"

Rick was standing now, torn between retreating into the bushes and reaching out for his brother's arm. Jerry came on, stumbling a little, but apparently determined. Rick shot another glance down into the town square and saw that several folks were already making their way up the grassy hillside towards the road. None of them was speaking. Nobody was making any sound of exertion. There were no calls of *Let's get 'em, men!* or *What are those guys doing up there watching us!* – only a strange and silent relentless movement towards them.

Geoff stepped back and held out his hands. "Jerry, it's me... Geoff."

"Geoff, we have to get back to the station."

"Jerry, *talk* to me for Chrissakes."

The thing that looked like Jerry Borgesson lifted its arms woodenly and slowly began to remove the gloves without stopping its ambling movement towards Geoff.

"Geoff, we have to get back to Mel."

Cynthia Crasznow's head appeared to the side of the road, her arm reaching out a gloved hand to grasp at tufts of weed and branches in an effort to pull herself up another few feet. She keeled over to one side, no expression on her face, and lay there for a few seconds, waving her arms and legs like a turtle that had been turned over on its back. Then she managed to right herself and shifted around to get a better grip. She was wearing the same dark glasses as Jerry Borgesson. And the same gloves, dark and skintight, but thick, making her hands look out of proportion to the rest of her body.

Over behind the filling station a throaty roar let out, too guttural for a regular sedan. Whatever was making the noise, a truly anguished bellyache of a noise, was bigger than any regular automobile.

"Geoff..."

Geoff turned around and looked at his brother. The look said everything that Rick felt. It held a deep sadness and an almost primal fear. The sadness was for the world that had suddenly seemed to go all to hell. And the fear was of something that was completely unknown and unfathomable.

Jerry pulled off one glove and dropped it to the ground. The second one followed. Then the arms stretched out again, reaching for Geoff's back.

Without stopping to think, Rick leapt forward, stumbling on a tuft and completely losing balance, pinwheeling his arms like he was going to take off and fly up into the night. A sharp pain hit Rick's side and he rolled over, grunting in pain. As he started to pull himself to his feet, Rick saw Geoff start to turn.

But it was a microsecond too late.

Rick watched as Jerry Borgesson's hands took hold of his brother's head, one hand at each side, holding it almost tenderly, like it was an overripe pumpkin that Jerry didn't want to squeeze too hard.

As Cynthia Crasznow lifted to her full height and started tugging at her own gloves, pushing her feet one in front of the other through the thick grass, and as Gram Kramer's pickup tow truck appeared over Main Street and began a slow slide over to the left, towards the radio station, Geoff Grisham threw his arms forward and opened his eyes and mouth wide.

"Riiiiii–"

Rick got to his knees and looked around. He found a thick gnarled branch and lifted it with both hands, lurching forward in a variation on Chuck Berry's famed duckwalk and, pulling himself upright at the last second, took a swing that would have shamed Yogi Berra. The branch hit Jerry Borgesson on the side of his head and Geoff could have sworn he heard something crack. As Rick's arms reached their full extent, he drew the branch back into view, fully expecting to find it had shattered. But it was still whole. The crack had been something else, something from inside Jerry Borgesson's head, but whatever it had been didn't seem to be causing Jerry any problems.

Jerry continued to hold Geoff's head, and Geoff's eyes rolled upwards, showing white. His entire body was shaking, like he had his fingers jammed into a wall socket, soaking up a few thousand volts.

Rick took another swing, this time catching Jerry full in the face, and jumped sideways, shoulder-charging his brother. Jerry stumbled backwards, his face suddenly dark and wet, letting go of Geoff's head but his arms still stretched out. Geoff slumped to the ground like a sack of potatoes.

But the damage was done.

Geoff's right eye slid back into view and Rick saw it catch his own.

In that brief instant, Rick felt as though he was looking into his brother's soul. The expression told him to get away, to get away as fast as he could, and to look after Geoff's wife and keep her safe. But there was also pain in there, a lot of pain. Rick could feel it in his own head, could feel it shriveling his insides, turning them to mush. Then the expression faded and, as though on autopilot, Geoff shuffled around on the floor, trying to get up.

Rick didn't think there was any real understanding in Geoff's mind at that point, just a simple reflex mechanism. He'd heard of it before, read about it in books about the war in Vietnam, people fatally wounded pulling their exposed intestines together and trying to stuff them back through their ruined shirts and into their stomach or bending down to retrieve limbs blown off by mortar shell or landmines.

He'd seen a bird doing the very same thing one time, back in the house in Providence when he was just a kid. A cat had got the bird, a big white cat that he had used to like stroking and listening to it purr. The cat had torn off one of the bird's wings and gouged a big chunk out of the side of its face, just next to the tiny beak. For what seemed like an age, the bird had shuffled around on the spot – watched quietly by the cat lying right next to it on the lawn – lifting its one good wing and trying to flap the exposed muscle of the other, just going through the motions as it tried to get back to normal, slumping as its legs kept giving way first to one side and then the other. Meanwhile, all of the bird's systems were mercifully closing down.

Rick figured that his brother's systems were being closed down in exactly the same way, the little men inside his body turning off all the power, all the screens, watching them go blank and flatlining one by one.

Then Geoff's eye plopped out onto his cheek like the crazy glasses you could buy in joke stores, and a thick dark substance oozed out after it. He lifted a hand to his face and patted the gunk gently, then shuddered. He moved his hand away and rested it on the ground, seemingly trying to get his breath.

As Rick watched, Cynthia Crasznow stumbled towards him, closing the ten yards that separated them.

Meanwhile, Jerry Borgesson shuffled into a sitting position. The dark glasses were gone, knocked off into the long grass. He started to lever himself up onto his knees, one arm waving around in front of him as though he was blind, the fingers on the hand constantly grasping.

Geoff projectile-vomited over his own legs, a long string of something solid-looking hanging from his mouth. He paused for a second, ignoring what was dangling from his mouth – and still bubbling in waves – while he patted his face again, sticking a finger patterned with leaf and grass shards into the empty eye socket. He suddenly shuddered uncontrollably and his other eye dropped onto his lap. More ooze followed and Geoff slowly lay back on the ground.

Ed Donahue stepped from around a thick tree trunk, having climbed up from the road. Next to Ed were little Janie Sullivan and Marcy Culpepper, two little blonde girls of around ten years old that Melanie had said would be breaking a lot of hearts in just a few short years. All of them were wearing dark glasses and gloves, although Marcy and Ed were already beginning to remove them.

Rick got to his feet and swung the branch at Cynthia Crasznow, catching her in the chest on the second attempt. Cynthia faltered, took an involuntary step backwards and then lifted her foot to move forward again. Rick brought the branch down on the top of the woman's head and brought her to her knees. One final blow sent her face forward onto the grass.

He took a final look at his brother, the vomit still pulsing from the mouth like a well, and it was vomit that no man had any right throwing up. It didn't look like the usual stuff – carrots, corn kernels, that sort of thing, all held together in a gelatinous brown wash. This vomit looked like stuff that a man really couldn't afford to be without – gray, concertinaed tubing and tubular valves dripping with viscous fluid, all of it steaming as it lay on Geoff's chest.

Rick turned around in time to see Jerry get to his feet. His eyes narrowed and, swinging his club-branch behind his head, he took two steps and brought it round into the side of Jerry's head. The head snapped sideways and flopped over, the ear torn off and a thick chasm opened up from Jerry's jawbone right the way to his eyebrow. Even as Jerry was falling, the branch came down one more, this time in the opposite direction, and caught Jerry full in the face. He went back and down, and didn't move.

Marcy Culpepper had managed to remove her gloves and was daintily stepping around Geoff to get to Rick, her arms outstretched.

Behind her came Ed Donahue and Janie, and behind them came other shadowy figures just appearing over the rise, all of them wearing dark glasses, all of their faces expressionless, and all of their arms held out in front of them. Rick felt a wave of panic when he saw that a lot of them had already removed their gloves.

He turned and plunged into the thick bushes and branches, heading away from town and the road that led back to the station. There was a ravine somewhere up ahead, and the trees got so thick it wouldn't be possible for a man to break through them – at least not without a lot of effort. Rick was confident that he would have the energy when the need arose but he wasn't too sure about the time it would take to do the job.

But somewhere in the back of his head, he knew the first thing was to head directly away from town and the road that he would eventually need to take. The road was exposed, that was the first thing. And Rick was very aware of the cars and trucks that the townsfolk already had in the air, maybe patrolling the open land. Here in the dense woodland he was safe from that at least.

But the road held other dangers. The townsfolk may already be making their way back that way on foot, breaking off up the hillside to the forest path in little splinter groups, their arms outstretched before them.

Branches tore at him, scratching his face and tearing his shirt, and he had the old familiar feeling of something coming up behind him, reaching out for him. This time, however, it wasn't the two cyclists he had run down. This time it was something altogether different.

Every few steps, he tried to move to his right, aiming to travel in a wide circle that would eventually bring him out onto the bridge road that led back to the station. He heard himself moaning and couldn't stop it. Then the tears came and he replayed Geoff's death in his mind. "Stop it, stop it for Chrissakes!" he shouted, wiping snot from his nose and mouth with the back of his hand. "Got to keep moving," he said, "got to keep heading forward and right, forward and right… that'll do it. That'll be OK." But he wasn't too sure.

He burst through a waist-high bank of gorse, grimacing as the thorns raked his thighs, and plunged head first down a steep incline.

He closed his eyes and tried to turn himself around, swinging out with his right hand to grasp something, anything. But the only things there to grasp were far too busy tearing his clothes and his flesh.

He bounced against trees, thankfully only glancing them, and was repeatedly spun around and over, lashed by branches and hit by rocks that tumbled after him. He eventually came to a halt in a narrow gully along which water trickled soundlessly. He waited, half-expecting to set off again, and opened his eyes. Miraculously, he didn't seem to have broken anything though both legs and his right arm felt almost numb with constant small collisions and, whenever he tried to move, a thick stabbing pain flashed across his lower back.

"Got to... got to keep my head clear," Rick whispered to the night. "Got to get back to the station."

He spat dirt and leaves and sat up, moaning when his back complained. He leaned forward and twisted his left arm around to rub the small of his back and to feel for protruding bones. There weren't any and, after a couple of minutes, his breathing became more regular. The image of his brother's eyeball plopping out flashed into his mind. He screwed his eyes shut, fighting back the tears, and leaned his head against his knees while he searched inside himself for strength.

A rustle from somewhere nearby made him look up.

Where normally he might have said, in a soft voice, "Geoff?" he had to bite his tongue. Geoff wasn't coming. Christ, Geoff was dead. What the hell was Mel going to say? How was he going to break it to her?

The noise came again, somewhere over to the left. It sounded too small to be a person. And anyway, he figured it was in the wrong direction for it to be one of the townsfolk, or whatever they were now. Paradoxically, of course, it was the other direction – the one from which the townsfolk *might* be coming, all gloves and dark glasses – that he now needed to go.

The rustle came again and something small scurried across a piece of open ground to his left before disappearing into a thick clump of bushes.

The sound of a motor drifted into earshot and Rick looked up at the canopy of trees, delighted to see that the covering was so think nobody had any chance to see him.

It was surprisingly light down here, with the real darkness beginning only three or four layers of trees in any direction. He took a deep breath and considered his plan.

In order to get back to the station he had to go right, to follow the gully. If the gully veered off to the left, away from the station, then it must eventually hit the bridge road or at least run within sight of it. And morning couldn't be too far away now – he grimaced involuntarily at the thought: it was already morning, with only the light that was still yet to appear. He looked at his left wrist and saw a thick welt where his watch strap usually sat. He must have lost it on the way down.

He looked up again in the hope that maybe he would see the first telltale signs of sunrise but there was only a dark sky overlaid with silhouettes of branches. That and the sound of a distant motor, quickly joined by a second, like a pair of dogs growling in annoyance that their prey had gone to ground.

He leaned over to his right, resting his weak arm, and levered himself to a kneeling position. It was uncomfortable but not impossible. He pulled his left leg so that the foot was on the ground and pulled himself upright by holding onto a long branch that swept the ground from high up. The branch rustled like a reluctant horse letting its passenger know it had some reservations about carrying him, but eventually he was standing on both feet, albeit crouched over like an old man and shaking at the knees. He let go of the branch and straightened up, waiting for a stab of pain. The stab didn't come.

Rick lifted each leg in turn and rubbed the calf muscles and the ankle, feeling for strains or lumps. Everything seemed to be intact. With a quick look around, he unzipped his pants and took a pee. The sound of the water pooling on the ground was familiar and reassuring. He zipped up, took a deep breath and moved off, carefully at first and then speeding up as he grew used to the terrain. He tried to concentrate on keeping his breathing even and deep, filling his lungs and breathing out, building his stamina and his reserve. Never mind whoever or whatever he might encounter on the way: he would need everything he could muster the time came for him to face Melanie.

(22)

Johnny smacked his head against one of the high cupboards, the one with the door that wouldn't close properly. Everyone in the station knew it didn't close properly but the advantage they usually had was that they could see the damned thing hanging out there, right at head height. Rick had been promising to fit a new magnetic catch switch on it but, like so many little things, it hadn't been done.

He rubbed his head and cursed.

"Damned thing could've put my fucking eye out."

Thuuuum! Thuuuum!

More thuds echoed through the station. The visitors were getting impatient.

Mel's voice chimed in and Johnny could hear it now. "Just hold your horses for a second will you?" That meant two things: one was that he was closing the distance and the other was that Mel hadn't yet managed to shift the deadbolt.

He reached across and ran his hand along the wall until he found the light switch and flicked it. The overhead tubes sprang to life, their light flickering on in stages and humming. The hum sounded good.

Johnny reached the end of the corridor and opened the door.

Thuuuum! Thuuuum!

The thuds were louder now and it sounded for all the world as though they were already inside, big feet stomping up the stairs towards him.

"Mel?"

He flicked on the switch for the staircase and started down.

"Yeah? Ah... this goddam bolt!"

"Mel, don't open the door."

There was a pause. "What?"

He rounded the bend in the stairs and started down to the ground floor, taking them two at a time. The darkness ahead looked threatening.

"I said–"

Thuuuum! Thuuuum!

"Jesus Christ, what's the *matter* with those guys! *Will you–*"

"Mel, don't open the fucking door!"

Johnny skidded into the corridor alongside the spare studio downstairs and hit the light switch. As he ran past the studio window he glanced in. Everything looked so normal in there: stacks of CDs – even though the studio had not been used for more than a year – playing decks, microphone. What the hell had happened to the world, and how had it happened in so short a time? Maybe they were all going to wake–

Thuuuum! Thuuuum! Thuuuum!

Then again, maybe they weren't.

He pulled the door open at the end of the corridor and came face to face with Melanie. She was standing between the door that led into the garage and the main door, frowning. Johnny saw fear in her eyes.

He glanced at the bolt and saw that it was almost clear of the housing and her hand was still on it. He stopped and looked at her, raised his arms. "Mel, don't open the door." He felt the indescribable and completely incomprehensible urge to laugh.

Thuuuum! Thuuuum!

"Why not?"

He was ten maybe fifteen yards away from her. If she decided to pull the bolt – he couldn't see whether the key had already been turned but he suspected that it had – then he may not get to her in time.

"Mel, trust me on this, OK?"

"Johnny, you're... you're frightening me."

He took a step forward.

Thuuuum! Thuuuum!

"Mel, I don't mean to frighten you–"

The hell you don't, a tiny voice said in the back of Johnny's head, *you mean to scare her shitless, cos if she opens that fucking door you've got a whole heap of trouble, compadre, and you can take that to the bank.*

"–but I don't think we should open the door until we figure out what they want. That's all I'm saying."

"What they *want*! Jesus Christ, Johnny–" Melanie pulled the bolt and it slipped out of the housing. "–it's Gram and Troy…"

Thuuuum! Thuuuum! the barrage sounded, as though to confirm.

"*… Gram and Troy*!" She nodded to the door. "*Listen* to them! What the hell's the matter with you?"

Melanie reached down to the key as Johnny gave a shrug and walked quickly towards her. *Hey, OK, you're right,* the shrug said. *What* is *the hell matter with me… gee, I dunno, maybe I'm coming down with an attack of anxiety.*

Melanie's face softened when she saw Johnny's apparent resignation. She shook her head, muttering, and turned the key.

Thuuuum!

Johnny leapt forward.

Melanie let go of the key and started to turn the handle.

Thuuuum!

"*Mel!* Get out–"

The throaty growl of an engine slowly grew outside but it sounded like it was coming from above, like a helicopter maybe.

"–of the way!"

Melanie started to turn in shock, letting go of the door handle.

Thuuuum! Thuuu–

But the door was already ajar.

Silence settled on the scene and it settled awkwardly.

Johnny stopped dead, watching the open door and expecting to see it burst fully open, expecting to see Gram and Troy standing there, looking like a cross between the Blues Brothers and a couple of Herman Munster lookalikes, complete with axes and chainsaws.

Melanie looked at the door and then at Johnny, her initial smile faltering a little. "What?"

Johnny waved for her to move back.

Melanie did as she was told but repeated her question. "What?"

Outside, the helicopter was beginning to sound as though it was about to land on the roof.

"What the hell is the matter with you?" Melanie shouted to be heard over the noise. She jerked a finger upwards. "Hear that? We're gonna be rescued and you're behaving paranoid."

Johnny took a faltering step forward and then another.

Maybe he *was* being paranoid. Maybe the guys in town had decided to give them an early Halloween scare, making out they were pod people or something.

Yeah, and maybe you'll win the lottery next week and there's something in your genes that'll mean you live till you're a thousand, the small voice said in Johnny's head, *but don't take* that *to the bank.*

Two more steps took him right up to the door.

Holding his arms straight out, and flattening his hands against the door, he stooped to look out of the peephole.

As he looked, the noise of the engine changed into a thundering crash of splintered stone, fractured metal and breaking glass, coming from directly overhead.

Melanie screamed as dust and fragments of plaster showered down on them. But Johnny didn't turn around. He was too busy looking into the face of Troy Vilawsky. He was standing right up against the other side of the door, pulling off his gloves. Johnny couldn't see Troy's eyes – the dark glasses were still firmly in place, flashy-looking things, wraparound with strange markings – but he knew–

Here come de Lizard Man, the small voice whispered, *and he mighty pissed at all this work he's had to do just to get inside to meet you.*

–that it wasn't the Troy Vilawsky he'd known these past years. Aside from the gut feeling that he had, Troy's face was smashed and bleeding, his shirt stained black, as though someone had pounded his head with a bar–

Or maybe he been pounding his head on something else, the voice chuckled, *like the door, f'rinstance...*

"But the glasses..." Johnny said softly. "They're not even scratched."

"Johnny!"

From upstairs came the sound of things falling over.

Johnny started to push the door forward as gently as he could.

Then, from just to Troy's side, Gram Kramer stepped into view, his arm held out in front of him. Gram's lower jaw was hanging down, the teeth broken and the gums dripping blood. Gram's arm was heading for the gap in the doorway.

Pushing as hard as he could, Johnny shouted, "Mel, get out of the way."

A gloved hand snaked through the gap and around the door, the fingers grasping.

The door hit the arm close to the elbow. Johnny leaned to the side and looked through the peephole. Gram was reaching up with his free hand, holding it palm out ready to push. He didn't seem to be in any pain.

Melanie screamed again.

Something crashed upstairs, something in the corridor leading to the staircase, and fresh clouds of dust fell around them.

Johnny took hold of the door handle and, with his other hand primed to push, he pulled the door off Gram's arm, waited a second until the arm fell a little – it didn't seem to be visibly damaged but at least only one of the fingers was still grasping, and grasping feebly. Then he pushed with all of his might.

The door knocked the arm back out of sight and hit firmly into the jamb.

He turned the key. And slid the deadbolt home.

Outside, something crashed to the ground from upstairs.

Thuuuum! Thuuuum! Thuuuum! Thuuuum!

Melanie was crying. "Johnny... what's happ–"

A crash of breaking glass from upstairs drowned out her question.

Thuuuum! Thuuuum!

Johnny looked out of the peephole and saw Gram and Troy calmly smashing their heads against the door. Pieces of bone and tissue flecked their shirts and hung from their faces, but the expressions showed no pain or fear or anger or even intent. There was just nothing there at all. He turned around and took hold of Melanie's shoulders.

"Mel, we have to get out."

Thuuuum! Thuuuum!

Melanie looked up at him, her face a mask of terror. All she could think of to say was, "Where's Geoff?"

"Mel–"

Thuuuum! Thuuuum!

"Johnnyohjohnnyjohnnyjohnny." She gulped in air. "Where's Geoff? I'm so frightened. Geoffgeoffgeoffgeoffgeoffgeoff–" As she wailed, saliva flecked her anguished mouth in thin strands, the words merging into and even becoming each other, so that her cry was more a mantra of grief and regret and fear than the simple question it had set out to pose. "–geoffgeoffgeo–"

Johnny slapped her hard across the face and, momentarily silenced, she slipped from the grasp of his left hand, sagging to her hands and knees on the floor, where she began to sob.

Thuuuum! Thuuuum!

"Mel."

Johnny looked down the corridor to where the stairs led upstairs – or, more importantly, to where the stairs led down from upstairs – half-expecting to see feet descending slowly towards them.

Thuuuum! Thuuuum!

"Mel," he said, as softly as he could, crouching down in front of her and gently taking hold of her shoulder. "First off, I think that the helicopter or whatever it was has crashed into the station. *Numero deux,* they're inside, and I don't think they're here to rescue us." He held up three fingers in front of her face. "And three, we have to get the hell out of here pronto, yeah?"

Mel continued to sob and Johnny took a look around.

There was a single *Thuuuum!* on the door and then silence, broken only by a solitary rattle of some small object falling to the floor upstairs.

Melanie looked up and wiped her eyes. "He's dead, isn't he?"

"We don't know that, Mel."

She nodded, her eyes blinking their confidence. "I know it, Johnny. I can *feel* it... can feel it *here*." She placed a hand on her left breast.

Johnny didn't say anything.

Melanie looked across at the door. "It's stopped. The noise."

He nodded.

"I think I preferred it to the silence." She shook her head and ran her fingers through her hair. "Who are they, Johnny? What do they want?"

"I don't know. I'm pretty sure they're not who they appear to be – not the folks from town." He thought of Troy and Gram beating their heads to a pulp on the door and managing not to get a single mark on their sunglasses.

Johnny waited a few seconds and then said, "We have to leave the station."

"What if he comes back and we're not here?"

Johnny ignored the fact that Melanie had referred only to Geoff and bit the bullet. "If he's... if *they're* dead, then they won't be coming back," he said. "That's... that's just a simple fact, Mel. But if they are *not* dead – and we don't know that they are – then we don't want for Geoff to have to come back to you being dead. Are you following me here, Melvin?"

She sat back on the floor with her back against the wall and, just for a second, a tiny smile tugged at her mouth the way it always did whenever Johnny called her "Melvin". She nodded and wiped her cheeks and eyes with her hands. "Yes, I'm following you."

He took hold of her hands in his own and pulled Melanie to her feet.

"OK. We need to get the keys to the Dodge – you know where they are?"

"Shit! Did Geoff take them?"

"Why would Geoff take the keys?"

"I don't know. I don't know that he did. I just–"

She looked up the corridor towards the stairs.

"Did you hear that? I thought I heard something."

"Don't worry about that – I'm keeping an ear open for anyone coming down. I think they're busy checking the place out... the studio. And they don't seem to move too fast."

Melanie considered asking what made him say that and thought better of it. "Who put the car away?"

"You or Geoff. I didn't do it, and that leaves only you two."

"Geoff did it. You know, I think they might be in the ignition?"

Johnny shook his head at the questioning lilt of Melanie's statement. "Thinking isn't enough, Mel. We need to have the keys before we go into the garage. Once we're in there, the only way we're coming out–"

Aside from maybe coming out in the Lizard Men's lunch boxes, he thought with an involuntary shudder.

"–is in the Dodge. I don't want to get in there and find I have to sneak back into the station for the fucking car keys – pardon my French."

Johnny raised his hand and shook his head as Melanie was about to speak.

The shuffling sound upstairs had stopped and had been replaced by a constant but strangely gentle and hypnotic droning noise, which seemed to be getting louder. Then the noise turned into a *plunk, plunkplunk–*

They both looked across at the stairs–

–plunk, plunkplunk–

–and watched as Geoff's lucky baseball came into view–

–plunkplunkplunk, plunk–

–tumbling carelessly down towards them, missing stairs occasionally, before–

–plunk, plunk, plunkplunk–

–reaching the corridor in front of them and rolling gently to a halt by the side of the bureau standing against the wall just a few yards away.

"The decision's made for us," Johnny whispered, nodding to the garage door. "We'll chance to luck that the keys are in the ignition."

"And if they're not?"

Johnny shrugged. "Then we're up shit creek without a paddle."

The shuffling had started again, moving along the corridor above, a cumbersome sound apparently without much coordination. Johnny tried not to think about who – or what–

It's the Lizard Men!

–might be making that awkward movement, and just why the movement should sound quite so difficult.

"Hey, I've got an idea."

"What?"

Johnny trotted across to the big bureau standing against the wall next to Geoff's lucky baseball. He took hold of the bureau sides and was delighted when he discovered it was on casters: the thing not only moved easily but soundlessly as well. "The garage door opens inwards," Johnny said as he pulled the bureau along. "We'll stand this right in front of the door and hope it takes them a little time before they figure out where we are."

Melanie frowned. "You're making them sound like first graders," she said.

"Well," Johnny said, puffing as he maneuvered the bureau into place, "it took Geoff's baseball for them to hit on the concept of going down the stairs."

As if on cue, a loud clump rattled on the stairs, followed by another. Then, at the same time, another clump and then another.

"Three of them," Johnny said.

Several more clumps sounded.

Melanie shook her head. "More."

Johnny nodded.

Melanie turned the key in the door to the garage and pushed it open. Then she helped Johnny pull the bureau into place behind them, before gently closing the door again. Just as the door closed to and last vestiges of light faded, Melanie saw shadows coming down the staircase at the end of the corridor. She slipped the key into the lock on the garage side of the door and turned it quietly. The darkness felt good. Safe.

"The bulb is gone in here," Melanie whispered.

She sensed Johnny nodding, sensed his head pressed against the door listening for sounds from the corridor beyond.

"We won't need light to get into the car and we'll get all we need once we're outside."

Melanie felt a thick column of iced water begin around her shoulder blades and travel quickly down the full length of her spine. "Johnny..."

"Mmm?"

"We don't have the remote for the door."

Something in the station, on the other side of the door, had come across Geoff's lucky baseball. His ear pressed against the wood, Johnny listened to it rolling and rolling, rolling and rolling until, at last, it clunked loudly against the door.

Which meant it had rolled under the bureau.

Which might also mean that whoever or whatever had kicked or knocked the ball had seen it. And had possibly seen where it went. And had possibly noticed, above the bureau, the unmistakable outline of a door in the wall.

Johnny hoped that wasn't significant.

(23)

Rick had made slow progress along the gully before branching off to the right up a wide avenue between the trees, as though someone – a long time ago, because the avenue was grassed and heavily cambered – had been considering creating a spur to the road down into Jesman's Bend.

That might have made sense: it would have meant a direct route straight into Dawson, creating a dogleg with the Bend right on the knee-joint. But then maybe it was something else entirely, such as a simple track once used by natives of the area or loggers perhaps.

The track kept narrow for a long time and Rick was nervous about how close the trees were as he passed them. Close enough to touch in some places… or for something to reach out a hand – an ungloved hand – to touch *him*. Or maybe one of the rag dolls he'd left on the road through the mountains all that time ago – seemed like another lifetime – stepping out from behind the tree and–

Hey, asshole, whyn't you come back and finish the job… think there's a couple of bones here seem to be still in one piece…

–giving him a piece of their mind.

Once or twice he thought he saw shapes moving behind the trees, but they were squat shapes and not even remotely human-like – unless the townsfolk had taken to moving around on all fours, which Rick didn't think was necessarily as unlikely as it sounded.

And there were constant engine noises passing overhead, though after a while, particularly as he started to move up towards the road again, the noises seemed to be further back. He presumed the townsfolk – or whatever they were now – were still busy patrolling the lower woods for signs of him. After all, they must surely think that anyone in his or her right mind would not head back to civilization, particularly after the events overlooking the town. And maybe that was his ace in the hole.

Rick wiped his nose and squinted into the gloom.

The trees seemed to be thinning out up ahead, sufficiently so for him to make out a space in the distance which gave onto more trees. That space could simply be a clearing, of course. But it could also be the road.

The big question here, audience, is a two-parter: first part, for ten points – what part of the road, or even which *road, is it? And for tonight's star prize, who or* what *else is watching it?*

Rick walked slowly and stealthily, picking his steps carefully amidst the twigs and bracken. Eventually, he saw that it was indeed a road. He sat down and settled into a cross-legged position, pulling his wet and torn trousers so that they were not touching his leg, and waited.

A dark shape passed overhead, purring softly in a hovering position before banking off to its right across the trees at the other side of the road. Rick couldn't tell what the vehicle was nor could he understand how the occupants could see anything – the car (if it *was* a car) was displaying no lights nor any search beams. A thought struggled to express itself, as though this discovery were in some way significant, but another engine noise caused Rick to flop back prone amidst the trees and the thought – something to do with the absence of light – faded away for a few moments.

When he was satisfied that the engine had moved off, Rick dismissed the thought completely and stood up. He stepped carefully down the slight bank and onto the road.

The pavement felt good under his feet – felt right.

He looked to the right and saw the road bend around, sloping downhill. To Rick's left it went pretty straight and always gently uphill. He'd come back onto the Jesman's Bend road and he had mixed feelings about that. On the one hand it made things a lot easier; on the other, it made him feel more vulnerable. Rick didn't think there would be much if any traffic from the Bend on the road that went straight out from the station and over the bridge. But this one could be different.

He turned around, checking the treetops for the amount of cover they provided and considered moving back into the woods and making his way through the trees. Each way had its advantages and disadvantages. The bottom line was weighing up speed against safety, bearing in mind that being safe wasn't much help if it delayed him to such an extent that everyone in the station was dead by the time he got there.

Clearly a balance between the two was called for.

He would move along the road, keeping a close eye on the woods so that he could duck into the trees at the first sign – visible or audible – of anyone coming along.

"Well, what is it they say about every great journey starting with but a single step?" Rick whispered to the night.

He was answered with a distant hum coming up from the right. Head down, he ran across the road, dived into the bushes – narrowly missing a thick trunk that had been sawn off at around waist height – and rolled beneath swaying fern fronds and bush branches. Holding his breath and not daring to move, he looked between the leaves.

It seemed like only seconds later – so quickly, in fact, that Rick was sure he must have been spotted – that Daryl Engstrom's 1970 tomato-red Plymouth 'Cuda came up the road. Rick knew it was the 'Cuda even though he couldn't make out the color – Daryl's cheesy swinging furry dice hanging from the rear view kind of gave it away. But it wasn't Daryl driving. In fact, Rick couldn't make out who was but the car was full – three men and one woman it looked like, the woman's hair long and tied back in a ponytail.

The three men – one of whom was driving – seemed to be looking straight ahead. The woman, sitting in the front passenger seat, was staring out of the window in what appeared to be a contradictory mixture of intent and disinterest but, just for a second as the car drifted by, her dark glasses faced directly towards Rick's position and he felt the eyes behind those black frames boring into him. He ducked down further, setting a branch to swaying right above where he was laid.

It was Jennifer Bacquirez, one of the Bend's most eligible spinsters: as he crouched, heart beating, Rick idly wondered whether spinsters could be said to eligible in the same that bachelors could. For the briefest instant, it seemed an important consideration and he yearned for the times, so recently ended, when such thoughts were worthwhile. And then the instant was gone.

Rick waited for the car to stop or turn around and head back to his hiding place, but it didn't. The sound of the engine grew fainter until it was gone and the silence flooded in again.

He waited, then raised his head.

The road was deserted again. They hadn't seemed to be looking for him.

Rick got onto his knees and then stood up, shaking from head to foot.

Suddenly, it made sense.

It was the road down into town, which also meant that it was the road heading out to the station. And Daryl Engstrom and his friends *weren't* looking for him – they were heading specifically for the station.

Heading for Melanie and Johnny.

Without another thought, he trotted down onto the pavement, glanced back once and then set off. He would be there in five or maybe ten minutes. And in another few yards, when he rounded the next bend in the road, he could cut across over the old fence, drop down through the trees and come up on the station from a position of cover.

Ten minutes maximum.

He hoped that would be fast enough – and tried hard not to think about exactly what he was supposed to do when he got there.

(24)

Outside of Sally Davis's hotel room, the man she had been watching bent down and thrust his head into the spyhole. The door shook and Sally turned around.

OK, what were the options?

She went to the window and looked out onto the street. Then glanced at her watch. After two o'clock in the morning: there should be cars out there – movement, sound (muted sound, distant sound, but sound certainly) the auditory proof of life. There was none.

Whoa, horse! Strike that last one. A yellow cab just turned the corner of the building, a mere two floors down from where she was, its headlights washing the street independently of each other. Not much in or of itself but, of course, with Sally snugly settled on the eighth floor, two floors down meant six floors up.

It didn't take too much effort to reach the conclusion that whoever was out there in the corridor wasn't normal. They didn't speak – that was the first thing. And when Sally thought back to the slack-faced boy with his head on one side, she wasn't even sure he *could* speak. And those dark glasses? There was no sunshine. OK, they could be musicians or celebrities – that would make the kid some kind of dwarf, of course – but dark glasses in a darkened hotel corridor? Nope. It didn't compute. And she decided that they were not trying to get into the room to offer her extra nights free of charge.

Are we going to hide, mommy?

She looked around the suite and assessed what was available to her. She could hide behind the shower curtain – not ideal. In the closet – even more not ideal. She remembered Jamie Lee Curtis in *Halloween*

Is he the bogeyman, mommy? The man smashing his head against our door?

–and checked the beds: no room to slide a newspaper under those.

The door rattled some more. And now she heard the sound of a motor. She decided that she didn't want to go back to the spyhole. While she couldn't see them, they were far away and she wanted to keep them like that. Just like that.

A thought was forming at the back of her mind and she didn't like it. Didn't like it one bit.

She considered shouting through the door to them, telling them to go away, or maybe making a growling sound like a dog. It wouldn't hurt – they knew she was here. Well, maybe so, but they hadn't had any proof. Perhaps if she just stonewalled it then they'd go away and beat on somebody else's door.

The door rattled again, three times in succession. Either they'd got reinforcements or something bigger was attacking the door. No, they weren't going to go away.

Sally checked the windows, half-imagining Gerry sitting on the bed behind her, hands still smelling of gunpowder, top and left back of his head blown away, shaking what was left and about to ask her if she wanted him to help. Things were looking slightly up – there was a ledge around the hotel right outside her window. Her luck was staying in. Then she looked up and saw exactly the same ledge running around the building on the next floor. Well, so what.

The noise behind her, from the door, did not sound good. It was the unmistakable sound of splintering. Any minute now and the boy and the black man, plus whoever else they'd got out there, would be in the room, and they'd get whatever it was they wanted. Well, she preferred not to think of that, putting it just barely in front of who or what they were and where they were from. "Not from around here," she muttered. She watched the tail lights of the yellow cab growing smaller as it turned into Broadway. It was joined by another car, a dark color, exactly the same height from the ground.

Sally refocused her attention on the windows.

The windows were two-pane side-sliders – the inside pane slid to the left and hit a stop, and the outside pane slid to the right and hit a stop. As far as Sally could see it wasn't possible to crawl out of the window.

She looked around for a tool – there wasn't one.

What there was, however, was a brace of beautiful carved Queen Anne chairs, upholstered in Regency stripe and polished until you could see your reflection. Sally took a hold of the back of one and, amazed at her own strength, swung it for all she was worth against the wall-corner. The chair broke immediately, falling to the ground in pieces: the back (with rear legs an integral part), the seat – with one front leg still attached – and the other front leg by itself. Sally picked the solo front leg and hefted it a couple of times. She turned to face the door.

OK, what was it to be? Stand here and face them down? Or attempt to dislodge the window blocks and crawl out onto the ledge? She'd be OK so long as she didn't look down. It wasn't windy. These sounded distinctly like famous last words so she put them from her mind.

The staccato rhythm on the door was drums, beating from somewhere over an impossibly high ravine, way, way across the jungle. She faced forward, watching the windows of the buildings across the street with calm fascination, half expecting to see someone watching her, someone who would lift a hand to his or her mouth, wave to her to cease and desist at once, turn back, mouthing dire warnings as he or she glanced down at the chasm below, before looking back, eyes wide in horror as he or she reached for a telephone and feverishly punched in a nine and a one and then another one, then explained to the person on the other end of the line that some fruitcake was about to step out onto the ledge of the Brown Palace and could someone come quick?

But there wasn't anyone in the windows.

Sally raised a knee, her left knee, and raised herself up onto the sill.

(25)

"Now what?"

"Now," Johnny whispered, matter-of-factly, "we get in the car and see if the keys are in the ignition."

Melanie nodded. "Good plan, Captain."

"It's always good to have a good plan."

"They're the best kind."

"Uh huh."

"Johnny?"

"Yeah?"

"Are you scared?"

Johnny couldn't stop the smile. "Constipation seems like a luxury right now. Like, mightily desirable."

He moved silently and slowly along the side of the Dodge to the driver's door and took hold of the handle.

"Can you see them, the keys?"

He turned around from trying to stare through the window. "Can you see me, Mel?"

"Nope. I can tell where you are, but I can't actually see you."

"Right. So how do you think I can see the fucking keys inside the car, in the ignition, hidden behind the steering wheel?" He hoped she hadn't realized that he was actually pressed against the glass trying to find out for himself.

"Sorry."

"No, *I'm* sorry. I didn't mean to snap."

"S'OK."

"I have to open the door."

"Well, we always knew we'd have to do that."

"True. But now that it's come to it, I can't help wondering whether we should just sit tight and hope that everyone goes."

Melanie's voice sounded disconsolate in the darkness of the garage. "Not much chance of that, I fear."

"I fear your fear is well-founded, Lady Melvin," Johnny agreed.

And he pulled the handle.

The Dodge's interior light glimmered until he pulled the door fully open, and then it shone as bright as a lighthouse beacon. He leaned on the seat and shuffled his shoulders across.

"The keys are here."

Melanie threw back her head and thanked whatever gods were in charge of giving suckers an occasional even break.

Johnny shuffled around a little. Melanie heard the lid of the glove compartment open and close, and then things being moved around in the small recess which straddled the transmission – sunglasses, packs of gum, biro pens. She knew what he was looking for, watched his back moving around intent on searching.

"Is it there?"

Johnny backed out of the car and closed the door gently. The darkness was immediate and absolute. He pulled it ajar again and the light returned, quelling the sudden flurry of panic in Melanie's chest.

"Can't see it if it is." He stood up and moved back to where Melanie was standing. "Where would he put it?"

She shrugged and then said, "Christ, it's anyone's guess."

"Here? In the garage?" She looked around at the clutter of forgotten and stored items hanging from the center beam or propped against the walls.

"I– I wouldn't have thought so."

Johnny let out a deep sigh.

"Sorry."

Johnny looked into her eyes and smiled. "It'll be OK."

"Will it?" she asked pleadingly.

He let the question hang and said, "I have to go back."

"Into the station?"

"What else can I do?"

"Can't we... can't we ram the door?"

"Oh, sure... but it won't give. It might, after a few dozen attempts – assuming we don't damage something under the hood, or chew the wheel arches up so's they ride on the tires." He walked to a chest of drawers standing in the corner and rummaged about in the cans and glasses of paint, each one boasting an abandoned brush standing to attention, its bristles long ago hardened. "The thing is, what'll they be doing while we're doing that?"

"Well, we have to–"

It was an easy thing to do. And normally, it wouldn't have mattered.

But, of course, this time it did.

Johnny was reaching for what looked like a piece of plastic that could have been the remote control for the door mechanism.

But it wasn't.

And nor was the goofy-looking cross-eyed reindeer standing on the shelf below, the shelf against which Johnny's flapping shirt sleeve brushed. The forgotten Christmas decoration slid drunkenly to one side, Johnny's eyes widening as he saw what was happening and–

"Johnny!"

–it lurched fully over, rolled the few inches to the shelf's edge and, even as Johnny shot out his free hand, dropped.

Johnny's hand missed, hit a can of America's Finest gloss paint that Geoff had used to paint the sills outside the studio a couple springs ago, which in turn knocked over a bottle.

The reindeer hit the floor with hardly a sound.

The bottle didn't.

Johnny cringed at the sound of breaking glass and the additional, almost musical–

Hey viewers, what sounds like a bell and smells like shit?

–duuh-uuh-uuhung! as it bounced first onto the metal tub containing cloths and a vicious-looking tangle of old clothes that Geoff and Melanie had either grown out of or which had been left behind by the fickle whims of fashion, and then onto the floor.

The silence which followed that seemingly endless reverberation was pure and, in and of itself, a noise all of its own. And it was perhaps *that* noise – the calm that trailed in the wake of the storm – that drew the most attention.

"Shit!" Melanie said.

It was a lot more appropriate than some idiotic question like, *D'you think they heard?* – particularly as that question was answered almost immediately.

Thuuuum! Thuuuum!

"Shitshitshitshi–"

"Shh," Johnny hissed. "If we can't get out, then they can't get in. The garage door's metal, for Chrissakes."

And then somebody started to move the bureau from the station door behind them.

"That one isn't," Melanie said without a single trace of emotion.

(26)

Sally's voices chorused. They were scared, but Sally sought to calm them, to reassure them. They did not become calm. They were not reassured.

The metal ridge bit into the soft skin beneath her kneecap but when she raised her second leg up and rested that knee on the sill, the pain eased. She hunkered up with both feet on the sill and gingerly placed a foot out onto the ledge. It was cool out here, not too cold and not too warm. Refreshing, under any other circumstances.

Now the noise against the room door behind her was deafening.

Sally eased her second foot out onto the ledge, trying to ignore the flurry of nervous questioning from the ever-present voices.

"Dontlookdowndontlookdowndontlookdowndontlookdown..." she told them, and herself, in a whispered litany.

Holding tightly onto either side of the outer pane, Sally slowly moved herself fully out onto the ledge, equally slowly straightening her legs to allow her to achieve a standing position. She kept watching the building opposite, thinking that if she saw movement now she would plunge forward.

She recalled a one page six-panel cartoon strip in Gerry's *Mad* magazine from many years ago. Entitled "Self Portrait", the strip showed a beatnik type arrive outside the Empire State Building with a framed blank canvas which he laid on the sidewalk. The remaining panels showed him going up in the elevator to the top floor and jumping out so that he landed right in the middle of the canvas. It seemed darkly amusing back then; not so amusing now.

The wind gently blew her hair and cooled the droplets of sweat on her forehead.

Close the window, mommy, one of the voices insisted.

It seemed like an unnecessary effort – when they got into the suite (which she was absolutely damned certain they would, and fairly soon) they would quickly deduce that she had to have left by another exit, and the only other exit was the window.

No, they won't think so logically, the voice countered.

On reflection, that seemed like a reasonable assumption. After all, the two people in the hall – plus however many others had arrived since she last looked through the spyhole – had hardly displayed profound levels of intellect. In fact, far from it. It was more as though everything they encountered was completely alien to them, and the simple act of logic-streaming was something of which they had no experience.

Alien, she thought.

That's what they are, mommy – they look human but they're not. You need to close the window and get out of sight.

"Alien," she said to the night.

She let go of the pane and, keeping her head, back and neck ramrod straight, and her backside pressed against the glass, outstretched her arms as though she were about to fly from the ledge and began to shuffle her feet sideways, turning herself around to face the glass. As she moved around, trying not to snivel, she noted in that kind of absentminded way one notes things of complete non-importance, that her pants felt wet – she wished briefly that she had gone to the bathroom before embarking on this route, but it was too late now. It was too late now for a lot of things.

Sally managed to get around in hardly any time at all and she now faced the window, her face pressed against the glass and her arms still stretched out to either side, palms flat against the wall on either side of the panes. The door was holding but she could see it moving with each hit it suffered. The noise now was an endless stream of crashes and she noticed that the carpet immediately in front of the two sides was sprinkled with wood dust and shavings.

Keeping her face against the outer pane, Sally reached in and pushed the inner pane until it secured into the slot. Then, still holding her face against the outer pane, she pushed it gently across using the palms of her hands. At least it hadn't been raining – meaning her hands would probably not have been able to gain any purchase – so Sally thanked God for small mercies. In just a few seconds, the outer pane slid into the metal slot down the right hand side of the window and Sally straightened up again. Now came the tricky bit: she had to edge her way along to her right and thus away from the window. A sudden ping against the inner pane made her lean back just for a moment. Immediately realizing the folly of such a movement, she thrust herself back against the glass, heart beating so wildly that she imagined the people out in the corridor would be able to hear.

When it seemed that she was steady again, Sally eased herself straight and saw a twisted screw on the sill inside the room. She looked up and saw that the door was now drunkenly weaving and waving, its top hinge completely free of the jamb. She could see a pair of arms flailing at the top of the door on the hall side but, thankfully, no faces. If she could see faces then it followed that the faces could see her. In which case, she would simply have been sidestepping the inevitable outcome. Of course, if they were not as stupid as she hoped – and as her phantom progeny had assured her they were – then she was doing that anyway.

Somewhere off behind her, an engine hummed. Sally dared not turn around – not least because she felt she would probably fall – mainly because, after all of this, she could not bear to face up to a flying yellow cab hovering right next to her, with its driver, complete with dark glasses and gloves, waving a finger at her – *Naughty naughty!* – but whatever it was, the vehicle passed by, its engine becoming more and more muted until it disappeared completely. That made sense. From what she had seen of the other two airborne cars, they were looking for something down on street level and, clinging onto the side of a building eight floors up, Sally was hardly that.

The door was buckling now. She had to move fast.

She edged along the ledge, suddenly delighted to discover that the glass had gone from in front of her to be replaced by brickwork. Encouraged by this, she moved faster until, within just a few seconds, her left hand left the pane behind and itself moved onto the brickwork. No sooner had she edged just another few inches than there sounded an almighty crashing from the window she had just left behind. They were into the suite.

Sally imagined the boy with the sunglasses slouching across to the window and looking out, his eyes suddenly focusing on the smashed catches, the wrecked leg of the delightfully ornate Queen Anne chair, and then he would raise a gloved hand, or perhaps two gloved hands, and he would ease open the windows, peer out (though only if he were able to stand on something, she remembered) and look first one way (where she wasn't) and then the other (where she was). And soon after that there would be hell to pay, maybe with the people coming out onto the ledge – she didn't think they would be worried about falling: she wouldn't have been able to say why, she just felt that way – or maybe with a whole posse of flying cars and trucks crowding her in and, eventually, nudging her from her ledge.

Sally remembered that terrible photograph soon after 9/11 – the one showing a man who had voluntarily leapt from one of the twin towers of the World Trade Center to plunge to certain death many stories below, his arms outstretched before him as he plummeted to an unforgiving sidewalk, legs pumping as though to slow him down (or hasten the descent), necktie blowing in the wind. What did it feel like? she wondered, that sudden cessation of motion when the body and all its myriad organs and arteries, bones and muscles, was pulverized. The face, smashing into the paving slabs, the brain going from thirty-two feet per second per second to a stationary state – and a stationary state brought on by a gazillion tons of planet that just wasn't ever going to budge, or even shudder, when you hit it.

Turning her head the other way – making sure she didn't look down and so scraping her nose on the bricks in the process – Sally saw that she was about twenty feet from the corner of the building. She could only hope that the ledge continued around the other side. There was no reason why it shouldn't, of course, but it seemed just the kind of capricious trick that might be played by gods who would have you watch the ghost of your husband blow his brains out while mouthing to you that he had never loved you.

She edged along, right foot exploring first, tapping the ledge every few inches to make sure it was there and that it was secure, placing that foot down and then sliding along the wall and dragging her left foot after. The noise from the room had either ceased or she had gotten too far from the window to be able to hear it.

Then, just as she was nearing the corner – her fingers actually curling themselves around the brickwork – a vintage car, two-tone, all polished chrome and tailfins, drifted around just below her and she stopped dead. She caught sight of a woman wearing a white blouse, or maybe a cream one, Sally couldn't be sure, her head turned to look out of her side window at the ground. The car's headlights had been pulled out of their frames and were somehow suspended on some kind of concertinaed latticework of metal, and they worked independently of each other, one of them scanning the side of the building that Sally was clinging to (albeit a few floors down from where she was) and the other washing over a covered eating area on the opposite sidewalk. The woman was wearing dark glasses – Sally couldn't see whether she had gloves on – and, just for a moment, Sally fully expected her to look up and–

Well, now, what do we have here?

–do a turn and maybe drift upwards a couple of floors hell-bent on giving her a little nudge behind the knees.

She waited until the car went fully by, sounding as soft and smooth as her mother's old Singer sowing machine, barely ticking over. As it moved along, the woman must have let her attention lapse a little because the car veered a little too close to the next building along: there was a dull crunch and Sally watched as the car straightened up, moving slightly away from the building, and pieces of concrete dropped down onto the street in a flurry of noise and dust, and, seconds later, the car was gone, having turned down one of the side streets up ahead.

(27)

The first thing Rick noticed was the trunk of Daryl Engstrom's 1970 tomato-red Plymouth 'Cuda hanging out of the upper floor side of the station. If the situation had not been so difficult, the scene might have been comical, the car stuck onto the building's roof like a huge boil or an unsightly canker on the side of a favorite tree.

Rick had come up on the station from the woods, with the building taking shape from the top down behind the trees, etched against the steadily lightening eastern sky like an apocalyptic drawing sketched perhaps after the very same tornado that had taken Dorothy and Toto from the safety of Kansas to the harsh landscape of Oz had hit twenty-first century Jesman's Bend and the immediate area.

He sidled his way between trees and bushes, being careful to avoid disturbing the foliage. As the concrete aproned entrance and the adjoining garage door came into view he was glad of his stealth.

There were about half a dozen of them shuffling around at the main doorway into the station.

Two more – one of whom was Troy and the other Rick didn't... no, it was Gram Kramer – were wandering across to the garage door. Troy seemed to have been in some kind of accident – Gram, too, he saw. It was clear even from where Rick crouched that the heads and shirt fronts of Jesman's Bend's favorite deputy and gas jockey were covered in blood. Had there been some kind of fight? And if so, had it happened in town or here at the station? Rick feared that the latter was the most likely – he couldn't imagine the townsfolk beating each other up, and certainly not to the extent that Troy had been beaten.

A loud creak sounded from above the throng and Rick looked up in time to see Jennifer Bacquirez push open the 'Cuda's warped door and start to get out of the car. He felt a sudden urge to shout and tell her–

Hey, Jenny, don't do that!

–that the particular section of Daryl Engstrom's pride and joy she was struggling to exit was suspended some fifteen feet or more above solid concrete. Nobody else seemed to be paying any attention.

In fact, Troy was now apparently concentrating on the garage door, his head tilted to one side. He was listening for something.

A dull thudding crack snapped out as Jennifer Bacquirez fell to the concrete. Nobody turned around.

Gram Kramer wandered over to stand beside Troy and the pair of them started banging their heads–

Thuuuum! Thuuuum!

–against the garage door.

Now Rick understood where the blood had come from. He looked across at the station door and saw the dark stains – he knew what those stains were.

Gram lifted his arms and slammed them against the garage door, thrust his head forward and rammed it. Troy did the same.

On the concrete apron, the prone figure of Jennifer Bacquirez struggled to right herself. She was lying on her back, one leg doubled up beneath her and the other one – her left – thrashing up and down. She looked for all the world like an upturned insect trying to turn itself over.

Rick watched others from the group wander across to the garage where Troy and Gram had built up an obtuse rhythm. Sally Pennington and Grace Sheffield joined them and commenced to provide a counter-beat. Nobody was saying anything – stranger still, nobody was screaming at the pain they were inflicting on themselves. The same went for the smashed Jennifer Bacquirez, who still flapped arms and single leg from the concrete, groping around for some means of support. She was still wearing her dark glasses. And her gloves.

Rick glanced around at each member of the group. All had on their dark glasses and all were wearing gloves.

Now there were four of them banging away at the garage door with various parts of their anatomy. One thing above all else was starting to worry Rick: and that was the fact that, slowly and surely, their movement seemed to be improving.

Back at the spot where he and Geoff had been watching the people from town, their coordination had been more stilted. What he was watching now was still a far cry from complete coordination, but it was drastically improved and more fluid. Rick didn't think that was a good sign.

A loud crash sounded from inside the station.

Troy and Gram stopped their beating and tilted their heads until two more crashes rang out. Then they recommenced.

More crashes came from inside the garage. The activity could mean only one thing: Johnny and Melanie were inside the garage. The trick was how to get them out.

Then there was a loud shout and the sound of things falling and breaking, and a high-pitched scream which turned into Johnny's name. That was followed by more smashing.

A single clunk from the garage door stopped Troy and Gram and their activity once again, this time inspiring them to stagger backwards and stare at the door. It had moved. That meant that Johnny and Mel–

Rick looked across to his left and saw Jennifer Bacquirez holding something in the air. She had shuffled her way around so that she now lay on her side.

Sally Pennington and Grace Sheffield turned around and looked at Jennifer without Jennifer having said anything. Troy looked as well, and Gram. Jennifer moved the object in her hand towards her until she was holding it right in front of her glasses. She shook the thing, shook it harder, then tapped it – surprisingly gently – on the concrete. Then she switched hands, like a baby trying to figure out how her favorite toy worked, and–

clunk, rackerrackerrack–

–the door moved again.

Sammy Lescombe emerged soundlessly from the bushes over to Rick's right. Everyone turned to face him without Sammy having said anything. He was carrying an armful of thick branches which he proceeded to hand out to the people at the garage door. Now Gram walked up to the door and, with what appeared to be a superhuman effort, brought his arm back and swung his branch – a thick piece of tree bole – forward to crash against the door. It made a loud reverberation. There was a shrill scream from the other side of the door, followed by a chorus of crashes.

Troy followed Gram's example with his own stick.

Jennifer took hold of the object in both hands, held it steady and–

Clunk, rackerrackerrackerrackerracker!

–pressed.

The garage door was moving upwards.

Troy and Gram, Sally, Grace and Sammy shuffled forward, holding their branches menacingly.

It was now or never.

Rick burst from the bushes and headed for Jennifer and the remote.

Abby Buchanan stepped from the shadows of the station doorway even before Rick was onto the concrete, striding her legs by swinging them out and forward, like the knees were locked and wouldn't bend. She lifted her arms out in front of her and started pulling off her gloves.

On the floor, Jennifer Bacquirez stopped waving her arm around and turned her head to face in Rick's direction. Rick noticed that the banging on the garage door had stopped.

He reached where Jennifer was lying and stopped to glance back at the garage door. Troy had moved away from the door and was walking in Rick's direction. His movements seemed a little stiff but generally OK, certainly a lot better than the movements Rick had seen back at the clearing just a couple of hours ago.

Troy hefted his branch and did a trial swing with it. There looked to be a lot of power in those arms, and Rick didn't want to be anywhere near.

Gram stepped over near the door and just stood there like a sentry on guard duty, his own branch resting in his arms like it was a rifle. Sally, Grace and Sammy fanned out into a horseshoe configuration making it so there was no way Rick could get to the garage door without encountering at least one of them. Sally removed her gloves and dropped them onto the floor. Grace did the same.

When Rick looked back he saw that Jennifer had pulled off one of her own gloves and was reaching the bare hand out towards Rick's leg. He kicked at the hand, felt it connect and watched her arm fly backwards behind her head. It was only a momentary retreat, though. Meanwhile, Abby Buchanan was shuffling her way to cover Jennifer's back.

Rick looked down and saw that Jennifer had switched the remote into her other hand, the one whose arm was pinned beneath her. She was holding the remote close to her chest – Rick saw the swell of her breasts, the slight point on the nipples, and realized that Jennifer was not wearing a brassiere. In any other circumstances, such a revelation would have prompted other thoughts, a drying up of saliva, maybe even an exploratory movement from behind his pants zipper. But now it didn't do diddly. He pulled back his foot again and kicked Jennifer in the face. Rick didn't pause to check the damage he had done – Jennifer had rolled over fully onto her back and old Abby was getting too close for comfort. He bent down, retrieved the remote which was now held very loosely, and turned around – just in time to see Troy making his swing.

How the hell had he gotten over here so fast?

Rick dodged backwards and sidestepped back towards the bushes.

Troy swung his branch – Rick heard it funneling the wind right in front of him – and adjusted his direction.

Abby had stopped to help pull Jennifer to her feet but as soon as she moved away the temporarily erect siren of Jesman's Bend slipped sideways on her ruined right leg and landed back on the ground. Abby paid her no more heed.

Rick looked across at the garage door, back to the side at the steadily-advancing Abby and then at Troy. There was nothing else for it. He needed something – anything – that he could use as a weapon and the only thing he could see was Troy's branch.

He slipped the remote in his trouser pocket and made like he was going to tackle Troy. The deputy swung the branch but Rick had already stopped. As the branch flew by, Rick jumped forward and slammed into Troy's belly, his head tucked down so that it crunched into deputy's chest.

They both flailed backwards a couple of steps and fell onto the floor before Troy could get his branch back in action.

Abby adjusted her direction and shifted around.

Sally and Sammy started forward from the garage door.

Rick pulled at the branch but Troy held it up over his head with one arm. He wrapped the other around Rick's back.

The hold was like a vice. Rick couldn't move. And there was the strangest smell coming from the deputy – a staleness, like old clothes that needed a wash or flowers that had been left too long in a vase whose water had evaporated in the heat.

Rick tried to push himself up but couldn't break Troy's hold.

Eventually, his left hand hit something solid amidst the cold shirt. Troy's holster. And in Troy's holster was–

Rick pulled the gun and jammed it into the deputy's side.

Abby was now just a few yards away.

In the other direction, Sammy and Sally were holding out their arms expectantly, stumbling forward, reaching for him.

Rick tried to pull the trigger but it wouldn't move.

Safety catch!

He snuggled in tighter to Troy's belly so that he could get his other hand around to the gun. If only he knew something about these things but he didn't. He arched his back, trying to make his middle narrower so that Troy's bone-crushing hold wouldn't be so intense.

Melanie's voice screamed from the garage, Johnny's name.

Rick found the catch on the gun, fumbled with it until it moved and then pushed it all the way.

Something dropped in the garage, echoing in the gloom.

Rick pulled the trigger.

A muffled explosion cut through the early-morning air.

Troy lurched and, from somewhere deep inside of the deputy's stomach, Rick heard a groan.

The hold relaxed, but only a little.

Sammy and Sally were now only a few yards away, their hands bare and clawing at the air greedily.

Rick pushed himself and the arm loosened still more. He pulled his arm from the side of Troy's belly and held the gun with both hands, pointing the barrel into the deputy's gut. "This is for Geoff," he whispered. The gun exploded and threw him backwards.

Something brushed his shoulder as he bounced back onto the ground. Right in front of him, old Abby was bent over reaching down to where he had been. He lifted the gun, both hands again, and fired into the old woman's back. She lurched forward, arms outstretched, and landed on top of Troy.

Rick rolled over and jumped to his feet. He looked down at the gun – three shots. He had fired three shots – which meant, how many were left? Three? Was it a six-shooter? He felt like an old-time gunfighter.

Over to his right, Sammy Lescombe moved to one side, covering Rick in case he ran wide back to the safety of the trees.

Sally Pennington widened her arms like she was about to try taking off.

Rick lifted the gun and fired at her.

The shot went wide.

He staggered forward, holding onto his back with his left hand, and held the gun as steady as he could in front of him. He pulled the trigger and Sally lifted from her feet and hit the ground skidding.

Rick started to run, the remote suddenly in his left hand, the gun still held in his right, heading for the garage door and for Grace Sheffield, standing with her arms held out to greet him.

Sally rolled over onto her side and tried to stand up. Blood was streaming down the front of her dress, running down the folds and onto her legs.

Sammy Lescombe turned around and started to close the gap between himself and Rick.

"Melanie!" Rick screamed. "I'm coming!"

(28)

The muted shuffling around the door leading back into the station was suddenly replaced by a loud crash.

"Oh, wonderful!" Johnny said. "They know we're in here."

There were two more crashes.

"And they're not using their hands," Melanie added. "They're trying to smash it down with something."

Johnny pulled open the Dodge's door so that they had some light. He pointed to one of the four inlaid wooden panels: it had splintered, a thick shard of wood bellying out at a right angle to the door. "And they're doing a good job."

"What do we do?"

"Fight for it?"

"How?"

Johnny walked across to the door and took hold of the key. "We open the door and–"

Another crash drowned out his words.

"And we charge them."

"We don't know how many there are out there."

Johnny nodded. He looked back at the car and then at the door.

Crash! Crash!

When he looked back at the door into the station, he saw the unshaven face of Daryl Engstrom peering through a wide crack in the left hand panel. The face pulled back and another crash took out the panel completely, the wood flying past Melanie's head and bouncing onto the Dodge's trunk.

"There's not much choice," he said. "There's no way out through the garage door, not without the remote. Got to do it before they have a chance to think about it."

Johnny breathed in deeply, smiling at Melanie's outstretched hand as she grabbed his arm. Melanie loosened her grip and patted his arm.

Johnny took hold of the key and turned it gently, making sure there was no noise. Then, with his hand on the handle, he pulled the door wide open.

There were three of them, Daryl Engstrom at the front with Jimmy James Poskett and little Elsie Weebershand flanking him. The most striking thing about them – aside from the fact that they were all holding either pieces of broken up chair or, in Daryl's case, the metal hat stand christened "Bullwinkle" by Rick – was the entire lack of anything even resembling personality on their faces.

Daryl's stubbly chin was thrust before him in a manner of confrontation but there was no other sign of aggression, though Rick couldn't see his eyes. The thin-lipped mouth was clamped shut – even though Daryl should have been surprised, shocked even, by Johnny's sudden appearance – and Daryl's hair, a thick thatch of wheat that was graying slightly around the ears, was unkempt and hanging over his forehead.

"Daryl, what's goin–"

Jesman's Bend's brawny odd-jobber cut off the pleading question with a two-handed swipe of the hat stand into Johnny's shoulder that sent him staggering backwards through the doorway. Daryl swung the hat stand back and stepped forward. Elsie Weebershand, fourteen years old and, Johnny knew, sporting a silver brace behind that cold and tight-lipped half-smile, sidled through at the same time, brandishing what the dazed Johnny quickly recognized as a chair leg from the studio. The leg came down on Johnny's shin and he heard rather than felt a dull crack: the pain came a few seconds later, washing up his leg like flood water.

Melanie grabbed a shovel from the wall, dislodging a metal watering can which rattled onto the floor nearly deafening her. She leapt forward as the small girl, very small for her years, was pulling back for another swipe. The metal end of the shovel struck Elsie full in the chest, momentarily pinning her against the door jamb before Melanie's forward momentum sent her back through the doorway. Melanie swung around and hit Daryl in the cheek but it was only a glancing blow. Daryl hefted the hat stand forward, an over-the-head thrust like he was hammering stakes into the ground. The hat stand hit the top of the doorway and he lost grip with one hand which flew forward clenched into a half-fist.

Johnny groaned from the floor. "Oh, Jesus Christ!"

From somewhere behind them – maybe in another county or an alternative universe, Melanie thought – the familiar clunk of the garage door opening joined the confusion and then stopped.

Melanie tried to ignore the fact that–

Oh, great, now they're coming in behind *us.*

–the garage door was opening. She swung the shovel back and slapped it onto the top of Daryl's head but it barely caught his skull and, instead, raked the side of his head and thudded ineffectively on the big man's shoulder. When she pulled the shovel back to try again, Melanie saw that Daryl's right ear was partly severed, blood dripping down the side of his head onto his pale blue collarless shirt.

As Daryl staggered, losing hold of the hat stand which clattered to the floor, Jimmy James Poskett powered through and swung Geoff's baseball bat, the tip connecting with Melanie's elbow and continuing until it reached little Elsie Weebershand's face. Blood and bits of what could only be bone – plus Elsie's teeth brace – skittered across the floor and sprayed the door jamb and a cabinet containing screws and nails, all in neat little jars, which Geoff kept just inside the garage. Elsie dropped her chair leg and fell backwards, arms pinwheeling, until she hit the floor.

Melanie jabbed the shovel forward, grunting, and smiled when it sank into Jimmy James's neck. The shovel took him back, pushing Daryl back fully into the station even as he tried to reach the hat stand. Melanie pulled back and jabbed forward again, the curve of the shovel lodging itself in Jimmy James's eyes snapping the intricate and expensive-looking shades. The glasses fell to the floor and Jimmy James dropped the baseball bat and threw up his hands, trying to cover his eyes, but catching a shard of thick, black glass that was lodged at the bridge of his nose and pushing it deep into the left socket.

Melanie closed her own eyes and held back the bile.

The garage door started to move again.

She span around. "Johnny... the door!"

"I– I know," Johnny grunted. "Can't move. My leg..."

Melanie turned back and, grunting, swung the shovel at Daryl who was pushing his way into the garage. The shovel caught him fully in the stomach. The big man staggered backwards, turning in an attempt to remain upright, and fell over the crouched figure of Jimmy James – still fumbling with his ruined eye socket – who, in turn, tottered over the prone body of little Elsie Weebershand.

There was a loud *crack*, like a car backfiring and someone was screaming but Melanie ignored the noise, only distantly aware in another part of herself that it was coming from her own mouth.

She stepped forward and brought the shovel down on the back of Daryl's head, lifted it, and swung it across and at an angle, catching the back of Daryl's neck. The blade of the shovel dug into the flesh and jarred on the spinal column. Daryl's dark glasses tumbled from his face onto the floor and, although seemingly oblivious to the damage, exposed tendons and cartilage in his neck, he lifted his hands to his face even as it connected with the floor.

From behind her came another *crack*, but it wasn't a car backfiring. She knew that now. It was a gunshot. Then another. And another.

She shifted the shovel to her right hand and picked up her husband's baseball bat with the left. Then she dropped the shovel and hefted the bat in both hands. It felt good. It had been a long time since she and Geoff had played softball but it was coming back to her. She took a few practice swings, keeping an eye on the trio twitching on the floor in front of her. Daryl lifted himself up and turned his head towards her, and blinked.

The two red blobs where pupil and iris should be were not like anything she had ever seen before – at least nothing that didn't appear in a movie theater. Daryl shifted himself to one side, with no grunt or sign of exertion, and he started to pull off one of his gloves. Jimmy James lay where he had fallen, moving his head from side to side. Little Elsie Weebershand didn't appear to be moving at all.

"Mel…"

Ignoring Johnny's call she took an image of exactly where Daryl's head was, closed her eyes and swung the bat as hard as she could. In her imagination, she heard a pumpkin split open, pieces of it hitting the corridor walls. Seconds later came the unmistakable sound of something falling to the floor. She turned around and opened her eyes.

Johnny was pointing at the door.

"I know… it moved. I heard it. Gunshots. The cavalry must be on its way." She moved over to where Johnny lay on the floor next to the Dodge and crouched down beside him. "You OK?"

He shook his head. "Leg… hurts like hell."

"Can you move?"

He laughed without humor. "Well, there's no way I'm staying here."

"Melanie!" a voice screamed from outside. "I'm coming!"

The door started to move upwards.

Melanie turned to watch it, a smile breaking out on her face. She ran to the door, holding her hands on the metal as it slid upwards. "Geoff? Geoff, I'm OK."

Outside the garage, Rick stopped dead in his tracks.

Melanie's voice… he 'd heard it. But she was shouting for Geoff. How was he going to tell her? Grace Sheffield ambled from side to side, moving her legs up and down like pistons, her gloves on the floor by her feet. She raised her arms and opened them towards him.

Over to Rick's right, Sammy Lescombe was still moving forward with just a few yards to cover before those welcoming arms and hands would reach him.

Rick tilted his head and listened to the wind. There was a sound on it – no, more than one sound – there were *several* sounds riding the breeze. Engines.

He looked up and saw the sky lightening to the east.

He looked back at the road that wound down first to the bridge and then on into town. Engines were coming but they weren't coming up the road. He lifted his head and watched the treetops. They were coming up there.

There wasn't much time.

Rick turned to Sammy Lescombe – the same Sammy Lescombe that he'd bought provisions from and talked baseball statistics and chewed the fat about the weather – steadied his hands and aimed for his chest. The bullet took off the right side of Sammy's head, his dark glasses with it. Sammy shuddered, took a step or two back, and then three wavering steps to the side, his right leg buckling as though about to give way. Then he fell forward, stiff as a board, arms still outstretched, and didn't move.

Rick stepped forward and picked up Sammy's branch, hefted it to test the weight. Then he turned to face Grace – Grace Sheffield with her powder-white hair and her delicately-patterned dress of fine cotton, wafting around her legs.

"Grace... back up now," Rick shouted. He slipped the gun into his pants pocket and waved the branch with his right hand. "I don't want to use this but I will if I have to. Now just let me by."

He trained the remote at the garage and pressed.

The door moved upwards, clanking.

The sound of engines was getting louder.

Melanie emerged from beneath the door, a baseball bat in her hands. She looked left and right and then across at Rick.

Rick saw the smile falter a little and then return, but when it returned it was a false smile. "Geoff?" She craned her head to look behind Rick and took a step forward, following Grace who still doggedly closed the gap between herself and Rick. "Where's Geoff?"

Rick sighed, both at the fact that he was going to have to deal with Grace and the fact that he was going to have to deal with Melanie. He wasn't sure which one he was looking forward to the least.

"Rick, where's Geoff?"

"Back up, Grace," Rick snapped. "I mean it."

"Rick!"

"He didn't make it, Mel." He waited for a few seconds, watched Melanie's face take on a quizzical expression. *Didn't make it? What kind of shit was that?*

"How do you–"

"He's dead, Mel. Geoff's dead."

Melanie dropped the bat.

Grace staggered another couple of steps, just a few feet away now. Rick shook his head. He waited for her to take another step, braced himself and swung the branch, clipping the side of her head and knocking the dark glasses across the concrete. Grace staggered, partially bent forward, and then straightened up. When she turned to look at him she lifted her hands to her face, but not before Rick saw the woman's eyes. They looked like coals, hot coals, red and black. She rubbed her face, swiveled around, clawing at her eyes.

"Grace..."

Melanie had retrieved the bat. She walked calmly forward until she was standing in front of Grace Sheffield. Then she brought the bat down on top of the woman's head with all of her might. Even with the sound of the engines, Rick could hear her sobbing. Melanie lifted her arms back behind her head to take another swing but Grace had fallen face forward, a thick black pool forming beneath her head.

"Mel, she's finished."

As Melanie brought the bat down and pulverized the back of Grace's head, Jack DiChapperlain's Camaro appeared over the trees. Behind the Camaro was Suzie Mendohlson's open-sided Jeepster, with Roy Clubb hanging out of the passenger side. There was something in Roy's hand.

A loud report echoed and a thick cloud of brick and dust exploded from the side of the station.

Rick dived forward, dropping the branch, and grabbed Melanie.

"Shit, now they've got firepower."

Another shot rang out but Rick didn't see where it went.

"Inside," he shouted over the roar of the engines. Another one was coming up from the bridge road but Rick wasn't about to waste time by turning around to see what it was.

Melanie was sobbing, the bat still clutched in her hands, repeating Geoff's name over and over again.

Roy Clubb's rifle snapped at the night again and a piece of masonry bounced inches from Rick's foot as he dragged Melanie across to the garage, all but throwing her inside.

"Where's Johnny?"

"GeoffGeoffGeoff... oh my *god*... he *can't* be–"

Rick slapped her and grabbed her shoulders before she could fall over.

Craaack!

One of the old paint cans leapt into the air, bounced against the Dodge's windshield and rolled down the hood.

"Over here," Johnny said, his voice weak.

Rick pulled open the Dodge's left-hand rear door and pushed Melanie inside. He slammed the door and edged his way around to the back of the car to where Johnny was laid out, almost unconscious.

"What is it? Bullet?" He searched Johnny's shirt-front for signs of blood. "Knife?"

Johnny shook his head. "Broke my leg. Daryl–"

"Doesn't matter who did it, Johnny." He looked around. One of the cars was landing – he could see dust billowing up just outside the garage door.

Craaaack!

Melanie screamed.

When Rick looked through the back window he saw the windshield was a mosaic of tiny lines.

"Shit," Rick said. "We have to move."

Another shot rang out, followed by another.

"Rick... I don't think I'm gonna be–"

"I know. I'm gonna have to do it."

(29)

Sally watched the departing car and breathed a sigh of relief. She looked back, carefully avoiding repeating the nose-collision, and was delighted to see no activity around her old window. She turned around again and shuffled to the corner, pausing to sneak a quick glance around it just to make sure there was nobody heading her way, and then moved around. It proved to be more difficult that she had imagined, mainly because there was a time when the only point of wall contact was the ninety degree sharp edge that travelled the full length of her body, occupying a knife-edge line down between her breasts and to between her legs: the rest of her – aside from her hands and knees, all of which she used to keep as tight a grasp on the hotel as possible – seemed to be abandoned out in space. But it didn't last long before she was around the corner and resting her face on the brick.

This was a side street, lacking in the grandeur of the main drag she had just left. A quick glance down revealed cars parked in bays, a collection of large trash dumpsters huddled in an alcove. But best of all – joy of joys! – there was a fire escape ladder that appeared to run down to the second floor where it would then have to be released in order to drop the final few yards to the ground. Sally sighed and closed her eyes. But she didn't want to hang around too long: the people (*were* they people?) out in the hallway – and latterly, in her private suite, for Chrissakes – were slow but she wasn't sure how slow they would be when they got back onto the luggage trolley and hightailed it back to the elevators to head downstairs.

They may not have figured out where she had gone – though she couldn't figure that out at all – but they sure as shooting knew she was around someplace. It figured that the place to set up camp to catch her would be the lobby, but then that assumed a whole lot of understanding that Sally wasn't sure they possessed.

After a few seconds, she edged along the ledge, pleased to see that she seemed to have gotten the hang of it. She reached the fire escape without incident and started down, trying to keep the noise down as much as possible. Releasing the final section from the holding clips, however, did prove to be a noisy affair and, as soon as she reached the ground – feeling decidedly shaky – Sally ran across the street and back up onto the main drag. She stopped at the corner and glanced up at the ledge: what she had just achieved looked an impossible feat. But she had done it. Now she needed to find somewhere to hide.

Looking around, worrying that any moment one of those airborne cabs would come scooting around one of the buildings, flashing its headlights all over the ground and–

Hey, look! There she is! Now let's just nip on down there and–

–she figured it would be curtains.

All the stores were closed so getting inside would involve breaking in, and that required something to smash glass with plus, most important of all, making noise.

We shouldn't make any noise, should we mommy?

"No," she said to the silent street. "No noise."

Somewhere far away, the sound of an engine could be heard, but it didn't seem to be getting any louder – maybe it was just moving cross-streets.

Then she saw it.

24 Hour, it said, in bold purple and green neons.

Movies! it said, in flashing yellow bulbs that ran like a wave, falling in on itself only to return to the beginning and start again.

"Perfect," she whispered. "A movie theater."

And after a final quick glance around, Sally Davis removed her pumps and set off at a trot, heading for – she now saw – the rather quaintly named Bijou Theater. She just hoped the movies were not art house or – even worse – porn.

What's porn, mommy?

Don't ask her that, answered another voice.

It worried Sally sometimes that she could not always identify the owners of some of her internal voices.

She reached the multiple-doored entrance just as what sounded like a helicopter came over the roof above her, Sally stepping through the doors and diving behind a stand-up cardboard advertisement for a Woody Allen Season as a pair of independently operated light beams played across the street like living things.

She saw the kiosk – noting with some sadness that it was empty (she imagined the girl – or boy, she supposed, but doubted – being spirited away in that flash, leaving the theater frontage silent and deserted). She glanced around the cardboard and watched the lights. They were still there.

"I need to get inside," she said. And then, softer, she added, "I need to sleep."

After one final check, Sally scurried crablike past the roped off section onto the carpeted area and headed for the double doors at the end of the corridor, drinking in the familiar movie theater smell of popcorn and disinfectant.

I wonder what they're showing, she thought, suddenly realizing that she hadn't noticed.

And then she was through the doors and into the darkness.

(30)

Rick lifted Johnny by the armpits and dragged him around to the other side of the car. He pulled open the door and dropped him onto the back seat, cracking Johnny's head on the door surround and wincing as Johnny screamed out in pain when he lifted Johnny's twisted leg and jammed it into the footwell so he could close the door.

Rick pulled open the front passenger door and fell in, dragging himself across the seats and the center panel. He was shaking as he slipped into the driver's seat and rested his feet on the pedals.

A loud *crummmmp!* came from somewhere up above and a thin cloud of dust drifted down onto the windshield and the back window. Johnny leaned forward and looked up through the windshield.

"Something's landed on the roof," he said. It sounded so casual and–

Hey, some pod people have souped up a whole bunch of the townsfolks' autos so's they can fly and they've landed one of them on the garage roof...

–matter-of-fact, and Rick didn't feel that way at all. Mostly, he felt tired.

Outside the garage door, Martha McNeil's rusted old Chevy flatbed did a shaky three-point landing, with Martha at the wheel and Frank and Eleanor Dawson crouched down in the back. Frank and Ellie were over the sides of the Chevy even before Martha had turned off the engine, and Frank was carrying a shotgun.

He shouldered the piece and brought it straight, letting off the barrels one at a time, taking a thick chunk of masonry and wood out of the top left of the garage door frame, and doing some damage to the Dodge's grill. Rick felt the car jolt and hoped it was only lights that had caught the blast.

"I don't care," Melanie was saying between tears. "I don't care about anything. I don't–"

"Shut up, Mel," Rick snapped. Then, "Johnny, I don't know as I can do this."

Johnny shuffled himself into an upright position and faced forward. "Sure you–" He broke off and winced at the stabbing pain that shot up his thigh. "Sure you can. Just like riding a bike – you never forget."

Frank and Ellie Dawson were striding across the concrete towards the garage, Ellie dragging a long-handled ax along behind her and Frank busy trying to load cartridges into his 12-bore.

Rick turned the ignition and–

Just like riding a bike.

–felt the Dodge thrum into life. He placed his hands at ten before two on the wheel, gritted his teeth, shifted the gear lever into drive and–

You never forget.

–looked outside.

Frank and Ellie Dawson had gone. In their place were the shimmering memories of two bedraggled figures, covered in blood, thick slices of flesh hanging from them. One of them – the girl; couldn't have been more than 22, 23 – was wearing cut-off blue denims and–

She had freckles, didn't she Rick? You remember that, don'tcha... You remember seeing her face in that much detail just before?

–the guy was lifting something up–

"Rick–"

–like he was waving–

Hey, asshole, whyn't you come back and finish the job... Think there's a couple of bones here seem to be still in one piece...

–to him but no, he was holding something out towards him...

"Rick! For Christ's sake... He's gonna–"

Johnny's voice broke the spell.

Melanie screamed and Rick felt her head come forward into the back of his seat.

In front of the car, Frank Dawson was clipping the stock into place.

Jim Ferumern walked stiff-legged around the garage door, coming out of nowhere, his gun in his hand. He let off a shot.

Somewhere behind them, in the garage, something gave a thin *thunk!* and whined.

Now out of the flatbed's cab, Martha McNeil walked jauntily up behind Frank like she was going to tell him something, let him into a secret.

"Rick, drive the fucking car!"

Ellie Dawson reached the hood and brought her ax down into the windshield. The Plexiglas buckled.

Johnny leaned forward and pressed the door catch, listening with satisfaction as all four of the Dodge's doors locked.

In a daze, Rick released the parking brake.

Jim Ferumern lifted his gun and tried to train it. Frank did the same with his 12-bore.

Martha McNeil came up behind Frank and brushed his shoulder, Frank shifting the 12-bore just a fraction to the right as he pulled the trigger for the first barrel, the shot taking off the top of Ellie's head, even as Ellie was hauling back with her ax. She stopped for a second, staggered a little, and then continued to heft the ax.

"*Drive* for crying–"

Rick stepped on the gas and the Dodge leapt forward, spinning Ellie Dawson around and smacking her into a run of shelving – pots and cans and drill bits spilling onto her and onto the side of the car.

Johnny shouted out in pain as he leaned to the side, resting his head on Melanie's hip.

The Dodge hit Frank in the crotch, doubling him over, the 12-bore skittering across the hood to the windshield and then rolling off of the driver's side.

Frank held on as the car screeched out of the station garage, side-swiping Martha's flatbed, the wheels spinning, burning rubber.

Jim Ferumern stood watching, apparently taking everything in, his gun still trained, his eyes unseen behind the dark glasses, holding the gun level with the side windows.

Melanie screamed again.

Jim got off a shot. It went wild.

Rick braked, watching Frank slide forward off the hood.

In the rearview, Rick saw Jim training the gun again, saw Ellie, the top of her head gone and no hair at all, saw her heft the ax and stagger out of the garage. He floored the gas pedal just as Frank slid off the hood, felt the car bump – twice – over the body–

Hey, you're getting real good at this kind of thing, Rick.

–as they spun around on the concrete apron.

Overhead, another car was circling – Rick didn't know what it was.

He heard shots, heard a dull *thunnnng!* on the roof, and aimed the car for Jack DiChapperlain's Camaro which was parked up outside the station door, all four doors wide open.

Rick took one of the doors clean off, felt the Dodge judder, and bent the other one on that side back flat against the front side-panel.

Roy Clubb stood up from behind the Camaro. He was holding a rifle.

Something went *ziiiinnng* across the hood and Rick spun the wheel, fanning the Dodge's rear end just as Suzie Mendohlson climbed up from the woods – glancing down, Rick caught sight of Suzie's open-sided Jeepster, lying in the trees on its side. The Dodge hit her legs and sent Suzie up into the air and back down to rejoin her car.

Rick checked the rearview.

There were two cars on the garage roof!

Ellie was lying on the floor.

Jim was walking after them, the gun hanging by his side. Then Roy appeared in the mirror, the rifle held slack. Neither of them appeared to be in any rush.

You heard another engine, didn't you drive-boy?

Rick hammered the gas and spun the wheel to head for the road. As he turned the corner, he saw Jack DiChapperlain waiting for them.

Jack was standing in front of a battered blue-and-white, the furry tail on the antenna telling Rick it was Don Patterson's. The car was parked right across the road. Jack pulled his rifle up into sight and fired.

Rick lurched to one side and the shot hit the windshield.

Hey, drive-boy, whyn't you fire back?

He reached into his pocket, pulled out Sammy Lescombe's gun. He slammed the brakes and knocked out the buckled Plexiglas just as Jack was preparing for another shot.

Rick held the gun as steady as he could and pulled the trigger.

The shot went wild.

"Rick!"

Jack tilted his head and lifted the rifle.

Rick fired again.

Jack staggered, a red patch spreading around his gut. He looked down at himself, regained his balance, and lifted the rifle again.

Rick pulled the trigger.

Nothing happened.

"Hit the fucker!" Johnny screamed from the back seat.

Rick stomped on the gas and drove. He was suddenly aware he was screaming, and Johnny was screaming, and now Melanie, she was screaming too.

The Dodge caught Jack DiChapperlain and carried him the three or four yards to the blue-and-white and squashed him like a bug. Rick lurched forward, his head colliding with the rearview and swiveling it out of place, just as Jack slumped forward onto the hood. The blue-and-white hadn't moved.

Rick adjusted the rearview and checked the road behind. It looked crowded.

Now, alongside or slightly behind Frank Dawson, came Daryl Engstrom – carrying what looked like the old hat stand from the station – J. J. Poskett, some kid whose name Rick couldn't remember, Shirley Pakard and three or four more people – Eddie from the sheriff's office, Luke Napier, Janey from the deli, and someone else that Rick didn't recognize. They looked for all the world like the Wild Bunch or the Dirty Dozen, walking down the road with the station in the background, various articles in their hands. Frank raised his shotgun and let off a shot. It didn't connect with anything.

Rick faced forward and stared at the blue-and-white.

Then he glanced up at the rearview.

He shifted the lever into reverse and hit the gas.

"What the *fuck…*"

"No choice, amigo," Rick said to Johnny, half turned around in his seat, his arm resting on the back of the empty passenger seat alongside him. "Got to build up some speed if we're gonna move the patrol car." He gave a little shrug.

The Dodge careened back up the road, the townsfolk growing bigger through the back window.

Melanie shook her head. "You think you'll do it?"

Rick didn't answer. He hit the brake about ten or twelve feet away from Frank Dawson, and shifted into forward gear again.

"Do or die," Rick said as they started forward again.

Someone fired a shot but it didn't hit them.

"Amen to that," Johnny said.

Melanie patted Rick's shoulder and braced herself against his seat-back.

Rick aimed the Dodge at the blue-and-white's hood. "Hold on!" he shouted.

Jack DiChapperlain's body was still twitching when the Dodge hit it, jerked a foot or so into the air and sent the blue-and-white's front end spinning. The Dodge was almost by before the blue-and-white's trunk jackknifed around from the other direction and hit their trunk, sending the Dodge's wheels spinning dangerously close to the edge of the grass which fell away sharply on the left down to the woods. But Rick kept control, twisting the steering wheel first one way and then the other, the wind blowing in his face through the smashed windshield.

They lurched down the road until they came to the bridge and the fork left down into Jesman's Bend. Rick brought the Dodge to a halt.

"Where to?" Melanie asked.

Rick shook his head.

They all turned around and looked back up the road. The sun's rays were clear from behind the station, a bright glow of hope.

"Uh oh," Rick said, a cold knot in his gut.

"Oh no," Melanie said.

The familiar sight of Martha McNeil's Chevy rose up, swaying side to side in the first touch of dawn's light, and then veered off towards town.

"They're– they're not coming after us," Johnny said.

Rick watched as the Jeepster rose up and followed the Chevy. "Doesn't look like it." He shielded his eyes against the still watery light, and thought of all the dark glasses the townsfolk were wearing, even at night.

He turned back to face front and leaned forward looking up into the sky. It was blue now – still a murky blue with shades of night mixed in, but the blackness had gone. He pressed down on the gas.

"The interstate," he said.

Johnny tried to straighten his leg and yelped. "Then where?"

"Then we need to find others... we need to find out what's happening, why it's happening and what we can do about it."

By the time they pulled onto the Interstate, the sun was coming up on a world that was both empty and, aside from the occasional car and truck smashed through the central barrier or upturned on the grass at the side of the road, deserted.

"You know," Rick said into the wind buffeting his face, "I'd forgotten just how much I like driving."

(31)

Sally opened her eyes and blinked.

She had heard something but she wasn't sure whether it had been in her dreams or somewhere around her. Without moving, she held her breath and scanned the area around her.

There seemed to be no movement, but it wasn't that easy to make everything out. She would have to wait until her eyes adjusted.

The movie theatre had seemed lighter than this when she had come in off the street. How long ago was that? Sally twisted her wrist and, without moving her head, jiggled her hand until the watch face presented itself to her. Not much use. It could be something after five o'clock or something to eight o'clock. It could, in fact, be any damn time at all. How long had she been in here, for Chriss–

There it was again. This time she heard it for sure. It wasn't a single sharp sound, like something maybe falling over – something that had been sitting there, in the same position that someone had put it into before the light, and had finally succumbed to the gentlest breeze and tipped over. No, it was nothing like that. It was a prolonged sound of movement. And it reminded Sally of the sound of the people walking down the corridor of the Brown Palace Hotel.

There was someone in here with her.

Maybe they were not close by and maybe they were not even aware she was here, but there was definitely someone else.

Or very heavy-footed rats, one of Sally's cerebral progeny offered.

Sally was curled up in one of the bench seats in the back row and she was pleased to note that, if she couldn't see the person in here with her, then it followed that the person in here with her probably couldn't see her. Very carefully, she lifted her head while strenuously avoiding moving any of the rest of her body. It didn't help.

One of the doors at the front of the theater, at the side of the screen – it was the right side, she thought; that was the direction of the noise – clunked closed. So someone had either come into the theatre from wherever or they were already here and they had just left. Paradoxically, she liked the sound of the latter even less than the former. Sally didn't like to think of herself snuggling down for a little shut-eye off the streets when someone else – perhaps even *several* someone elses – was sitting just a few rows away from her. It felt like the old silent comedy screen gag of the hapless explorer finding a cave to get out of the elements and, in the darkness, settling down using a bear's back as a pillow thinking it was a convenient rock outcrop.

Mommy, I'm frightened, whispered one of Sally's constant children, somewhere deep in the back of her brain.

Without thinking, she let out the start of a *shhh*! before she realized she was doing it. Sally clamped her lips tightly closed and buried her head back into the muscle of her upper arm, which was crooked beneath as a support.

He's heard me, she thought. It was a certainty, she realized. There was the unmistakable sound of a *cessation* of sound. Somebody had been moving, slowly, shuffling along, and now they had stopped. She could imagine the scene without even lifting her head. Someone was standing at the front of the theater and, right at this very instant, they were scanning the spread of rows of seats stretching all the way to the back wall, from which, through two small square windows, the projectors beamed the moving images onto the giant screen.

Sally placed her right hand on the floor and shifted her weight onto it, easing her body up from the seat in preparation for moving completely to the floor. The sound the seat made was not loud, not by any stretch of the imagination. Nor was it sinister. It was little more than a small creak, a squeak, perhaps, a breath of material and spring, hinge and wood, moving in its time-honored fashion from the pulled-down position into the folded-back position. But it was tantamount to a fanfare of trumpets or a seismic shifting of the San Andreas plates. And the slurring started up again, this time with seeming determination, and Sally heard it shift from the carpeted central aisle onto the wooden flooring – that meant that whoever it was had moved into one of the rows. She contemplated dropping to the floor but that would mean the seat would make an even louder noise. She could lift her head but that would only serve in delaying the inevitable. Wherever the person was that was looking for her, he or she or it was not about to abandon the hunt if Sally wasn't in one particular row. They'd simply try another row. And Sally thought that "they" was pretty much the case. She was sure there were two, maybe three of them. Hell, maybe there were four of them.

Once she had made the decision, all the anxiety evaporated.

In one perfectly fluid motion, Sally jumped from the double seat, hoisted her pumps from the floor and stood up to her full height.

The old woman edging her way along two or three rows in front of Sally seemed almost as surprised as Sally herself, but appeared also to recognize Sally, tilting her head to one side and then, pulling off her gloves very slowly, holding her arms out in front of her as though to embrace Sally like a long lost friend or distant relative come to visit. The woman was wearing dark glasses, just like the people in the hotel corridor – and just like, Sally now saw, the old man walking up the main aisle and the neatly suited gentleman threading his way between the seats of the right hand side block.

Up in front of her, the old woman was holding onto a seat-back as she hoisted a leg and prepared to clamber over – an action that would then leave a further two similar seats to be hurdled. In the dim light given out by the myriad tiny bulbs in the theater's ceiling, Sally watched in a kind of rapt fascination as the wood beneath the woman's fingers seemed to flake and then collapse to the floor in a shower of slivers and shavings.

The man in the aisle removed his gloves and slid them into the pockets of his white coveralls. Maybe he was a doctor… or an ice cream seller? Whatever, Sally didn't think he now operated under any "good humor" or Hippocratic oath. Holding his arms straight out in front of him, he lumbered up the aisle slowly but with a grim determination. And the same could be said of the man in the suit, now nearing the end of his row, thereby leaving him with just the center aisle to cross and two rows to move up: he would reach Sally first, she reckoned, unless the old woman got the hang of straddling seats.

She glanced back and saw the woman fall over backwards, just toppling over like a tall statue placed on an uneven surface, her legs going up into the air, dress flying up in a flurry, pants and hose showing, one shoe falling off, and the woman's head hitting another seat-back with a blow that Sally thought would have felled most linebackers, never mind a little old woman who looked like the real life counterpart of the granny figure who used to look out for Tweety Pie and take a broom to Sylvester the cat in the old cartoon shows.

We have to get out, mommy, someone said in the back of Sally Davis's head. She nodded. But which way was going to be best? That was the jackpot question.

Suit Man had reached the aisle. He had removed his gloves – no surprise there – and was reaching out ahead of him as he emerged from between the seats and headed diagonally for Sally's row-end. He would reach it seconds before the old man who might be a doctor.

Sally heard a clatter from her left and she spun around just in time to see a young woman with a milky-pale complexion wrong-foot herself on soda cups and popcorn cartons and keel over like a tree being felled just a few feet away from her in the row in front. The girl hit her head on one of the chair backs in front of her – a hard hit, Sally thought, and one which brought with it a dull and sickening thud – as she went down, her right hand straining upwards from where she now lay on the floor, groping towards Sally.

Now the doctor had reached the end of Sally's row and Suit Man was hot on his heels, the two of them shambling along like store window dummies, walking as though they had never done it before and were not altogether impressed.

Over towards the screen, the old woman seemed to be stuck astride a seat back, her dress hoisted clear up to a pair of voluminous pants and exposing wattled, flabby-skinned legs the color of alabaster. She was adjusting her sunglasses–

Why's she wearing sunglasses, mommy?

–with hands that appeared totally new to the task they had undertaken.

Without even thinking about what she was about to do, Sally slipped her feet into her pumps and stepped first onto the seat next to her. Then she pulled her dress up, the material bunched in her right hand and the left held out beside her as a balancing stick, and she stepped up onto the seat back in front of her. Then, realizing that momentum was the only thing that was going to work here (and even that was a tall order), she started forward towards the screen, stepping from row to row by chair back to chair back, suddenly aware from her eye corner that two more "people" had entered the theater by the door at the right of the screen.

There was no noise from the old woman, the pasty-faced girl, the doctor or Suit Man, and Sally determined not to look back to see what they had made of her escape. What were the people aiming to do to her? Whatever had happened to them, she thought, why had it not happened to her?

Five or six rows along, one of the chair backs was loose.

There was no way Sally would have been able to tell even if all of the lights had been blazing bright. The first intimation was when Sally placed her not inconsiderable weight on the very tip of the bowed wooden back and used it as a springboard to throw her other leg – the left one on this occasion – forward to another row. And so on.

She was mindful of the pasty-faced girl, the doctor, the old woman in the big pants and Suit Man – not to mention the assorted wanderers gathering in the dip immediately in front of the screen – and was busy spreading her concentration between them (and whatever it was that they had in mind for her), the reasons for the gloves and the glasses, the need to stay balanced and place her feet correctly on the seat-backs, and a consideration as to which route seemed most likely to get her out of here. Thus, when the seat clicked once and, with a dull but discernable *ping*, fired its sheared holding bolt across the dusty floor space beneath the seat, and then yawned backwards until it collided with the upraised seat in the row behind, Sally was pitched unceremoniously forward, landing in a heap around twelve rows from the front.

The pain hit three areas pretty much all at the same time: her face collided with the edge of a seat-back two rows further on, her left breast received a wooden sucker-punch from the chair arm one row behind that one, and her right knee took the full brunt of that chair's back with such force (and noise; Sally didn't expect ever to walk again) that, when she finally hit the popcorn-littered floor in a chaotic bundle of arms and legs and pain and blood, a dim-and-distant part of her was half-prepared to lie still and play dead. But she didn't think she would be able to maintain that level of dummy-playing with any believability – particularly if they were able to feel pulses and watch for signs of breathing.

And the sunglasses, mommy... and the gloves.

Yes, those too.

Shaking her head, Sally got immediately to her feet and took stock of the situation, drinking in the scene around her as fast as she could. The shapes were moving around clumsily and slowly – that was the good news. The bad news was that they seemed to be covering most throughways – the main aisle on the right, the one on the left, several of the individual rows, the wide passageway directly in front of the screen and the two exit doors on either side of it. Aside from the exit doors, which led additionally to restrooms and presumably storage and office facilities, there were only the main double doors Sally had come in by – which meant finding an unoccupied row and heading left to join the aisle leading to it. In turn, that also meant having to deal with whatever was in the foyer.

Why are they walking that way, mommy? one of the voices asked.

Before Sally could formulate an answer, a bitter hardened voice chimed in with a response all of its own. *Because they're a bunch of sick puppies, kiddo,* it said. *They're dead – dead and lost and changed – they aren't pulling off those gloves to shake your hand, and they aren't wearing those glasses to protect against glaucoma.*

No, the only sensible way was up. *And why not?* she thought, glancing up at the ornately patterned ceiling. After all, she had just walked along a ledge eight floors up on the side of a building: no point in stopping now, not when she was on such a roll.

The aisle leading back out to the foyer looked busy now, people starting to thread along the row that she was standing in and the ones on either side of it. When she turned around, she saw they were coming from the other direction.

A strange calm descended on her, and she looked back up the seated area towards the two projection windows. The windows fronted a rectangular outcropping that stood off from the wall. Sally could see a faint green glow on the outside wall facing the left side of the outcropping. There were doors there. She couldn't see them, not exactly (though there were different tones of dark set against the wall) but she just figured a door had to be there. She figured that because if there was no door over there – which, it had to be said, didn't make much sense at all – then her goose was cooked.

Our goose as well, mommy?

"There is a door!" Sally said, defiantly.

As she had opened her mouth, she had tasted liquid, warm and thick liquid. It tasted metallic. She wiped her nose and cried out in pain. It was definitely broken. Plus her knee hurt, both shins were throbbing, and – as she discovered when she bent down to retrieve her lost pump – her left hip would not allow any sudden movements without sending shafts of pain across her midriff and a wave of nausea welling up her throat.

"We have to go back," Sally said.

There was muttering in her head.

Somewhere behind her, a seat twanged and rattled.

Sally dropped the pump onto the floor again, slipped her foot inside and stepped gingerly onto the seat in front of her. Once there, feeling a little unsteady but increasingly aware of the shuffling coming ever closer (she dared not turn around to see what the ones in the row behind her were doing but on one occasion she thought she felt something brush her back) she stepped up onto the seat back and headed back the way she had come, facing the twin windows of the projection room and moving diagonally now toward the green light on the far wall.

Every step was profound agony but after a few rows she was in the clear from the shufflers. She reached the aisle four rows from the back and, just for a second, she considered jumping down onto the floor. But the pain in her hip said that such a move would undoubtedly be foolhardy–

Foolhardy?

You're *a fool, Hardy!*

Sniggers.

–because she felt that she would then be unable to move at all.

She pushed the seat down with her foot, balancing on the chair-arm with her good (or better!) foot and leg, and then stepped down onto the seat, her arms held out wide alongside her. Once there, she sat down carefully on the wooden back, the chair threatening to tilt suddenly and Sally throwing her arms up in horror (thereby causing more pain in every area), and then stepped onto the floor of the aisle. Shambling up towards her were around a dozen or maybe fifteen people, all wearing sunglasses and all with their arms stretched out in front of them.

Sally turned and headed for the green light and the doors beneath it.

Each step brought with it an involuntary yelp but she reached the green light in surprisingly fast time. The folks in the aisle had only barely reached where she had been but she didn't waste any time. She pulled on both of the two doors behind the closed curtains but only one – the right one – would open. She stepped through into a long corridor that sloped upwards. This corridor, too, was in darkness, without even the tiny spot bulbs to give at least a little light, and whatever pale illumination was available from behind her was fast disappearing as the door squeaked closed. In that brief glimpse, Sally had seen that the corridor was empty. But there had been a bundle of what appeared to be some kind of material in a heap over on the left. And as the door reached its inevitable conclusion, the bundle had moved.

Sally reached out to the walls on either side of the corridor, sweeping the Hessian covering for a light-switch. It was then that she heard the shuffling from in front of her.

Sally stopped and remained perfectly still with her nose, arms, legs and hip screaming out inside her in absolute agony.

"Hello? Is somebody there?" she whispered.

Nobody answered, but the shuffling continued.

Sally spun around and pushed the doors slightly ajar – the others had reached the end of the aisle and were even now making a drunken left turn to head towards the green light. The green light! That was it. If she could manage to get both doors open then there might be sufficient glow from the green exit sign for Sally to see what she was doing.

She pushed open the door she had used and flipped the retainer bolts from the top and bottom of the secured one: Sally was sure there must be some kind of law against bolting what appeared to be fire doors in a public place, but she didn't think she would ever have an opportunity to complain.

Mommy, one of the voices whispered, *somebody wants to–*

Sally turned and stepped back just as two bare hands reached for her, reached up to her, from a little old man wearing dark glasses and – Sally saw in the surreal green glow from behind her head – a pair of light colored trousers (stained wet around the crotch area) sitting on top of a pair of symmetrically patterned carpet slippers.

Sally knocked the hands aside and ducked around the old man, who momentarily was now facing the corridor wall. As she shot forward, Sally felt something cold grip the flesh on the lower left side of her back, grip it through her blouse. And just for that split second, Sally knew that it was only her momentum that saved her. If she had been standing still when the hand had grabbed her back then she would have sunk to the floor beneath that strange concordance of darkness and light, heat and cold, pain and pleasure. And even running along the corridor to the end, seeing the faint glimmer of the metal crash bars that she knew would lead to the outside, there was a part of her that almost bemoaned that loss of opportunity – of being able to stop, to finish it all, to face whatever it was – maybe even join Gerry. But all of that was gone when Sally hit the bars and emerged into the early Denver morning, all elements of pain from anywhere in her body were but dim and distant memories. She was braced for more of them, her hands clenched into tiny fists, her muscles charged and waiting to swing, to power, to crash and to maim. But the street was empty and, best of all, over the rooftops eastwards, a lightness was gathering on the horizon.

Sally stopped, took a couple more steps and then slumped onto her knees, oblivious of the concrete hitting cartilage and bone, and then she slid onto her left arm, head held low, and she looked back at the theater's fire exit. Just for the briefest of moments, the gathered people seemed about to step out to follow her but then, then they seemed to waver and pause, their feet hitting the first part of paving slab and stopping. Sally recalled a long ago movie, a foreign film, subtitles, about a group of people in a dinner party who, when they had finished eating, were unable to leave the room even though there was nothing standing in their way.

As one, the figures backed into the theater and two arms – from different people, Sally noted – reached out and pulled the doors closed again.

Sally stretched out where she lay, rested her head on her arm and closed her eyes to the muted sunshine.

(32)

It was after seven o'clock when they finally decided it was safe to stop.

Rick waited until he saw a car that he liked the look of and then pulled in.

But, each time, the car had been damaged, running into metal fence posts or outcroppings of rock, and the ignitions had all been left on and the batteries were stone dead. Rick decided they would have to wait until they hit a stop somewhere and, sure enough, one came up.

The place appeared to be called, somewhat unimaginatively, "Diner", and the car was a shiny blue Cadillac Seville, a late '70s model that had clearly been cherished by its owner, he or she having moved on to the same place everyone else had gone.

It was parked up alongside four 18-wheelers, a little foreign job with a stick-shift, and a couple of rust buckets, all sitting outside a coffee house with a curling "Help Wanted" sign taped to the window. Four sets of keys had been on the counter, sitting beside half-eaten plates of food or newspapers open to the sports pages. The process of elimination had identified the ones that belonged to the Seville, a fob which also contained house keys for an unknown home and a bendy Bugs Bunny figurine.

The place was deserted and, after clearing the counter of greasy plates and cups of cold coffee, Melanie made them fresh coffee, poured orange juice, and put together a plate of sandwiches and stale Danishes while Rick checked over the Seville for gas and oil.

They had strapped up Johnny's leg as best they could and pumped him up with painkillers from a machine on the wall, but the pills were really only meant for headaches brought on by driving, not for broken shinbones and they were having only a limited effect.

Nobody said much at all.

They used the washrooms to freshen up and ate in silence, each of them lost in their own thoughts and Melanie spending most of the time turning the dial on an old radio set on the shelf behind the counter. All she got was static. When it got to nine o'clock, Rick said that it was time to be moving on.

The Seville's dashboard clock registered 9.08 as they pulled out onto I-90 again, heading east.

The sun was blistering.

The sky was a pure blue unbroken by clouds.

And the road stretched off into the distance.

They didn't know quite where they were heading but Melanie and Geoff had honeymooned in New Orleans and she had expressed a desire to go visit again. Rick and Johnny had shrugged together at that: hell, one place was as good as another, though they all felt that they needed a big city to try come to terms with what had happened.

Up ahead, down the long miles that lay before them, a telephone was ringing in the concourse of the 16th Street Mall in the deserted city of Denver – the very same way it had been ringing, off and on, for the past couple of days...

(33)

"What do you think?"

Virgil Banders shielded his eyes from the sun and looked around the road. He shook his head. "Can't be sure," he said.

They were standing right in the middle of the pavement, Virgil holding a little foldout map of downtown Denver. The airplane was six or seven blocks behind them, the 16th Street Mall maybe another few miles ahead of them. Right alongside them, turned crossways across the street, was a bus.

With his hand on the side of the bus, Ronnie made a clicking sound with his mouth and then stood back, hands on his hips. "We'd have seen it."

"We had a lot on our mind," Virgil said.

Ronnie grunted. He wasn't convinced.

"Look at its lights," Samantha the doll squawked. She was being held up in front of the bus by Angel Wurst, and Angel had the doll move its head side to side in exasperation. "They're a mess."

"Yeah." Virgil moved over to stand beside the girl and Angel took a few steps back, watching him carefully. "How did they *get* like that?"

"Somebody pulled them out of the sockets," Ronnie said. He hunkered down and looked at the lights more closely. "See this?" He took a hold of one of the sealed beam units and pulled it slightly to one side. "There's a kind of girder-support system going on back here." He reached into the socket where the wires were all wound up and exposed a tiny mechanical grid that went right out of sight.

"See, this allows the lights to move side to side and up and down." He demonstrated.

"Huh," Virgil said. "Never seen nothing like that before."

Ronnie grunted again and then said, "Never *has* been anything like that before. Not that I've heard of."

They had been on the road for around an hour, taking it slow and easy and checking out the stores along the way. They'd already found a deli with a freezer full of bread and rolls, and a fridge heaving with salad and meats, so lunch was assured. Right now, it was a little after nine in the morning and Virgil was hankering for his first coffee of the day. He turned around and looked across the street to the *Mile High Café*. Karl was busy levering one of the windows open.

"How you doing, map-man?" Virgil shouted.

"OK. Nearly in. But I'm only going to give it another few minutes and then I'm breaking the glass."

"Need any help?"

Karl turned around and grimaced, holding his left shoulder. He shook his head. "Let me see how I get on."

Virgil nodded. "Be prepared for an alarm."

Karl waved and returned his attention to the glass doors.

"Door's open," Angel announced, this time in her own voice.

Ronnie straightened up and let go of the headlight, and he and Virgil moved around to the entry steps and looked in. The driving section had been torn apart. It didn't look as though the bus would ever move again. Ronnie suggested that maybe it was vandals. Virgil said not.

"Why would they do that, man? I mean, you know, there's no gain."

"There's all too often no logical reason for people–"

Virgil shook his head. "No, I mean..." He stepped up onto the first step and pulled himself up by the handrails onto the bus. "... there must be a gain, that's what I mean." He plopped into the driver's seat and looked at the dashboard. "Like, it's a mess. But, then again... it isn't."

Ronnie climbed up, followed by Angel.

"I don't follow you."

Virgil took hold of clumps of wiring and balanced them in his hand. "See, it's pulled free but it isn't severed." He leaned sideways to follow a trail of wires under the dash. "It's a good job."

"You call trashing a bus a good job?"

"It's not trashed. That's the whole point. Things haven't been removed, they've been added."

"You mean to tell me that it's customized? Somebody has customized a damn bus?"

"Looks that way," Virgil said, his voice muffled from under the dash.

"Customized to do what?"

"What are 'custom eyes'?"

Virgil sat up and leaned on the steering wheel. "I have no–" He stopped and lifted his arms quickly.

"What is it?"

"I *said*, what are 'custom eyes'?"

"Not now, honey," Ronnie said.

Angel flounced around and, as she whispered something into Samantha's ear, she looked down the bus.

"Get a load of this," Virgil Banders was saying behind her.

"It's a box," Angel whispered. She glanced around, suddenly realizing that the box was maybe what the young man had been talking about. But it wasn't, she could see now, and she snapped her head back quickly.

At the very back of the bus, on the back seat, was a large box.

Angel took a step forward. And then another step. She was delighted to see that nobody was paying any attention to *her* discovery.

"What is it?"

"The steering wheel. It goes up and down."

Ronnie pressed down on the wheel and it moved downwards slowly, as though on some kind of pneumatic air system.

"You feel that? You feel what it did? Just then?"

Ronnie was nodding. "It did something." He reached over with his other hand and used both to lift the wheel back to its original position.

"It did it again, man? What *is* that?"

Angel was now just a few seats away from the box, tiptoeing.

She held Samantha in front of her. "What's in the box?" the doll whispered.

"I don't know, Samantha," Angel answered. "Should we find out?"

"Yes," said the squawky voice.

Across the street, an alarm sounded, dopplering in and out of intensity. "Jesus, that's loud," Virgil shouted. He and Ronnie looked out of the side window just in time to see Karl push open one of the doors and disappear into the café. Ronnie leaned out of the bus window and looked back up the street. He felt nervous with that noise and he couldn't explain why. When he looked back at Virgil he saw that the boy too seemed a little apprehensive, looking over his shoulder at the steps and then leaning across to check the side street across from them.

Angel Wurst had flopped onto the seat just two seats in front of the ornate box, her hands clasped tightly to her ears and her eyes squeezed shut. Samantha the doll seemed unperturbed.

Suddenly the sound stopped and silence flooded in, like the ghost of a sound that had once been there but which was now disappearing, slowly, until it became something that maybe happened and then again maybe didn't.

"Oww!" Angel announced. "That hurt!"

Virgil leaned out of the door and shouted across to Karl. "You OK in there?"

"Yeah, all OK." Karl's voice was muffled until he reappeared at the café doorway, arms raised up as he leaned on the door jamb window edging on the one side and the still-intact glass door on the other. "Had to knock the box off of the wall."

"Just think," Ronnie was muttering as he checked the steering column, "any other time and we'd have cop cars screeching up all around us."

"Any other time, there'd be people out there," Virgil said.

Angel got to her feet and turned back to the box on the back seat.

"You see anything in there?"

Ronnie shook his head. "Someone's disconnected the drive shaft and then re-connected it so that you can't fix it into one position." He moved the wheel up and then down, feeling it click in the middle of the range. "See, it sticks around here–" He did it again. "–and then moves freely up and– Hey! Hold on a minute..."

"What?"

"Look." Ronnie moved the wheel first to the left and then to the right, feeling the same click again when he passed the middle point of the range. "It moves sideways as well as up and down." He did it again.

Virgil held onto the tubular steel handrail and said, "There. You feel that? It's like the bus judders somehow when you move the wheel. Shouldn't do that if it's stationary. Should it?"

Ronnie shrugged. "Who knows."

"Who knows what?" Karl said. With a deep groan, he pulled himself up onto the bus steps with one arm and slumped against the handrail. He glanced down the bus and saw Angel on the back seat, making her doll dance around on some kind of box. "Hey, I got coffee percolating in there." He jerked a thumb back at the café.

"Sounds good," Virgil said. "I'd kill for a cup of coffee." He felt his neck and ears redden at that and glanced quickly at the others to see if they had noticed but Ronnie was still jiggling the steering wheel and Karl was watching him.

"Somebody's been messing with the steering mechanism," Ronnie said. "First the headlights and now the steering column," he added.

"What's up with the steering?"

Ronnie showed him.

At the back of the bus, Angel had Samantha sit on the seat while she looked around the box some more. It was around five feet long, a couple feet wide and maybe the same height off the seat. It was smooth all over except for a series of what appeared to be little glass portholes. And there was no handle. She checked the top and then the sides. Maybe the handle was on the other side, the side that's against the seat, she thought. "Or maybe some dummy put the box on the seat upside down," Samantha squawked helpfully.

"Can someone come help me?" she shouted.

Karl had moved across and was swapping places with Ronnie on the driver's seat. Virgil turned to Angel and smiled coldly.

Not you, she thought. *I don't want your kind of help.*

"You know what?" Karl said. Without waiting for an answer, he added, "Let's start her up and see what's what."

"Hell-*low*?" Angel's voice was lost in the sound of the engine's throaty roar.

"Christ, sounds more like an eight cylinder Mustang than a courtesy bus," Virgil said.

Angel turned her attention back to the box and ran her hands along the side. There was definitely a thin line where the top and bottom parts of the box joined but there was no way she was going to be able to prize them apart.

At the front of the bus, Karl said, "OK, let's make a move," and shifted the gear stick into drive. The bus moved forward slowly. He turned the wheel and the bus's direction moved the way he wanted it.

"Try lifting it," Ronnie shouted.

Angel had crawled on top of the box, her full length covering its surface. And all of the little glass portholes.

The bus lurched forward.

"I don't believe this," Karl said.

"What?"

The map reader looked over at Ronnie and said, "I suggest you take a hold of something."

Virgil said, "What are you going to–"

Karl pulled the steering column back and down.

Angel frowned. The bus was doing something to make the box jar against her stomach.

"Jesus H. *Christ*!" Ronnie said, and he grabbed a hold of the upper curtain rail around the driver's area. "What the *hell*..."

The bus lifted slowly from the street, the engine whining.

"I think it's going to be better in the manual gears," Karl shouted, and he shifted the lever into second. The bus shuddered and then clanked. They were some four or five feet above the ground, heading for a women's clothing store and a Mexican restaurant on the opposite side of the road.

"Jesus Christ!" Ronnie said again. "We're actually flying."

Angel sat up on the box and leaned on the back of the seat. They had taken off... in a bus.

"Better sit down," Karl said through clenched teeth. "I'm not too sure how steady this is going to be."

Virgil slid into the seat next to the door, still holding tight onto the upright handrail at the top of the steps. Ronnie looked around and saw that Angel had perched herself on some kind of box on the back seat.

"You OK back there, honey?" he shouted.

Angel nodded emphatically but her furrowed brow and hands tightly clenched on the seat backs in front of her suggested that she felt like she was on some kind of rollercoaster ride.

"Take it easy, Karl," he said.

Karl nodded. "I'm taking it down again," he said.

A few seconds later, they touched down again in the street just a couple of hundred yards from where they had started.

Karl reached out a jittery hand and turned off the ignition.

Nobody said anything for a while, they just sat and listened to the engine ticking. It sounded just like any other engine settling down after a little exercise – but, of course, the bus's customized engine wasn't like any engine any of them had ever experienced before in a road vehicle.

"Who on earth fixed this heap up to fly?"

"That's only half of the question," Karl said, turning to face Virgil.

"What's the other half?"

Karl looked away out of the windshield onto the empty pavement surrounding them. "Where are they?" he said.

"Hey!" Angel Wurst shouted from the back of the bus. "I'm hungry." And she jumped down from the box and headed for the front.

(34)

The I-25 freeway had been a ghost road and they were glad to get off of it, though they knew that the new route would eventually cause them some problems.

And so it was that, under a midday sky the color of gunmetal and bruising, they pulled the Seville into a mini-mall parking lot in a little town on the outskirts of Denver to empty bladders, grab some refreshments and generally gather their thoughts. Rick stood alongside the car and marveled at the fact he'd driven all the way from the station. He wasn't going to get too confident right now but he figured that maybe he was over the worst where the accident was concerned. Accident, he thought. Strange how people came up with these little euphemisms for the various unpleasantnesses that plagued them from time to time.

"Shee-it, my goddam leg is killing me here," Johnny hissed from the Seville's back seat. "I'm gonna have to get something stronger for it."

Melanie leaned in and looked at Johnny's face. It was ashen and he was perspiring badly. "How'd you feel otherwise?"

"How do I feel *otherwise*? Is that like, a *joke*?" He shook his head and laughed without any trace of humor. "What does that mean, exactly? How do I feel otherwise from *what*?"

"Hey, take it easy, Johnny. Mel doesn't–"

Melanie flashed her eyes at Rick and crouched down, watching Johnny between the front passenger seat edge and the door surround.

Johnny leaned over and placed his hands gently on either side of his knee. "It's killing me, Mel," he said. There were tears in his eyes.

"I know, honey," she said, and she reached over to run her fingers through his hair. She felt tears brim in her own eyes and, just for a second, she pretended it was Geoff's head she was stoking. She closed her eyes and swallowed hard.

It had been a long couple of days.

The first light had hit when she was doing her early morning stint on the radio and it had left the world empty. OK, it probably figured that there were some other people who had been bypassed by whatever it was – they still didn't know, didn't even have a clue, nor any idea what it was they all had in common to sidestep the light – but the ratio had to be small. After all, Jesman's Bend was *deserted* – no, *emptied* was a better word: she didn't think the townsfolk had had much of a say in the matter.

The second appearance of the light had come almost one day later – pretty much to the minute, she'd have said if she'd have been asked. And that was when things had gotten kind of back to normal – or, at least, as far as they knew normal to be at that stage. They had seen the car on the road set off down into town, and that was when Rick and Geoff had gone off to see what was happening. A little after that, Melanie's personal world had ended right along with – or so it seemed to be stacking up – the regular one.

Rick leaned on the roof and rubbed his stomach. "We gonna eat something here? I'm feeling a little faint."

Melanie nodded and looked up at the sky.

"Is it my imagination or does it seem to be getting dark early? I mean, *too* early."

Johnny groaned as he leaned over and rolled down the window. "Could be a storm coming," he said, wincing slightly when he leaned his leg against the car's side-panel.

Melanie didn't comment on the idea of a storm. "Too early for sunset." She stepped back from the car and scanned the sky. The funny thing was that the darkness seemed to be, well, darker than usual. She knew that didn't make any sense but that was just the way it was.

She clapped her hands together. "Well, I think we should move."

"And I think we should get food," Rick said.

"Well, if everyone can wait for me, I need to pee."

They were driving again, eating prepackaged sandwiches from a convenience store, when they saw the smoke from the eighteen-wheeler. But it was still several miles before they reached it, by which time Johnny – having eaten two pre-packaged baguette sandwiches and a blueberry muffin – was feeling a little better.

"Jeez," he said from the back seat, his voice low. "What a mess."

Oil was still burning in some places and in others just pumping out a funereal pall way up into the otherwise clear blue Colorado sky. Whatever it was that had removed the population of Jesman's Bend had clearly seen fit to take the driver from behind the wheel of the rig in that same instant, out here in Denver, and the rig had jackknifed across all four lanes. A couple of other cars had slammed into it, others had gone off the road at the side a good way before. Johnny tried to picture the scene, the blinding light and the ensuing explosion.

They stopped the car, simply because there was nothing else they could do, and then checked the wreckage to see if there was any way they could get the Seville onto the clear road beyond. There wasn't. And up ahead, they could see other cars, 4x4's, pickups and even a couple of twelve- and eighteen-wheelers covering the blacktop, with one trailer home upended on its roof and hanging out of the front window of a big display store filled with John Deere tractors.

"Didn't know the twenty-five was so busy that time of night," Rick said, shielding his eyes against the sun's glare.

"Lot of folks heading for Denver," Mel said. "All day, every day," she added, nodding as though to underline that a couple times.

They scanned the road beyond the jackknifed rig but there was nothing up ahead that looked drivable.

Johnny pointed over to a pull-in on the other side of the highway, and the familiar sign of the Taco Bell franchise. "Hungry?" he said.

"We only just ate," Mel said, unable to hide her incredulity.

"I'm feeding an injury," Johnny said. "You know how to work these big ovens?" he shouted over his shoulder as he limped toward the sidewalk.

Mel turned to Rick and shook her head. "Whatever happened to New Age Man?"

Rick smiled and shrugged. "I think he just left the building."

They started after Johnny, both of them noting that he seemed to be walking a little easier now. He was still hobbling, but the limp wasn't quite so severe.

Johnny stopped when he reached the sidewalk, stretched a little and looked down at his exposed shin. The shinbone was swollen up like someone had inserted a short banana under the skin where Elsie Weebershand – or whatever it was that Elsie had become – had hit it with one of the chair legs from the radio station's studio. "You think maybe it isn't broken after all?" he asked of nobody in particular, marveling at the colors of the bruising that stretched down below his sock and way up over his knee.

"If it was broken, you wouldn't be able to put any pressure on it at all," Mel said, "never mind walk on it."

Rick read out from the menu. "He's inspired by the culinary expertise on offer – chimichangas, burritos, fajitas, soured cream, refried beans–"

"Gonna be good fun in the car," Mel said. She was trying to put on a brave face but the situation seemed hopeless. And every time she started to feel a little lighter, the whole thing washed over her again.

She recalled smiling at Geoff, and him smiling back, as though they both of them knew that it was going to be the last smile they exchanged. And she remembered stroking his arm before stepping back inside the radio station and watching Johnny secure the door. And then that was it. He was gone. According to Rick, her husband hadn't died for a couple of hours after that but the departure was enough. That was the moment, the door closing slowly on Geoff's face, Geoff watching her and she watching him, until the door fitted itself neatly into the frame and Johnny turned the key and flicked the deadbolt. She kept having to check herself from wishing that Johnny had gone – which, of course, really meant her wishing that Johnny was dead. The thought made her feel guilty and she had to shake her head to loosen it, to dislodge its talons from holding onto the soft flesh of her brain and insinuating itself into her psyche.

"You thinking about Geoff?"

"What?" Melanie started at the touch of Rick's hand, gentle on her shoulder, and at the softness of his voice. "Oh–" Well what was there to say? She forced a smile, a weak one which she could already feel shivering a little at the sides of her mouth, her bottom lip trembling. She shrugged and looked away, focusing instead on Johnny, standing over there on the sidewalk as though nothing mattered at all, as though the world was just the way it had always been – filled with people and all the normal hopes and fears that made up life.

"It'll get easier," Rick whispered. "Just give it time."

She nodded. "I know," she said, though, deep inside her, deep down where Geoff's removal from her life burned in her gut like battery acid, she didn't think it was ever going to get better. That maybe even it was going to get worse. And maybe one other thing: maybe she didn't *want* it to get better. Maybe she just wanted to wallow in it from here on in, drinking the grief in deep draughts, feeling it pool in her gut and just sit there, still and growing stagnant.

Melanie turned and looked down the street.

"You think they're around here? More of them?"

Rick nodded slowly. "No reason why not."

"Hiding," Melanie said, her voice little more than a whisper.

When she turned back to Rick, Melanie's eyes were hard, like a shark's eyes, black and merciless. "I want to kill them all," she said then, matter-of-factly.

"I know," was all Rick could think of to say to her. He could have initiated a conversation about them – about all their one-time neighbors, the good folks of Jesman's Bend – and about how they had killed Melanie's husband and attacked the station, dragging themselves around like mindless zombies (but, hey, lest we forget, not so mindless that they couldn't turn their collective hand to souping up the local vehicular motorcade so that it could fly over the rooftops). And what was the deal with the dark glasses and the gloves? And where were they during the daytime? Vampire zombies, that was what they were, with no trace of the original person left behind. But none of this was worth putting into words. It was best left unspoken. They all knew each of them was thinking about it but a group debate didn't seem to have anything going for it.

Rick put an arm around Melanie's shoulder and said it once more – "I know..." – but softer this time.

Johnny appeared in the doorway and slumped dramatically against the door. "Hey? We eating or not?"

"Seems to me like you got a worm in there, the food you're packing away."

Johnny leaned on the door frame and lifted his right leg, holding it under the thigh and shaking his head. "Shit, it's throbbing like a bastard," Johnny said. Even as the words left his mouth, wondering what on earth had made him use such a nonsensical relationship. It was just the dull ache that seemed to wash over every part of him. He needed some painkillers. "I need some painkillers," he said.

Rick nodded and stepped forward, squeezing his sister-in-law's shoulder twice before letting his arm drop down by his side. "Let's get inside, figure out some food, and then I'll go hunt out a drugstore, get some bandages, ibuprofen, stuff like that."

"I think I need the painkillers *now*, Rick," Johnny said, his voice filled with apology.

"You take him inside and see about the food. I'll go find a pharmacy."

Melanie nodded. "OK. Be careful," she said as she walked over to where Johnny was trying to rest his right foot on the Taco Bell's window ledge.

"You too."

In the Taco Bell, Mel and Johnny had done the restrooms while Rick was scouting for drugstores, and Melanie had managed to throw together a few plates of food – mostly salad, cheese and tacos: no fajitas, much to Johnny's dismay – and cartons of soda. It was while they were busy working their way through this feast, sitting at a table alongside a large window that looked out onto Main Street, that they saw Rick marching along the opposite sidewalk carrying a large brown bag. He held the bag aloft triumphantly when he saw Melanie and Johnny in the window, and they waved back to him.

"I feel as excited as when I was a kid at Christmas," Johnny said as Rick came into the restaurant.

"Any food left for me?"

Melanie stood and made to walk to the counter.

"Hey, no, finish up. I'll do Johnny first, keep him quiet."

"Muchos gracias, compadre."

"Just like a native," Melanie said, adding a small handclap to supplement the words. "But, unfortunately, *not* a native of Mexico."

"Let's move you over to this table and get you stretched out," Rick said. He leaned over and pushed his shoulder until it slipped under Johnny's armpit. "You'll soon feel better with food inside of you."

"Yeah, but I'm pissed about the fajitas."

"I did the best I cou–" Melanie started.

"Hey, I'm just kidding you," Johnny said. "You did great."

Melanie walked back out onto the sidewalk to allow the two men to concentrate on binding Johnny's leg. When they emerged from the Taco Bell, Johnny looked definitely better and Melanie told him so.

"It's the ibuprofen." He held up his hand, palm facing Melanie, and wiggled the fingers.

"*Five*? You took *five* painkillers?"

Johnny shrugged. "The warden wouldn't let me have any more." He jerked his thumb back at Rick.

"How's it feel? Now you're standing on it?"

"Hey, what can I tell ya, doc. It's felt better. But believe me, it felt a whole lot worse a half hour ago."

"You want something to eat, Rick?"

Rick made a face and shrugged. "I'm OK. I had a Snickers bar from the drugstore."

"OK. Then are we good to move?" Melanie seemed tense.

"Sure. But what's the hurry?"

It was only approaching mid-afternoon now but already the sky over to the east looked like a mud hole.

Melanie pointed. "See that?" Without waiting for a response as the two men turned to look, she said, "That is most definitely not right."

Halfway back to the car they saw, a little way down from them, slewed right into the center rail, a buckled Escort gleaming in the sun, lying on its side heading up to the way they had come. At first, Johnny couldn't see what she was pointing at but then, just as Rick said "Hey," he spotted the hand up against the glass on the front passenger window.

"Someone's in the car," was all he could think of to say and, just for a few seconds, the realization scared him. All he could think of was Daryl Engstrom's torn-eared face and his blood spattered blue shirt as Daryl doggedly came on brandishing the station hat stand, seemingly hell bent on doing away with everyone inside. Everyone not wearing gloves and dark glasses anyways.

"Are they wearing sunglasses?" Johnny asked.

"Can't see from here." Mel moved across their side of the highway, keeping a wide berth between her and the Escort. She felt her heart hammering. For some ridiculous reason, she couldn't fight off the feeling that the Escort's door was going to creak open, spilling powdered glass and dashboard junk, and the figure that was going to roll out onto the blacktop was her husband, Geoff.

Of course, Geoff was dead. Rick had said so. Rick had seen it *happen*. All of that *plus* they were miles away. And finally, Geoff would not have been seen in an Escort. More to the point, no, ladies and gentlemen, he wouldn't even have been seen *dead* in one.

Johnny limped over alongside as Mel and Rick walked closer to the Escort on their left.

"Hello?" Rick shouted. "You OK in there?"

Of course, it could be the guy–

Hey, asshole, here we are once again... thought maybe you'd like to mash me up a little more just in case you left a couple of intact bones someplace...

–he ran over all that time ago, come back to have his revenge. Or maybe just to make him feel bad. Without thinking or even realizing he was doing it, Rick held back.

Mel shouted, "Can you see any movement?"

Johnny shook his head. "I'm going to get down and take a look."

"Go easy on that leg, Johnny," Rick called. And then he jogged forward until he had caught them up.

"Whoever they are and wherever they're from, I think it's safe to say they're on the home team." He took another step closer to the Escort. "At least, they don't have dark glasses and gloves."

Melanie shuddered. She was thinking back to how Geoff must have felt when Jerry Borgesson had started to remove his gloves. Only it wasn't Jerry Borgesson–

"Mel?"

–it was one of those things, things from – she couldn't even bring herself to say another world – or alien beings from a dying planet (she thought the line in the narrator's voice from the old *Invaders* TV show), so how must he have felt when–

"Melster? Hey... Mel!"

–the thing had taken hold of her husband's hea–

"*Mel*!" Johnny shook her and she turned to him as though waking from a dream, a slight frown as, just for a nanosecond, she tried to place his face.

"Let it go, Melvin," Johnny said.

Rick crouched down by the Escort and craned his neck. Even from where they were standing, Mel and Johnny saw Rick grimace and turn away for a few seconds. In that short time, it looked as though Rick was about to throw up but he seemed to regain control. When he turned his head back to look inside the car, Melanie gave silent thanks that Rick had not stuffed himself full of cheese, soured cream and cold refried beans.

"There's a piece of windshield just about taken his head off and–" He moved to the side and pointed at something Melanie decided she would be better off not seeing. "–there's also a piece of metal tubing's gone right through his eye socket."

Mel turned away to face the littered roadway.

"How about the driver?" Johnny called.

Rick shook his head. "No driver."

He lay completely down on the road and shuffled closer to the car.

"Jeez, Louise!"

"There's a lot of blood in here, let me tell you." He moved a little closer and tried the door. "Uh uh," he shouted. "Locked tight." He shook his head again and stood up, started to walk back towards them, dusting his hands. "Looks like someone killed a herd of steers in there."

As Rick reached them, Johnny said, "Any sign that the driver got out?"

"Nope. Believe me, if he – or she – hadn't got out before the impact, then there's no way they'd have got out after it. The foot pedals are up in the air, steering column is fractured and bent to hell and it's been hammered in a good few feet." He looked from one to the other. "If the driver had still been there when that happened, well, let's just say he'd be a lot shorter."

"How about the collision bag?" Mel asked.

"Blown up on the driver's side. Doesn't seem to be one on the passenger's." Rick shuffled further into the car. "Ah," he said, his voice muffled. "That clinches it." He started to pull out.

"What?" Johnny accepted Melanie's shoulder to lean on.

"The driver's seatbelt is still engaged."

"So that's four we know of – sorry, five," Johnny said. "That's us three and Geoff, and now the guy in the Escort."

Rick pulled himself up by the Escort's roof and dusted himself down. "Five?"

"Five of us who were not affected by the light."

Melanie looked around at the Escort. "What if the guy in there died *before* the light, or maybe *during* it?"

Rick shook his head. "No," he said, straightening up. In that instant, Melanie suddenly felt safer with her husband's brother. She thought of all the times the two men – or even two boys – had spent together, all the words they had spoken to each other, all the confidences they had shared. There would be confidences in there that concerned her, too. Early conversations when Geoff must have told Rick that he had met a new woman. She imagined Rick saying, in response to that, *What's her name?* And then, in her head, she heard Geoff whisper, *Melanie*.

"–as we can figure it out," Rick was saying, "it was a pretty instantaneous thing." He clicked his fingers. "And you're gone. History. Just disappeared. And if the driver went, then the car would continue rolling on, maybe doing forty, fifty miles an hour..." He let his voice trail off and looked at the Escort.

"Until it stopped," Melanie said.

"Until it stopped," Rick agreed, "or until something got in its way."

"And it's lights out," Johnny said.

"And still no logical reason for any of us still being here," Melanie said.

Everyone stayed silent until Rick looked over towards the east. "It's getting dark. Sun must be going down," he said.

"What time is it?" Johnny asked.

Mel checked her watch. "Hey, it's only a little after four."

"Hey, hold on a second," Rick said. He pointed over to the west. "See the sky over there?" Then he turned and pointed in the opposite direction. "Doesn't it look darker east to you?"

Mel and Johnny did a double take in each direction and then had to agree. It did look slightly duskier in the east than it did in the west. At first Mel was just going to shrug it off and then she stopped. "The sun rises in the east and sets in the west," she said, immediately feeling dumb for pointing out the obvious. So she scooted along as fast as she could and added, "So it figures that the sunset will spread from the east the same way as the dawn spreads from the east."

"Yeah, but it's only four in the goddam afternoon, Mel."

She nodded. Johnny had a point.

"Maybe it's just a–" Johnny was stumped for words. What exactly could it be, *maybe*? An optical illusion? Global warming? No illusion: it definitely was darker in the east than it was in the west. Not by a whole lot but enough to make it noticeable. Johnny wished he was able to see the sun. That might make things a little easier to figure out.

"You know," Rick said, "I think we should get the car off the roads and hole up someplace."

"You got a feeling about this?" Mel said.

Rick looked to the east again, scanning the sky on the horizon. Was it his imagination or did there seem to be a gentle darkening – no, not exactly a darkening; a shading was more like it – spreading over the distant sky?

"I dunno. I just think we should get off the road."

A couple of minutes later they were back in the car heading north again, checking the cross streets for a clear way through towards the city.

(35)

They were sitting in the *Mile High Café.*

They had tentatively touched on such mundane matters as how long the power was going to last. Presumably nobody was overseeing power supplies – how did that work? Light, heating, refrigeration... they didn't know but they guessed that eventually it would all stop. That seemed like bad enough news in itself until Virgil Banders suggested that maybe someone would come in and fix it.

Angel Wurst wasn't sure she liked the sound of that and she said so. She had a feeling that the power wasn't the only thing they'd fix. Ronnie made a *shh!* face and smiled at her. It didn't look like there was any warmth behind it.

The girl was sipping a mango and pineapple smoothie from the refrigerated cabinet over by the door that Karl had smashed in order to get inside. Her face was smeared with chocolate from the enormous piece of cake from a different cabinet. They watched her for a while, Ronnie and Karl eating cinnamon pastries and Virgil Banders smoking a cigarette. The smoke smelled good to Ronnie: he had half a mind to ask for one when he'd finished his coffee. He would see how he felt. Right now, the pastry tasted heavenly, and the coffee was a life-saver. He told the map reader as much.

"My wife used to say coffee was the only thing I didn't burn."

Noting the past tense, Ronnie said, "Divorced?" He suddenly thought about Martha and was surprised to find that her image was a poignant one rather than one of loathing. Perhaps it was true that absence did indeed make the heart grow fonder. He suspected that his own heart was going to get mighty fond – he did not expect to see Martha again.

Karl shook his head and looked down into his coffee cup. "Died." He lifted the cup and swirled the contents around a couple of times before returning it to the table.

Ronnie winced and made a face. "Hey, sorry I–"

Karl waved him never mind. "Nothing for you to apologize for," he said. "It was a good few years back now. Never found anyone else – never even *looked*, for that matter."

"How did she die?"

Ronnie looked around at Virgil Banders and flashed his eyes at him. What was the boy thinking, for Chrissakes? And was it Ronnie's imagination or did Virgil's voice sound suddenly different – excited, perhaps?

"That's OK," Karl said. Turning to Virgil, he said, "Elaine keeled right over in the middle of a meal – lasagne, as I recall. Heh, I say 'as I recall' like there's a possibility I might have gotten it wrong." He shook his head. "There's no way that could ever happen. I remember every single second of that evening… play the whole thing back now and again… sometimes intentionally, other times in my dreams. And every time I do the same thing: I sit at the table and I say to her, 'Elaine? You OK, honey?' And Elaine is slumped forward with her head right in the middle of the pasta, her glass of merlot knocked over and steadily spreading on the table like blood, her fork – with pieces of food still on it and scattered around it – lying on the floor next to her drooped hand."

Ronnie reached over and rubbed Angel Wurst's head. "You OK, honey?" he said, suddenly realizing that those were the very same words that the map-man had just used. The girl nodded, took another sip of her smoothie and returned to adjusting Samantha the doll's attire.

Virgil Banders cleared his throat and shuffled around in his seat.

Karl sat upright and clapped his hands. "Hey, sorry. I just pissed on the campfire."

"My fault," Virgil said. "I shouldn't have asked."

Ronnie thought, *No, you fucking shouldn't,* but he didn't say anything. There was something not altogether to his liking about the boy, he realized. Maybe Angel had been right all along. He glanced sideways at the girl as the thought drifted first into and then out of his head, and he saw her looking at him. As their eyes met, hers darted to the side and widened. Ronnie turned around and saw Virgil was watching the pair of them. He smiled, but it was a smile completely without humor.

Angel looked directly at Ronnie and said, "Hey, you wanna look in my box?"

There was something vaguely ambiguous about that innocent inquiry and Ronnie felt that Virgil had felt it too. Out of the corner of his eye, he saw the boy uncross and recross his legs.

"What box is that, honey?" Ronnie asked.

"The box on the bus."

"Box on the bus?"

Angel nodded.

"What's in there?"

Angel shrugged and twisted Samantha around to face Ronnie. "We don't know," said the squawky voice. "No," Angel added, "we can't get into it."

"Maybe it's just a part of the bus."

"Uh uh."

"Where they put the bags, maybe."

She shook her head again.

"You sure it's not a part of the bus, Angel?" Karl had a point. Perhaps it was part of the heating system, dressed up nattily but only accessible through the back of the bus or maybe the side-panels, where the long haul passengers would store their bags.

"It moves."

"You mean it's not fixed in place?"

Angel frowned and made an exasperated face. "I mean, there's something inside it. Something that moves."

"You were bouncing it around back there," Virgil said by way of an explanation, the general theory being that when Karl was maneuvering the bus from side to side, whatever was in the box was sliding around.

Angel looked across all of their faces, one by one, moving the doll around constantly. "No, it didn't move when you were driving. It moved when I laid on top of the box."

Karl sighed and stood up from the table. "Let's take a look," he said, stretching his arms up and wincing at his right shoulder. "Then we need to make a move."

"Need to make a move? We on a deadline?"

Karl smiled at the boy. "Well, I just thought that–" He stopped and looked at Angel. He was about to say that it might be best to make a move – with or without the flying bus – before whoever made it *into* a flying bus came back to claim it.

He moved around the table and hunkered down beside Angel, looking straight out of the *Mile High Café* window into the street – at the bus. "How big is your box, Angel?" he asked.

This time, there was no awkward movement from Virgil Banders and Ronnie wondered if maybe he had imagined the boy's reaction earlier.

Angel held her hands wide apart and then tried to stretch even further. "This big," she announced proudly, "but even bigger."

The men exchanged glances. "Let's go take a look," Karl said. And they walked out into a darkening street.

(36)

"She dead?"

"Can't see from here," Rick said.

"But she isn't wearing sunglasses," Melanie offered.

"Amen to that, Melvin," said Johnny. He rubbed his leg and although he still winced a little as his hand passed over his shin, it didn't seem quite so bad as it was. "You know, I think I'm gonna live."

"Thank you, Lord," Rick muttered. He turned to face the back seat, where Johnny was sitting with his leg up. "Well, we know she wasn't taken. And that's all we know." He turned back to watch the prone figure lying almost spread eagled outside the movie theater. "She *looks* dead to me."

"Shit, I'll go check her out, man," Johnny said as he shifted his leg back onto the floor. "It's daylight out there and, like you say, she isn't wearing glasses – nor gloves, far as I can make out."

Rick held him back. "No," he said, tiredly, rubbing his eyes, "I guess I should go."

Johnny started to ask why but it was obvious: if anything did require fast movement then the chances were that Johnny wouldn't be able to do it.

"Go easy," Melanie said, patting Rick's knee.

It was intended as a purely platonic gesture but there was more to it than that and both of them knew it. Rick was a part of Melanie's husband, skin created by the same genes, experiences they had both lived through,. some of which Melanie might not even know about.

So the pat was not entirely selfless and as she withdrew her hand, Melanie's slight coloring reflected that knowledge.

"Don't worry, sis," Rick said, using a term he had never – to Melanie's knowledge – used before, "I'll look after myself."

They watched him get out of the car, close the door and stretch, looking around in every direction. After a few seconds, he seemed to have satisfied himself. But he still turned to Melanie and, frowning, pointed at the group door-locking button on Rick's door frame. Melanie pushed it down.

Rick took a couple of steps and then kind of crouched and leaned forward. "Hello?"

They could hear him clearly inside the car.

"Damnedest weather," Johnny said. He nodded over in the direction of Melanie's side. Thick black tendrils were snaking around on the horizon.

"Storm coming," Melanie said. She turned around to watch Rick, who had taken another couple of steps.

"Doesn't look like a storm to me."

"Hey... you OK?" Rick was shouting.

Melanie gasped and pointed. "She moved."

Rick stopped dead and turned to the car, eyebrows raised.

"The wind," Johnny said, "blowing her clothes."

Melanie shook her head. "Uh uh. She moved."

They watched.

"Lady?" Rick shouted.

Sally Davis lifted her head and looked up at the man standing above her. He looked young – about mid-twenties, maybe thirty – and fit, a craggy face with softness around the eyes.

"You're not... you're not," Sally began. And then she slumped her head onto her arms.

Rick turned and waved for Melanie and Johnny to come out.

The woman lifted her head again and licked her lips. "Sunglasses?" she said.

Rick nodded. Then he shook his head. "Nope," he said. "No sunglasses."

He's *a nice man*, one of the voices said. But Sally ignored it.

(37)

"Getting late," Ronnie said.

Karl the map reader grunted an acknowledgement of that and persevered with his latest attempt at prizing the girl's box open.

"Light's beginning to go," Virgil Banders added. He wasn't quite sure why that concerned him so, but it *did* concern him.

Angel Wurst sat on one of the seats swinging her legs as she watched Karl work. "It did move," she said.

Nobody said anything to that.

"You know what it looks like to me?"

Ronnie knew damn well what it looked like and he was pissed at the boy for making it official. Once someone else commented on it then it became a pretty sure thing. Well, three pretty sure things, he was now thinking.

The first one was, it looked like a goddam coffin. Now that one right there was bad enough. But the second one was a little more uncomfortable. It didn't look like it had been made from any material Ronnie Mortenson had ever seen. OK, so coffin-making materials were a long way outside his sphere of reference, but some things you just knew. And this was one of them.

But it was the third thing that made Ronnie the most apprehensive. He believed Angel Wurst. He believed her when she said that something had moved in there. And now, the afternoon was moving along and the light was fading and they were in what appeared to be a bus that had been customized by aliens and, well, my oh my, what do we have here, snuck away on the back seat in his or her (or maybe its) very own little home from home? Could it possibly be the driver?

"Yeah," he said, "it looks that way to me, too."

"There's someone in there, isn't there?"

"It's getting dark outside," Angel Wurst announced.

Karl tried to stifle a cough but, in the end, had to take out his handkerchief and clear his throat into it. When he glanced down into the material before returning it to his pocket he saw blood. He folded it up and put it away quickly, glancing around at the others. The boy, Virgil Banders, was studying the box. But Ronnie was watching him. Neither of them said anything but Karl gave a little movement with his mouth – a kind of *oh well, that's the ball game!* sort of movement – and Ronnie's face grew suddenly soft and concerned. Karl looked away.

"Have you tried to lift it?" Virgil asked.

Karl got to his feet but Ronnie stepped in his way. "Here," Ronnie said, "you're the brains of the outfit. Let me do the lifting." He hefted it and jiggled it a couple of times.

"Is there anything inside?"

It was Samantha the doll that had asked the question and Ronnie was tempted to mimic that squawky voice right back at her, but he thought better of it. "Can't say," he said.

"There's something in there, I know there is." Angel's voice emerged from out of Samantha the doll's strangled squawk.

"Well," Karl said as Ronnie rested the box back onto the seat, "I'm damned if I know how to get in there." He pointed to the side. "There's definitely a join – see?"

Ronnie leaned forward, squinting, trying to figure out what Karl was referring to. He kind of half fancied he could see an occasional hairline but nothing that appeared to travel the full length.

Karl nodded, more to himself than to anyone else.

"You OK?" Ronnie kept his voice low. Virgil Banders had gone back to the front of the bus for a smoke and Angel Wurst had shuffled back into her seat to converse with Samantha.

"OK?"

"Sure. OK."

"Why wouldn't I be OK?"

"Well, I mean. I saw you–" He waved his hand. "–back then."

"Yeah?" Karl frowned at him and then looked at the box again. "You know," he went on, "we're all in super deep shit if what you said was right."

"What did I say?"

"That I was the brains of the outfit."

Ronnie couldn't help but smile.

He patted the map-reader on the shoulder. "You up to driving?"

"Is that a brains of the outfit's job?"

Ronnie nodded. "One of many."

When they went to the front of the bus, Virgil tossed his cigarette butt out into the street. Angel had fallen asleep. Everything seemed calm, even serene.

We're like a family, Ronnie thought. A real honest to God family.

Nobody had seen the slow thickening of the tiny pencil-line crack on the side of the box on the back seat. And when Karl slid into the driver's seat and the three men concentrated on getting the bus airborne, the noise drowned out the gentle creaking coming from the rear of the bus.

(38)

Darkness had snuck up on them while they were driving. It had slithered in on them hands-in-pockets, casually whistling an off-key tune and insinuating itself when their attention was elsewhere. That elsewhere was on Sally Davis's story.

The woman sounded more like Lara Croft than a mid-fifties woman in a plain skirt, blouse and sweater. What a story it was! Walking around a high ledge seconds before the sunglasses zombies broke into her hotel room and then battling across theater seats pursued by a whole horde of them seemingly out to touch her and weave their special magic on her. Sitting behind the wheel, listening, Rick's mind drifted back to seeing Jerry Borgesson – or whatever it was that Jerry had turned into – reaching out both hands and taking a hold of Rick's brother's head, one hand on each side, holding it almost tenderly, like it was an overripe pumpkin that he didn't want to squeeze too hard. And as Sally Davis's voice droned on and they drove past endless crashed cars – some of them still smoking, though the fires had long since burned out – Rick recalled watching his brother's eyes roll upwards, showing white, and his body shaking like he'd taken a hold of a live wire.

Rick had managed to dislodge Borgesson's hold but the damage had already been done.

Geoff's right eye had slid back into view and Rick had seen it catch his own.

In that brief instant, Rick had felt as though he was looking into his brother's soul. The expression told him to get away, to get away as fast as he could, and to look after Geoff's wife and keep her safe – he turned to the side and looked at Melanie, watching out of the windscreen as she listened to their new passenger, oblivious to her brother-in-law's thoughts. Rick turned away before Melanie could turn to him and smile, maybe frown that *what's up?* look of hers.

There had been a world of pain in that final glance from Geoff. Rick had been almost able to feel it in his own head, feel it shriveling his insides, turning them to mush. Then the expression had faded and, as though on autopilot, Rick's brother had shuffled around on the ground, trying to get up.

Rick didn't think there was any real understanding in Geoff's mind at that point, just a simple reflex mechanism.

He had seen a bird doing the very same thing one time, back in the house in Providence when he was just a kid. A cat had got the bird, a big white cat that he had used to like stroking and listening to it purr. The cat had torn off one of the bird's wings and gouged a big chunk out of the side of its face, just next to the tiny beak. For what seemed like an age, the bird had shuffled around on the spot – watched quietly by the cat lying right next to it on the lawn – lifting its one good wing and trying to flap the exposed muscle of the other, just going through the motions as it tried to get back to normal, slumping as its legs kept giving way first to one side and then the other. Meanwhile, all of the bird's systems were mercifully closing down.

Rick figured that his brother's systems had been closing down in exactly the same way, the little men inside Geoff's body turning off all the power, all the screens, watching them flatline and go blank, one by one.

He remembered Geoff's eye plopping out onto his cheek like the crazy glasses you could buy in joke stores, and a thick dark substance oozing out after it. Geoff had lifted a hand to his face and patted the gunk gently. Then, with a tiny shudder that seemed to pass through his entire body like a wave, he had moved his hand away and rested it on the ground, seemingly trying to get his breath.

In his final brief seconds, Geoff had projectile vomited over his own legs, a long string of something solid-looking hanging from his mouth. He had paused for a second, ignoring what was dangling from his mouth – and which was still bubbling in waves down his chin – while he patted his face again, sticking a finger patterned with leaf and grass shards into the empty eye socket. Then he had shuddered uncontrollably and his other eye dropped onto his lap. More ooze followed and Geoff–

"Rick?"

"Oh, sorry... miles away."

In a low voice, Melanie asked what he was thinking about.

"Oh," Rick responded, without so much as a second's hesitation, "I was thinking about how great it is to be driving again. Particularly on these ro–" He stopped, and leaned forward so that his face was almost on the windshield, slamming his foot hard down on the brake pedal. "What the *fuck...?*"

Johnny leaned forward as well. He gave a little whistle and then let out a throaty laugh. "Now there's something you don't see every day," he said.

"What *is* it?" said Sally Davis.

"Unless I'm very much mistaken," said Rick, "that is the guy out of *American Splendor...* and he's driving a flying bus."

The Seville screeched and swung around on the road to a stop, narrowly missing the tail end of a UPS delivery truck that was lying on its side across the center line. They all leaned over to watch the bus as it swung over them.

"Hey, anyone see if the guy was wearing any sunglasses?"

"He wasn't," Melanie said. "Least, I don't think he was. It's pretty dark, and those headlights are everywhere."

"He wasn't," Johnny said, turning to Sally Davis, who seemed to be muttering to herself.

"And how about gloves?"

Johnny shrugged. "No idea. Too dark."

Rick breathed in nervously. "Well, we're gonna find out soon enough. Because I think he's trying to lan–"

Just as he was about to finish, the bus rocked side to side mid-air about sixty or seventy yards down the road.

"Scratch that," said Rick. "He's about to crash."

(39)

As they flew along, Ronnie and Virgil Banders looked out onto the deserted city while Angel Wurst played with Samantha the doll. She had moved closer to the front of the bus – around the mid-way point – because she felt kind of lonely back there, but it was too noisy right up at the front. She'd leave the three men to get on with things and she would sit with Samantha.

The twilight was pronounced now, and still only about 6.00am. But store windows were still lit up, and traffic signals continued to change colors while little metallic voices instructed the empty street to "walk" and "do not walk."

"It's like a ghost town," Ronnie said, shaking his head, sending the words out to nobody in particular. "All that's missing is sagebrush."

Karl coughed a rattling cough and wiped his mouth again with his handkerchief, making sure he kept one hand on the steering wheel. He switched on the lights so that the dials on the dashboard lit up and the twin beams from the headlamps illuminated the ground but working independently of each other.

"How the hell do the lights work?" Virgil asked.

"You got me," said Karl. "They seem to be on some kind of system, roaming around the ground in a loop." He coughed again, his hand lifting the handkerchief to his mouth, and swallowed with apparent difficulty.

"Wouldn't we be better on the ground?"

Returning the handkerchief to his pants pocket and clearing his throat with a loud *harrumph!*, Karl agreed. "But I'm guessing we could need this mode of transportation sometime in the future," he explained, "and I'd sooner get the hang of it now, when the pressure isn't as bad."

He looked around at Ronnie, wheezed a little, and said hoarsely, "You know, could be a good idea for *you* to get the hang of this."

Ronnie held his hands up and forced himself to look away from the tiny flecks of blood on the map-reader's lips. "No way."

"You did OK in the plane."

"Yeah, well, that was an emergency. It's surprising the things you find out you can do when the chips are down."

"Hey," Karl said, reaching over to pull Ronnie across to the driver's seat. "You do need to do this. You know you do."

Ronnie allowed himself to be pulled.

"It's actually pretty easy," Karl said, now standing behind Ronnie but keeping his hands on the wheel. "God knows how they've done it but it just responds to the way you push or pull the steering–" He suddenly bent forward.

Virgil Banders moved across from the long seat next to the steps, where he had been lounging, feet on the seat. He grabbed a hold of Karl's shoulders.

"You OK, man?"

Karl removed his hands from the wheel leaving Ronnie to take over full control. The bus juddered and lurched a little but pretty soon Ronnie had it going smoothly. The only trouble was that he'd ended up going across to the right, over buildings. He didn't think that was too good an idea – the buildings were all different heights and he felt that it would be easier keeping mid-height along the regular street grid.

Angel wasn't sure what it was that made her turn around when she did. It could have been some tiny noise coming from behind her, or it could have been that she wanted to look through the rear windows as they moved along – she had never flown in a bus before! – or it could have been one of her little pre-man-ishons. It could even have been that she saw a strange cold fear creep over the face of Samantha the doll and she was simply turning around to assure her that they were going to be OK. And what do you know – there was a man walking down the aisle between the seats.

"Are you the con-doctor?" Angel asked.

The man didn't look like a con-doctor. He looked old, for a start, and he was wearing a pair of fancy-looking sunglasses that didn't look right on him. Didn't look right on him at all. Angel did a double take at the windows and, sure enough, as she thought, it was getting dark outside.

The man looked unsteady on his feet, holding his hands out in front of–

And hey, wait a minute there, where did this guy *come* from? Angel leaned over and looked down the shadowy aisle all the way to the back seat. And there, sure enough, was the box – *her* box. Only now, the lid was open.

Angel pushed herself back against the side of the bus, frowning. The man had almost reached her seat – too close for her to slide out into the aisle and head for the front.

When she looked down at the front she saw that the map-reader was being hoisted out of the driver's seat and the other man – the nice one who took her to the mall: Ronnie – was sliding behind the controls. All of them had their backs to her and the noise of the engine – much louder than the bus that took her to Fremont Elementary School back home – was far too loud for her to be able to make herself heard. And that was if she could speak, because right now she couldn't.

Angel opened her mouth and made to shout to someone but nothing came out. She looked back, made to stand up and then sat down again. The man was shuffling along like a snail, hands outstretched in front of him. And now he was taking off his gloves. What the heck was he wearing gloves for? It wasn't cold, not in the slightest. Maybe he had some kind of a skin thing. Angel didn't like the idea of touching those hands – or, more particularly, being touched *by* them.

She wished the nasty man – Virgil Banders – she wished even *he* would turn around. As Angel got to her feet she saw that the man was now at the seat behind her. She started to clamber up the back of the seat in front, looking back to see where he was, then looking forward again, trying to pull herself on the metal pole attached to the end of the seat in front. It was no good. She stopped and turned. Of course! The seat, her own seat. She could stand on that and fall forward onto the seat in front and then kind of somersault over. But the man was at her seat now, still standing in the aisle. He was turning towards her, reaching out those ungloved hands.

Angel looked back at the front and saw that Ronnie was busy driving the bus. Virgil Banders was crouched beside Karl the map-man in the seat across the aisle and next to the steps that led down to the door. She opened her mouth again and screamed but it was a silent scream, just air. In desperation, she looked down at Samantha the doll and, without another second's hesitation, she threw it at Virgil Banders and Karl the map-man.

The old man stopped dead, one leg already into the leg area of Angel's seat, and his head turned and followed the path of the strange projectile, watched it fly across the seats and over the aisle to bounce once on Virgil's head and shoulder and then drop down across Karl's face and onto his lap.

When Virgil looked up, there was something flaring in his eyes but it immediately went out when he saw the old man. "Ronnie," Virgil snapped. "We got company."

"Not now," Ronnie hissed as he negotiated overhead wires hanging across the street. The bus lurched and Virgil staggered backwards at exactly the same time as the old man lost some of his footing – and boy, he was very steady for such an old man – and he must be around a hundred and fifty years old if he was a day.

Karl spun around, saw the man, watched him starting to get up, saw his arms reaching out for the girl.

"Get away from him," Karl shouted over the engines' roar, and the bus lurched again, only this time, it lurched the little old man back onto his feet and clear across the aisle.

"Which is the switch for the interior lights?" Ronnie shouted.

Nobody answered.

Angel screamed, and this time it was a doozy. What her mommy used to call her *earshplittenloudenboomer* cry. Karl turned into the aisle and pulled himself upright. He started down the aisle, clapping his hands loudly.

"Hey!" he shouted. "Here!" The bus lurched to the side and Karl took a dive onto the seat, catching his forehead on the handrail.

His chest felt as though someone had just dropped a grand piano onto it from a second floor window.

The old man had not faltered at all in the sudden lurch but he had stopped, his hands now barely a couple of feet from Angel Wurst, and he turned to face the origin of the sound, his head on one side, moving slowly until the man obviously locked onto Karl's legs sticking out into the aisle.

Karl struggled to a sitting position, holding onto his chest. He waved for the old man to come forward.

Virgil stepped into the aisle behind Karl. "You OK?" Virgil kept his voice low.

"We have to get him away from the girl."

"Hey, what can he do to her? I mean, an old fart like that?"

"I don't think he's an old fart at all," Karl whispered.

Angel was sobbing over on the other side of the aisle, apparently unable – or unwilling – to move.

Virgil suddenly realized that, here they were, two reasonably fit people – even with Karl clearly not on top form, he was undoubtedly more than a match for this old dodderer – and yet neither of them was making any kind of attempt to walk down the twenty feet or so of aisle to smack the guy into his seat. And why was that? he wondered.

It's those hands, he thought. *I don't like those hands.* He, better than anyone, knew what some folks were capable of doing with their hands. And old fart or not, the guy in the aisle seemed fairly confident about his hands.

"Shit!" Ronnie was having problems at the front. "Can't keep the damn thing in a straight line." The bus lurched again and this time scraped right alongside the upper floors of a savings and loan building, pieces of masonry and concrete showering down onto the sidewalk and several parked or just abandoned cars, some of them overturned, some half inside stores and others jammed up against each other as though in drunken tryst.

"Mister, back up," Virgil shouted.

"Where did he come from?" Karl asked, unsure as to whether he was aiming the question at Virgil, in front of him, or at Ronnie, busily maneuvering the bus.

Virgil spoke over his shoulder, keeping his voice to a whisper. "Out of that box," he said.

"I know, out of the box," Karl said. "I mean, *before* that."

The man had kept his head twisted to one side, his hands held out in front of him so that, if Karl or Virgil were to charge him then they would encounter the hands first. He gave another jiggle of his head and then turned away from the two men, swinging his hands around like an airplane gunner until they faced the young girl.

Then he started to shuffle in towards her.

Karl coughed and wiped more specks of blood from his mouth. He stared at the flecks and then looked at the man: another three steps, four at the outside, and the guy would be right up at the girl close enough to take her dancing. "Fuck it," he said.

Karl lurched forward as Ronnie brought the bus's head back up again and shattered an overhead streetlight. They could hear broken glass and metal fixtures sliding across the bus's roof. He sidestepped the boy and moved straight for the old man, a sudden constriction in his chest as though he had been roped like a hog and the rope pulled tight. He staggered for a moment, his head lolloping forward and, just for a second or two, Karl thought he was simply going to fall head first to the floor. But he managed to keep upright and reached the man as the man started to turn again, this time towards Karl.

And now the man was smiling.

It wasn't a happy smile or a friendly smile, and, if he had been pushed, Karl wouldn't have been able to explain why that thought was paramount in his mind at that point – just as he was entering the final few minutes of what had been, until this past 36 hours, a singularly uneventful but wonderfully enjoyable life.

As Karl took a hold of the man's shoulder and collar, the man grasped Karl's left cheek with his right hand, the left hand barely missing a similar handhold on the other side of the cartographer's face.

Immediately, Karl began to shake. His own hands dropped from the old man's clothes, flopping by his side and twitching spasmodically. And now the rest of him began to gyrate.

"Hey, map-man," Virgil Banders shouted. To no avail.

Ronnie managed to manipulate the steering wheel to bring the bus around in a small turning circle in the middle of a four-lane road leading into downtown Denver. His muscles were aching and his back felt as though he'd been digging the yard back in Atlanta for two days straight without so much as a break for sleeping, eating or even taking a dump. He heard the girl scream again but he didn't know why – the bus seemed to be settling down into the roadway pretty evenly. He even managed to avoid hitting a FedEx van that was leaning at a rakish angle into a jeweler's store window, broken glass now lying amidst the diamonds.

And what do you know, he thought as the wheels touched the blacktop and the bus settled. There were some people out there.

"Hey," he shouted. "There are some–"

That's when he saw his new friend, Karl, shaking like a bowl of jello, his right eyeball popped right out of its socket and hanging down the side of the map-reader's face on what appeared to be a piece of orangey-brown coiled string.

The girl was now falling over the seat in front of her and screaming hysterically.

Virgil Banders was backing away from a little old man – where the fuck did that guy come from? – who appeared to have Karl in a death grip.

"Let him go!" Ronnie shouted. He stepped from the driver's seat immediately into the aisle.

The old man looked at him, turning his attention from Karl and a careful eye on the stealthy but retreating figure of Virgil Banders to focus on the driver of the bus.

It's his *bus,* Ronnie realized – or, at least, it was the vehicle into which the bus had been customized, presumably by him. It came in one fleeting second, quickly followed by other thoughts. *He's not just an old fart,* was the first one. The next was simply, *Those hands…*

Ronnie reached his right arm back and, fist clenched tight, he swung it with all his might, right into the side of the old guy's face. He felt like he was beating up his grandfather, or smacking some old rest home geriatric who hadn't ever hurt a soul. But he knew better than that.

He had expected it to hurt like hell but, surprisingly, it was OK. The old guy's face went with the force of the punch to the side, turning his head to the right. But his hands still reached forward.

"Get the girl," Ronnie shouted, and he swung his right hand again, the hand open this time, swiping at one of the old guy's own hands, which had now let go of Karl – and Ronnie would have put money on the map-reader never again reading any maps.

When Ronnie's hand connected with the old guy's splayed-out fingers, he felt an excruciating blast of pain – it was only for a few seconds but it made him cry out. The man's hand shot outwards and collided with the vertical tubular rail.

Virgil said, "His glasses. Go for his glasses."

The old man steadied himself and turned to Ronnie. There was a thick gouge on the side of his heavily jowled face but there was no blood. It just looked like a tear in the skin, like a rip in the side of a kid's nighttime cuddly toy, with stuffing exposed instead of tissue and artery and vein.

His glasses?

Ronnie looked at the old man as he took a step forward.

Somewhere from behind him, Ronnie heard Angel Wurst scream and then lots of feet clumping on the steps of the bus. Then he heard Virgil say, "Who the hell are–"

(40)

"Move away from the door."

It was the only thing Junior Talbert could think of to say to his kid brother, little Wayne, huddled up and cowering beneath the frosted glass that lay between him and the screen door, the door still perplexingly shut tight even though someone clearly wanted to come into the house.

Hey, who'th that knocking at the door? lisped the hippified Garcia Gopher in the constant TV screen playing way in the back of Junior's head, the goateed Garcia wrapping an implausibly long arm around his cereal bowl. *Lookth like thomeone'th after my Gopher Nut Cluthterth. Mmm, neckthtt to tree bark, they're the betht!*

But Junior figured the person at their front door this early evening – *ridiculously* early, come to think of it, but much darker than usual at this time – was not after breakfast cereal. In fact, Junior reckoned they were after something a whole lot more substantial.

The knocking grew louder but not faster. Still leisurely, kind of. *Hey, we know you're there... so just make this easy and open the damn door, OK?*

The figure out in the cold night banged on the screen door twice and then let out some kind of yowl sound, like a wolf or maybe a bear. Truth be known, neither of the Talbert boys had heard either, leastways not outside of the *National Geographic* channel. But one thing was for sure: it didn't sound like anything they'd heard or might expect to hear from Mr Yovingham. But then again, they neither of them thought that the guy out there was Mr Yovingham. Sure, he looked just like him, but it wasn't him. Nossir. Not at all. It was someone or something completely different come to pay a social call on the boys. Both Junior and little Wayne the Dwain knew that one because they knew damn well – down there in the darkness where facts is facts and you just don't question them – that this version of Mr Yovingham knew all too well that the boys' folks were not at home and was about to capitalize on that information. In fact, the boys figured that Mr Yovingham knew all too well about the whole city being empty.

"I said, get away from *the door*!" Junior hissed.

"You don't have to *yell*," Wayne hissed back, stretching his neck out like the bendy man in their dad's old *Flash* comic books. "Why don't we let him in?"

"We don't know who he *is*."

Wayne drew in his head at that one, frowned and said, "It's Mr Yovingham," waving his arm out and pointing at the door. Then, lowering his arm again, adding, "Isn't it?"

"Uh uh," was all Junior said to that one. Junior had known it wasn't Mr Yovingham as soon as they had first seen their neighbor moving slowly along the early evening street in his car, sometimes getting out and checking the doors like a prison guard, checking the doors and giving them a good rattle before moving off. Meanwhile, all around, the light had started to fade and then had pretty much just gone out, like someone flicked a switch someplace.

It was around twelve hours before the sun snaked its head up on the horizon between the familiar shapes of the Civic Center and the Mint, and Junior had a strong feeling in his gut that it was going to be a long night.

The car, a beat-up old Toyota that Junior's dad said was being held together by spit and brown tape, had appeared around from 18th Street with the driver, cunningly disguised as Dick Yovingham, apparently checking the houses as he drifted along the street, veering across from side to side every few yards. With just a couple of exceptions, the scene was profoundly optimistic and heartwarming for Junior and for Wayne too – and save for the marked lack of glorious tailfins and good primary coloring, the whole thing could have been a cover for the old *Saturday Evening Post* magazines that Grandpa August kept in a box in the cupboard up in Hudson. But those two exceptions kind of nixed the initial euphoria.

The first one was small: the car's driver was wearing dark glasses so Junior figured he had some kind of eye problem that meant he couldn't stand to look at bright lights as he moved along the street as quiet as you please. (Junior wasn't happy about this particular slice of reasoning because there were no bright lights along Market, just a couple of streetlamps and maybe one or two warm glows behind closed drapes and blinds, all houses on whose doors Junior and Wayne had hammered throughout the day.)

But the second exception was pretty fundamental: the car's wheels were not actually touching the ground, old man Yovingham staring out of the side window at each place as he passed it by, holding his car steady just a few feet above the blacktop and the sidewalk, checking the properties as he passed them by like he was in a neighborhood watch scheme.

And that was the problem right there, wasn't it?

Oh, there were strangenesses, sure, but then life was kind of filled up with strangenesses – even a life as relatively short as Junior Talbert's. No, the problem here wasn't the fact that everyone had disappeared – and that wasn't simply everyone on the street; it was, as far as the Talbert brothers could ascertain, the whole of Denver, plus everyone they could think of calling on the telephone, people out of state, even (Junior just hadn't had the stomach to call his Uncle Pete over in London, England, but he couldn't help feeling that he'd get an answerphone, even though, over the Atlantic, it was well beyond breakfast time right now).

It wasn't the fact that no TV stations were on the air, and no radio shows appeared when he spun the dial. Wasn't even the blinding flash of light that had turned the world white for a few seconds just a couple of hours ago. And it didn't matter that, after the light – and Junior believed with all of his heart that the two things were somehow connected – folks had come back. A few of them, anyways.

It was the car that had done it. The car and the simple fact that it was flying. As far as Junior was concerned, that just had to register a pretty impressive nine on Ripley's Sphincter Scale of Unusual Occurrences.

"Junior–" Wayne started. He didn't need to complete the sentence. Junior knew what that meant. It meant that his kid brother was pissed at him.

Junior shook his head and flared his eyes. If he'd been that guy in the X Men, he'd have burned his kid brother into a little pile of ashes. And truth be told, it was Junior who had every reason to be pissed at Wayne, not the other way around.

They had been sitting in the darkened front room, eating peanuts and drinking Dr Pepper while they watched their way through the second season box set of *24*, featuring a suddenly pleasantly normal-seeming world. OK, maybe the world of Jack whatever-his-name *was* preposterous – their father's word, but Junior had adopted it – but at least it was filled with people and cars and noise and McDonald's outlets and Burger Kings and movie theaters and drugstores. Sure it was just more aural and visual wallpaper presented for suckers of the glass teat (their father again) but at least it seemed real, seemed to be happening.

And then a single light, muted, as though a flashlight were running down its battery, had played briefly on the bushes across the street. The two of them, Junior and Wayne the Dwain, had gone to the window and there was the car. Junior had told Wayne to stay where he was. Then he had turned off the TV set and gone upstairs to see if he could get a better look. And it was while he was up in their parents' bedroom, craning his neck around his mom and dad's table (his mom's making-up table, as she was always kind of keen to point out) that he suddenly noticed his kid brother on his hands and knees crawling away from the front of the house towards the street. Even as Junior started to think that there was some reason his brother should not be doing that (he later wondered how long it would have been before he'd worked that reason out for himself), the Talberts' security light flashed on with all the intensity of a baseball stadium's floodlights.

Junior had barely managed to refrain from rapping hard on the window glass, thereby inevitably drawing even more attention to them – or, at least, to their house. Just before he turned to look up the street, Junior saw his brother hightail it into the shrubbery, where he turned to one side and looked contritely up at Junior. Junior shook his head and waved him back to the house exaggeratedly. Then he had looked up the street just in time to see Mr Yovingham's car bank to one side, cross the street and move slowly (but Junior thought "purposefully") up to outside their own home.

Still on all fours, Wayne had banged his way back into the house through the side door. "Junior!" He closed the door, turned the key in the lock and – *This'll stop 'em!* – shuffled his backside up against it.

But Junior wasn't listening. He reached up and switched off the little nightlight in the hallway before dropping to his brother's level and crawling crablike towards the sofa in front of the street windows by the front door.

"Junior," Wayne said, the word coming out like a whine now, "I'm getting scared."

"Don't be," he said. "Just do as I say and–" He eased himself up against the sofa and peered around the side through the window into the street. It was deserted – no people, anyways. But Dick Yovingham's Toyota was there, its headlights on, its taillights on and, who'd have thought it, ladeez and genteelmen, even the lights mounted on the *side panels* were on, sweeping the Talberts' front yard like a jailbreak movie. Oh, and one more thing, unbelievers: the Toyota was not exactly parked normally. It was floating some four feet or so above Junior's mom's rosebushes.

Nah, this was not Old Man Yovingham. This was a real life version of Mork from Ork. *Nanoo nanoo.*

Another howl from the porch. Junior glanced across at the front door.

Behind him, Wayne said, "You know what's funny?" When Junior didn't answer, Wayne continued anyway. "Have you noticed? How he hasn't tried the door?" Wayne sniffed alongside his brother and rubbed his nose on the sleeve of his sweater. "Have you seen him try the door?"

Junior didn't answer.

"It's like he doesn't know how a handle works."

Without responding, Junior allowed his eyes to fall to the handle and, below that, the key in the lock. "Hey," he whispered, "did you lock the door?"

"Did *you*?" Wayne sniffed again, like he was coming down with a head cold. "I'm the kid, remember. Someone's supposed to be looking after me."

"Shit." Junior flattened himself on the floor and edged around the sofa.

"I locked the side door," Wayne said in a conciliatory tone.

"I have to check the door," Junior said, and without further comment, he edged out from in front of the sofa and began crawling across the wilderness of carpet between the sofa and the front door.

The closer he got to the door, the more Junior's neck ached. He was craning his head backwards and a little to the side, just so that he could keep an eye on what the figure outside was doing. Right now, the figure outside wasn't doing much of anything. Come to think of it, the figure seemed to have stopped, or at least slowed down a little. It was standing on the porch step, partly jammed inside the screen door, with its head on one side, as though it was listening.

Junior stopped in his tracks, glancing down at the handle and the key below it.

Wayne hissed from behind him. "You OK, Ju?"

Junior hissed *shhhh* over his right shoulder. Dick Yovingham's head had tilted sideways when Wayne had spoken and was now looking over, through the darkness, in the direction of the sofa. Wayne stayed as still as he could and dropped his head so that his chin was now resting on the carpet. The figure's head moved again, first down a little to the left and then down a little in the other direction, like a swimmer trying to get rid of water collected in his ears. Then he lifted his arms and beat on the door so hard that Junior was frightened the glass panels would shatter.

"Move away from the sofa," Junior shouted, hoping that his voice would be lost beneath the clamor of hammering, and he lurched forward the final few feet to reach the door, reaching out and taking hold of the key fob and turning the key in the lock as slowly and as quietly as he could. The key turned part of the way and then stuck – it did that sometimes but Junior didn't want now to be one of those times.

He pulled his head back and over to the doorjamb, trying to see if he could see the telltale glint of metal that signified the lock was thrown across. But it was too dark. Junior fished in his pocket and found a folded piece of paper. He unfolded the paper and saw that it had a phone number scribbled on it but he had no idea whose number it was. The sudden realization that it didn't matter and would probably never matter ever again sent a cold chill across his shoulder blades, though maybe that was a draft from around the door. He refolded the paper and slid it between the door and the door surround. It passed right down without any obstruction. So the door was unlocked.

He had known that was a distinct possibility when he had set out from the sofa but now that he knew for sure, he suddenly felt vulnerable. But there was nothing to be gained just lying here in front of the door. It was put up or shut up time. He shuffled himself closer to the door and edged his head up towards the handle before taking hold of the key again.

"Come on," he whispered to the key, lifting himself up so that his left shoulder, arm and cheek were up against the door paneling, feeling it judder with every strike from the man on the porch. He turned the key back to the left, gave it a little jiggle – that worked sometimes. Other times, he had seen his mom or his dad remove the key, rub it with their hands and then reinsert it in the lock. After that, it invariably worked. He gave it one more jiggle, exactly at the same time that Yovingham ceased his pounding and an eerie silence fell over the proceedings.

The sound the key made in the lock seemed huge, almost deafening, and Junior saw the thing that was almost certainly not Dick Yovingham drop its head. With glass being frosted, there were no details available, only a dark outline set against the streetlights and the moon. But it was clear that the man out on the porch was looking down at the point where the sound had come from: the lock. And right above the lock was–

"The handle," Junior said, softly.

Junior jiggled the key some more, no longer bothering to be silent. He didn't think he had time to be silent.

He could see what was happening in the thing's head. It was just the same kind of thing that various filmmakers had put into the zombie movies that constantly filled movie theatres: that magical moment when the mindless living dead suddenly discover a simple something that can swing things their way.

A simple something like a door handle.

Junior had a feeling that the door might well just push right open. But most fascinating of all was that the door glass had not been smashed inwards. Something else that was clearly new to the thing on the porch. In light of that, he made a decision to leave the key. After all, he was drawing more attention to both the fact that there was someone inside and also that the general area of the key (which is where the sound would come from) might well hold the means to get in – i.e. the handle.

"See anything out of the window?" Junior asked, crouching low and crab-walking back towards his brother.

"Just Yovingham's car."

Even as the last word was leaving Wayne's mouth, he could see that the statement was not completely true. Kayla Jekt stepped from around the back of the beamer and straight-leg-walked over to the bushes that fed onto the sidewalk along the front of the house.

"Kayla," Wayne whispered, the word sounding like a mantra, some utterance without any meaning. Wayne had had this strange situation occur on more than one occasion in the past – like that episode of *The Twilight Zone*, when everyone started calling dogs "encyclopedias" and their lunch "dinosaur". The most memorable of blankouts took place around the word "door", when Wayne was curled up in his bed, staring at the object in question, and repeating its name ("...door, door, door, door, door ...") over and over again, until at last the word ceased to mean anything to him.

And then another car – some kind of a little delivery truck – drifted over the top of the widow McCarthy's house across the street, sidling down onto the old woman's lawn in a flurry of steam jets.

"Oh, shit," was all Junior could think of to say.

"She doesn't find any of that strange, Ju," Wayne said in a low voice. "The van over the roof. Kayla doesn't find it odd, does she?"

Junior looked at his brother, saw the pleading in the boy's eyes and, welling up from nowhere, he felt a sudden rush of strength. "No, she doesn't," he said. But then Junior didn't think that the tall and gangly teenaged girl walking over their lawn was the same one who had pulled down her pants for a five dollar bill a couple years back and let Junior and Arnie Kahn play with the first signs of wispy brown hair she'd got growing down there. "You wanna put your finger inside it'll cost you another five," she told Junior and Arnie. If they'd had the extra five then they'd have willingly done it.

But that was then and this was now. The girl out there in the evening street looked like she could be Kayla's twin sister but she wasn't Kayla. And you could take that one to the bank.

"Junior, I'm scared."

Junior nodded. "Me, too. But we have to keep our heads."

Old Man Yovingham howled some more. Junior thought maybe the good neighbor had heard his last remark – maybe heads were a delicacy where he came from. *Headth – they're the betht!*

Kayla Jekt turned her own head sideways like she was trying to see something that had rolled under someone's car only there were no cars there to see. All the cars owned by the folks along the street were tucked up in their garages the way all cars were tucked up at night in this affluent suburb of Denver, barely a car ride from the city's sprawling center. And they'd been that way for a whole day now, until the light.

"We have to get out," Junior said, surprised at how calm he sounded. He didn't feel calm.

"Where we going?"

Junior thought about that a few seconds before he shrugged. "Away from here," he said at last. "Maybe into town."

"How we gonna do that?"

"Well, first off, we're gonna hole up in the drugstore. They got food and stuff in there so at least we won't starve."

"And how we gonna get to the drugstore?" Even with his very limited take on what was happening out there in the night – I mean, flying cars anyone? – Wayne didn't think the folks walking out on the street, all of them wearing dark glasses when there was no sun, and gloves when it wasn't cold, he didn't think they'd stand back and wave a couple of kids through – *You all come back now, you hear?* No, Wayne didn't think that was going to happen *at all.*

"We have to create a diversion."

They both reflected on that for a while, listening to Mr Yovingham howl out back. Then there was a thud on the window at the front of the house.

And then it sounded as though someone had kicked over the trashcan down the side of the house near the garage.

And then, finally, they heard the squeak of the handle turning.

"I think now would be a good idea," Junior said, and he reached over to tug his brother by his t-shirt and drag him towards the stairs.

"I have to pee."

"No time," said Junior, scanning the front door and the downstairs area to make sure nobody was standing there waiting for them.

"I'll do it in my pants," Wayne moaned.

"So do it in your pants. We'll get new ones at the mall."

"We're going to the mall? Not the drugstore?" Wayne suddenly sounded excited.

"That's the plan."

Wayne nodded. "Always good to have a plan," he said. It was what their father always said – always said about *any*thing, calling to mind that cheesy old TV show starring Mr. T.

"We gonna see Mom?"

Junior wondered a little too long on answering that one so his brother decided to push a little.

"You think she's hiding? In the mall?"

"Hiding?"

Wayne nodded and held onto his pecker through his bunched-up trousers. "Like maybe that's why she didn't answer the phone when you called."

Wayne felt a sliver of pain through his guts. Their mom wasn't hiding. He'd pretty much figured out that one for himself. His dad wasn't hiding either. They were gone – gone to wherever everyone else had gone. After all, someone would have answered the telephone down in the mall offices, even if his mom was – he couldn't bring himself to think of her "taking a pee" so, instead, he thought the phrase "using the bathroom".

"Could be," he said at last. "You better go pee."

Wayne stared at Junior's eyes, glancing from one to the other.

"Yeah," he said. He relaxed his grip on his pants' crotch as though he'd never needed to pee in his whole life.

They turned together and stared at the glass door, saw Mr Yovingham – *Hey, how you boys doin' this fine day, huh?*

They didn't think the man – thing? – standing out on the front porch was all that concerned about how Junior and Wayne were doing. And the day was not fine. It wasn't even day any more. And as for having a plan, well...

Right now – even though it was, what, around six or seven in the evening? – it felt like that graveyard time that Grampa August used to tell them about – a little after three in the morning to be precise, the time when, according Grampa August, the corpses in the graveyards rolled back the turf, opened their coffin lids and stepped out to scratch blackened fingernails, all encrusted with soil, on the windowpanes of kids' bedrooms. Kids like them. And corpses like that guy out in front of them right now, beating on the doorframe and howling like a coyote.

"You know," Wayne said, kind of matter-of-factly, "I was wondering."

Without turning from the front door, Junior said, "Yeah?"

"If that's a corpse out there – you know, like Gramps August used to say."

Junior turned around to stare at his brother, his face twisted in a grimace of incredulity.

"I was wondering how they could roll back the grass and then open their coffin." He shrugged, suddenly aware of Junior's staring eyes. "Just wondering, that's all."

"It's Mr Yovingham."

Wayne looked at him then, and, for just a few seconds, Junior felt like the kid with his hand caught in the cookie jar. Worse still, he felt that Wayne had assumed the role of parent. Or teacher. Hell, maybe even principal! They both knew it wasn't old man Yovingham out there, just like they knew that something bad had happened. Something real bad.

Junior had no idea why he and his brother seemed to have been ignored or left behind by this thing, whatever it was that had happened. He only knew that they had. Just as he knew that the something bad that had already happened didn't measure up diddly to the something bad that seemed right now to be sizing itself up – and sizing itself up just for the two of them.

"Come on!" Junior snapped, and he grabbed his brother by the sleeve and tugged him away from the door. But even as they moved towards the stairs, the thing that wasn't Mr Yovingham was turning the handle some more.

Junior pushed his brother ahead of him towards the stairs and turned to watch the handle.

Wayne climbed two stairs and, his hand on the banister, turned to watch the handle and his brother, right there in front of it, like he was going to pray to it. And sure enough, the handle was turning.

Junior slowly moved himself into a kneeling position and pulled his hand back from the door, as though the slightest jarring movement might cause the thing to explode in his face. Actually, Junior figured that was probably what *would* happen, and it would happen soon. As soon as Mork from Ork figured that turning the handle at the same time as pushing would gain him access to the goodies inside.

Mmm, neckthht to tree bark, they're the betht!

Wayne edged up to the third stair, and then the fourth, hanging onto the banister as though he were facing a cyclone wind that was about to tear him free and way up into space, like the house in the old *Wizard of Oz* movie. And now he had remembered his full bladder.

Junior kept edging back from the door, keeping his eyes fixed on the shadow in the glass, watching the shadow tilt its head to one side as it reached out – he could see the thing's arm lift and move towards the door. Still moving, as slowly as he could – so that Yovingham didn't notice he was there.

Yeah, right. And what exactly did the guy think had been banging on the key? Termites?

Junior dropped his gaze to the handle and, as if by magic, the door started to move forward, very slightly, as the handle continued to turn.

"Wayne, get up the stairs."

"Ju, I–"

"Wayne, this is not the time for bullshitting me, now get up the stairs and go pee."

Wayne moved up to the fifth stair and then the sixth, still holding tight onto the banister with one hand and his pants crotch with the other.

If the figure suddenly decided, right now, to combine a strong forward motion at the same time as he turned the handle then that would be it. All bets would be off and the tiger would be loose in the house. That, and the first few stairs leading up to the bedrooms would be awash with Wayne the Dwain's pee.

The handle turned noisily a couple of times and then, after one more squeaky turn, there was a dull thud followed by a sharp clatter, and then a creaking noise as the door drifted slowly open.

Junior could smell the outside, suddenly.

It came into the house on a cool breeze that smelled of new mown grass and maybe just a hint of rain. There were other things on that breeze though, things that Junior could not identify. He hissed at his brother to get up the stairs and clambered across the hallway floor like a crab, skidding slightly on the throw-rug Alice Talbert had placed midway between the stairs and the front door.

By the time Junior reached the top of the first long flight and was standing hugging the newel post just before the short flight up to the main landing, Wayne was mostly in shadow, although a thin shaft of moonlight was illuminating his left side all the way up to his chin – his head was totally in shadow, though Junior could make out the shape of his brother's head. Junior took a couple of steps and was then aware that there had been no noise from the doorway behind him. He paused where he was and looked around.

Dick Yovingham was still standing out on the porch, the screen door still open and resting against his right side. In the street behind him, lights – searchlights – washed the roadway and the tops of the bushes before moving up the side of the house towards the bedroom windows and, Junior presumed, the roof. There was no engine noise, only the sound of something passing through air, though the speed that whatever was out there was moving hardly suggested great wind friction.

Yovingham moved his head side to side again, jerky movements, like the mime artists with the painted faces made up to look like statues or robots that they used to hire in down at the mall around

Christmastime, and then he straightened his head and looked right across at Junior. Junior knew the man was looking at him even though he couldn't see his eyes. It was the slight hint of a smile on the man's face that gave him away.

And then he started into the house, striding slowly – and, it seemed, a little awkwardly – along the hallway. "Hey," Wayne said, almost forgetting to whisper, "we got all the lights switched off and he's still wearing his sunglasses."

"Get into one of the bedrooms," Junior hissed. And he ran up the last few stairs to the landing, taking two steps at a time, after Wayne's disappearing figure.

A dull clump sounded on the stairs. Then another.

The boys raced into their parents' room – chosen unconsciously because it had a lock and an en suite bathroom – and immediately skidded to a halt.

Outside and directly in front of the window were two cars, hovering about twenty feet from the house. In addition, above the house right across the street, a flatbed pickup was swooping around to move closer to the Talberts' stronghold – there were three men and a woman standing in back, none of them holding onto anything. Junior couldn't help thinking of the young men who rode the carnie rides out in the park come the Fourth and Thanksgiving – that kind of balance was a real art.

"Uh oh," Wayne said.

"Don't worry about *them*," Junior said, his words not particularly convincing.

"It's not them I'm worried about," Wayne said, "it's *them*!" And he pointed to the right.

A large fire engine had just made the turn out of Walnut, dragging with it a whole mess of overhead wires and its ladder – bearing two men outstretched on the rungs – already extending and scraping along the tops of trees as it snaked its way towards the house.

The clumping on the stairs was getting louder.

Junior turned around and closed the door as quietly as he could. As he turned the key in the lock, his brother began to cry.

(41)

"–the hell are *you*?" the boy said to Rick as Rick pulled himself up the bus's steps.

The boy was good looking, lean and muscular. He was standing facing Rick as he reached the main flooring. Behind him, over by the window, was a young girl – a child, couldn't have been more than seven or eight years old. She was sobbing into a doll that she was holding up to her face. Kneeling on the floor was Paul Giamatti – or what must have been his doppelganger – his arms folded around his gut, shaking like a bowl of jello.

Rick felt a hand pushing him from behind.

"What is it?" Melanie shouted.

"He's right," Rick shouted to the guy facing off against an old man wearing a corduroy jacket. The old man looked like he'd just stepped out of a boxing ring – there was a thick gash down the left hand side of his face but no blood that Rick could see.

Melanie pushed herself onto the bus and squeezed under around Rick.

"Get the glasses," Mel shouted.

The old man turned in Mel's direction and she saw him smile at her, saw his mouth move and–

The man standing in the aisle hauled off and drove his fist right into the old man's face. The sound of his nose breaking could be heard through the bus and, at the same time, the dark glasses flew from the man's face and clattered under one of the seats. The old man howled.

"Bastard!" Melanie shouted. "I saw what you said."

The old man bent forward and buried his face in his upheld arms. The other man clasped his hands together and brought them down onto the top of the old man's head, catching him between the base of his skull and his neck. The old man crashed to the ground without another sound.

Melanie rushed forward even as the man – a good-looking guy of around thirty-five years old, maybe even touching the big four-oh – lifted his foot and, holding onto the tubular bars for support, drove his foot down repeatedly onto the prone old man, grunting with each new contact.

Rick grabbed a hold of Melanie's jacket, his fingers slipping free almost immediately. Melanie pushed the man out of the way and reached down for the old guy, grabbing a hold of the corduroy jacket's collar and yanking it upwards. "What did you *say*?" she screamed at him. "What did you–"

"Hey, Mel, take it easy," Rick said, pulling her back from the man.

Melanie turned to Rick, her eyes wide and teary. "He said my name, Rick," she said. "These bastards killed my husband, and now, miles from home, one them mouths my fucking name at me. So how does *that* fucking work?" She lowered her voice. "Now get your hands off of me."

Rick glanced over at the young girl but figured there were things far worse happening in front of her on this bus than hearing a few "fuck" words. He let go of Melanie's arm and stood to one side until she elbowed herself in front of the man, crouched down and turned the old guy over. As she did that, Rick stepped onto the old guy's arms, pinning his hands to the floor of the bus.

They watched, the two of them, as the old guy lifted his head.

With the dark glasses now consigned to the dusty floor beneath one of the seats, the old man's eyes were unprotected. But they weren't there.

"His eyes..." somebody said from up near the front of the bus. Rick wasn't sure who it was – one of the men: there were three to choose from, not counting Johnny, though Paul Giamatti hadn't looked in a talking mood when they'd come onto the bus.

"His eyes are gone," Sally Davis's voice whispered.

That wasn't exactly true, but it was close. The bulbous crimson gelatinous blobs that now occupied the old guy's sockets were a far cry from what anyone would consider regular eyes.

"They're all red," was all Ronnie could say, looking down over Rick's shoulder at the old man.

"Not like real eyes at all," Sally Davis added, her voice little more than a whisper.

The man seemed to affect a smile, though it was without warmth or humor, and, his voice strangled and guttural-sounding, he screeched a single word.

Karl's scream answered him, puncturing the stillness even further, and then Angel Wurst began to sob.

"Jesus Christ!" Virgil Banders offered.

Sally bent down to the stricken map-reader and lifted him so that she could see his face. "Oh, my," she said.

What is it, mommy? the voices seemed to ask in unison, a cadence and cascade of tones and ages, all of them reacting to the sight of the man's eyeball plopped right out onto his cheek without so much as a how-do-you-do?

"He's not well," she said.

Virgil Banders frowned. Jesus Christ, now some old broad had come in to broadcast the goddam obvious. You didn't need to be House MD to figure that one out. But he didn't say anything.

"What did he say?" Ronnie asked, nodding at the old man who was still writhing on the floor, his arms still pinned down by the new man's boots.

"Did he say anything at all?" Johnny asked. That sound – that screech – was that words? Was that any language at all? It had sounded familiar, though, that single exclamation: it had sounded for all the world, God help him, like–

"It was my name," Melanie said. "He knows my name."

As if on cue, the old man gave what could possibly have been construed as a laugh. Or maybe a wave of pain.

"His eyes are getting fainter," Johnny said. "Like, less red, I mean."

It was true. The bright and almost incandescent glow in the old man's sockets had diminished considerably. And the globs seemed to be settling back, like a rising cake freshly removed from the oven. Plus he wasn't squirming as much.

Johnny knelt down between the seats to get a better look, grimacing when he twisted his knee.

"Don't let him touch you," Rick said.

Angel had stopped crying and was now sitting on one of the bench seats, Samantha the doll pressed close to her chest and chin.

"This man..." Sally Davis said, turning away from Karl.

Ronnie turned around. "What about him? He's going to be OK, isn't he?"

"From what I can see, his entire system has gone into some kind of cardiac arrest."

"Are you–"

Sally smiled at Ronnie, thinking to herself how nice it felt to smile that way. She didn't do it very often these days. "*Was,*" she said. "I was a nurse. Twenty-two years," she added. Implicit in that was *yes, I do know what the fuck I'm talking about.* "I've managed to get his eye back into the socket but there's almost certain to be dirt in there and, as you can see, it's moving independently of its partner." She looked back at the map-reader – he looked familiar, like maybe a movie star, from some film she'd rented from the local Blockbusters, about two guys on a wine drinking trip around California – and shrugged.

"Doesn't matter," she said, resignedly.

Ronnie and Johnny and Virgil Banders crouched down and looked at Karl's face, alongside Sally Davis.

"He gonna be OK?" Virgil asked.

Sally shook her head.

"Shit," Ronnie whispered.

But it figured. Karl the cartographer looked a mess. His good eye was moving from one of them to another, and then to another, before returning to the first one and so on. The other eye was sliding around in the socket, sometimes moving up, sometimes down, sometimes seemingly going right over, showing white, plus a little flurry of colored wiring. Meanwhile, the man was shaking head to foot.

From behind them, Rick said, "I think he's dead," to which Virgil Banders snorted, "Uh uh, he's still moving for Chrissakes," before realizing that this new guy was talking about the old dude on the aisle floor.

"Give me a hand pulling this guy up," Rick said to Johnny. "You sure he's not going to reach out and–"

Rick brought a clenched fist down into the old man's face and it folded in on itself. "He won't now," he said, with a tone of grim satisfaction.

"What the hell..."

"I think that once the lights go out, nobody's home," Rick said.

They hefted the man onto one of the seats while, still on the floor a little way up the aisle, Ronnie asked Sally Davis if Karl was still aware of where he was.

She looked at Karl and watched the single eye dart from side to side, the forehead furrowed. "I really have no idea."

"He feels like–" Johnny paused and straightened up, looking down at the old man crumpled up on the seat like an inflatable grandfather who'd sprung a leak. "–like there's nothing *in* there."

"Hey," Rick said, his voice lowered, his finger pointing. "You see that?"

Johnny frowned and took a small step backwards, away from the seat.

"What? He's not dead after all?"

"I don't–" Rick crouched down next to the old man's head, now slumped over onto the seat. He patted his pockets and then turned to Johnny. "You got a pen?"

"I think... I think he knows what's happening," Ronnie said.

"Yeah? What *is* happening?" Virgil Banders said.

"He's dying. That's what's happening." He turned to Sally and watched the woman's face. There was something in that face, something over and above the fact that she was – was! – once a nurse, something he couldn't put his finger on. But why should it matter? It didn't matter, on the face of it, but Virgil felt there was more to this woman than what was on the face of it. "Isn't that right?" he said.

"That's right," said Sally. "Yes, he won't last long."

"Is he, you know, is he in pain?"

She looked at the man, the movie star from whatever movie it was that she had watched, alone, the way she watched all movies these long lonely days, watched his hands flickering and twitching, saw his eye darting, watched his chest heaving, saw the thick line of drool from his mouth, the single tear stream from his good eye and then, in the silence, he let out a loud fart that seemed to carry on and on.

"He foller through on that?" Virgil asked and then the smell provided an answer. "Hoo eee!"

"He's closing down," Sally said. "And I'm betting it's not pleasant."

"Can't you do anything?"

"I could go back out–" She nodded to the windows. It was getting dark now. "–try find a pharmacy, get some morphine. Don't know how long it would take me..."

"And those things'll be out there," Rick shouted from up the bus. "They come out at night." He nodded at Karl. "And you've seen what they can do."

Virgil shuffled closer and then knelt upright, placing the thumb and forefinger of his left hand tightly on Karl's nose. "Cover his eyes," he said.

Ronnie frowned, already fearing the worst even before he knew what was going to happen. "What?"

"Oh my God," Sally said.

"Cover his damn eyes!"

Ronnie started to reach for Virgil's hand but stopped when the boy turned to look at him. "You know what they are?" When Ronnie didn't say anything, Virgil said, "They're windows to the soul, and he's watching me. Now cover the fucking eyes."

Sally got to her feet and moved between the scene on the aisle and the girl on the seat. The girl's eyes were like saucers. She was holding a doll in her arms, cradling it tight against her chest, shaking her arms up and down. Sally sat next to her on the seat and gently eased an arm around the girl's shoulders.

"What's your name?" she said. When the girl didn't say anything, Sally said, "My name's Sally. Won't you tell me yours?"

Ronnie hung his head and placed his left hand over Karl's eyes. "Safe journey," he whispered.

"Here," Johnny said. He handed a cheap ballpoint over to Rick and then watched as Rick slowly moved the pen towards the old man's face.

"What the hell are you doing?" Johnny said.

"I think... I think I saw something move in there."

Virgil Banders waited until the map-reader seemed to have relaxed a little, and then he leaned forward and, still holding the man's nose, he pushed his right hand over Karl's mouth and pressed the man's head onto the floor, moving so that he now sat astride him.

Angel turned her eyes to the woman. There was something about her – something very sad about her. "Angel," Angel Wurst said. "My mommy and daddy have sneaked off someplace."

Angel, said the voices, *Angel Wurst,* they chorused.

"What a beautiful name," Sally Davis said.

Yes, whispered the voices. *Beautiful.*

"My mommy and daddy have sneaked off someplace," Angel said softly, as though she were betraying a trust and exposing a secret.

Perhaps she is, thought Sally.

There was a thick clopping sound, like someone dancing, from behind the Sally woman. Angel moved her head to the side to see what was happening, but the Sally woman moved at the same time.

"Sneaked off?"

"We were on an airplane," Angel Wurst said, "and that man–" She pointed through Sally to the aisle. "–he flew us down."

"Oh God," Ronnie said. "Oh God. Oh God."

Can she be ours, mommy? the voices asked. *Can she be our sister?*

Virgil grunted and pressed harder.

Rick slid the pen into the old man's empty right eye socket.

Johnny shuddered. "Jesus H. Chri–"

The thing was a dull orange color, as far as they could make out in the dim light – the interior of the bus was now very dark.

It flashed out of the old man's eye socket, seemingly attacking the pen – which Rick dropped as he fell backwards and struck his head on the vertical tubular bar. "What the hell…"

Angel turned just in time to see it, to see what looked like a large light-colored fish flash against the pen held by one of the new men and leap from the old man's face and eye socket and onto the floor. The fish was all bulbous, its back a single eyeball that swiveled around, and along the sides it had a fringe of tiny trailing tendrils flying behind it like a tasseled jacket. Worst of all, she would recall much later, when a bad dream awoke her screaming in the deserted city of New York, it looked right at her and, just for a second or maybe three, it considered her. That was the only way she would ever be able to explain the thing: *it considered me.*

The thing flashed once onto Johnny's arm – as Johnny bounced backwards – and scuttled further under the seats at the right of the bus. Johnny twisted around, jarring his damaged knee again, and yelped in pain. "What the *fuck* was that?"

"Where did it go?" Ronnie said.

Ronnie and Sally turned away, grateful for the distraction – though they didn't have any idea of what they were looking for – while Virgil pressed harder on Karl's face, riding him like a cowboy on a bucking bronco, the gyrations and grunts growing steadily weaker until, at last, they stopped completely.

"It was like... it was like some kind of... of..."

"Slug," Melanie offered. She scanned the seats leading down to the open door and saw the boy lift himself up from the guy on the floor.

"You OK up there?" she said.

Virgil nodded.

Ronnie looked first at Karl and then at Virgil Banders, and finally at Karl again. The map-reader looked calm now and, though he had never been what you might call a God-fearing man, he sensed a release from pain for the man. He looked back to Virgil again and fought a mixture of feelings: admiration and revulsion. The boy seemed entirely unperturbed by what he had just done: he had smothered another man to death without so much as a by your leave.

Sally moved back to the aisle, keeping herself between the body on the floor and the young girl, and felt the movie star's wrist. "He's dead," she said.

Somewhere outside the sound of a motor engine started up, distant but slowly increasing in volume.

"I don't think that's good news," Melanie said.

Outside, the world had gone dark, darker than it had any right to be at this time, Ronnie thought.

"They know we're here," Angel Wurst whispered. "And they're coming looking for us."

Nobody said anything to that one. They just let it sit a while, fading away like soap bubbles. And then Rick took charge.

"You want to get your people together?" he said to Ronnie.

Ronnie nodded, squinting in the direction of the other man's voice. "You know who they are? These people?"

"They're not people," Melanie said.

"What are they, then?"

Melanie looked over at the boy. He made her feel unclean but she put that down to the fact that he had just suffocated another man. She put it down to that but there was a gnawing feeling that there was more.

"'Alien beings from a dying planet'," Ronnie said softly.

"What?"

Ronnie shook his head in Sally Davis's direction. "An old TV show. *The Invaders.* That was one of the opening lines."

And nobody said anything to that, either.

Sally and Melanie moved across to the little girl and Melanie put her arm around her. The girl shrugged her shoulders a couple of times, like a dog preparing its sleeping arrangements, and then she leaned her head against Melanie's chest and watched Sally Davis.

"There are others," she said after a few seconds.

Melanie looked down at the top of the girl's head. "Others? You mean other people? People like us?" she added. She didn't feel they really wanted to find other people with big red slugs inside their eye sockets.

Angel pointed at Sally. "Others with *you,*" she said.

Sally stared at the girl, feeling a quickening in her heart.

We like her, the voices twittered.

Let's keep her, they said.

Please? they added.

She told on us though, one of them said. *We can't have that, can we?*

"No," Sally said at last. Then, "I'm all alone."

She ignored the frantic rustling of disagreement and turned back to watch the windows of the bus.

The engine sounded louder now and, just for a second, they saw the hint of a light.

"Something's coming," Rick said. "Everybody keep down."

He pushed the old man's body under one of the seats and crouched in the footwell against the bus side. Johnny came alongside him.

"We need to get the hell away," Virgil said, edging his eyes over the lower edge of one of the big side windows.

"Not now," Ronnie said. He hunkered down behind the boy, his back against the seat edge and his head resting against the rail.

"You think there *are* any others?" Virgil said. "Out there?" he said.

Ronnie remembered the phone ringing in the mall and he felt in his jean pockets for the piece of paper. It was there. He left it where it was and nodded before realizing that the boy undoubtedly could not see him. "I think so," he said.

"Yeah?"

"Yeah. I think so."

A light washed over the side of the bus and then across the roof before rolling onto the roadway at the other side and up across the building fronts. Something skittered across the floor in front of Virgil and the boy instinctively raised his leg and brought his foot down hard. The boot heel thudded into the object – barely a fuzzy shadow down below the windows – and gave a resounding *thuu-unnnkk!* on the floor.

"Shit," Virgil said.

Everyone stayed quiet, but the light on the other side of the bus moved quickly back and washed over them once again before spilling across a TJ Maxx store on the other side of the street.

"You think they heard us?"

Ronnie nodded, even though the boy hadn't turned to get an answer. He had raised his head against the metalwork between two big windows and was watching the light move slowly across the building front.

He tilted his head to see where the beam originated. "Must be high up," he said. "Can't see anything."

From across the aisle, Johnny said, "You think they know which vehicles they've souped up?" He cleared his throat. "You know, do they know that this is one of theirs? Cos if they do, then they may come down for a closer look."

"Thanks for that," Virgil said. "I feel better now."

"Shh!" Melanie hissed.

Outside, the light had moved back from the building and had returned to the bus. It was now moving slowly over the windows and spilling onto the aisle floor. Ronnie and Virgil Banders pressed themselves against the wall and hunkered over, while, on the other side, Ronnie and Rick and Melanie, Sally and Angel Wurst slid themselves beneath the seats.

"What the hell can they see?" Melanie asked nobody in particular. So nobody answered. But they were all thinking the same thing: whatever it was that had come out of the old man's eye sockets didn't look like anything that would – or maybe "should" – be able to see a bunch of people scrunched up under bus seats.

"You think they know where my mommy and daddy are?" Angel Wurst whispered.

Melanie squeezed her tightly and patted her shoulders. She didn't know what to say, so she just said, "Shhh," again, this time gentler.

Eventually, the light moved off again, over the road and then somewhere completely away from them. The bus was returned to darkness save for the glow from the store windows along the street.

Johnny started to shuffle out from beneath the seat.

"Stay put," Rick snapped.

"My bloody leg is killing me," Johnny whined. "I have to straighten it out."

"Can't you straighten it out without getting up?"

Johnny didn't answer. He pulled himself free and, with a long moan, he stretched his legs into the aisle.

"I think they've gone," Ronnie said to Virgil's face as it suddenly moved into his vision.

"Yeah, unless they're waiting above us with their lights switched off... waiting to pounce."

Rick twisted himself around and slowly edged his head up until his eyes were above the rim of the window.

"Nothing out he–" He paused. "Hey!"

Melanie pulled the girl tighter into her arms and patted her shoulder. "There," she said, "it'll be OK," even though she was not at all sure that it would be.

"What is it?" Johnny tried to lever himself up so that he could see but the pain in his knee was too sharp and he sank back onto the floor.

Sally Davis watched Melanie and the girl enviously while Angel Wurst stared solemnly across at Virgil Banders.

You're going to have to go, kid, Virgil thought. He was surprised to see Angel's eyes widen. He smiled. *You heard that, didn't you kid?* he thought at her, but there was no response. *Yeah, you heard it,* he thought.

"Mussellsky's Guns and Ammo," Rick said.

"Mussellsky?" Johnny's voice was a mixture of excitement and incredulity. "Sounds Russian. Wasn't he a composer?"

"That was Mussorgsky," Sally Davis whispered.

"I can't *believe* this shit," Virgil Banders muttered to himself, though not soft enough that Ronnie didn't pick it up.

"What's a comp-hoser?"

"Someone who writes music, honey," Melanie said.

The girl nodded and moved Samantha the doll around for a few seconds before asking, "He gone away, too?"

"Gone away?"

"She means," Ronnie said, "like her mommy and daddy."

Melanie laughed. "Oh no, sweetie."

"Mussorgsky is dead, Angel," Sally Davis said.

"Are my mommy and daddy dead?"

Nobody seemed in a big rush to pick up the question so it was left sitting in silence for more than a minute or maybe even two until Melanie turned the girl around and said to her face, "We just don't know, honey. That man–" She nodded to the pair of trousered legs protruding from beneath the seat. "–he wanted to hurt us. Men like him hurt my husband."

"Is *he* dead? Your husband?"

Melanie nodded. "Yes, he is." She waited for a few seconds before adding, "But that doesn't mean your mommy and daddy are dead."

"No, not at all," Sally agreed.

"No," Rick and Ronnie chorused emphatically.

Her eyes having moved from face to face and now settled on Ronnie, Angel said, "But they might be."

Ronnie nodded. "They might be."

"Well," Rick said with a sigh, "if nobody has any other suggestions, I'm gonna go get us some guns."

"Sounds like a plan," said Ronnie.

"I'll come with you," said Virgil.

Getting to his feet but staying crouched and scanning the windows, Rick said, "You know anything about guns, er..."

"Virgil," said Virgil. "And no, not really."

"Does anybody know anything about guns?" Rick said.

"I know a little," Ronnie said. "You know, basic stuff."

"Basic's good," said Rick. "That's more than I know. You come with me."

As Ronnie got to his feet, Virgil said, "Shall I come as well?"

Rick shook his head.

Virgil wanted to say, *who the fuck died and made you king, shitface?* but he didn't, though his scowl betrayed his feelings. "Whyn't you stand outside and watch the street while–" Rick frowned and pointed at Ronnie.

"Ronnie," Ronnie said.

"–while me and Ronnie pick up the ordnance."

Melanie watched the exchange. There was something different now about her husband's brother, like a coming of age. He was taking Geoff's death well but maybe only because he was concentrating so heavily. The fact that he had managed to drive the car all the way from Jesman's Bend showed that he had been able to banish one demon. And now, Melanie thought, here he was banishing another, and the Banders boy didn't seem particularly enamored with it.

There was no response. "OK," he said to Ronnie, "let's make a move."

A few seconds later they were out in the cool and dark Denver night, running along bent double towards Mussellsky's Guns and Ammo.

Virgil Banders stepped down onto the street after them, watching their figures grow smaller as they headed for the sidewalk.

(42)

As Wayne Talbert scurried under his parents' bed, he could hear shoes clattering on the polished wooden floor downstairs behind and below, making as much noise as Junior suspected Frankenstein's monster's boots might make. He covered his ears while Junior removed the key from the lock and peered through the key hole.

"Whatcha see?" Wayne wanted to know.

Mr Yovingham came into view and negotiated a turn towards the landing, moving clumsily and awkwardly, even though there was nothing in his way.

"It'll be OK," Junior lied. He didn't think it would be OK at all. But they had to try. "We just need to–"

"I've peed myself."

"What?" Junior had heard him but the revelation just didn't seem to be all that important right now. There was a clump from right outside, now – this time a dull one.

"I've pissed my fucking pants!" Wayne moaned, his legs ramrod straight and his body arched forward towards his brother as though this momentary loss of bladder control were somehow his responsibility.

"We'll get more–"

"I know. We'll get more at the mall."

"Right. Now hide."

Another clump from the stairs.

Then something rattled down the roof above them.

"Where?" Wayne asked.

Junior scanned the cupboard doors, some open and some closed. That was a good question. Where could they hide?

"Further under the bed," Junior said at last.

"That's the best you can come up with? Further under the bed?"

For a moment they wanted to laugh… laugh uncontrollably and let their bladders go in full force.

But then there was another thud on the door, this time sounding like it was about to break in pieces.

And was it Junior's imagination or did the handle turn?

A howl, this time much closer. A second howl answered, from somewhere outside. More clattering from the roof.

(43)

They had dumped Karl's body and the body of the little old man into a large flop-topped dumpster in an alleyway beside a Barnes & Noble bookstore. Ronnie had considered saying something but it just seemed like a cheesy thing to do. They had all got back onto the bus in silence.

The city sped by in a blaze of color and shape, like a showcase city, sterile and empty. The advantages of the airborne bus were obvious – the roads were littered with wrecks of all shapes and sizes, some on their sides or just smashed into other vehicles, and some through store windows, their wheels still turning and the store intruder alarms echoing through the stillness and dopplering as the bus passed them by.

A ruptured fire hydrant on the corner of Larimer and 19th still fountained a torrent of water while the cause of the disruption – an empty yellow cab – lay silent on the steps of a savings and loan building behind whose broken windows stood an array of mortgage rate offers extolling the virtues of home ownership.

"I still wish we could've gotten us some more rifles," Virgil Banders said as he steered the bus out of the downtown area and headed towards the suburbs. Sally Davis knelt next to him, her left hand on the tubular steel pole behind the driver's seat and her right, resting on the rubber matting in front of Virgil, clutching a creased slip of paper bearing a scribbled address which she squinted at earnestly through her dark glasses.

"You think we really need to wear these?" Melanie said. She

removed her own glasses and studied them for what was possibly the fourth or fifth time since they'd got the bus airborne after ditching the old man's body.

Rick grunted approval. "They're not fashion accessories," he said. "I'm not sure – hell, I have absolutely no idea – why the others wear them but I reckon it'll be a help if we come across too many of them."

"Is that what we're calling them? The others?"

Rick shrugged and gave Melanie a sad smile. "It's just a name. What do you suggest?"

Melanie shook her head and turned to look out of the window. She had some suggestions, of course, but the confines of a flying bus occupied by, amongst others, a young girl didn't seem to be the place to air them.

"If wearing the glasses gives us a few minutes' advantage, it'll be something," Johnny shouted. He rather liked himself in them, having chosen his own pair when Rick and Ronnie and Virgil – strange dude, Virgil; something about him that Johnny found creepy – had come back onto the bus loaded with enough firepower to take Fort Knox and Rick had suggested they get some sunglasses. Johnny had volunteered for the job, and he'd gone out into a steadily darkening Denver to a pharmacy with several spinning racks of the things.

"You know what we should have done?" he asked of nobody in particular. When nobody rose to the bait, he added, "We should have kept the old guy's glasses."

"Hey, good point," Rick said. "Were they in the box?"

Ronnie and Johnny were now sitting on the back seat, the two of them having ditched the box – and its one-time octogenarian contents – in an dumpster behind TJ Maxx. Ronnie had smashed the two rear windows of the bus and removed all the glass. He figured it was better that they had some clear firing opportunities, though he felt the whole thing was ludicrous. He glanced up the bus.

"Uh uh," Ronnie said.

"Did you check?"

Ronnie thought about that. And then shook his head.

The boy, Johnny, was stretched out across from him, his fingers tapping to an unheard rhythm; the woman, Sally something-or-other, was up at the front with Virgil, helping direct him. Ronnie had wondered about doing the driving himself but he decided it would be better if he were free to deal with any unwanted attention. After all, how difficult could it be to drive a flying bus through an empty city?

"I told you," he shouted down the bus in response to Virgil's moan about the shortage of rifles. "We took all they had. All we could find, anyways." He finished loading buckshot into a 12-gauge and laid it alongside him on the seat. He looked down at the Sam Browne shoulder rig, tore open the Velcro fastening and stuck it down again a little tighter this time.

"You know," he said across to Johnny, "I feel like... like, I dunno. Elliot Ness." He adjusted his dark glasses, removed the .38 special and checked the clip.

Johnny said, "You like doing that, don't you?"

Ronnie nodded. "Seen it enough times on TV." He slipped the special back into the holster and re-clipped the thumb-break snap release. "Don't know if I'll be able to use it, though."

Johnny struggled to his feet and moved forward down the bus. Rick turned around from his seat, a few seats in front of Ronnie, and smiled.

"You'll use it," Rick said. He lifted his glasses so they sat on his forehead just above the hairline, turned back around and checked the pump-action on a snub nosed shotgun, making a resoundingly solid *chunk chunk*. "You seen what they did to–" He let his voice trail off as he turned to look in Melanie's direction. "–what they did to Geoff–"

"He her husband?"

Rick nodded. "And my brother." He nodded at the memory of it while, up at the front of the bus, Johnny stared out of the big front windows. "Made a hell of a mess of him." He pointed to his face and said, "eyeball out on his cheek, shaking like he wasn't right in his head." He demonstrated. "I tell you, was a mercy when he died." Rick nodded and laid the shotgun across his lap. "Yep, you'll use it."

"How about you?" Ronnie asked.

"Me?"

"Family, I mean."

Rick shrugged and grabbed for the seat rail in front of him when the bus lurched downwards and to one side. "Jesus Christ, what the hell's going on up there?"

"Sorry," Virgil shouted back. "There's one of those, you know, street cleaning trucks? The ones that spray all the water as they move along."

Rick grunted an acknowledgement.

"Damn thing just moved across the intersection up ahead. Caught me napping."

"They see you?"

Virgil said, "Don't think so. Don't *know*, but don't think so."

"You wearing your glass–"

"Yes, I'm wearing my glasses."

"What would they do – if they saw us, I mean?" Sally Davis asked, her voice low. She didn't really want to know, Ronnie thought.

I won't let them hurt you, mommy, a strong voice in Sally's head assured her. She frowned. She didn't recall hearing the voice before. Sally looked back at the creased piece of paper and straightened it out.

"Should we drop down onto the street?"

Virgil shook his head. He liked Melanie. He wanted to spend an hour or so with her, just him and the girl, some rope maybe and a nice thick roll of brown ducting tape. "It's hell down there, down on the street," he said. "Cars everywhere. Why'd you think they went to all that trouble to make things fly?"

Melanie nodded.

"It's cos everything's all smashed up with hardly a clear road anyplace."

"There was back in Jesman's Bend?"

"*Excuse* me? Where the hell's *that*?"

"Back home," Melanie said, her voice wistful. She glanced out of the window at what looked like some kind of sports arena.

"Coors Field," Virgil said as he swung the wheel around to avoid hitting a bent metal post, its lamp ending still sputtering sparks. "Home of the Colorado Rockies." He turned to Melanie. "It's a ball team."

"I gathered," she said.

"Hell, we'd be sitting ducks, one of them saw us," Johnny said as he returned to the back seat. "Down on the road, I mean," he added.

"That's where the dark glasses should come in useful," Virgil said.

Rick turned to Johnny and frowned. "You OK?"

"Sure I'm OK." He patted his chest. "I just took a couple of painkillers. Damn leg feels like someone chopped it off and stuck it back on again with superglue."

Rick nodded.

"What could they do?"

"It wouldn't be good, I don't think," Sally Davis said. She pointed up ahead. "There's the market. We've come too far."

"Jesus H. Fucking Christ, lady–" Virgil began but Sally punched him in the shoulder.

"Mind your mouth, young man," she said. "You can do any better, then you do the map reading and let someone else fly the bus."

There was silence then for a few seconds before Virgil's face cracked into a big smile and then a burst of laughter.

Sally laughed as well.

"Tell me again where we're going," Johnny said.

"We were in the mall and a phone was ringing."

"This is you and the girl, right?"

Ronnie nodded. He looked up at Melanie, still watching out of the window, and saw little Angel Wurst leaning against her, Samantha the doll underneath her head.

"First time it rang, we missed it. Could have been anywhere." He flicked the hammer-guard on his holster. "Then we tracked the phone but missed the call." Ronnie smiled and, raising a finger, affected a eureka pose. "But we found out whose desk the phone was ringing at and then I found the personnel files."

"How'd you know which person sat at that desk?"

"World's Best Mom."

"Excuse me?"

"She was the world's best mom." He shrugged. "I'm guessing she's not anymore, though."

Johnny nodded. "No, not anymore."

Nobody said anything for a minute or two and then Ronnie said, "You know, I been thinking. You know how after 9/11 we had all those handwritten notes from folks who'd lost their loved ones all pasted up in New York asking if anyone had seen them?"

Rick nodded. Nobody else said anything.

"Well, I was thinking how this time, with–" He shrugged and jiggled his head side to side. "–with millions and maybe even *billions* of people gone… there are no notes."

"I think I found 'em," Virgil Banders said as he cruised the bus around a grove of trees and a traffic signal.

They had just crossed an intersection fed by two three-laners and two singles. Down the left-hand single there had been activity. A lot of activity – even Ronnie had noticed that from the corner of his eye while he was facing forward.

"Go past, go past," Rick snapped.

Virgil hit the gas pedal and lurched forward, swaying slightly. "It's hell keeping this damn thing in the air at the same time as I'm trying to make sure we go forward."

Sally Davis patted the boy's shoulder. "You're doing fine," she said. Her girls agreed enthusiastically.

"OK," Rick said, "bring it down."

Without answering, Virgil wrestled with the controls and slowed the bus, the back end swinging out, hitting a window and scoring a deep groove in the brickwork. He pushed forward on what he now considered to be the joystick and brought the bus to a bumpy landing alongside a small park and a parade of stores, most of which had corrugated metal shutters pulled down on the windows. He pulled on the brake and turned around, the bus letting out a loud *hissss* as though relieved.

Ronnie had his face against the side window trying to see if the collision had done any real damage.

Virgil said, "You want me to turn it off?"

Rick thought on that, and looked at Ronnie who, satisfied that they were still functioning in one piece, was facing forwards again.

"Make more noise starting it up again if we have to move fast," Ronnie ventured.

Rick nodded. He turned to Virgil. "Leave it idling."

Angel Wurst's head shuffled around against the bus window and her voice said, "Mommy?" softly.

Melanie's heart ached for the girl and she leaned across and, placing her face right next to Angel's ear, she whispered, "Mommy isn't here right now, sweetie."

Without turning around, Angel said, "No, she isn't. She's dead."

Melanie started to say something else but the girl cut her off, still staring out of the window.

"My daddy's dead, too."

"Angel, don't–"

"They're *all* dead," she said. And even at six years old, there was such a weathered finality to the girl's words that Melanie just didn't feel up to taking her to task on them. As if reading Melanie's thoughts, Angel Wurst turned around and looked up into the woman's eyes, saw the tears. "Every single one of them," she added with a slow but deliberate nod.

Standing in the aisle, his bad leg propped up on one of the seats, Johnny pointed at the rear window. "Hey, look!"

A fire engine was hammering along the road they were on, about thirty or maybe forty feet off the ground. There was no siren.

Ronnie backed away from the window and got to his feet, pulling the .38 from his holster. *This is it,* he thought. *I'm going to get killed in a blazing gun showdown on the deserted streets of Denver by a crazy bunch of–*

Of wacked-out aliens? Volunteer firefighters?

–brainwashed people who can make my eyeballs pop out if I let 'em get a hold on me.

Then he thought, *glasses,* and wildly ran his hand up to feel if they were there. They were. He dropped his arm and tried to look calm.

At the intersection, the engine turned left, taking a whole mess of overhead lines and cables down on the way, one cable bouncing and spitting on the ground like a rattler that had just had its tail bitten off. A tall pole that had buckled when the engine caught the wires leaned further over across the intersection. At first, Ronnie thought it was going to drop all the way but it didn't; it just hung there at a forty-five degree angle to the blacktop.

Johnny said, "Hey, you see that?"

Ronnie didn't move or say anything.

"The ladder was already extended and there were two guys lying on it."

"And I don't think they're attending a fire," Ronnie said.

"What did you see down there?" Rick asked Virgil.

Virgil Banders shrugged. "It was so fast, man," he said, and just for a second, Ronnie thought he was watching some burned out veteran high on sauce and weed explaining why he'd aced some old dear crossing in front of his Camaro. *It was so fast, man!*

"I saw," Sally said.

"I did, too," Angel Wurst said. "There are two boys in there."

Everyone went quiet. Following her last outburst, the girl had seemed to go off to sleep or, at best, be staring out of the window on the opposite side of the road to the one that led down the street the fire engine just went down.

"You were dreaming, honey," Melanie said.

Ronnie moved along the bus and slid into the seat in front of Melanie and the girl. When he was sure the girl wasn't watching him, Ronnie shook his head very gently at Melanie.

"Angel is a very clever girl," Ronnie said. He reached out a hand and smoothed the girl's hair out of her eyes.

Without looking away from Angel, Melanie said, "Angel's worried her mommy and daddy are de–"

Angel nodded. "They are," she said. "They all are. I told you." She looked outside. "They're making it all dark."

Johnny looked over at Rick, shaking his head.

"Who's making it dark, sweetie? Not your mommy and daddy?" Rick asked. He crouched down in the aisle, a pump-action shotgun on his knee, and gave the girl a big smile.

Angel shook her head and lifted her doll onto the seat-back rail in front of her. "The people," she said. "The bad people."

"Is she OK?" Johnny asked.

The girl sees things, mommy, one of Sally's own girls whispered to her. *I think she sees* us.

And right on cue, Angel turned her head in Sally's direction. For a second, Sally thought she was going to say something but then a man's face came up against the outside of the bus window on the driver's side.

(44)

Junior backed away from the door and reached an arm out for his brother.

"It'll be OK," he whispered.

"I wish... I wish mom and dad were here," Wayne said between racking sobs.

There was a crash from the door and Junior pulled Wayne even tighter to his chest.

Hey, who'th that knocking at the door? lisped Garcia the right-on goateed Gopher in Junior's Head-TV.

"It's the bogeyman," Junior whispered.

Behind them, glass shattered.

Above them, something clattered on the roof and slid over their heads towards the section overhanging the front of the house, and the Talberts' bedroom window.

And to cap it all, now the door handle was turning. He was a fast learner, the thing that wasn't Dick Yovingham.

(45)

Virgil was turned around in his seat, looking down the bus, but Angel saw the man's face and screamed. Virgil spun around and hoisted the revolver from the dashboard.

"Don't use the gun," Rick hissed. "There could be others."

"Move slowly," Johnny said. He suddenly remembered Gram Kramer and Jennifer Bacquirez back at the station, and how slow they moved.

Melanie pushed Angel away from her and made her crouch down in the footwell. Then she pulled out her gun, flipped the safety the way that Rick had showed her, and rested it on her lap. She felt surprisingly calm.

Rick moved up to the front of the bus alongside Virgil. "Sit down," Rick whispered. "But do it slowly."

"I can't believe we're doing this," Virgil whispered between clenched teeth as he slid into the bus's driving seat once more.

"Don't show any emotion," Rick said. "They don't seem to do emotion."

"Pisses them off," Johnny added, recalling the chaos at the radio station.

Virgil placed his hands on the steering wheel and faced forward, hardly moving a muscle.

Outside, the man moved his head to one side and just stared. They had no idea which one of them the man was watching because his glasses were so dark. But his head wasn't moving.

"Hi there," Melanie said loudly as she stood alongside Virgil Banders.

The man outside looked like some kind of truck driver, blue overalls, chin stubble, wispy hair and a receding hairline – just a Regular Joe like millions of others. The only thing was he was wearing a pair of what looked like thick asbestos gloves and a nifty pair of RayBan style dark glasses. The man straightened his head and shifted his attention to Melanie.

Melanie removed her glasses – at which the man outside made no reaction – lifted her .38, took a two-handed stance and aimed the gun right in front of Virgil's face at the man.

"Jesus Christ!" Virgil managed to get out before the gun went off and the side window flared into a mosaic of cracks.

Melanie fell backwards into the seats on the right hand side, still holding the gun, and loosed another shot into the bus's roof.

"Fuck!" Rick said. He hoisted the pump-action and pressed the button to open the door. The door swished open and he jumped down the three steps onto the road, shifting a load into the chamber as he started around the front of the bus.

The man had already removed one glove and was busy pulling up on the fingers of the second when Rick came face to face with him, pushed the barrels of the pump-action into his chest, edging the guy backwards, and pulled the triggers. The sound was deafening and Rick suddenly wished that he'd used a knife. They had picked up a dozen or so nice-looking Swiss sheaths at the store but hadn't gotten around to handing them out. Too late now. The man virtually flew backwards, landed flat on the sidewalk and skidded for a few yards before coming to rest with his head bent over on the kickboards of Paula's Patisserie. Rick did a double take on the name, half expecting the stores on either side to be a *boucherie* and a *boulangerie*. When he looked back at the ground he saw a wide stain leading from where the man had landed to where he now lay.

Rick pumped another load into the chambers and held the shotgun ready. They had made themselves known now: there was little to do but move into the street. The only question was whether to take the bus.

(46)

It was either a car backfiring or some kind of explosion – maybe even a gunshot. But whatever it was, it had a profound effect on the siege of the Talbert house. Two more followed.

Junior had pulled his kid brother close to him and was in the process of turning to the window for some other means of escape (he figured the door, when it opened, was going to be a little too busy to allow any additional personnel to pass through, even two small boys). And now he saw that the top of a ladder had smashed into his parents' window, scattering glass, wood frame and even bricks across Junior's mom's dressing table, the one with all the little glass animals that Junior and Wayne had bought for her (with help from their father) to mark special occasions such as Mothers' Day and her birthday. There was something particularly depressing – in a world that was fast becoming Depressopolis – about seeing all the dust and broken glass, and the deep gouges in the table itself. Mahogany, Junior seemed to recall his father saying on one occasion long ago, before a bright light changed the world forever. *Mahogany* – it was now just one of so many seemingly magical words that had once been possessed of great magic but which had now been shorn of their power.

There was clumping on the stairs, this time moving away, so that was something. But there was still the window to contend with and Junior now saw that more than a simple wood and metal ladder had invaded his parents' bedroom. As he backed away, a pair of gloved hands appeared amidst the swirling dust. The top of a head came soon after it.

"I know him, I know him!" Wayne shouted excitedly. "It's Mr–" What the hell was the guy's name? Worked in the drugstore around the corner, where Wayne and Richie Baynham filched comic books while eight year old Jerry Bockheimer – who, at almost five and a half feet, was something of a specialty in the neighborhood (he's a goddam freak, Lucy Myers protested) – sneaked a look into the girly magazines sitting on the top shelf that only he could reach.

"He isn't wearing any glasses," Junior whispered. That was significant, wasn't it? Not wearing any glasses? Even though it was X o'goddam clock and nobody with even half a brain should be wearing dark glasses – not unless they were maybe Tom Cruise and particularly when they just pushed a fire engine ladder through the second story window of a building where there wasn't even a fire.

The man held out a pair of gloved hands, waving them a little like he was searching for them, his face all screwed up, eyes clamped tight shut.

"Hey, Ju!"

Junior clamped his hand around his brother's mouth and gave him a shhh! "Don't let him know where we are," he whispered in Wayne's ear.

Wayne shook his head and started to pull back, his face averted from the man.

Junior felt like maybe giving Wayne a swift clip around the ear, the way their father did–

Hey, big guy, maybe we'd better make that used *to do…*

–whenever he stepped out of line.

Wayne was whimpering now. He turned around and writhed his mouth free of Junior's hand. "There's something on the floor!" he shouted.

Junior frowned. Something on the floor? Hell, half the fuckamamey house was on the floor and there'd be hell to pay when mom and dad got home. Junior kept that thought right at the front of his mind. It made him feel better. Made him feel like it was a little toehold on normality, a tiny grasp on the way things were. Particularly now that the man on the ladder had pretty much fallen into the bedroom, with a fine dust of plaster falling down on him like fog or fairy dust, and he had opened his eyes to reveal–

Hey, ladeez and gents, waddya think to this now, I aks ya, just two empty sockets! Guy's eyes gone bye-bye...

–there was nothing in them.

"Shitfuckshitfuckshitfu–"

Amazed at the sheer force of Wayne's outburst, Junior fell out of his little brother's way as the boy tumbled over, wrong-footing himself on pieces of concrete and plaster.

"It's on the fucking floor, Ju," the boy cried out. Without turning back, he stumbled towards the bedroom door.

Through the dust, Junior could see the door starting to open. Could it be mom and dad, come home to rescue them from people in flying cars who destroyed their home, and who – even worse, Judge – wore dark glasses in the nighttime when they weren't even movie stars but rather just local folks gone to hell in a handcart, and all wearing gloves? But even as the thought popped into his head, Junior popped it right back out again. He couldn't be sure who the heck it was out there on the landing, his or her outline blurred by dust, but it sure-as-shootin' wasn't Junior's parents.

"Wayne! Don't go out of the–"

And that's when he felt it, felt something brush against his folded knee on the floor. Junior turned around, ignoring the guy with the empty eye sockets who, even now, was getting to his feet, pulling himself upright with his gloved hands on the chest of drawers. It didn't seem important any more. What was important, Junior felt, was the large gelatinous orange eyeball-thing that was moving around in the debris, seemingly unsure of where it was going and its frilly jellyfish skirts rippling.

Someone screamed then.

Junior was only partly surprised to discover that it was himself.

(47)

Virgil was the second one down from the bus. He stood in the street, revolver in his hand hanging loose at his side, and surveyed the damage.

"Well," Rick said at last, "we're committed now. Stealth is no longer an option."

They moved back to the door of the bus and looked up at the faces clustered before them – the guy from the plane on the bottom step, Melanie and Johnny behind him, with little Angel Wurst and her ever present doll between them, and the older woman at the back, the plane guy craning his head around to look up the street along the side of the bus to see if the shots had brought any unwanted attention. Rick had a feeling that such attention would not be long in coming.

"What are we going to do?" the older woman asked of nobody in particular. In fact, Rick fancied it was not actually intended as a question, more an evaluation of their situation. Hell, it wasn't good.

"It's dark," Johnny said.

Sally Davis and Ronnie looked across at the young man.

Johnny shrugged. "They like the dark," he said. "It's their time."

Ronnie stepped forward and pulled his gun from the holster. "I feel ridiculous with this." He hefted it in his hand and shook his head.

"Nothing else gonna stop them," Rick said. He checked the street along the way they had come and then looked up the way they had been travelling. Ronnie pulled a crumpled piece of paper from his pocket and checked the street sign, nodding. He took in a deep breath and when he looked up, Angel Wurst was watching him. He gave her a smile and waggled the gun, trying to make light of what they were about to do. But the girl didn't seem able to see the funny side of it.

Rick said, "Someone's going to have to stay with the bus. Johnny, you take charge here. We'll be back as soon as we can." He checked his watch. "Give us fifteen minutes. If we're not back then–"

"Come and get us," Virgil said.

"I won't be going anyplace without you." Johnny shrugged. "One way or another, we'll be on the bus together or I'll know what's happened to you."

"Shee-it," Virgil said. He lifted the pump-action and cradled it.

"OK," Rick said. "Mel, you stay at the bus with–" He made a face and looked over at Sally.

"Sally," she said in a soft voice.

"You stay at the bus with Sally and Johnny."

"And me."

"Sure, and you, Angel." Rick grinned.

"The two boys are in a lot of trouble," the girl said.

Ronnie crouched down beside her. "Yeah?"

She nodded, her mouth clenched tightly shut.

Ronnie considered asking her how much trouble, exactly, but there was a part of him that just didn't want to know. The anxiety he felt was only partly for the two boys. The rest of it was for himself. Aside from fleeting dark thoughts every once in a while – very rarely, to be fair – Ronnie had not actually given much thought to the prospect of death and dying. And now, in the space of just two or three days, he had had to face it head-on on two occasions: once on the suddenly deserted plane plummeting out of the skies towards an unforgiving Denver ground, and now here, in some back of beyond suburban street proposing to face up to things that looked human but which stored eyeball creatures in their heads and could destroy your body simply by putting their hands on you.

"We better move," Rick said.

"Yeah." Ronnie wanted to say something else to the girl but he looked at her eyes and saw that she'd said all she wanted to say. He stood up and moved against the store window, lifting his gun to his face and staring at it in the gloom.

"You're still wearing your glasses," Melanie said.

Almost as soon as the words had left her mouth, Melanie clapped her hands. "Hey–"

"I'm with you, Mel." Rick reached into his breast pocket and lifted out his own dark glasses.

Sally Davis frowned. "You think they're going to buy that? The three of you walking down there carrying guns and–"

"And no gloves," Johnny added.

Rick said, "Maybe it's going to be better than nothing."

A small squawky voice said, "Wonder why they wear gloves anyway."

Ronnie looked over at Angel Wurst and saw the face of the doll they'd picked up at the mall. It seemed to be looking right at him.

"Hey," Ronnie said, "Samantha's right."

Johnny whispered, "Samantha? Who's Samantha?"

"The doll," Melanie hissed back at him.

Ronnie went on. "Why *do* they bother wearing gloves? They take them off when they want to hurt someone but otherwise they keep their hands covered." He nodded to Rick. "You said that they all wore gloves when they hit you at the radio station."

Rick nodded, glancing sideways at Melanie, who had hung her head.

"So that can only mean that not wearing gloves in some way diminishes them."

"Diminishes them?"

"Hurts them, even. Maybe even kills them."

Virgil threw his hands in the air. "Fantastic. So what are we worrying about? All we gotta do is persuade them all to take off their gloves and then we watch them die." He sniggered. "Shouldn't be too difficult – so long as we stay out of their grasp." He shook his head and hefted his pump-action. "Me, I'm just gonna blow them away with this."

Nobody said anything for a few seconds and then Rick said, "But it is worth bearing in mind. Same goes for the dark glasses. They're obviously not fashion accessories."

"They don't like the light," Angel Wurst said.

Everyone turned to face the girl, who was nodding. Samantha the doll, sitting on Angel's arm and held securely by Angel's right hand, was nodding too. "They're going to make it *all* dark."

"All dark, honey?" Melanie said. She didn't like the sound of that. Not at all.

Angel nodded. "All dark, all of the time," the squawky voice added. "And then they won't need their glasses."

That didn't sound too good at all.

Angel turned Samantha around and then lifted the doll to nuzzle into her neck.

"Time to go," Rick said.

Once everyone else was safely on board – Melanie, Angel and Sally Davis – Johnny climbed stiffly back onto the bus. At the top of the steps he nodded to Rick. "Take care."

Rick nodded back but didn't say anything and the three of them walked away from the doorway, and paused at the intersection, Ronnie leaning on the wall. Rick asked him if he was OK as Virgil eased the top of his head over the edge of the wall to see what was happening.

Ronnie patted his chest and let out a little laugh. "I think I'm just scared," he said. He held his right hand out in front of him. "See that? It's shaking."

"Shit, it's like a circus down there," Virgil hissed over his shoulder.

"We're all of us shaking," Rick said. "You gonna be OK?"

Ronnie smiled, shrugged and patted his pump-action. "I've got this, at least."

"Better than nothing," Rick said as he sidled over to Virgil.

When he reached the wall, Ronnie could not bring himself to peer around and instead waited for Rick or Virgil to report. He could feel his heart beating, in his chest and in his mouth, and he had to crouch down so as not to keel right over where he stood. He cradled the pump-action on his upper thighs and placed both hands on it. It was just metal, nothing more sinister than that. But it was a killing machine, a device designed and sculpted and built purely to cause pain and harm. Ronnie fancied he could feel the killing energy from the ribbed sleeve that pumped the next load into play.

They moved back from looking around the edge and crouched alongside Ronnie, Rick on Ronnie's right and Virgil on his left.

"You sure you're gonna be OK? You look a little pasty."

"Sure. I'm fine. Let's get on with it."

Rick nodded and went on. "OK, there are around twenty people, maybe more, wandering around about halfway down the street."

"What are they doing?"

"Nothing much." Virgil shook a cigarette out of a pack and lit it.

"Hey, you smoke," Rick said.

Virgil nodded and returned the pack to his jacket pocket. "There are several vehicles down there, a couple of regular cars circling the roof, a fire engine that's kind of parked on the guttering with a ladder through an upstairs window, and a van plus another couple cars down on the street."

Ronnie could feel his breath fading on him and he shuddered each time he breathed in, barely managing to maintain his smile.

"OK," Rick said. "Ronnie, we're gonna have to leave you here."

Ronnie started to protest but Rick was having none of it.

"Ronnie," he said, whispering now, "you're gonna fuck it all up, you go walking down the street tottering side to side."

Ronnie breathed in. And then he breathed in again. He held out his right hand and watched it for movement. There wasn't any. "I'm OK," he said. *Martha,* he thought, *I never wanted you by my side more than I do right now.* "Truly. I'm not going to be left here."

Rick looked over at Virgil, Virgil looked at Ronnie. Virgil made a "doesn't matter to me" face, shrugged and took a pull on his cigarette. "OK, let's get going."

The three men stood upright, their backs against the wall, and checked their weapons. Each of them carried a fourteen inch Ithaca pump-action. Rick also had a holster and 1911 handgun, plus a small .38 in his pants pocket. Ronnie wore a wide belt of bullets around his shoulder and a Dan Wesson .357 stuffed in his waistband. In addition to his pump-action, Virgil carried a Smith and Wesson 59.

Virgil said, "So what's the plan?"

"We walk," Rick said. "Until one of them figures out that we're playing for the other team. When that happens, you do whatever you have to do." He looked at the others and placed the pump's stock in his right hand, running the barrel up behind his arm. They followed suit. "OK," he said.

They stepped away from the wall, took a deep breath and turned the corner into Market Street.

A compact job appeared from behind a tall building to the left, veered over the rooftops, disappeared for a few seconds and then reappeared a couple of houses in front of them. They walked steadily and without any suggestion of urgency.

The car – maybe another Volkswagen, Virgil Banders thought, suddenly thinking of the dead body in the last one he'd used – seemed to slow down as it saw them. That was ridiculous, of course – cars did not see people.

"They're watching us," Virgil said between clenched teeth.

"They're *not* watching us."

"*You* think they're watching us?"

"I don't know," Ronnie whispered. He was actually feeling a little better for being on the move. It was the moment of decision that was the worst, he had decided as he walked along the street. While there was a chance to take either course of action – to get the hell away, in this case, being the other – there was anguish as to which course should be taken. But once the decision had been made it was simply a matter of continuing.

"Don't let anyone see you speaking," Rick snapped.

Another car, a wreck as far as they could make out, turned from the house and started back towards them. The VW just hung there like a magic trick, a car suspended without wires against the dark sky.

"Now I think we have a problem," Ronnie muttered without moving his lips or faltering his step. "There's nobody in the VW."

Virgil turned to him, amazed. "You can tell the make? From here? In the dark?"

Ronnie almost shrugged. "I like cars," he said. "Maybe I need to get out more." If all this mess sorted itself out then he would be getting out more, Ronnie thought. *I wonder if I'll ever see Martha again…*

Virgil hesitated, just for a second, and the VW flinched to the side, turning in the boy's direction.

"Keep walking," Rick said.

The VW straightened and lowered itself to the street a few feet in front of them. Up ahead, from the house where all the action seemed to be concentrated – *the home of the World's Greatest Mom,* Ronnie reasoned – two men staggered onto the sidewalk and looked in their direction.

"We gonna stop?"

Rick didn't say anything, just kept walking. Without any communication between them, they slowly drifted apart, Virgil moving to the left and Ronnie to the sidewalk at the right of the street next to a Presbyterian church with a small fenced garden area at the front. Rick stayed in the center of the road.

"Looks to me like we don't have much choice," Virgil said, shifting his gait from the stilted stagger to his usual walk as he stepped onto the sidewalk. He hefted the pump-action into plain view as the driver's door on the VW opened up.

"OK," Rick said. He pulled his own pump clear and loaded the chamber. "Fuck it."

"Is that the plan?" Ronnie hissed from his side of the road. He didn't feel in the least bit comical but he just couldn't resist it. He dropped the stock of his own pump into his hand and swung it up so that the barrel pointed at the driverless car. These people–

People? whispered a voice in the back of his head. *These are not* people, *compadre, these are* things – "alien beings from a dying planet" – *and all of 'em set on popping your eyeballs out of your head.*

–had somehow stolen his wife, the only recently re-loved Martha, and whatever it was they could do to him, he had this here pump-action gizmo (a device he had, alas, not yet fired, of course, but let's not worry our pointed little heads about that one, kiddies) and he would take more of them than they would take of him.

But what's it like to have your eyeball popped, oh great gunslinger? How does it feel when it plops right out onto your cheek on a little coil of slippery head-wire, maybe even looking right back up at the leaking socket it just came from?

But across the street, Virgil was just ahead of him. He let off three rounds, the first knocking him backwards so that the shot went wild and didn't connect. He steadied himself so that the second hit the VW's grill while the third took out the windscreen. It also made a splash of the head of the young boy – maybe six, seven years old – sitting behind the wheel as he made to step out of the car.

"That's why we couldn't see him," Ronnie said. "He's just a–"

The boy continued to move forward, his hand still on the top of the door, but he keeled right over after two steps and lay still on the sidewalk just a few yards in front of Ronnie, his head on the ground and his ass stuck up in the air.

"He's just dead," Virgil Banders said.

This isn't good, Ronnie thought. The body, when he reached it near the overhead streetlight, looked perfectly human. He couldn't see the face – or what was left of it following Virgil Banders's shots – but he knew from the mess of the back of the boy's head that it probably didn't look too good. *So the fuck what?* said the little voice. *We're playing for keeps, here. There's no standing up after the last reel and the cowboys having a coffee and a smoke with the Indians.*

As Ronnie watched, a fold of hairy skin lifted upwards and what looked like a large, frilly-sided anemone pushed itself free from the mess of brain tissue and bloody sinew. The thing had a large circular translucent ball set into the top of it but Ronnie could see that the ball had been punctured and a milky liquid was oozing out onto the paving slabs. As the thing moved completely out of the boy's head, Ronnie saw that one half of it was gone and it was trailing white slime over the kid's neck and jacket collar.

Without even thinking about what he was doing, Ronnie lifted the pump and fired at it point blank. The shot took off the boy's shoulder and pretty near dislocated Ronnie's. But the thing was unharmed – or, at least, no more harmed than it had been before the shot.

Ronnie pumped another round, leaned over so that the end of the barrel was just above the thing as it seemed to contemplate dropping itself onto the sidewalk, and pulled the trigger. Both the thing and the boy's head disappeared in a cloud of gelatin, bone and gristle.

He pumped the gun again, starting to feel like he was getting into it, his jaw set and his teeth clenched as he turned to face the street. *That was for Martha,* he thought, the words having a strange resonance that he would never have expected. Just for a few seconds there, he might even have cried.

He remembered, way, way back, back when they had just gotten married and things were still good, how he had woken up in the middle of the night in a sweat, with Martha lying alongside him, her breath soft and even tuneful. The boneyard blues was what Martha called it. What Martha *had* called it. Once. A long time ago.

Rick ran across Market Street to the sidewalk that the house was on, fired his pump a couple of times into the air and shouted, "Hey, in the–"

(48)

Junior had just taken hold of a piece of wood from amidst all the bricks and debris and tugged at it, eventually managing to yank it free. The man on the ladder end – the man who seemed to be having a hissy fit because he didn't have his glasses on (though why that should be important when you had a pair of empty eye sockets was anybody's guess – unless you wanted to keep from upsetting folks, and Junior didn't think that was likely in a man who had just crashed a fire engine into his mom and dad's house – *upstairs* window, no less) somehow sensed that Junior was close by, and he stretched out blindly, his face screwed up, empty eye sockets tight shut and squinting, and his hands snapping at the air like crab claws.

"Wayne!" Junior shouted on the fourth or fifth swing, pretty much most of the previous ones having connected but the man not seeming to be adversely affected, just reaching out with those snappy pincer hands trying to catch himself a nice juicy Junior.

All bets were now off. His kid brother was loose amidst a bunch of things that looked like people (though Junior didn't think they were people at all) and the rest of the world had disappeared or, at least, this particular suburb of Denver – Junior had checked the news channels when Wayne had been taking a dump and they were either dead (unfortunate choice of word, that one) or, in the case of Fox, showing an empty newsdesk set.

Junior stumbled back as the man on the ladder took a little tumble to the left and crumpled to the floor from his ladder aerie. Junior hefted the piece of wood and stepped forward purposefully.

The thing–

thwakkk!

–to make sure–

thwakkklshh!

–was that this guy didn't just stand up and–

swullthk!

–proceed to wandering around the house with–

thuunnnk!

–his arms stretched out in front of him.

Junior stood up, panting, and surveyed his work. The guy had to be dead – just had to be – but he was still twitching a little, particularly down at the hands. Junior looked at the hands and frowned. Why the hell was he wearing gloves, for Chrissakes?

"Hey, in the house!" someone shouted.

(49)

"You know," Sally Davis said as she watched the three men disappear around the corner of the intersection and into the street they had just passed, "there are times I miss my husband and there are times I *really* miss him?" She lifted the statement into a question with the last word.

She was leaning against the bus window, next to Melanie, the young woman from the radio station, the pair of them with their arms propped on the metalwork below the glass alongside their seats, one in front of the other, each of them watching the glass mist up from their breath. The little girl, Angel Wurst (*such a* lovely *name,* the voices in Sally's head crooned enthusiastically), was standing beside Sally with her doll pressed against the glass.

"You two not–" Melanie stopped and reconsidered before she went on to say, "–not together?"

Sally shook her head. "He died. Years ago."

"I'm sor–"

"Don't be." Sally's voice sounded calm and even a little dismissive. Then she said, "He killed himself." The voices whispered. *Killed himself? Had* we *known this? Our father* killed *himself? Why'd he do* that*?* Sally realized that she had probably never thought the truth to the voices, but rather had let them believe that Gerry had simply died. (Did anyone "simply die"? Surely the whole process of giving that final breath and the body commencing on its journey of decomposition was a complex affair. In that single split second, while she waited for some kind of reaction from Melanie, Sally wondered how it felt to die.)

When the reaction came, it was a muted "How?" that was hardly more than an exhalation of breath.

"He shot himself?" Sally said, once again turning a simple statement into a question. "With a shotgun? In his mouth." She didn't turn the last bit into a question. That was all there was. He shot himself in the mouth. End of story.

Sally thought of telling Melanie how she had driven out one night, long after Gerry had done the dastardly deed, and seen her husband's ghost appear in their old Chevy, but she thought better of it. What would it achieve? The answer was, of course, absolutely nothing.

"Hey, ladies?" Johnny's voice from the front of the bus sounded a little tense. "I think we may have a small problem."

"Small isn't too bad. Yeah, we can do 'small'."

"Well, dear Melvin, it's maybe a little more on the medium size. Plus there's a second problem."

Melanie slid out of her seat and duckwalked up the aisle of the bus. "Ah," she said as she reached the back of Johnny's driving seat and crouched next to him. Sally pulled the girl close to her and breathed in her youth and her innocence while the voices twittered.

Up ahead, maybe sixty or seventy yards, a man and a woman were walking down the street heading straight for the bus. They could have been out for a summer evening's stroll along the promenade at a fashionable seafront resort in the Hamptons, if the weather had not been so cold and the visibility so dark as to register sunglasses quite heavily into the "totally unnecessary" category. And despite the low temperature, the gloves looked out of place where the couple's other clothing suggested a warm evening.

"You think they've seen us?" Melanie whispered.

"They've seen the bus," Johnny said. "Whether they know it's one of theirs is anyone's guess but–"

"They know," said a squawky voice from the aisle behind them. Melanie and Johnny turned their heads in unison to see Angel Wurst having moved from her seat and Sally Davis and now standing holding her doll aloft. "They know we're here," Samantha the doll croaked menacingly.

"Get down, honey," Melanie hissed. She turned to Johnny. "What's the second problem?"

Johnny pointed to the ignition. "That," he said.

Melanie grunted, unable to see the difficulty.

"No key," he said.

"They took–" She stopped and lowered her voice. "They took the fucking *key*?"

"Not deliberately, Melvin. Cut them some slack here, OK?"

Outside, the man and the woman had almost reached the front of the bus. "I can't even close the door," Johnny said, unable to keep the moan from his voice. "The door relay is attached to the ignition."

"Angel, get down, honey," Sally Davis said as she took hold of the girl's shoulders and forced her down first to her hunkers and then onto her knees.

The man was close now, only fifteen or twenty feet from the front of the bus. Johnny lifted his gun and flicked the safety catch.

"You know how to use that thing?"

"I'll figure it out," he said. "How hard can it be?" He slumped down further into the driving chair and trained the gun on the open doorway. "Best get yours ready, Melvin," he said. "And yours, too," he added, pitching his voice a little higher and over his right shoulder to where he knew Sally Davis and Angel Wurst were crouching in the aisle. Sally lifted her gun and held it awkwardly, giving a little smile to the girl when she watched her.

In the street, the man had stopped while the woman continued towards them. Johnny looked around helplessly.

"Now we really do have problems," Melanie said. "Look."

Sally Davis looked up and saw three young men step out of a side alley onto the street, all nicely turned out (as Sally's mother used to say), swept-back hair, jerkin jackets and, in one case, a lettered sweater.

Johnny twisted himself out of his seat and onto the floor. He waved his hand – the one holding the gun – towards the back of the bus and snapped at Melanie and Sally Davis, "Get back in the seats – each of you in a different one – and keep the girl quiet."

Melanie said, "She *is* quiet."

Johnny nodded. "Well make sure she *stays* quiet."

"They know we're here," Angel Wurst said as Sally turned her around and walked her back down the aisle towards the rear seats. The girl's voice was calm and confident. She was *sure* that the people outside knew they were on the bus. So she didn't bother crouching over.

"How come she knows so much?" Johnny whispered to nobody in particular.

They heard gunshots from way over in back of where they were and Johnny looked meaningfully over at Melanie, who had just ensconced herself between a pair of seats down the left side of the bus. "Sounds like someone's having some fun," he said as he turned himself around at the head of the steps.

"You think that's *at* them or *from* them? The shots, I mean."

"You mean *our* guys? The *good* guys?" Johnny shrugged and, laying his gun on the floor next to him, he reached down to a lever alongside the pneumatic door and tugged at it. "Anybody's guess." The lever wouldn't budge. He glanced up at the people in the street – there were now eight of them, all heading for the bus, with two of the young men in the expensive threads leading the pack. "*They* don't seem to have guns–" He nodded at the blank faces now gathering on the road and sidewalk. "–so I'd guess that, back there, it's us doing the shooting."

"You think they have the keys?" Sally asked. For a second, Johnny thought the woman meant the two people who were at that moment negotiating the bottom of the bus steps, their arms outstretched to the handrail, one leg apiece suspended awkwardly as they made to mount the steps. And then he realized that the woman meant the others from the bus – Rick, and the guy from the plane (Johnny liked him). And Virgil Banders. He frowned when the mental image of Virgil Banders popped into his head and, without thinking, he lifted the gun, closed one eye and took aim, and fired. The force of the blast pushed Johnny back onto the floor, but it did far worse to the young man in the lettered sweater. The bullet took the man in the neck, laying it wide open and splattering the brass name and address plaque on the wall behind him with pieces of flesh and bone. The man lifted a gloved hand and seemed to be attempting to find the wound – and Johnny thought that, just for a moment or two there (and the dark glasses made it very difficult to be sure), the man had been frowning – and all as he had been slowly falling over backwards, his sweater now sprayed with darkness, until he hit the ground and didn't move again. Johnny knew that, under a decent light, that darkness would be a deep red.

"Sorry, what'd you say?" Johnny shouted as he pulled himself back into a sitting position.

"I was wondering if we knew where the keys were," Sally said, though it didn't seem so important any more.

Johnny nodded as he shifted onto his knees. "Uh huh," he said, and this time he rested his right arm on the tubular rail at the head of the steps. "Uh huh," he said again, and fired. The shot missed the girl completely but it must have been close because her auburn hair fluffed out on the left side of her head. The girl got a hand on the right rail and one on the left and then pulled herself onto the first step. Johnny shot her in the face and the girl fell back onto the other men behind her. He watched with a kind of detached interest as the girl's glasses flew from her face, and he barely raised his eyebrows at her blackened eye sockets: of far more interest was the smeared cavity where the girl's nose had been and the smashed teeth suddenly exposed by the flap of cheek-skin. He wasn't sure whether he saw anything move inside those eye sockets before the girl was lying on the ground, her arms and legs twitching. Then she was still.

Johnny shifted himself to one side and immediately grimaced at the sharp pain in his leg.

"You OK?" Melanie called and Johnny would have nodded but, out of the corner of his eye, he saw a youngish man move into view and stand on the sidewalk with his legs astride the girl's body.

And that's when he dropped the gun.

He wasn't quite sure how it happened. A silly thing, errant clumsiness, perhaps. Or a distraction – one of the women in the seats farther down the bus (maybe even the girl) diverting his attention. Or maybe it was the pain in his leg. Then again, maybe it was just a minor infarction in the cosmic comings and goings of the stars in the sky, wreaking their chaos on mankind (or what was left of it) far, far below. Or maybe it was none of the above.

Whatever, it didn't actually matter. Johnny's hand fumbled, turned on itself as the gun butt shifted itself from the soft pad of skin below his thumb, tried to grasp the butt, the butt catching a small flick of the thumb-end and shifting its trajectory, giving it a little spin.

He watched the gun twirling over and over itself, like something from one of the music videos they showed on MTV or maybe even something from a movie or a complex trick from Penn and Teller, the streetlights right outside of the bus occasionally catching the gun's blackness and giving little gleams.

Other eyes were watching it, too, Johnny saw. Or at least, they were aiming in the general direction of the gun – he couldn't be sure they were watching it exactly because of the dark glasses.

The gun hit the floor of the bus right on the barrel end, twirling the weapon back into the air. Johnny reached out to grab it but the lettered sweater-man thrust an arm forward and, gloved fist clenched, he brought it down onto Johnny's wrist. Johnny yelped and pulled his hand back, and the gun hit the deck again, this time on the grip. There was a loud explosion and the right-hand side of the windshield shattered, glass peppering the street.

Someone screamed from down the bus but Johnny didn't turn around. He got to his knees and threw his hand forward towards the man's face as the man scrabbled for the gun while trying to keep a hold on the rail. Johnny's hand was outstretched for some reason, instead of folded over in a fist, and the tip of his middle and index fingers hit the man's cheekbone. The impact was enough to dislodge the man from the bus stairs but it also sent waves of pain up Johnny's already tender arm.

As he pulled his arm back and slid the hand under his armpit, Johnny heard a dull thud from the front of the bus. When he looked over, expecting the worst (though exactly what that might be he couldn't even guess at), he saw an elderly man's head moving backwards away from the bus. After a few yards, the man stopped and ran forward, his arms in the air, until he crashed into the bus. The man seemed not to have felt anything. He just straightened himself up and walked backwards again.

"He's trying to get in through the broken window," Johnny said, the pain in his hand forgotten.

"Johnny!" Melanie shouted.

Johnny spun around and saw the letterman was back on the steps again, this time with his left arm wrapped around the rail. He was pulling at the fingers of the glove on his right hand, and just for a few seconds, Johnny could have sworn that the man was smiling.

"Don't let him touch you," Melanie shouted.

Johnny glanced down and saw the gun.

The glove came off just as the old man at the front of the bus managed to hook his hands over the window rim. He immediately started scrabbling for a foothold.

Sally Davis hoisted her gun and pointed it towards the front of the bus, her hand wobbling.

"Shoot it," Melanie said. "Shoot the fucking thing."

Nobody thought to apologize to Angel Wurst for the ribald language.

Sally tried to hold the gun steady but couldn't shake from her mind the image of her sad-faced husband Gerry sliding his lips around the barrel of the shotgun and–

Johnny's hand crept forward, finger-walking towards the gun grip teasingly just out of reach under the front seat, Johnny's breath coming in short bursts as he strained that little extra. He heard Melanie shout "Fucking *shoot* it, for Chrissakes!" behind him and heard a dull *doooiiing!* sound followed in rapid succession by two more and then the tinkling of breaking glass.

Just as Johnny felt his middle finger touch the gun butt, he heard the sound of running feet. Then another shot, this time Melanie following it up with "I think you got him!" And then the letterman's hand wrapped itself around Johnny's wrist and a tsunami of black pain washed through him with such ferocity he withdrew his hand from the gun (but, alas, not from the letterman's firm grasp) and sprang immediately to a semi-crouch, smacking his forehead and temple on the metal bar underneath the seat. The sound of his own voice – a wail of pain and misery – merged with a profound silence that was more a susurration, a myriad of paper-folders playing origami with a million sheets and turning them into dragons and birds and faces whose mouths opened and closed by the pulling of a small torn slip at the rear.

Johnny's perspective changed. He seemed to be looking at the seat in front of him as well as at the letterman alongside him, though the letterman seemed to sway almost drunkenly from side to side, together with the bus doorway. On one of these swings, he heard another gunshot – followed by two more metallic reverberations – and then from somewhere behind him the little girl's doll leapt into the fray, dashing itself against the letterman's nose and eyes.

Melanie said, "His eye."

Angel Wurst screamed.

The guy on the steps had let go of Johnny's arm. Johnny could see him sprawled half on the road and half on the sidewalk. But it was a strange image because it was lacking in perspective. Just a flat photo rendition of a dead man (Johnny was sure the man was dead) coupled, inside his head, with the floor of the bus. And then something moved into view – a knee and a shaking hand resting on it, and all the while, he could still see the dead man out on the street.

"We have to get it back in–"

"Shh," Sally Davis whispered.

Johnny started to lift his hand. He glanced to the left: the guy at the front of the bus was moving backward again (but he could still see his knee).

"Johnny..."

He glanced to the right: Angel Wurst stood watching him, her face a mask of horror, a broken doll cradled in her arms (and still he could see his knee).

Sally Davis placed a hand on his shoulder at exactly the same moment that the old guy out front ran into the bus again. The glass was now smeared in blood. Johnny started and looked down as the woman's hand reached toward him. As he followed the hand he saw her fingers curl out very gently toward his face – he could see it very clearly, the hand approaching him like a slow-motion snake. The only problem was that, while he kept on looking at that oh-so-slow snake-hand, he could also see his own knee and the floor. And that was when, as Melanie said his name yet again, and Sally Davis kept telling him it was going to be OK – catching a hold of his wrist as he lifted his hand to his face and pulling it back down – he started to hum.

Melanie got calmly to her feet and fired off several shots at someone trying to clamber over the body on the sidewalk and get to the bus steps.

Just as calmly, she ejected the magazine (now where the hell did she learn to do that? Johnny wondered), slipped a new one into the grip, and then she heard a familiar voice.

(50)

When Rick burst into the house he swung the gun out in front of him and fired, first three shots in fairly rapid succession and then another couple. The first went wild – he had no idea where. The second hit an old man in the back of his head and sent him face forward onto the staircase he was pulling himself up, hands clasping the banister. A young girl, sweet-looking thing with raven dark hair and a tooth-brace, turned and looked at Rick quizzically, head on one side and her hands outstretched.

For a second, Rick studied the girl's face. There was something about her that he recognized but it was something–

Hey, asshole, whyn't you come back and finish the job... think there's a couple bones here still seem to be in one piece...

–of course! The girl. The one on the road, way back. When he had been travelling up I-90, in that old DeSoto, with the Bighorn Mountains up there in the distance. And he'd reached for the stick of gum, Juicy Fruit chewing gum, and they had appeared, right in front of him – hell, man – what could he do? He'd stepped on the brakes – hah! *Stepped* on them? He just about stood upright on the fucking things and put his head through the roof of the goddam car, but it was no use. He'd hit the boy, the boy folding over the DeSoto's hood, and the girl had gone down under the wheels – *Ba-dump, Ba-dump* – Goodnight, sweetheart! – quizzical smile, freckles and all.

But this wasn't her, nossir. This wasn't any girl at all. This was a vegetable from space or someplace else – some wired-up and freaked-out fucker wearing a teeth-brace and a bunch of freckles like a Halloween mask.

That was what it had been, he now realized. The freckles.

Rick shot into the girl's midriff and she staggered backwards, hands moving to her stomach before she keeled right over. But she didn't lay still; she jiggled, like a windup toy that had been knocked over, her heels banging repeatedly into the rucked-up carpet beneath her while the red stain widened under her back, spreading all over the polished floorboards.

"Anyone in here?" Rick shouted.

An elderly Puerto Rican man with his flies undone and food stains down the front of a Hawaiian shirt emblazoned with scantily-clad girls appeared around the room corner and stopped, putting his head on one side as though studying Rick. For a few seconds, Rick considered saying something to the man but then he saw a young boy backing away from a young woman wearing hair-curlers and a baby doll nightdress. And gloves. The boy wasn't wearing gloves. Or glasses.

Rick glanced back at the Open Flies Man in time to see the man remove the glove from his left hand. Rick held his arm straight out, held onto the elbow with his left hand, and pulled the trigger. The gun – and his right arm – bucked, and the shot went wild. Rick had no idea where. He lowered his arm and fired again. The man folded over and staggered backwards, letting go of his glove and finally dropping to a sitting position against the wall, an additional deep redness blossoming amidst the myriad colors of his shirt.

At the top of the staircase, another boy appeared, this one a little older than the one backing into the kitchen and carrying a plank of wood that, even from where he was standing, Rick could see was dripping with gore.

"Wayne!" the boy shouted.

The kid over by the kitchen was crying.

Virgil Banders appeared at the front door and sideswiped a fat woman wearing what appeared to be a bathrobe and more hair curlers. *What the hell,* he thought. *This a hair curler convention or somethin'*? As the woman keeled over to one side, her glasses skittering across the floor, Virgil pumped and fired, and then pumped and fired again.

The first shot dislodged the left side of the woman's head, scattered her curlers (most of them still with hair attached) and sent her back against the front door, and the second hit her full on her very ample right breast. She was still in the process of sliding down the doorframe as Virgil turned, shouted, "Kid, get down on the floor!", pumped another round, and fired.

Feet clumped on the boards outside and Rick spun around to see Ronnie backing into the house.

"What the hell's going–"

He turned in time to see Virgil's blast take the young woman over by the kitchen on her left side – the shoulder – pushing her forward and spinning her around at the same time so that, just for a few moments, she was facing Virgil.

Virgil pumped another round. "Stay down, kid."

The second shot was low, taking off one of the woman's legs – her left one, same as the shoulder – around the knee. The woman fell over like she was in one of those speeded-up old movies.

Now the older boy was running down the stairs.

"You OK?"

Virgil answered Ronnie without turning around. OK? Hell, he was having a ball. It was like one of those games in the amusement arcades. And now, well, what have we here. Looked like a fireman – leastways he was wearing a fireman's tunic and breeches. But the guy looked like he'd spent the past week or so hammering in garden posts with his face. He was still wearing a pair of glasses but they were embedded into his forehead and right eye socket (the left half of the glasses was missing, the socket behind it black and cavernous – and was that just a hint of movement that Virgil saw in there?).

Rick shouted to the boy by the kitchen. "Over here, kid. Run! Now!"

The boy ran. Then, glancing up the stairs, he saw the other boy. "Junior!"

"Junior," Virgil said, pumping in another round. "Down."

Junior dropped.

Rick and Virgil fired at the same time, catching the fireman in the crotch and belly. Virgil pumped once more but his second shot missed. It didn't matter: the man fell backwards flat against the stairs and started to slide. But he was still moving his right arm, the hand fumbling at the glove on his left hand.

"I got it," Rick said. The shot shortened the man's head by a good couple of inches and sent splinters of wood into the air.

Ronnie motioned for the young boy to get over to them.

Rick put an arm around Junior's shoulders and turned around.

Standing in the center of the room, a tall man wearing a dark jacket, shirt and necktie, stood with his hands clasped and watched them. He made no attempt to move towards them.

Ronnie saw the guy first and he lifted his gun and held it as steady as he could, pointed at the man's face.

"Hey," Rick said. "What's going on?"

The activity around them had stopped.

Virgil moved so that his back was against Rick's and the older of the two boys. He pumped a round in and waited.

The smaller boy started to sob. Ronnie rubbed his shoulder and then gave him a little reassuring squeeze. The boy nestled harder into Ronnie's side, his arms around the man's leg.

"That's Mr Yovingham," Junior whispered.

Not any more, Ronnie thought.

As they started to move slowly towards the door, Mr Yovingham said, "Jerry?"

Rick frowned. He suddenly felt a little sick in his stomach.

The man took a steady step forward. "Jerry?" he said again.

"They're all saying it," Virgil Banders whispered.

"Jerry?" said Mr Yovingham again.

"Jerry?" inquired the man wearing carpet slippers.

A young barefoot boy dressed incongruously in a T-shirt and a pair of threadbare sleep-shorts said "Jerry?" as he took a step forward, saying it again – "Jerry?" – his head tipped to one side, one gloved hand pulling at the glove on the other.

"Who's Jerry?" Ronnie asked, his voice soft, not actually asking it of anyone in particular but rather merely giving sound to the strangeness that surrounded them.

"Jerry, it's me," the voices chorused, each of them now morphing so that they all sounded pretty much the same – the same timbre, the same inflections, the same curls to the letters and the vowels. "Geoff," they concluded. And then they said it again, a mantra of sorts.

"Now who the fuck is *Geoff?*" Virgil said.

Rick lifted his gun and pointed it at the young boy's head. He was pleased and maybe a little surprised to see that his hand was not shaking. "Geoff was my brother," he said. And then he pulled the trigger.

(51)

"Jerry?" Sally Davis said, addressing the fat Puerto Rican woman struggling her bulk onto the bus steps. "Are. You. Trying. To. Communicate. With. Me?" she asked, spreading out the words slowly. "Trying. To. *Talk.* To. Me?" she added, thinking that maybe "communicate" was a bit of a mouthful for your standard interstellar traveler – and possibly even your Monkey's Paw-type shade come to visit with a one-time loved one.

The fat woman rolled her head to one side, causing a large fold to appear on the left, and just for a few moments it seemed to Sally as though the woman was about to answer her.

Melanie was aware of someone shouting at her but the voice was distant, dim and hazy. She paid it no heed, treated it like a distant sound of no import, a car door way off in the distance or the muted mutter of a radio carried on the wind from a far-off open window.

"Mel," Johnny shouted.

Though she couldn't be sure because of the woman's dark glasses, Melanie could have sworn that the woman shifted her whole attention to her, now pulling off one of her gloves and seeming to lower her voice a little, making it more personal, softer, more gentle.

Somewhere off behind her, in that other world that was a bus interior – a flying bus's interior, no less – there was some crashing and banging, then a couple of gunshots and a few curses ("fucker", "motherfucker" and "cocksucker" figured heavily), and Melanie lowered her gun and started to reach out.

"I wouldn't do that, honey," the woman next to her told Melanie.

But Melanie didn't mind. Melanie didn't care.

"It's me," the fat Puerto Rican woman had explained to Melanie as she hoisted herself onto the bottom step. "Geoff," she had said.

Melanie saw that the woman had exposed her left hand and she was reaching out. Sally Davis made to knock the outstretched hand out of the way but Melanie pushed her back and returned her attention to the proffered hand – the woman intoning that mantra of hers: "Jerry, it's me... Geoff."

Sally Davis regained her position and started to grapple with Melanie. Then a voice behind her said, "Melanie, get out of the way," saying the words very calmly.

But Melanie didn't register this new intrusion. She wanted more than anything to sit down with this fat Puerto Rican woman and talk to her. She wanted – wanted more than anything in the world, she now realized – to sit and listen to that voice, that voice that in no way sounded like a fat Puerto Rican woman.

"Jerry, it's me... Geoff," the woman said.

"Jerry, it's me... Geoff," chorused an old man wearing nothing but a voluminous beer belly and a pair of boxer shorts with a distinctly yellowed fly, and from the bottoms of which a spindly pair of wattled legs protruded.

A small boy elbowed his way into view. "Jerry, it's–"

"Get the fuck–" Johnny said, his voice still calm. He thrust the gun between Sally's and Melanie's heads and fired. The boy flew backwards in a mist of darkness that Sally barely registered as blood.

Melanie started, as though waking from a dream, and put her hands over her ears, the right one still holding her gun.

"Sorry, Melvin," Johnny said. He rose to his full height and kicked out at a man wearing an ill-fitting dressing gown, his hair a wild birds' nest. "Jerry," the man was insisting as he tried to regain his footing, "it's me–" Sally's bullet took him in the face and the man caromed backwards.

"We have to get away from here," the squawky voice of Samantha the doll said. The words were matter-of-factly delivered but neither Johnny nor Sally Davis said anything. Johnny looked around at the toy's blank face, its heavily lashed eyes seeming to blink as Angel Wurst shifted her position.

"Wait a second," he said.

Johnny looked around back at the driver's seat. A pair of gloved hands was grappling with the window rim just a few inches from the steering wheel while, on the other side of the bus, a black girl wearing long earrings and an askew hairpiece, had actually made it to the point where she was almost fully into the bus. "Jerry," she was mouthing, the words lost in the sound of turmoil and gunshots – Melanie and Sally Davis had now assumed the roles of Davy Crockett and Jim Bowie, Johnny noted – "It's me... Geoff." The girl's arms were cut ragged, a long piece of flesh hanging from her left like loose meat. Just for a second, when Johnny moved back towards the seat, the girl seemed to pause. He lifted the gun – the smell of burning and, Johnny assumed, gunpowder was everywhere – and smiled at her. The girl didn't return the smile but instead pumped her out-of-sight legs and feet more frantically as she struggled for better purchase. The shot took her in the right shoulder and she spun around, the dark glasses flying from her head onto the street. Seconds later, the girl dropped out of sight and Johnny slid back into the driver's seat.

Amidst the grunts and the constant assurances to Jerry – coming from all directions – that it was, indeed, Geoff, Johnny started checking around the driving seat. He pulled down the visor but there was nothing there except a dog-eared photograph of two young black boys secured in the PVC strip, maybe seven years old the one of them and nine or ten the other. Jerry pushed the visor back up.

A painfully thin woman wearing a surgical gown was flattened against his side window, her arms spread across the glass as they felt for a means of ingress. Johnny watched her, just for a few seconds, and tried to get some inkling of what was going through her head. The woman seemed impervious to his interest, moving her head side to side, pressing it against the glass, while her mouth moved in that now familiar mantra and the dark glasses forbade any sense of purpose or thought.

He glanced back and saw Sally Davis now standing like a latter-day Annie Oakley, Angel Wurst secured beneath Sally's left arm (and Angel's constant doll companion similarly safe and protected beneath hers) while Sally brandished her gun and fired intermittently into the throng of muttering people. Sally's backwards glance at him said it all: they couldn't go on for too much longer like this. Ammunition would run out and then they'd all be caught like rabbits in a trap. They either had to get the bus moving – a little difficult without the keys – or it was getting close to time they needed to consider taking to the streets on foot.

He looked back at the bus dashboard and yet again at the visor. Looking to the side, he saw there was another visor over the right-hand side window. He reached over and pulled it down: nothing. He lifted a clipboard from the dashboard top and looked through the papers underneath: nada. He looked in the little recessed shelf, pulled out a creased and water-damaged paperback novel written by Fannie Flagg and checked underneath: zilch.

"I think we could use some help over here," Melanie called out.

Johnny retrieved his gun from the dash and, as he moved around on his chair, his finger touched what felt like a small taped corner underneath the seat. Without daring to look, he pushed his hand farther under the seat and followed the wedge of tape. It could be that it was just a piece of tape holding something together or possibly even a throwback to when the seat was newly installed into the bus. But then again, it could be something else. His fingers continued to explore and then...

He slid from the seat, placing the gun beside him on the floor, and reached under. In the center of a crossroads of old brown tape was the little lump of metal he'd felt: a pair of keys in a lighthouse fob.

"Hey," Johnny shouted, holding the keys aloft. "I think–"

The girl tumbled from the front window right next to him, her gloves already removed. "Jerry," she whispered to him, almost pleading, "it's–"

Johnny fell back and reached for his gun as he lifted his other arm to block those hands.

"–me... Geoff," the girl finished.

"Johnny!" Melanie's voice was shrill somewhere over to Johnny's right but he couldn't respond and dare not turn away.

Angel Wurst screamed. "Shoot her! With the gun," she added helpfully.

"Can't shoot her," Sally said. "I'd hit–" Damn! She'd forgotten the boy's name. She slipped the gun into her pocket just as a bare chested black youth, his upper arms and neck a mass of cuts and smeared blood, leapt from the smashed front window and started for her. Sally pulled Angel Wurst behind her and reached for her gun but Melanie had already turned in the boy's direction. She held the gun out in front of her and pulled the trigger. The first shot went wild – she had no idea where but was pleased there was no endless ricocheting, no cartoony *bdoing! bdoing!* as the bullet bounced around the bus interior – but the second hit the boy in his cheek (she would replay the scene in a mixture of fascination and horror as blood and pieces of tooth peppered the back and hair of the girl now virtually straddling Johnny) and toppled him against the dashboard and onto the floor, where he continued to thrash his arms, already managing to pull one glove free and reaching for Johnny.

Johnny pulled his knees up and managed to continue blocking the girl's snatching hands as he scrabbled on the floor for the gun.

Just briefly, he felt the black youth's fingers brush against his wrist and he received a jolt of searing pain that seemed to surge right up his left arm, through his shoulder, up the side of his face only to pool in his head, somewhere behind his eyes. He screamed out, but at the same time, he felt the gun's handle.

Sally moved quickly across the bus, pushed Angel Wurst into a seat as Johnny placed the gun somewhere in the region of the girl's head and fired. The girl lifted entirely up from him for a few seconds and then slumped back on him, her hair against his mouth. Sally stepped across and leaned over, holding her own gun against the black boy's neck right at the base of his skull. The shot jarred her shoulder and she staggered backwards but the boy now lay still, not even the slightest twitch of those outstretched fingers.

The susurrant muttering from the figures on the bus steps allowed little time for self-congratulation and Johnny took no time in sitting upright and letting off a shot into the stomach of an old man trying to negotiate his way over the prone figures of the girl and the black boy. "Jerry," the man muttered as he figured out he could step actually onto the bodies, "it's–" And then he fell backwards.

"Time to go time," Johnny said.

"What about–" Sally Davis began.

"We'll pick them up," Johnny said. He turned the ignition and the bus shuddered, coughed a couple times and then, with a loud whine, went quiet.

A young Hispanic woman wearing a postal clerk's uniform swung her leg through the smashed front window and lodged the foot between the dash and the ticket dispenser. "Jerry," she began.

"Fuck. Off." Melanie swung her gun by the barrel, the handle grip catching the bridge of the woman's nose and smashing the dark glasses.

Angel Wurst screamed and pointed at a side window, the glass of which bellied out in a single sheet, flopping out of its housing. "Look out!"

A small child (Johnny could not discern the gender) of around four or maybe five years old was being held up to the gap by an old woman wearing hair rollers and some kind of face mask. "Jerry," the two of them were intent on explaining, "it's me... Geoff."

The woman pushed the child through the gap and allowed the figure's small legs to piston themselves against her ample bosom as it reached in for a handhold.

Johnny gunned the engine again and this time it caught. He revved and pulled back on the elevation lever, the bus listing side to side as it lifted from the street.

"Jerry," the woman with the face mask seemed to plead.

"It's me," said the small child of indeterminate gender.

Angel Wurst stepped unsteadily forward and, just for a second, it seemed as though the girl and the child now clinging to the bus exterior locked eyes in a kind of mind-meld. "This is your stop, I think," Samantha the doll squawked as, with Angel's help, it swung itself into the child's face.

"Geoff!" the child yelped as its fingers scrabbled and finally lost purchase. The face, as expressionless as ever, dropped from view as Johnny started to turn the bus around.

"How we doing?" he shouted.

"Better," Melanie said. She leaned forward just in time to see the child crash onto the sidewalk and lay motionless. The group of people surrounding him (or her – she still had no idea as to the child's gender) lifted their heads as one and watched the bus as it banked to the left in a small circle and headed back to the side street behind them. As they lifted higher, she watched the mouths, all of them moving in perfect unison. "Jerry," Melanie whispered, "it's me... Geoff."

And then the mouth of the street loomed ahead of them.

As they turned the corner, they could see immediately that there were throngs of people down there, most of them walking in that stilted fashion pioneered in all the bad horror movies featuring zombies and ghouls.

Johnny leaned on the bus's horn. "Lock and load," he shouted.

"Have you always wanted to say that?"

Johnny turned briefly and nodded to Melanie. There was just the vaguest hint of a smile when he said "Always."

(52)

Ronnie was standing with his back against the wainscoting and fall pipes of the house when Rick, Virgil and two young boys spilled out onto the front yard.

The weathered fence that went around the coarse grass edges of the yard was now littered with bodies, either slumped over the actual fence itself or propped up against it as though they were taking a break from chores. One or two of them, however, did not seem to be enjoying a comfortable repose – one old woman of some considerable size, the back of her head a hairless and skinless affair that appeared to have been bludgeoned out of any resemblance to a head shape and then covered in crude oil, was lying with her head pinioned onto one of the pointed wooden slats, most of the slat inside her mouth and the point, presumably, having pierced and shattered the roof. The bend of the woman's body, lying like a banana, with her enormous pantaloons and suspenders exposed for all the world to see beneath the rumpled dress and a pair of dark glasses still fixed in place on her face, owed more to a Robert Crumb sketch than to any version of everyday society.

No sooner had Virgil and Rick made it down onto the grass with their charges huddled tightly to them than two women, arms outstretched before them, staggered drunkenly onto the porch, initially jamming themselves into the door jamb. If things had not been quite so frantic – not to mention, with all the ordnance flying around, dangerous – then the sight might well have been funny. Virgil pushed one of the boys – the smaller one – behind him and kept him tight against Rick's legs before spraying shot into the two women. One buckled forward and toppled over the wooden rail and the second one glided (and that was the only way to describe it) backwards until she crashed against the window, shattering the glass before she slid to the porch, her legs splayed out before her.

"That's Miss Chizzick."

"You know her?"

Wayne nodded. "She teaches us math."

For a second, the three of them just let that information sink in as they watched the woman's blood spread out across her blouse.

"She ain't gonna be teaching you no more math," Virgil said. As he watched, he almost succumbed to the desire to leap across to her and tape the woman's mouth and nostrils. It was just three or four steps and that would be it; he would–

"You never liked math," Junior said, turning to his brother.

Wayne nodded. "I never liked math," he agreed.

Rick turned around and looked down the street. "Hey, is it my imagination or is it starting to get lighter?"

Ronnie swung his rifle into an old man's face, watching the glasses skitter across the blacktop. The old man hit the ground sideways, reaching out a gloved hand for Ronnie's leg. Ronnie shouldered the rifle and fired into the man's head, twice.

"You got him the first time," Virgil shouted.

Ronnie nodded. "I got him the second time, too."

When it came, the horn sounded like the angels of Heaven announcing their presence. The bus came around the corner of the street, glancing a piece of boarding across the Pentecostal Church and sending two wires down onto the road where they sputtered a couple times and then lay still.

At the same time, coming from the opposite direction – somewhere across town, Junior thought absently – a pickup headed towards them, two headlights circling independently of each other, a bulked up shape behind the steering wheel.

"I was just about to say the cavalry is here but looks like we may have more injuns, too," Rick said.

As Johnny settled the bus down a few yards away from the

besieged house, Ronnie said, "Something's wrong." He reloaded his gun and held it at arm's length.

As one, the people on the street turned around and started walking towards the parked vehicles. Meanwhile, the pickup continued towards them, its engine sounding strained. The pickup slowed, banked to the left, did a 270 degree turn and settled on the other side of the street facing towards the ruined house.

The sound that Wayne made was not quite a word, but it was more than a grunt. Infinitely more, as it was to turn out. The driver kept the engine running and stepped out onto the pavement.

Junior said, "Gramps?" and made to move forward but Virgil caught a hold of his shirt and held him back.

A little way down the street, Johnny stepped down from the bus, closely followed by Melanie and then Angel Wurst and Sally Davis, Angel holding tight onto Samantha the doll and all three of them watching the people.

"They've stopped," Sally Davis whispered. The voices chorused excitedly in her head, and Sally was forced to issue a stern rebuke that sounded like a radiator letting off steam.

"Hey, dad, we thought you were dead," the thing that looked like August Talbert announced as he stepped from the running board of the pickup. "What the hell you doing down he–?" The last word was cut off, making it sound like "hit". *What the hell you doing down hit*? It didn't make any sense.

"That isn't Gramps," Wayne whispered.

"No," his brother said. "It's dad."

"That's your *dad*?" Virgil reckoned this guy was clocking up into his eighties so he must have some very choice lead in his pencil if he was able to father a couple of scrotes like these two when he was well into his seventies.

"The sun's definitely coming up," Ronnie said.

"You OK over there?" Johnny shouted.

Rick waved them to stay back.

The people standing in the street turned in the direction of Johnny's voice, their faces impassive. "Hey, dad," they said, their voices in almost perfect harmony. "We thought you were dead. What the hell you doing down he–?"

There were high voices and low voices, old voices that shuddered a little and voices that sounded full of youth. There were voices with the unmistakable patois of the African American communities, the vibrant trill of the Puerto Rican and Mexican areas, and maybe even a few Asian, Chinese and Japanese. Rick could hear them all, could discern the inflections and the intonations. But, somehow, the words lacked any real substance. They were like parrot-speak, words picked up by being overheard without any understanding of their meaning.

"Boys, stay put," Ronnie said.

"But that's my dad's voi–" Junior Talbert began until he was interrupted.

"Hey, dad," their father said as he turned around from them.

"We thought–" continued an overweight little girl in pajamas festooned with images of cats and dogs playing and leaping around.

"–you were dead," chorused an elderly man in a checkered work shirt, the arms rolled up to reveal white sleeves beneath.

"What the hell–" added a woman in a brassiere and a slip as she retook her place on the pickup.

"–you doing down he–" a swarthy-looking old man finished as he sat down on the pickup's passenger seat.

"Why are they doing that?" Melanie asked, directing the question to nobody in particular, just letting the early morning and any gods listening know that she didn't understand. "Why are they saying that? Saying it over and over?"

Angel Wurst hugged Samantha tight. "The man said it," she offered.

"What man, honey?" Sally Davis looked around but could only see the people turning away from the rest of her party – the boy called Virgil (who, it had to be said, made her skin crawl a little), and the man who Melanie had brought with her, and the man from the plane. And the two boys, new additions.

Angel nodded at the boys. "Their daddy," she said. "Their daddy said those words to the old man."

Melanie crouched down and pulled Angel gently towards her, one hand on each of the girl's shoulders. "Where's their daddy now, honey? Do you know that?"

"What's she talking–"

Melanie shot a glare at Johnny. "You can see things can't you, honey?"

Angel Wurst nodded. She turned Samantha the doll's head around so that its shiny eyes were looking right at Melanie. "Things that have happened already," the doll said in that squawky voice. "Sometimes things that haven't happened yet."

"Where's the boy's father now, sweetie?" Sally asked.

"Oh," Angel said, matter-of-factly, "*he's* dead."

Melanie couldn't help doing it – didn't even know she was doing it until it was all over – but she just had to do it. There was something in the back of her head that flicked over, like a binary switch, and she shook the little girl so hard that the doll fell out onto the pavement.

"Mel, take it easy."

"How do you *know* that?"

Sally Davis placed a hand on Melanie's shoulder and squeezed.

Angel Wurst's bottom lip started to quiver and a tear appeared on each of the girl's lower eyelids.

"How do you know, honey?" It was Sally who asked this time, her voice softer.

"My mummy and daddy are dead, too," she said.

"Shit!" Johnny turned around and shifted another round into the rifle. "Who *are* these bastards?" he said as he started to walk the couple hundred or so yards to where the others were standing, standing watching the townsfolk walk back to an old Toyota, a pickup, a fire engine and who the hell knew what else those damn contraptions were – or had been once upon a time, in a galaxy a fucking long ways away from where they were now.

Johnny fired the gun, a single explosion, and the shot peppered the backs of two men, one in a suit jacket and one in a shirt, sending them flailing forwards face-first onto the roadway. The jacketed man didn't move, just lay there. The man in the shirt – who, Johnny now saw, was wearing a toupee – tried to pull himself forward, scrabbling his fingertips on the road towards the far sidewalk where a Chevy Camaro sat with its engine idling. A woman in the front seat watched the man and then lifted her head. Johnny thought she was looking at him, could feel the woman's eyes behind those fucking glasses, but he couldn't be sure. When she opened the car door, she did so without any noise or display of emotion.

"Hey, Johnny, leave them," Rick shouted. "They're going."

Johnny didn't respond. By the time he had reached the crawling man's side, he had chambered another round. He put his foot on the man's back, around about the bottom of his spine, and then fired the rifle into the back of the man's head.

"Johnny!" Melanie shouted.

The man jerked once as his head split wide open, and then he slumped against the blacktop and lay still.

The woman in the Camaro got to her feet, the car door still open, and stood there. She still showed no emotion. Didn't move.

Johnny chambered another two shells.

Somewhere behind him – he didn't turn around – an engine started up. But he ignored it and pulled the trigger.

The pellets hit the woman right across her chest and shattered the glass of the passenger window. She bounced back against the car, slid onto the seat and then fell forward onto the road, her ass up in the air.

Rick stepped away from the wall and out onto the blacktop, his handgun hanging by his side. He was around halfway across when Johnny caught sight of an elderly woman in a nightdress, her hair in rollers. She seemed to be in the process of walking back, away from the melee in the street, pausing at the entrance to an alleyway between a five-and-dime store and a little drugstore that looked bereft of products. Johnny fished in his pocket for two more cases. He had almost got them slid into place when Rick took hold of his arm.

Johnny turned around in terror, staring at the hand on his arm. When he looked up at the hand's owner, he visibly relaxed. That was when he noticed that he was humming. Rick took the shotgun from him and said, "She's going."

"And now she's *gone*," Melanie said quietly from just alongside. She pulled the trigger on her handgun four times. Two of the bullets hit the woman, one ricocheted off of the wall with a high pitched whine, and the other just kept traveling. The woman spun half around when the first bullet made contact, in her left side, and then the second one got her in the belly. The woman was already falling when the third one hit the wall in a small explosion of brick dust and shards of cement.

Melanie threw the weapon onto the blacktop and buried her face in her hands.

"Mel," Rick shouted. "Get the gun. We may need it later."

Virgil nodded without saying anything. Hell, it was as sure as shooting they'd need it later. And probably just as sure that it wouldn't be enough.

As a revving sound started up from the fire engine, the cars in the street began to move off into the now lightening air.

(53)

The skies were clear when they finally lifted up from the street.

Johnny was driving again, the two young boys – Junior and Wayne, they'd finally confessed – standing just behind him and watching through the smashed front windows as the buildings moved downwards alongside them until, at last, there was just air and, way over behind them, the tall buildings of Denver.

"Another day," Ronnie said. He couldn't help thinking about Martha, wondering where she was, knowing that he would never see her again. *No,* a tiny voice in the back of his mind corrected, *you're* hoping *you'll never see her again.*

Melanie was shaking, shuddering like jello, the occasional ripple rolling through the length of her body and finishing at her neck and head with a flick. Virgil watched her from across the aisle, his back against a window that showed tiny fractures where bullets had hit the glass. The Sally Davis woman was consoling Melanie but that was a job that Virgil would have enjoyed himself. And for once – perhaps the very first time, in fact – he thought of what life might be like with this woman, here in this brave new empty world.

Sally Davis watched him.

Watch him, mommy, one of her voices insisted.

I'm watching him, honey, Sally thought back to them. *I'm watching him.*

Virgil saw that the girl was watching him, too – the girl and her fucking doll. Seeing that Sally had closed her eyes as she stroked the trembling Melanie, he stuck his tongue out at Angel Wurst and imagined the brat's eyes bulging as she strained for breath against the surgical tape he would so dearly love to spread across her mouth and nose. The girl narrowed her eyes and then quickly looked away. But the doll stayed facing in Virgil's direction. Virgil stuck his tongue out at that as well and then turned to look out of the window himself.

"Hey, they're out on the streets," Virgil said.

Down below them, gathered in small pockets in the shaded areas of building doorways and alley entrances as though avoiding the steadily growing lightness, people stood motionless and watched them pass by. And as though as one, they then turned and drifted away into buildings.

"I think they're... they're singing?" Virgil got up from his seat and pulled at the sliding window section above his head. "Can you see that?" he said, pulling it open and pointing. "Their mouths are moving."

"Bastards," Melanie said softly.

"Should I drop lower?"

"Be careful," Rick said and he nodded to a small park over to the right, between two banks of single- and two-story buildings. "I don't really think we want to come down into that lot." A small bandshell in the middle of the rolling greenery housed a large group of people, all of them standing in the shadow of the bandshell's roof, most of them either naked or semi-naked or dressed in what was obviously nightwear. Plus the gloves. Plus the sunglasses. The grass around the bandshell was strewn with vehicles, some with their doors open but all of them empty, parked up with no apparent thoughts of neatness. *Not so much parked as abandoned,* Martha Mortenson used to delight in saying when she and Ronnie used to pull Ronnie's old Corvette up near the golf course in Cuyahoga Falls, Ronnie shaking so hard with the anticipation of getting into Martha's pants that she thought he was likely to have a cardiac arrest. Those, of course, had been the days when she might have cared about such an eventuality.

Ronnie pulled the door open as Johnny banked the bus to the right.

"Hey, I think I'm getting the hang of this," Johnny said.

"I think we need to change our transportation as soon as we're able," Rick said. He held onto the leather strap from the overhead rail and bent forward to look at the people in the bandshell.

"What the hell are they look–"

Ronnie waved a hand behind his back. "Listen."

It was a symphony of sorts, and perhaps a prayer – far off voices speaking as one, with no intonations or emphasis or emotion. Just words, spoken in perfect harmony by every single man, woman and child in the shadowed recesses of the bandshell – and, Virgil Banders now noted, by all the similarly poorly attired folks huddled in store doorways and even, he now saw, standing in huge trash bins down an alleyway, their elbows propped on the edges and the heavy lids resting on their heads. He could see the first faint display of sunshine creeping along the opposite wall in the alley and he knew, before too long, those folks now standing in the trash bins would hunker down and wait once more for night. For darkness.

"Jerry," the voices sing-songed, a choir now.

"It's me," they insisted.

"Oh God," Melanie moaned.

"Geoff," the voices said.

Melanie sprang to her feet and pulled open her own window, straining her face so that her mouth could almost taste the fresh early morning air. "No, you're not him," she screamed. "You'll never be–"

"Jerry," they said once more, their one collective voice a towering testament of timing.

"Close the window," Virgil snapped.

"It's me," the voices confided.

Sally struggled to push closed the small window above Melanie's head.

"Geoff."

The window banged shut and Melanie slumped onto her seat, sobbing.

Ronnie managed to close the concertinaed entrance doorway, blocking out the bulk of the sound. "How we doing for gas?" he said as he stepped back onto the bus's deck and slid onto one of the bench seats. "I don't relish the idea of another forced landing so soon after the first one."

Johnny tapped the dial and nodded. "Fine. No gas required. Not for another hundred or maybe hundred and fifty miles."

"It's OK, honey," Sally Davis cooed to Melanie. "It's good to cry."

"They've stopped," Rick said. He moved over behind Johnny, pushed open the window by the driver's left shoulder and put his head out. The air tasted good, fresh. And best of all, the voices had stopped.

Johnny said, "You see how they all just turned away from us? Back there?"

Virgil nodded.

"I don't think we scared them off, if that's what you were thinking."

"No, I wasn't thinking tha–"

"More like they knew that dealing with us wasn't urgent," Junior said, his voice low.

His brother Wayne looked up at him but failed to register any real understanding. His eyes were lifeless.

"Like they had plenty of time," Junior finished.

"And right now – right *then*, I mean," Rick said, "they had to get out of the light."

"Hence the dark glasses," Johnny suggested.

They all nodded. And then Rick said, "Hence the dark glasses."

Nobody showed any desire to consider the relevance of the gloves.

EPILOGUE

They brought the bus down on a vehicle-littered stretch of Highway 34 outside of Greeley, just a few miles south of where the Pawnee National Grassland began. Nobody said anything. Only the noise of the wind in the muffle of an upturned Dodge Rambler and various members of the party stretching legs and arms disturbed the stillness. Ronnie couldn't help but imagine the ghosts of the Pawnee and maybe the buffalo that used to roam the southwest. Although nobody said anything for a few minutes, they all felt the same way: lonely.

They had made a decision that they'd look for a vehicle that was not anywhere near someplace where people could hole up out of the sun. The logic was that they simply were not sure how these folks worked and they would simply feel a lot easier in their minds if they knew that firstly the sun was up – that was a key point, Rick said – and secondly, that all buildings and anywhere else that a person could hide were more than a long sprint distant. (That, according to Virgil Banders, was belt and braces.)

Of course, what it also meant was that the vehicles they had a choice of had not been "souped up" – Virgil again – and a lot of them were pretty banged up. And it also meant that they all, every single damned one, had a flat battery.

"All had their lights on," Ronnie said.

The rest of them nodded, even Angel Wurst and the two boys.

"So what do we do?" Sally asked.

It was Rick who answered.

"We get back in the bus and head for Greeley, pick up a couple of cars that were parked up when the–" He looked around for someone to finish his sentence for him but they just nodded some more. "And maybe we'll be able to freshen up, too."

It was a longer job than they would have liked it to be.

Sally, Melanie and Angel Wurst went into 1298 Medicine Road – once Rick and Johnny had confirmed that the house was indeed as empty as it first appeared – and then Rick, Ronnie, Johnny and the two boys went into number 1296. With there being more of the guys than the girls, by the time Rick and Ronnie emerged with car keys for a bottle green Pontiac Grand Am Melanie was already leaning against the door jamb brandishing a plate of thick sandwiches.

By the time the clock ticked over into the afternoon, they were all showered and shaved and sporting fresh clothes. They set off with Rick leading in the Pontiac and Sally following in a Nissan Pathfinder. All three children were with Sally and Melanie. After one more stop for gas at a filling station at Fort Morgan, they continued on the I-70 heading for–

"Where *are* we heading for?" Virgil asked when they'd gotten moving again.

"East," Rick said. Johnny was asleep in the Grand Am's back seat.

Virgil nodded and looked straight ahead as Rick negotiated the car around a truck lying on its side. "What happens when we reach the ocean?"

When Rick didn't answer, Virgil said, "It shouldn't be dark like that, should it?"

"Nope."

"You think something's happening out there?"

"Yep."

They were silent for a while and then Virgil said, "You don't talk much, do you?"

"Well, you pretty much said it all. The sun rises in the east and it sets in the west. So, sure, the dark rises in the east just the same way." He shrugged and leaned forward so that he could look straight up into the sky. "See that?" he said.

Virgil craned his neck and looked up. "The sun."

"Right. The sun's overhead – in other words, it's not going down in the west – and yet over there–" He nodded in the direction they were travelling – darkness covered the sky way over in the distance: it wasn't dark clouds, not a storm or anything resembling it – just rather an absence of light.

"Over there it's dark."

"Very dark," Rick corrected.

"And it shouldn't be."

"It shouldn't be."

It was several miles before either of them spoke again.

Virgil said, "I guess we need to get the cars off the road before the dark comes."

"Yep." Rick checked the mirror to make sure the Nissan was still following him. "And we also need to find ourselves a better mode of travel." He glanced sideways at Virgil. "You follow me?"

"You mean we need to get ourselves one of those flying vee-hickles? Hoo-eee, Musky, that could be a mite tricky."

Rick nodded. "Yep," he said.

And as they continued on into Kansas, the sun moved across them heading for California and all points west. Up ahead, the darkness seemed to be waiting for them like a feral animal, knowing that they were heading its way.

About the Author

Peter Crowther wrote short stories in the Seventies before embarking on a sixteen year career in music and arts journalism and as the head of corporate communications for one of the UK's biggest financial institutions, before releasing his first fiction work for more than a decade in 1990.

Since then he has sold more than one hundred stories, novelettes and novellas to a variety of anthologies and magazines and has had work reprinted in *Year's Best Fantasy and Horror* (three times), *25 Finest Crime and Mystery Stories* (twice) and *Year's Best Crime and Mystery Stories*.

In addition to his own writing, Peter is also a prolific editor of other people's work. His PS Publishing imprint has received the British Fantasy Award for Best Small Press seven times while Peter himself received the 2004 and 2008 World Fantasy Award for Best Professional. In fact, since its inception in 1999, the PS imprint and many of its almost 200 titles have picked up almost thirty awards.

Peter lives about five hundred yards from the sea in Hornsea, England with his wife, Nicky – their two sons (Oliver and Timothy) having flown the coop for solo adventures – and several thousand books, magazines, comic books, graphic novels, vinyl records and CDs. He enjoys reading virtually anything, but also listens to a lot of music (again virtually anything... although he writes only to jazz), and loves watching old black and white movies and reruns of *Sgt Bilko* and *The Twilight Zone*.

petercrowther.com

Tell us!

Talk about this book on Twitter using the tag **#darknessfalling**

Acknowledgments

This book (three separate volumes in its first incarnation) has been a long time coming – my thanks to everyone involved for displaying patience that borders on the Biblical. As ever, I've had help along the way: special thanks then to Marc Gascoigne and Lee Harris at Angry Robot, Richard Chizmar at CD and Bill Schafer at Subterranean Press, plus Nathan Blumenfeld, Nick Gevers, and, most of all, Nicky.